CANARY

TIJAN

Edited by Jessica Royer Ocken
Proofread and beta read: Paige Maroney Smith, Crystal R Solis, Eileen
Robinson, Serena McDonald, Ashley Scales, Amy English, Kimberley Holm

DEDICATION

Dedicated to all my readers who continue to buy my books and support me. Without you, I wouldn't be able to keep doing what I love to do. This is my most violent book that I've ever written.
I hope you enjoy!

1

GIRL

I should've been fazed that I was about to witness a murder. I wasn't.

Sad to say, but this was my new normal.

I was in a motel room. A large plastic sheet covered the floor, and a guy sat on his knees in the middle of it. My boss stood over him. He took his gun out, pressing it into Knee Guy's mouth.

He leaned forward.

"You're going to tell me who sent you, you motherfucker," he growled.

That was my boss. Raize. He was on a kick today. The "motherfucker" bit was new.

He'd used it to the point that I wondered if he called his mother *motherfucker*, and if so, did she reply with who actually fucked her? Probably not.

I couldn't see Raize having a mother.

Knee Guy was sobbing, making pleading sounds around the gun's muzzle, and a distinct smell filled the room.

"Ah, man." One of Raize's henchmen groaned, shifting on his feet. "He just pissed himself."

Henchman Two gave him a look. "Shut up."

Henchman One was new. I called him Henchman One because he acted like there was a hierarchy, and he was on top. I didn't know his name. I'd learned it was easier not knowing their names. Raize had hired him a week ago, and I was surprised he was griping so much. Raize didn't put up with attitude from his goons. Maybe this one hadn't been around long enough to realize that.

Raize took the gun out of the guy's mouth and turned, pinning Henchman One with a look. "You got a problem?"

Henchman Two glanced my way. Then we both made sure not to make eye contact with Henchman One while he was looking around for allies.

Oh, wow. Look at that floor.

It was a beautiful myriad of...plastic. All different colors in that plastic down there.

Yep.

Plastic.

"Can't hear you, motherfucker." Raize took the safety off his gun.

Yep. I recognized the slight sound of that by now. This was something else that should've fazed me. But all I did was move to the side, farther away from Henchman One.

Knowing my boss, I knew Raize didn't miss. But the blood would be a bitch to wash out. I'd have to shower here, and there was an ick factor involved with showering a door away from two dead bodies.

Henchman Two moved with me.

He'd been with Raize for the last month and was proving to be smart. He'd last longer than Henchman One, that was for sure.

There were two main rules you had to follow if you worked with Raize. One, do whatever he tells you to do. And two, don't bitch about it. This guy was bitching. Our boss did not have patience, hence why this guy had been hired in the first place. He was filling another guy's spot who hadn't followed one of those two rules. I didn't know which. But he was there one day and gone the next. This new guy showed up for lunch, and then we were off to do whatever Raize needed us to do.

"I—I'm sorry, Raize."

Raize glowered at him, and it was ugly.

Not that Raize was ugly. One night when I was drunk, I realized that Raize was good looking—hot even, but he was dead inside. That was obvious, and the fact that he had no problem killing snuffed out any attraction I might've had. I tended *not* to look at Raize, or did it the least amount I could.

Another unofficial rule of mine? Don't make eye contact with Raize. He might think you're issuing him a challenge.

I'd been working for him for six months, almost seven. In this world, that was just about tenure. I was pretty sure I'd been won in a bet. I'd gone to a poker game with my previous boss. He went inside a room. Eight hours later, Raize came out, grabbed my arm, and we left.

I'd looked back, but my boss' guys were just standing and staring. If they'd been going to put up a fight, they would've done so the second Raize touched my arm.

And, well, anticlimactic, but that's how I came to work for Raize.

He'd turned to me in the car after I left with him. "You got a place here?"

I'd eyed him, warily, as I shook my head. "I was staying at Slim's." That was my previous boss from an hour earlier.

He'd grunted. "I got a room. You can use that." But he must've had a new thought come to mind because he'd squinted at me after that. "You want your own place?"

I'd wanted to ask why. I'd come into this world knowing the score. If I worked for someone, I worked wholeheartedly for them. There was no half-in or half-out. We didn't do taxes. Forms of ID were issued from what was 'heard' about you. Everything was cash. There was a normal world, that wasn't this. We were all the way in the 'other' side of society.

You were all in or all out. And all out meant death.

I wasn't ready to die, not yet.

I still had shit to do.

So I'd shrugged. "What's the point?"

He'd grunted, his mouth curving up in a slight grin.

That'd been the only time I saw Raize come close to smiling, and it wasn't even a half-smile. It'd been a hint of a smile, like a glimmer and then poof—it was gone. He'd returned to being scary the next second when he'd pulled a gun out and aimed it at the guy in front of him in the car.

I sat behind the driver. Raize was behind the front passenger.

There was no warning.

He'd put the end of his gun against the headrest and pulled the trigger—I'd missed the silencer on top.

White fuzz and blood went everywhere. The guy's body slumped forward.

Raize had settled back, cleaning his gun. He'd wiped blood from his face and hands.

The car made a turn and pulled over in an alley.

"You want?"

My heart had been in my damn throat, my body on the razor's edge of flight or fight. Everything around me had intensified. Colors were brighter. Voices were louder. Stronger. I was on a stimulus overload, so it had taken a second to realize that as the driver opened his door, Raize offered me a piece of cloth—the same one he'd just used to clean his gun and face. He had folded it back so a clean section faced out.

He held it up. "We're going to stop for food. If your face isn't clean, you can't come."

Of course.

Food.

With blood on me.

That wasn't good.

I'd shaken myself out of the weird state I was in and reached for the cloth.

The driver had walked around, opened the front passenger seat door, and taken the dead body out of the car.

I'd started to wipe my face.

Raize had been watching, seeming almost bemused by me. Then he'd offered up some alcohol.

I'd been confused, but hell, I'd figured it might help at this point.

I took the bottle and dipped my head back, taking a long drink. The burn was good, warming.

Raize had frowned. "You need it to wash your face. The blood is caking. I don't have anything else to offer you."

Oh.

Oh!

I'd snorted and poured some of the whiskey onto the washcloth. I'd never needed alcohol to wash my face before. It wasn't the first time I'd seen someone executed in front of me, but it was the first time Raize had killed a man in front of me, and the first time I'd used alcohol as a cleanser.

New things.

Exciting.

By the time I'd finished, the driver had returned.

He'd leaned over, grabbed some wipes from inside one of the car's compartments, and started cleaning off the dashboard, the seat, everything around him. He'd used one to clean his face as well, and then he'd looked back at us.

"Chicken nuggets?"

Raize had grunted again, settling back, and we'd gone to get chicken nuggets.

I never asked why that guy was killed. No questions. It was a rule, but in working for Raize, I had learned that he didn't kill unless there was a reason. A further 'problem' that might happen. There'd been no warning that first night when he'd killed the guy in the car. So as Raize stared at Henchman One now, I was ready.

His eyes narrowed, and for a moment, the guy kneeling seemed forgotten.

Raize lifted his gun toward Henchman One. "You got a big mouth on you?"

This guy was fucked. He'd be a 'problem' and Raize knew it in the way he worded that question.

I also knew what else was coming.

My stomach clenched in preparation.

The guy swallowed. I could see the sweat pouring off of him. His hands twitched, and he shifted his feet around, the plastic crackling underneath him. "No. No, sir. No, boss."

"You've been having a lot to say." Raize's gaze was cold, but there was a twitch beside his mouth, and he turned his eyes to me. "You."

Fuck.

But I'd known.

He nodded toward Henchman One. "He gonna be a problem for me?" he asked me.

Shit.

Fuck.

Shit.

Fuck.

This. This was what I did for these men. It was something they'd learned right away. Or almost right away. When they asked me a question, I always knew the answer in my gut, and I hated it.

Hated it. Hated. It.

I hated being the reason there'd be another body to clean up today.

"Girl!"

I jerked at Raize's bark and answered, because if I wanted to remain alive, I had to be truthful. "Yes."

I'd barely gotten the word out before *bang!*

Henchman One's body fell against the door behind him, then slid to the side and down, a dark, red hole smack in the middle of his forehead. His eyes remained wide, as if watching us, but he was gone.

Raize was an ace shot.

I bit back my remorse. Dammit. But I'd told the truth because this guy would've been a problem. When I'd gone against my gut in the past, I was always proven wrong, and my bosses tended to get pissed at me.

I wasn't psychic, but my gut knew the true answer to any question. If it was a yes/no question, I'd know.

Raize sighed, his gaze lingering on the blood that left a trail down the wall behind Henchman One. It'd be a long night of cleaning. With all that done, he turned and stuck his gun back into Knee Guy's mouth again. He cocked it and raised an eyebrow. "You gonna tell me now, motherfucker?"

The guy's mouth moved around the muzzle, his words unclear.

Raize took the gun out, his face locked down, waiting.

The guy coughed and said, "Bronski sent me."

"Why?"

The guy glanced up at me, and I felt a chill pass through me. Nausea rose up, my stomach churning and twisting. I knew Bronski. He'd been my first boss, and the worst boss. He hadn't known about my gut. That shit was discovered by my second boss. It was the reason he'd taken me to work for him.

My time with Bronski had been short, *thankfully*.

"He wants her back."

Raize swung his head my way. "You worked for him?"

I had to tell the truth, and it tasted bitter coming out. "Yeah."

"As?"

"As nothing. I wasn't with him long, a few days."

"What'd you do for him?" He cocked his head.

"Not what I do for you."

He didn't comment on that, but his gaze traveled down and up my body.

Another blast of cold seared my insides.

Then he turned back to the guy and *bang!* A second body collapsed.

Henchman Two went to work. He started rolling up the kneeling guy first since he was smack in the middle of the plastic. That was an easier cleanup job. Henchman One would be last.

Raize stuck his gun back in his pocket as he crossed the room to me. "Bronski ever fuck you?" he asked, his voice gruff.

My stomach twisted again. "Yes."

"You wanted it?"

I looked up at him, wanting to be a smartass because no one wanted to think back on memories like that. "No," I said instead, hating that my voice came out sounding the way it did.

Henchman Two stilled and turned to look at Raize.

A vein throbbed in Raize's neck as he turned away, motioning to the body. "Clean it up. Get this shit done."

Henchman Two went back to work.

Raize focused on me again. "Hey."

I looked up to him. I'd never seen Raize soften, ever, and I knew this was probably the closest I'd ever get. He wasn't soft, but he was less hard than he usually looked.

"I don't want to go to war with Bronski, but we'll make this right. Yeah?"

I had no idea what he was talking about, but I nodded.

Raize wasn't about using girls or forcing them. He didn't need to. He had a slew of women who came and went from his place whenever he wanted them. That wasn't his business.

He motioned to Henchman One's body. "Help clean that fucker up."

As I did, he went outside for a smoke.

Forty minutes later, both bodies were gone, the room was clean, and we left, leaving no trace of the two murders just committed there.

Then we went for chicken nuggets.

I didn't have any.

2

GIRL

I knew this life wasn't for everyone. It was barely for me, but I'd made the decision to enter this other world so long ago... It was cold and harsh, but if you got over caring when you died, it could be freeing at the same time. No government except not getting caught by the government. No parents. No rules to follow —except the boss'. So maybe it wasn't that freeing after all.

Maybe I was just deluding myself.

Maybe I'd been deluding myself this whole time...

"Girl."

I looked up from the book I was reading on my bed. I'd opened my bedroom door once I heard Raize's girls leave this morning. No one alive could've missed them. They made so much noise. They were all the same. Loud. Annoying. High heels clomping on the floor, giggles, and slurred speech. There was a thud by the wall on their way down the hall, so one must have fallen over. Raize liked to party when he had his women, so she was probably still drunk or high.

That was one thing I appreciated about working for Raize. When he partied, it was just him—his business. Lines were blurred so much in this world, but he had some professional boundaries. Some bosses made their employees party with them, and that was just bad. But not Raize. Once we got to the house, we were on our own until he needed us to do something.

So after we'd returned from the motel, Henchman ~~Two~~ One had taken his food to the kitchen table to eat. Raize had disappeared. He usually ate in his living room with the television blaring or music blasting.

I'd gone to my room, where I usually went after days like that. It wasn't much.

A simple room.

A bed. A desk. I had some clothes in the closet. Sneakers if I wanted to exercise. A phone. And some books. I liked to have maybe two or three. Wherever I was, I got a library card. I'd been eyeing one of those e-readers, but I hadn't made the jump yet.

Simple meant survival in this life. I liked to survive.

The girls that came over last night were gone, so after getting ready for the day, I went to the kitchen for coffee. I'd left the door open after I went back, figuring if Raize needed something, he'd holler or show up.

After a little while he showed up. He stood in the hallway, not even coming into my doorway, dressed in his typical uniform: dark jeans, a shirt, and a leather jacket. The jacket and jeans were always frayed, having that worn-in look, and the shirts changed. Some days it was a Henley. Other days, a T-shirt. And the colors were either white, gray, or black.

I'd never seen him in anything else.

His hair was always the same, too. Cropped close on the sides with the top just long enough to have some volume. He ran his fingers through it, and that was it. It was a mess, but it worked for him.

Today it was jeans and a gray Henley. No leather jacket. And he had sunglasses on.

He checked his phone once he had my attention. "I reached out to Bronski's boss. We have a meet with him in thirty." He put his phone away and slid his sunglasses down so his eyes could meet mine. He studied me. "You're gonna have to talk. You good with that?"

Talk?

Fuck.

I knew what he meant, and I looked away in response.

"Hey." He raised his voice, but I looked back and he lowered it to normal. "I killed Bronski's guy, and that means Bronksi could claim you as his or go to war. I don't want war with that fucker, but he stepped to me when he sent that guy in the first place. I don't work that way, and I'm not done using you, so that means you gotta talk. I'm asking now. Can you handle that?"

I swallowed over the knot in my throat. "Yeah. I'll talk."

Fuck, I'd talk.

I hated that shit, which was ironic considering that's the entire reason I'd signed up for this life. Talking. Snitching. I hated it. It always felt wrong unless it was against a guy like Bronski, but even then, my stomach still felt sick.

"It's not the police," Raize reminded me. "Deal with it."

Right. Deal with it. Easy for him to say. He had a dick and I didn't think a lot of women were forcing him to put it in their vaginas.

But whatever.

Talk.

Fine.

Fuck.

I'd have to talk.

I sighed as Raize headed for the kitchen, hollering, "Let's go, Jake."

I followed, and Henchman Now-One swung in line, shoving his gun behind his back as he joined us from the living room. We left like that, Raize, Henchman Now-One (or Jake, since I knew his name now), and me bringing up the rear. Raize had other staff, and they were staying in the house. Their job was to bag the blow and watch so no one stole it. Me and Henchman Now-One were Raize's traveling team, but I knew we'd have another guy joining us within a couple hours.

There was a job opening.

WE WENT TO A HOUSE, and—no shock here—it was surrounded by guards. Anyone who was anyone had security, but as we parked the car and we got out, I noted that these guards looked Russian.

I felt a tickle that ran down the length of my spine, waiting, pooling at the end.

Every sense in me heightened to full alert as we were led through the door, down a hallway, and into a back office. Music came from elsewhere in the house, but it was muffled. I could hear people. Conversations. The clinking of glasses. Footsteps. Heels on the floor. Wafts of cigar and other smoke in the air.

There were two men in the office. One stood at the desk, waiting as the other, sitting behind the desk, wrote something down. As we walked in, two guards entered behind us. I noted that Henchman One remained outside—Jake.

The standing guy gave us a glance, but soon went back to waiting, his hands at his side, his head down.

He reminded me of a soldier.

The guy behind the desk looked up as well, then finished and handed the piece of paper to the waiting guy. He took off, and the door closed behind him.

The guy behind the desk leaned back, his eyes hooded. He was young, maybe early thirties. Mid thirties.

I was bad at guessing ages. Everyone looked older than they were in this world. A fourteen year old looked like a thirty year old, but this guy truly did seem in his thirties. Dark hair combed back. Business suit.

He was smart, and cold.

I could feel it in the air around him, and I suppressed a shiver.

His gaze locked on me, skimming over my body before looking back to Raize. "Why are you here?"

Raize looked at me, his gaze blank as usual. He often reminded me of a robot, with no emotions—even when he killed. He did it sensibly.

"Bronski sent a man for one of mine."

See? He spoke like he was giving an order at the drive-thru.

"What man?"

Raize shrugged. "I didn't get his name."

The guy made a point of looking around before raising his eyebrows. "Where is this guy?"

"I killed him."

No emotion. None. So matter of fact.

The desk guy regarded Raize for a moment before sighing and scooting his chair back. He didn't stand. He remained sitting and gazing off into the distance.

Then he turned back. "What was the reason for you killing one of Bronski's men?"

"Because if I didn't, Bronski would've gotten to you before I could."

Desk guy's mouth pursed, and he nodded as he stood. He stayed behind the desk, his gaze falling to me again. "Are you going to fill in the dots as to why Bronski sent a man for one of yours?"

"It's the girl," Raize noted.

So flat.

Desk Guy's eyes skirted back to Raize. "Are you fucking her?"

"No."

Desk Guy asked me, "Is he fucking you?"

"No."

"Was Bronski fucking you?"

I didn't answer.

Desk Guy noted this before turning back to Raize. "Was he fucking her?"

Raize nodded once. "Against her will."

Back to me. "He raped you?"

He did not seem like he gave a fuck.

My tongue grew heavy. My throat started to swell. This wasn't a conversation any survivor or victim wanted to have, but here it was so blasé that I wanted to vomit all over everyone in the room.

I was quiet a moment.

Raize's jaw tightened.

They were all waiting.

I shifted on my feet, but maintained eye contact with the head boss. "Yes, it was rape."

"You fought?"

Really, *really* wanted to vomit.

Everywhere.

Bile moved up in my throat. I rasped out, "Yes."

Images of us came back to me.

Him on top. Holding my arms down.

Me kicking, straining.

The smell of his breath. God. His horrible, *horrible* breath.

"You said no?"

God, he was so cold.

Raize swore under his breath. "Rape is rape, Carl. They say no and anything after is rape, whether they fight, flee, or freeze. It's rape."

Carl. That was his name.

That name was now on my list.

I'd had one name on my list when I started this life. One. My sister's boyfriend. Then his boss got added to the list. Bronski was put on there. A few other guys, and now Carl. One day, somehow, I'd cross out each and every one.

One day.

"Why's he want her back?" Carl asked.

I almost sagged in relief, wanting to take a step back, as if I could melt into the background. But I couldn't. That wasn't how it worked, so I stayed firm, but I was thankful that question had gone to Raize.

He shrugged. "I don't know. He wants to fuck her again?"

Raize was lying. And he wasn't looking at me on purpose, or I guessed it was on purpose.

Carl studied him, then turned and studied me.

I felt seared from the inside out by the time he sighed. "You're lying to me."

I gasped, trying to remain silent, but the sound was out.

He turned that accusation toward Raize, who didn't flinch, who didn't gasp, who didn't react at all. Total stone robot.

"Bronski got rid of her," Raize said. "He sold her to Nelly to be a mule."

"That true?" Carl asked me.

I nodded. "Yes." Also, how did Raize know this? I'd already been with Slim before Raize got me.

So many bosses.

"Were you a mule for him?"

Shit. That's when I knew.

Carl knew. He knew everything.

Fuck, fuck, fuck.

"I wasn't, no."

He raised an eyebrow and leaned forward, resting his hands on his desk. His fingers spread. "You both have one more chance at being truthful here. Why does Bronski want you?" He glared at Raize. "Start filling in the blanks."

I opened my mouth—

"She's got good hunches." Raize beat me to it.

Carl's shoulders lost some of their tension, and he eased back, standing upright again. He folded his arms over his chest. "Keep going."

Raize looked like he was eating wood chips as he ground out,

"She knows shit. Ask her a question, and she'll know the answer. She has good instincts."

"You psychic?" Carl asked.

I opened my mouth, again.

"No."

Raize beat me to it, again.

"She doesn't see the future or talk to dead people," he explained. "But ask her a question with a yes or no answer and she's right."

"How right?"

"Nine out of ten, she'll be correct."

"You've tested this?" Carl was starting to sound impressed.

"Test her yourself."

I hated when they did this. Despised it.

His first question was like a bullet. "Do I have a middle name?"

"No."

He grinned briefly. "You're right, I don't."

Question two. "I have a gift for my lady friend. Is she going to like it?"

"No." And I did *not* want to know anything more about that situation.

He didn't respond right away, but then came a third question. He spoke more slowly this time. "There's a guy behind you. Turn and look at him. Then turn back to me and tell me if he's skimming from me or not."

I turned, but my gut already knew.

The guy held a gun and at my look, he started to bristle. He grew red in the face.

I turned back, finding Carl watching me intently.

"Yes." I moved aside.

"Wha— I didn't! The bitch is lying."

Carl asked Raize, "She's not wrong?"

"Nine out of ten."

"Carl." The gun guy stepped forward, his arm hitting me on purpose. The tendons in his neck bulged. "I'm not lying. I never skimmed on you. Ever! She's a whackjob. You can't believe her."

"The question was if you *were* skimming me, not if you *had* skimmed me. Your answer confirmed hers." He reached into his desk drawer and produced a gun.

A hand grabbed my arm.

He raised it, and I was pulled to the side just as he pulled the trigger and shot the guy in the forehead. Raize had yanked me out of the way.

Just like that, *again*, I had blood and brain matter on my face, hair, and shirt.

I was so sick of seeing people killed in front of me.

The door opened. Another security guy poked his head in with Jake.

Jake looked at Raize and me. Raize motioned to him, and he stepped back outside.

Carl motioned to the body. "Take that out of here. Dispose of it."

The security guy looked back into the hallway, and two more guys stepped in, picked up the body, and carried it out. One guy cleaned the blood as they went.

Carl leaned back against the wall, folding his arms over his chest. "I need a reason why you killed Bronski's man, Raize."

"I told you."

"Bronski fucked up. He didn't know what she could do. He raped her, then sold her. He's too stupid to have her. I'm not."

I studied Carl, searching for a clue as to what he would do. He was Bronski and Raize's boss. I knew the stakes here, or I was getting them at least. If Carl found in favor of Bronski, I'd be returned to him, and Raize would get a bullet in the head. That was how it worked. If he didn't find in favor of Bronski... I didn't know. Probably nothing would happen because Bronski was the one wronged by Raize.

They didn't give a fuck what Bronski did to me.

Women had minimal uses in this world. Being a mule or a sex worker were the two most common options. I had a different purpose, and thank fucking God for it or I'd probably be dead with a busted drug bag in my stomach or hooked on drugs and pimped out on some corner, in some bed, in some motel, or in some gambling game. Who the fuck knew. I'd hit the jackpot with Raize, I was finding out.

Carl sighed, nodding. "Fine. You can keep her, but on one condition."

Raize stiffened.

I held my breath, too scared to do anything else.

"I have a job for you in Texas." He pointed to me, his finger extending lazily. "And you're going to use her."

Raize's jaw tightened. "What's the job?"

"We'll talk more later. Go and get your things ready. You'll be leaving tomorrow."

With that, Carl left the office, and Raize finally turned to me.

I was still holding my breath.

"We're going to Texas." He brushed past me, and I swayed back and forth on my feet for a second.

Texas.

What was in Texas?

"Breathe, Girl." Jake's voice drifted in from the hallway. "We all lived another day."

Right.

Living another day was also on my list of things to accomplish, but I was going to keep Carl's name there anyway. 'Cause fuck him.

I bet he'd never been raped.

3

CARRIE

"You got family here?"

I was surprised at the question and also who was asking. It was Jake.

Looks wise, he was six feet. Not as tall as Raize, but not short. Medium build. I'd guess that he worked out, or lifted on a regular basis. He was black. Dark eyes. His face was a little round and high cheekbones.

Did I mention he lifted? Because his shoulders were defined. He wore baggier clothes that didn't show the definition, but I knew it was there. I saw it when he was lifting a body one time. He was a bit bulkier than Raize, but both were defined. Cut.

I didn't know much about Jake. He came in and he was quiet.

He never said anything to me, and now he was asking questions like that?

People didn't ask questions. Nosy snitches and all that.

He turned around as we waited outside yet another house. Raize had gone inside, and he'd been in there for a good long time.

I was getting restless. Also, I needed to piss.

"Shouldn't you be in there?" I motioned with my head toward the house. "Since you're security."

Jake snorted, hiding a smile. "Raize doesn't need my help. I'm more the take-out-the-body guy and the driver. But between you and me, I'm hoping he gets a new guy that'll do the driving. I get antsy, want my hands free in case we need to shoot, you know?"

I'd have liked to say I didn't know because needing to shoot a gun at a second's notice wasn't normal. But it was for us.

So I nodded, settling back in the seat. "What's he doing in there, anyway?"

I wasn't looking at him, but I could feel Jake's look sharpen. "You never ask questions. This because I asked about your family?"

I met his eyes, and no words were needed. It was the reason, or most of the reason. I might have had a small trace of worry about Raize, since I now knew he was the reason I wasn't with Bronski again. It would suck if I had to go back to him. I'd probably have to kill him, and then who the fuck knew what would happen.

I had an agenda. There was a reason I was sitting on my ass in the cold car, or at least I hoped there still was. I wanted in with the Russians—just not through Bronski—and if we went to Texas, there were no Russians down there.

"*You* got family up here?" There might've been some attitude with that question.

He grinned. "Nah. My parents divorced. Mom's gone—left our asses long ago. She's got a new family out in Oregon or somewhere." He turned back to looking out the front, his head bobbing. "And good for her, you know? My old man and me...we ain't close."

I narrowed my eyes. "Why are you telling me this?"

"You asked."

I shifted again. It was getting hot in this damn car. "You know what I mean."

He didn't answer right away.

I started to think he wouldn't.

Then, still facing forward, he spoke. "I've been here a bit. You more. And I don't know... We're going to Texas, and it's obvious we've all hitched our wagons to Raize, and he's hitched his to you, so I figure what's the harm in getting to know each other a bit? It's not like any of us are leaving any time soon, you know?"

Yeah... I knew.

Still, I didn't like talking about family. My mouth was tight, my answer even tighter. "No family."

"Yeah." He sounded tired and sad at the same time, but then he glanced at the house. "Raize got a new man."

I looked.

Raize was headed our way, a big guy right behind him. The new guy looked uncomfortable in an oversized suit. But his face was bland—no tattoos, no scars. He was white, with some redness on his face like he'd been out in the sun too long. He had dark-blond hair that was flapping all over the place in the wind. He was a good five inches taller than Raize, who was over six feet, so the dude was big. He had a slight stomach on him, but that could've been muscle. The big clothes might've been picked on purpose, to trick anyone assessing into thinking he was chunky and not big and muscular. You couldn't tell from his face, though his neck was just huge.

We were in Philly, so it was effing cold—a smattering of snow on the ground, chilly air. But as Raize walked toward us, it was like nothing touched him. His dead eyes met mine, lingered, and then he motioned to the guy. His words were muffled through the glass, but I heard him say "front seat" as he walked around the car and got in behind Jake.

Raize glanced my way once, then sat back. "Airport, Jake. We're flying."

Jake looked in the rearview mirror. "Papers?"

"I got 'em." Then, "This is Cavers."

Jake nodded to him.

Cavers nodded back.

"Jake, you'll continue to be driver," Raize added.

Jake's eyes flicked to mine, but I looked away.

Cavers turned to look at me.

"She's none of your business," Raize said.

Cavers' face closed up, and he faced forward like he'd been slapped.

He'd just been expecting the same introduction he got for Jake. Raize must've sensed this, because he didn't say or do anything the whole way to the airport.

"Park in the long-term lot. We'll be leaving the vehicle here. And, Jake, wipe it down."

That meant we'd never be coming back to this car, ever.

I felt a whole new foreboding feeling, an itch down my spine, but what else was new in this world? I needed to get used to it.

No. That wasn't true.

I never needed to get used to it. When I did, that's when I'd be dead. I suppressed the tension that created, stuffing it to the back of my mind.

Could not go there.

Would not go there.

Jake pulled in, and we all got out.

Raize went to the back of the vehicle as Jake started wiping the inside of it.

We'd been told to pack light. I had a small backpack with a book and a change of clothes. Some toiletries. Raize was just as light. Cavers had nothing, and I assumed he hadn't known we'd be traveling, because he was looking around, shifting on his feet.

At least I hoped that was the reason he was doing the nervous dance. The other reason meant a bullet in his forehead, and I did not want that to happen—not because of him, but because I lost my appetite every time a body dropped dead in front of me.

Raize handed me my bag, and I put it on my back. He did the same with his bag. Jake's bag went on the ground, and then Raize rifled through another smaller bag.

He pulled out packets, handing one to each of us. "These are your traveling papers. These were taken care of by Carloni, so don't get a big head thinking you have fake papers and you can head out from us."

The warning there? These papers could be traced. Got it. Also, Carloni would be pissed about the lost investment.

I was also going out on a limb and guessing that Carloni was also Carl. It made sense.

"You sit by me," Raize said, looking at me.

I nodded, taking my new driver's license out.

My name was Carrie Smith. I was from Kentucky, and I was now twenty-three.

"You can call her Carrie," Raize told Cavers.

Cavers frowned, but didn't reply.

He also gave us new phones and took our old ones, which he put in a baggie and stuffed into his coat pocket.

It took Jake about an hour to finish with the car.

We waited to the side.

Raize was on his phone, standing away from us with his head down. Cavers was a smoker. I could smell the cigarettes on him, and wondered if he was itching to light up. Probably. Maybe that was why he was shifting on his feet. He stuffed his hands in his pockets, and I caught the bulge from his gun...which made me wonder what Raize was going to do about their guns. Unless we were checking a bag?

That proved to be the case once Jake was done.

Raize ended his call, shoving his phone into his pocket. He jerked his head toward Jake. "You're checking your bag. Everyone, put your guns inside. Wrap them up in some clothing. Give me the keys, Jake."

He handed them over.

Raize went to the front and ducked inside to leave the bag of phones under the seat. He put the keys in a zipped compartment behind the front seat. Then he locked the doors before giving everything a once-over.

After that, we were ready for the airport.

RAIZE HAD us each enter through different doors and different security entrances. He and I stayed together, and he sent Cavers off first. Jake went next, with instructions to keep an eye on Cavers, from a distance. He nodded, heading off to check his bag.

Raize and I moved past him and through the farthest door and the farthest security checkpoint. I used to fly, back when I lived normally, so I knew not all airports were the same. Some had different security stations set up around the whole airport, which helped cut down the lines, but others had one large security line. Those were horrible to go through—they took forever.

I was glad these were sectioned off.

"Move."

The command wasn't loud or even a bark, but I jerked because I'd been daydreaming. *So* not something I did.

I picked up my pace, settling behind a group of ladies who looked like they were off on a girls' weekend. They looked rich, mid-thirties, and they were eyeing Raize behind me. A couple seemed already sloshed, the others ready to get sloshed. I hoped they wouldn't be on the same plane as us.

"You nervous to fly?"

I was surprised by Raize's question, and turned toward him.

His dark eyes assessed me, but he didn't seem as cold as he usually did.

I didn't know how I felt about that.

I raised a shoulder. "No, just thinking about life before."

He stared at me, then nodded and looked forward.

The women were openly staring at him now, whispering together.

I didn't know women could still whisper like schoolgirls, but these ladies were doing it.

A couple of them smiled at Raize, who cursed under his breath. "Come on."

"What?"

"I don't want attention. Let's do another security gate."

We shifted forward, and I said, "We're two groups away. Ignore them."

He glared at me. "They want to flirt with me."

"Duh."

"I don't flirt."

I almost grinned at that. He was outright annoyed.

One of the women fell back, and I knew she was doing it to overhear our conversation.

The front of her group started through the security line, and that's when she turned back. "Where y'all traveling to?"

"None of your business." Raize's hand touched the small of my back, and I almost jumped into the lady. But then I settled back and felt his hand open up, his fingers spreading wide.

His touch didn't make my skin crawl. That was a shock. I pasted a smile on my face as the lady gasped. "We just got bad news from a family member. You'll have to excuse my..."

"Husband," Raize announced.

"Husband." *Seriously? Husband?*

The lady stepped back at my statement, but her eyes darted to our fingers. No rings. She frowned, and I saw more questions coming.

I got there first. "Where are you all headed?"

"Oh!" She lit up as we progressed through the line. "My friend over there, Sadie, she's getting a divorce, so we thought a trip down to Mexico would be the best way to celebrate. We love to go down there. We go once a year, sometimes more. You ever been?" She was asking me, but her eyes had returned to Raize, who shifted farther behind me.

I had to smother my grin. I shouldn't be enjoying this reaction from him, but I couldn't stop myself.

It was so...normal.

That was it.

This was a momentary escape from our lives, and I was going with it.

I moved forward as the woman did, after introducing herself as Mary. She asked our names, but the guard called for her. It was perfect timing. After that, she and her friends went down the right lane, and after handing over our identification and showing the tickets on Raize's phone, we were sent to the left lane.

I didn't have anything to pull from my bag, so I left it the way it was. No computer. Nothing like that. I didn't have any liquids, so I toed off my shoes and put them next to my bag in the same bin. Raize did the same, putting his leather jacket in a separate bin.

"Did you send the tickets to the guys?" I asked as we waited our turn.

He nodded, touching my back again, and as the guard waved me forward, he gently pushed me ahead.

Going through, I spread my legs and put my hands above my head, barely letting myself think how this would be how I'd stand to have handcuffs put on. Nope. I wasn't going there. When I got the clear, I moved forward and grabbed my stuff from the bin.

The ladies were waiting a few feet away. Mary migrated over, giving me a small smile as we watched Raize get waved through. They took longer checking him, waving him to the side for a further inspection. I kept an eye on his bin as Mary asked, "So where are y'all heading to?"

I started to answer, but realized I didn't know. *Shit*. That was something I should know, but Raize had the tickets.

"We're headed to Texas."

"Really? We're not flying into Mexico. We're heading to Texas for a few days first. One of our girlfriends has a house down there, in Corpus Christi. Where in Texas are you going? Maybe we're on the same flight."

Fuuuuck. I needed to stall, but then I felt a familiar presence behind me. Raize's hand touched my back as his rough voice answered for me, "Excuse us. We're meeting some people."

So abrupt, but so perfect.

He pushed me forward, still gently, and Mary stepped back. "Sure. Yeah... Have a good trip."

He didn't respond, directing me toward a busy walkway as he pulled his backpack back on.

"Where are we going?" I asked.

"We're flying into San Antonio and then driving down."

"Down where?"

As the crowd swarmed around us, Raize moved to walk beside me. He dropped his hand and gave me a look. "Since when do you care about that shit?"

Right.

I'd forgotten. I was an employee, nothing more.

My moment of normalcy was gone.

"I don't." I shrugged it off, feeling the usual cold, numb wall sliding over me. Once it was locked in place, I could feel the distance between myself and these other travelers. I was standing almost shoulder to shoulder with them, but they had no idea how far away I actually was.

When we got to our gate, Raize had me wait in the open area just outside it. Jake and Cavers were already there, sitting in opposite sections from each other. I didn't look at them after an initial glance to see they were there. I tuned out my surroundings.

"Do you have any headphones?" I asked Raize.

He frowned, but dug into his bag. He held them out, and I took them, not saying thanks.

I slid down to sit on the floor and took out my new phone. This life or a different life, I could still enjoy music.

4

CARRIE

The divorce-party ladies were on our flight.

I was ten minutes into enjoying my music when they showed up. Raize immediately moved away, bending and telling me to watch his bag. I smiled because seeing Raize uncomfortable was just funny at this point. I was starting to like these ladies.

They continued looking him over, and I tried to see it.

I did.

I mean...

No. I didn't see it.

He might've been attractive, but Raize was just cold, too dead on the inside.

Mary saw me and came over, bending down and taking a seat beside me. "Hey."

Headphones. Did she not see the headphones in my ears?

I pulled one bud out. "Hey?"

She jerked her chin up toward Raize. "It looks like we're on the same flight. How awesome is that? Where are y'all sitting?" She pulled her ticket out, showing me. "We're in the comfort zone. Sabrina didn't want to spring for first class, but are we close?" Her head bent toward me. She lowered her voice. "Are you two really married?"

Her eyes dipped down, lingering on my finger. The one that did not have a ring on it.

"Uh." I needed to up my game on lying. "We are, but we just had an anniversary, so we're getting a little update on them." I gazed over at Raize, making sure the look seemed loving and warm.

As if sensing it, he turned toward me and then halted, his eyes narrowing.

I pasted a big, wide smile on my face. "He's so romantic. He won't tell me what's being done to the ring, but then we got the call about our family, and now we're here."

She sighed, fanning herself. "Oh my. That's just swoon-worthy." Her eyebrows dipped down, and she tensed for a second. "He seems a bit cold, though. Doesn't he?" Her voice fluttered, literally fluttered.

I could feel the excitement from her, and I suddenly understood.

The more of a dick Raize was, the more intriguing he was to her. Turn him into a good guy, a nice guy, and their whole group would lose interest. I could make the recommendation to Raize, but that wasn't something he could fake. It'd be painful to see him try.

Women weren't something Raize ever needed to work for, but I always figured it was because of what he did. Those women wanted drugs, or so I'd assumed, but maybe not. Maybe they just wanted Raize.

It was a weird sensation, looking at him the way normal women viewed him. Then again, he hadn't shot someone in cold blood minutes after they met him. And they hadn't seen him continue to murder people for the sole reason that they might be a problem in the future.

Mary sidled a bit closer to me. "He seems dangerous. Ruthless." She was eye-fucking him, but glanced to me as she asked, "What's the worst thing he's done?"

This woman was deranged. But then I noticed a white line above her top lip. It was faint, but it was there. I could only see it because she'd scooted so close to me.

Ah. *Now* it made sense.

Could she sense he dealt drugs?

I reexamined her gaze. She'd gone back to eye-fucking Raize, and the lust was palpable.

Maybe it was the danger Raize gave off?

Or could she sense he was a killer? Was that it?

She drew in a sharp breath and moved back, her head straightening as if she'd been struck. She blinked rapidly, looking past my shoulder, and a pair of shoes came to my other side.

"They're calling our seats," Raize said.

I hadn't noticed the announcements, but he was right. A line had started to form to board the plane. Cavers and Jake were already in line, five passengers between them. Cavers stared blankly forward, but Jake glanced back at us.

I flashed him a look. He grinned before facing forward. A wall slid back in place, and he was a stranger once more.

Raize bent, grabbing my bag. "Come on."

I had my phone and his headphones in hand.

Mary had jumped to her feet, smoothing her shirt and running her hands over her skirt. "Hey there. Fancy seeing you guys again."

Raize gave her the chilliest of chilly looks ever, ignored her, and touched my back. He herded me forward. "Let's go."

"Hey—"

He stopped, twisting around. "Don't, you fucking coke skank." She gasped, but he wasn't done. "Walk away and forget we exist. Got it?"

"Oh, come on." A nervous laugh hitched in her voice. "Don't be like that."

"Keep looking at me or her, and I'll put a bullet in your forehead."

Her second gasp sounded more shocked. Reality had started to set in for her, but still, she murmured, "We're going to be on an airplane. No guns."

Joking.

She was joking?!

I went back to my first thought. Forget the coke habit; she needed to be in a mental hospital.

Raize's voice was low, and filled with warning. "I'll improvise."

The line began moving forward, so I went to stand behind a lady. A second later, I felt Raize's presence at my back.

"Don't talk to her or any of them. They're trouble," he said quietly.

Uh, yeah. I was getting that.

I didn't respond, but he didn't seem to care.

The line progressed and when we came to our row, there was a guy in the aisle seat. He looked up, and his eyes widened.

Raize leaned around me. "You just got the window seat."

"But..." Panic flashed on his face, but he was smarter than Mary. He shut up, grabbed his tablet, and moved to the window seat.

I took middle and Raize had the aisle.

I glanced back once and saw Jake laughing, his head shaking before he ducked down in his seat.

I felt myself starting to grin with him.

This whole thing was just nuts.

At one point during the flight, Mary needed to go past us to use the bathroom. She averted her eyes as she did. That made me smile, too.

5

CARRIE

When we deplaned, Mary and her group got off before we did.

We walked past them on the jetway where they were waiting for their bags. Mary averted her gaze, same as on her bathroom trip. I noticed another less-faint white line over her lip, but that was for her friends to handle. It might even be picked up by drug dogs, if this airport had them. One of her friends noticed my look and realized what I saw. Her eyes went big, but then we were past them and up the ramp.

Stepping into the airport, Raize pulled his phone out and kept walking. I moved behind him. I knew my place, but I glanced back to see if I could see Jake or Cavers.

My phone buzzed, and I pulled it out. Raize had texted all of us.

Raize: Walk out, wait by the cab line. Jake, get your bag and find us. Cavers, stand fifty yards away. Jake, the same.

He had already put his phone away by the time I finished reading, and he'd picked up his pace. I hurried to catch up. Raize moved through crowds like I did. He kept to the side and found the path of least resistance through the oncoming people. His head was down, but when a security guy stepped out, Raize guided me to join a crowd in front of us, our heads turned to the side.

We didn't want attention.

I doubted there were arrest warrants out for us, but in our world, you never knew.

I had to hand it to Raize, because while he was now moving not to attract attention, people around us still reacted. They instinctively moved aside for us, and they often wore a look of confusion as we slipped past, as if their bodies made the decision for them.

That was Raize, not me. People didn't move for me. They didn't notice I was there. I could stand in a shadow for hours.

I realized I was thinking too much. I needed to turn off my mind and go with Raize as if we were two ends of the same wave, one starting and one ending.

I could tell Raize noticed when I managed this because his shoulders relaxed, and he began walking more smoothly. He looked up, no longer hiding as much, and we moved as one when a security guard appeared. I almost faltered when we went past a guard with a dog in front of him, but Raize didn't likely have anything on him. That'd be stupid. We'd pick up product or whatever his orders were after we left the airport. If we'd been transporting, we would've driven down.

As we got to the exit of the airport, the attention began to return.

People were looking for their loved ones. I could feel eyes on us, and no matter how or where I moved, those eyes never left. My forehead started itching. I didn't like it, but I stayed with Raize, and as we stepped outside, he had his phone again.

He stopped, read whatever was on the screen, and looked up.

A blue truck waited by the curb.

Raize cursed under his breath. "Wait here."

I shifted back, standing by the wall as people leaving moved past me. Raize went over to the blue truck.

The passenger window rolled down, and he bent forward, but stayed on the curb. The driver spoke to him, motioning, but Raize wasn't moving. He was not happy. I knew that much. His back was straight, and he was alert. If he'd had a gun, he would've had it out by now.

Feeling a presence on my left, I looked.

Cavers stood ten yards away from me, waiting just outside the doors. He blocked the flow of people behind him, so they were moving around him. He looked at me first, then slid his gaze to Raize. His mouth pressed into a line, and he stepped away to the other side of the doors.

He stopped twenty yards away, but instead of moving to the wall, he took position just behind a post. He looked as if he were waiting for a ride to pick him up.

I went back to watching Raize, whose hand jerked at his side.

I gasped.

His hand flexed before he shook it out, and he moved his head from side to side as he turned and walked back my way. His jaw was tight.

Coming toward me, he saw Cavers and pulled his phone back out.

Another text came through.

Raize: Carrie, wait for Jake. Get a cab and I'll send directions.

Raize: Cavers, grab a cab. I'm with you.

Cavers had his phone out and immediately switched position, going for the cab line.

Raize didn't say anything, just made eye contact as he walked past me, following Cavers at a good distance.

I settled back against the wall. Who knew how long the baggage claim line would be.

THE WAIT WAS THIRTY MINUTES.

Jake came out, bag over his shoulder, and he was pissed. When he saw me, we walked together toward where the cabs were waiting.

We needed to be talking.

Normal passengers who traveled together talked. They didn't move silently, like they were oddly synchronized by the same thoughts.

Musing on that, I stepped up next to Jake. "How was the baggage claim?"

He cut his eyes my way. "Why?"

I lowered my voice. "Everyone is talking to the people they're traveling with."

He looked, too, and I felt some of his edge fading. He eased up and nodded. "Those bitches were there that were talking you up. They noticed me looking at you, and the cokehead wanted to know who I was."

"Are you serious?"

He dipped his head in a quick nod, his tension coming back. "What'd Raize say to that one? She looked out for blood, thinking I knew you or something."

"He threatened to kill her."

He grinned, snorting. "Bitches don't like threats like that. Think they're above that shit. Fucking socialite princesses."

"I think they're just sheltered."

We stepped forward, and I felt Jake studying me. "You know from experience?"

I opened my mouth to say, "My sister was the same." But I caught my words.

Holy—I'd been about to spill to him.

I didn't spill to anyone.

I'd gotten comfortable—comfortable enough that it was dangerous.

No one could know about my sister. No one.

But Jake was still studying me, still waiting.

I lifted a shoulder. "She's a cokehead. What am I thinking?"

He frowned and murmured, "Those bitches are the kind that want your blow, but want you to fuck 'em while they snort it. She was frothing at the mouth, thinking Raize was her new drug dealer."

I glanced sharply at him. "He comes off like that?"

"No. He comes off like an asshole or a soldier, but she saw what she wanted to see."

Then the worker motioned for us, and we were at the front of the line.

A cab rolled up, and Jake waved him to stay in his seat. We held our bags with us and slid into the back. Jake pulled out his phone, reading the address Raize had sent in a text, and then we settled back.

We were on our way.

We were now in San Antonio.

I just didn't know why we were here.

CARRIE

W e stayed in a rundown motel the first night, in two rooms that had an adjoining door. Raize and Cavers in one; Jake and me in the other. The door between the two rooms was open the whole time.

It was late at night, but it didn't matter. Raize went to work.

He drove off and came back an hour later in an SUV. He picked up Jake, and they returned a while later with an older brown truck as well. I just sat back, watching through my window as Raize continuously left and came back with something else: a bag, a second bag.

Jake laid out our guns on his bed, going through and checking each one. Cavers went with Raize on his last two runs, and I was bored. I could've read. I didn't want to read.

I started watching Jake, meticulously going over each gun. "I want to learn to shoot," I told him.

He swung surprised eyes my way. "You don't know?"

I shook my head. "I never wanted to learn."

He whistled, going back to cleaning. "Girl, you *loca*. This life —how the fuck you still alive?"

"I'm more useful alive than dead."

He grunted and bobbed his head, still cleaning. "That's true, for sure."

I waited.

He kept cleaning.

I leaned forward, resting my elbows on my knees. "I mean it. I want to learn how to shoot."

He gave me another long, lingering perusal as he dipped his head slowly forward. "Girl, I ain't the one who's going to be teaching you. I ain't the boss here."

"You can still teach me."

"When?" His sarcasm was thick. "This is the most he's left you alone. You're boss' secret weapon. Why do you think I'm with you?" He motioned with his rag to the other room, currently empty. "He don't trust Cavers with you, and he don't trust Cavers not to kill me. That's why we got the cab assignments and room assignments we got. You and me tomorrow will be in one truck and those two will be in the other."

That all made sense. But that wasn't what I was asking about.

I leaned back. "Teach me to shoot."

"No."

"Yes."

When I started on this journey, that had been my one thing I tried to stay away from. I was a year and a half in and learning how stupid that'd been. I should've learned before going to work for Bronski. That would've been the smart thing to do. Know how to use a gun, but act like I didn't. Be underestimated. It would've been an ace up my sleeve, and in this world, that could keep me alive.

I needed to learn how to shoot a gun.

He sighed. "Girl."

"Carrie."

He frowned, lowering the gun he was cleaning. "Excuse me?"

"My new name. Carrie. What's your name?"

He continued to stare at me, like I'd told him to figure out a puzzle before we could keep talking. But then he pulled out his new license. "Brad Watowski. I'm a Norwegian piece of shit."

"Brad."

He nodded to me, returning to the gun. "Carrie."

I stood from my chair. "Teach me to shoot a gun, Brad."

His eyes went flat. "Don't do this, Girl."

"Teach me."

"You know I can't." He went back to cleaning.

I bit back frustration.

"But I guarantee that if you ask the boss, he'll teach you to shoot, or he'll okay me teaching you."

Relief warmed my chest. "So you're not saying yes because you need approval?"

He whistled, shaking his head. "You've seen our boss in action. I ain't doing shit without his say-so." He gave me a dark look. "You been watching Cavers?"

A chill went through me.

The answer was no, because I didn't like Cavers. I didn't know why, but I knew I didn't like him.

Seeing my look, understanding my look, Jake kept on rubbing that barrel. "Boss don't want him with us, but he's not asked you about him because he can't get rid of him yet. I don't know what we're doing here, but I can tell that Cavers guy is a big part of it."

That gave me a bad taste in my mouth.

Whatever or whoever Cavers was, none of us wanted him with us. A person didn't need my gut instinct to know that. Cavers was either going to bring about our death or he was going to die by our hands. One or the other. A guy like that, there was no other way.

Jake reached for a new rag. "I'll tell you right now, though. I'll be happy when I get the go-ahead to put a bullet in that guy's forehead. We'll *all* be better off. You. Me. *El Jefe*."

I reached for my phone as I glanced out the window. Two trucks had pulled in, and they drove slowly past our rooms.

"What is it?" Jake asked.

I found myself standing, though I hadn't realized it.

I motioned to the window. "Those trucks look friendly to you?"

Jake was all business, moving to the window with a gun raised. He eased back the curtain, looked, and cursed.

That was all I needed.

I was on the move, grabbing the bags.

Jake put the rest of the guns in a bag and pulled it onto his back. He was facing the door with a gun in each hand as I came back with Cavers and Raize's bags. I was wearing mine.

"You need me to take anything?"

He was looking outside. "No, but text the boss. Let him know we might be running."

I did, and got a near immediate response.

Raize: Kill them if need be. If not, get away. Take a pic of them if you can.

I told Jake what he'd said, and he gave me a hard look.

The truck stopped outside our room.

We could leave through the back window. Everything was in our bags. The only thing we'd be leaving behind was our DNA, but I could tell Jake didn't want to do that.

"Can you take a pic for him?" Jake asked softly.

I nodded, going to the other room.

A guy was getting out of the truck. He wore tight jeans, a big belt, a white button down shirt, and a cowboy hat. He walked toward the room where Jake was and peeked inside. I took my phone out, positioning it just beyond the curtain, and I took the pictures Raize wanted.

The truck.

The guy walking.

The license plate.

The driver still in the truck.

The images were clear enough, and I shot them off to Raize.

He responded as I returned to the other room.

Raize: Leave. Now.

I shared this with Jake, and he took one last look out the window before motioning to me. "Let's go out their bathroom window."

We went back to Cavers and Raize's room. Jake shut the adjoining door, locking it without making a sound. We went to the bathroom. It was a small window, but big enough for both of us. I went first, falling into a crouch on the ground outside. Jake tossed all the bags to me, and I kept a lookout as he climbed through.

I had a moment to reflect as I did so, and this was *so* not normal.

Here I was, escaping through a shitty motel bathroom window, and I knew it wasn't luck that we had this exit. Raize wouldn't have picked a motel where we could've been cornered. We were probably running from local drug enforcers, and if anyone came to check the back, I'd have to shoot.

So I should probably have a weapon. Jake had his back to me, and I reached up, taking one of his guns from him.

He cursed, falling the rest of the way, and then glared as he swiped his gun back. Raising it to me, he warned, "You don't touch this until you know how to shoot it. I'm not going to be taken out by a girl named Carrie. Got me?"

For some reason, I found that endearing. I grinned. "Got it."

He rolled his eyes and reached up, grabbing the window so it closed somewhat.

Then we took off down the alley, which connected to another alley, and we crossed a parking lot before hitting the street.

I didn't know how to feel about what had just happened, but my stomach growled, and I decided that was more important right now.

I motioned to a late night taco truck. Since we were here, why not?

There were a few buzzed or drunk people also there so we'd have cover.

While we were at a picnic table eating our tacos, those guys drove past and took a left at the intersection. I nabbed a pic of that and sent it to Raize.

My phone rang a second later.

I answered it on speaker, knowing who it was. "Yeah?"

"Where are you guys?"

I told him the taco place's name. "We're outside, sitting at a table."

"Those guys left?"

"Yeah."

"They didn't see you eating?"

Jake had stopped eating, waiting.

"I don't think they know who we are." Not that I knew who we were either. "They were just looking in the rooms when we left."

"Is Jake there?"

"Aye," he called.

"Listen, we can't get away right now. Get a cab, go to a *nice* hotel. She's going to stay in the lobby, and I need you to go buy a car. Local. Cash. No paperback."

Jake's gaze met mine. "Got it."

"After you get the vehicle, go to a different motel. Have the girl pick it. Text me where you are."

Jake's gaze narrowed and his chewing slowed. He lowered his taco. "You and Cavers need backup?"

Raize's response was brisk right before he hung up. "No. Do as I say." And then dial tone.

Jake sighed, raising his taco again. "I ain't doing shit until I finish my third taco."

That sounded about right to me, too.

Tacos should always come first.

7

CARRIE

After we finished eating, we did as Raize had instructed. I babysat our bags in the front lobby of a Milton—sitting far, far off in a corner because I had no clue what was in these bags—and Jake went to get us a new set of wheels.

He came back with an older, black Honda Civic, the engine sounding like it was trying to eat its way out of the car.

I didn't say anything as he approached me in the lobby, just focused on not laughing.

Jake snorted. "Shut it. It's the best I could do. Boss is going to have to deal."

We were just settling in at a motel on the outskirts of San Antonio when Raize and Cavers pulled up. Neither seemed happy when they saw us.

"What car did you get?" Raize asked.

Jake nodded to the black one parked in the lot. "That beautiful masterpiece."

Raize gave him a second look before assessing the car. His lips pressed into a line, but he nodded. "Fine." He was back to business, stepping inside our room. We'd gotten the same setup with a connecting door between the rooms. Cavers immediately went to the other room, and I could hear him opening some bags.

Raize shut the door and stood with his back against it for a second, his eyes downcast.

Jake and I shared a look. This wasn't a good sign.

We heard the bathroom door shut in the other room. The fan clicked on, and Raize lifted his head. His eyes were blazing.

This was so not good.

"Go and get a tracker," he told Jake softly. "I want one on his phone and one on his truck. Now."

Jake nodded, grabbing his things on the way out.

Raize stepped away from the door and came closer to me. "You and he need to know what we're walking into, but I can't." His eyes flicked over my shoulder, and I knew what he was saying. He couldn't when a certain someone was close enough to eavesdrop.

I nodded. "What do you need from me?"

"Pack a small bag—bare necessities. We'll leave it somewhere you can grab it if you need to run."

Run?

Fuck.

Run. Running was bad.

I swallowed over a knot. "I didn't get into this life to run."

"Whatever the reason, you need to live to do it." His eyes went back over my shoulder. "Pack the bag," he repeated as he stepped back.

It didn't take me long, and I used the plastic bag that went over the motel's hair dryer. Cavers was still in the bathroom when I showed it to Raize. "Done."

His eyebrows pulled in. "There's nothing in there."

"I don't have anything to start with."

He gave me a look. "What do you have?"

"Two pairs of underwear, one pair of socks, a sports bra, and two changes of clothes."

"Money?"

"Whatever you give me."

He shook his head. "That's it? You don't have anything extra on you?"

"You're the only boss that's paid me."

His eyes went flat at that, and he ran a hand over his face. "There's nothing in here. There's no point in even doing this bag." He nodded to the bathroom door. "He comes out, you tell him I went to get food."

I glanced to the door, but felt Raize move up behind me.

My shirt lifted.

I stiffened, holding my breath.

He pushed something cold and firm into the back of my pants and returned my shirt to its proper place. "You sit. If he moves at you, you shoot him. Got me?"

Fuuck. My mouth was so dry, but I nodded. "Got it."

He was gone in the next second, and I was left with the shower running in Cavers' bathroom and my heart pounding in my chest. It was deafening.

I HEARD Cavers come out of the bathroom and walk through his room. He came to the doorway of my room with a wet head and new clothes on.

He glanced around. "Where'd they go?"

My mouth was so dry. I could feel the weight of that gun against my back. "Raize went to get food. Jake's doing an errand." I didn't know if I was supposed to share that last bit, but lying came naturally to me—another skill I didn't like, but needed for survival.

Also, I didn't even know if I was lying. Raize might've actually gone for food.

He nodded, blinking. I noticed the deep bags under his eyes.

"Good. I'm fucking tired and hungry. Mind if I close this so I can take a nap?"

"Raize doesn't want that closed."

He narrowed his eyes. I tensed, expecting a fight, but he only nodded again. "Okay. Ignore my snores then."

I nodded, but didn't move—not even when I heard him collapse on the bed I couldn't see. A minute or so later, when I heard his snores, some of my stiffness loosened. There'd be no fight, no sudden... I didn't know what I was expecting. Still, I sat in the same position until forty minutes later when Raize came through the door.

It opened soundlessly, and he paused, taking everything in.

He didn't speak. I didn't speak. He came in, shut the door, still silent, and moved to glance into the other room.

He had another two guns on him, both handguns. He also had food with him and he tossed the bag of food on the table in front of me. He put one of the guns on the dresser and disappeared into the other room for a bit. When he came back, he had all the bags with him. He set them in the corner before going back and returning with Cavers' personal bag and phone. He put everything on the counter before closing the door and locking it.

After that, he closed his eyes, resting his forehead to the door for a millisecond. Then his neck straightened, his back went rigid again, and he turned, skimming his dead eyes over me before going to the bathroom. He kept one of the guns on him, while he washed up.

"Do you need to take a shower?" he asked after a moment

It was then that I felt like I could relax, as much as I normally could.

I stood and pulled his gun from my jeans.

He waved at me. "You need to keep that."

"I don't know how to shoot it."

He narrowed his eyes, his head cocking to the side. "You don't?"

I shook my head. "It was my line. Before." I handed him the gun.

He took it. "Your line?"

"You know, we all have a line we won't cross. Shooting a gun was mine."

His eyes darkened, and he gave me the gun back. "That's a seriously stupid line. You need to learn how to shoot."

I was aware, but I just didn't want to tell him that. Or, not yet. I'd wait until Jake became a pain in my ass about getting Raize's approval before he taught me to shoot. I didn't know why I was doing this, but I dunno. Maybe it was a new line?

I yawned, lying down on the bed by the door.

"Switch."

"What?"

Raize took his bag and the guns he'd put on the other bed, the one closer to the bathroom. "Sleep here." He put everything on the end of the bed I was currently lying on. "I'll do watch until Jake gets back."

I was not going to argue with that. My head was now bobbing since I'd given myself permission to let the exhaustion seep in. It came hard and fast.

I lay down, my shoes on, fully dressed. I could be asleep within seconds, and I yawned. Still, if we had to run, I wanted to be ready. I skipped the blanket and turned to lie on my side.

I watched Raize for a beat.

I'd never seen anyone like him.

He was lean, but he had broad shoulders. He moved around without moving around, if that made sense. He had a pretty face. Tan skin. Dark eyes. His hair was left alone. It was brown and he let it be. It wasn't long or anything, but it wasn't a crew cut. He was rough without not being rough at all. I knew he had tattoos, some on his arm, I saw one on his back one time, but nothing on his neck or face. He kept them where they could be hidden. And his body, it was lean and cut. Right now, shadows cast down over his forehead and his cheekbones, giving him this whole dark angel look.

I suppressed a shiver and turned away. What was going on with me?

He settled at the table by the window, moving the curtain so he could see outside.

"What are we doing here?"

He looked over, a flicker in his eyes.

Normally, I would never ask. Raize always provided information as needed. But my gut told me this was a whole different ballgame.

There was a moment of quiet before he said, "The Russians want to set up a business relationship down here. We were sent to set up that connection."

I frowned. "Here? Who runs San Antonio?"

"Not here. We're leaving once we've all gotten sleep."

"Where?" I pressed.

"The Valley. Carloni wants us to work with the Estrada Cartel."

He stared at me. I stared back.

Cartel.

That was a whole different ball game.

Those words hung between us, because we both knew what that meant.

I started this journey to find my sister.

There were a lot of details about the who, the why, the where, etc., but it's why I was standing in this motel room staring at this guy.

Jesus.

There'd been many times that I wished I had never started this journey. But never once had I considered giving up the search for my sister. But today, right now, hearing where our path was taking us, I thought about letting her go.

Maybe it was time.

She'd made her decision so long ago, but...

Not yet.

I rolled over, curled into a ball, and fell asleep.

I was going to need the rest.

8

CARRIE

W e were parked outside a gas station. Me and Jake. I was in the front with the door open, my feet up on the dashboard. We were waiting for Raize and Cavers to return from inside.

It was almost eleven in the morning.

We only had another hour to go. The drive hadn't been long, but Raize said we needed to stop, so we did.

Jake climbed back behind the wheel with his food. He handed me a bag and put his coffee in the drink holder. He handed over the second for me.

"I added some of the sugary shit for you."

I took it, surprised at the gesture. "Thank you."

I hadn't thought about getting anything. I went in, went to the bathroom, washed up, and came back out. I hadn't needed to get the keys from Jake. Raize had sent Jake to make extra copies while I was sleeping. We each got a set of keys to both vehicles, and once Jake had slept enough to drive, we were off.

"So?" he asked as he looked my way.

I sipped my coffee, grimacing at its heat and his question. "I haven't asked."

His eyes shifted to my bag, where he knew my gun was. When we'd taken everything out to the vehicles, Raize had added a gun to my bag. *"That is yours now,"* he'd told me. *"You will need it."*

Jake shook his head. "Girl."

I grinned. I'd grown attached to being called Girl. "It's Carrie now."

He huffed, rolling his eyes. "I don't get this, whatever you're doing."

"What am I doing?"

"I don't know. That's why I don't get it. What are you doing? He gave you a gun. Does he know you don't know how to use it?"

I took another sip. It was still hot. "He knows."

"And?"

"And what?"

"I still can't teach you unless you ask him or he gives me the order. You know that. What's this weird resistance from you?"

I sighed, putting my feet down and sitting up in my seat. I rested my head against the backrest. "It's just another milestone I don't want to cross yet."

"Milestone?"

"Yeah. You know, in this world, it's all a slippery slope. Me learning how to shoot a gun is the milestone before I actually *use* the gun." My stomach clenched, knowing what was on the other side of *that* milestone.

Understanding flared in his eyes. "Look, you're never gonna be the girl he sends out to kill someone. When it comes to it, the boss is going to do his own dirty work. That's how he got his come-up anyway, but you need to learn. When it's you or the guy who's trying to kill you, the other guy has to go. And you ain't dumb. You know that."

I knew that. Of course I did, but it was another step toward losing my soul, too.

I frowned. "His come-up?"

He reached for his bag, taking out a sandwich and unwrapping it. "You know."

I shook my head. "I don't."

"That's how he got in the business. He's from the cartel." He kept watching me, and seeing my confusion, his lips pressed together. "You didn't know?"

I shook my head. *Raize came from the cartel?* What did that mean?

I felt like it meant something... Cartels were a whole other level of vicious.

Wow. The *cartel*. In our business, they were avoided. The Russians were bad, but the cartel was different. They didn't just kill *you*. They went after your family. They went after anyone you loved, and they did their research.

I was doubly glad no one knew my real name.

I'd been Brooke when I started down this path. There had been a few other names before Raize started calling me Girl. Now I was Carrie.

"He was the guy they sent in to take someone out. The dude's good at killing people."

I suppressed a shiver. "How'd he get out?"

"I don't know. There were rumors he got out because his boss was indebted to him. Others say he was sold like you were to Carloni. I think the only one who really knows is him." Jake side-eyed me. "He might tell you. He likes you."

I jerked in surprise. "What?"

He nodded. "He's got a soft spot for you. Don't know why. I don't think he wants to fuck you. Maybe you remind him of someone?"

That was weirdly unsettling.

We both stopped talking.

Jake ate his food, and I sipped my coffee as we waited for Cavers and Raize to show.

Raize came out first, but waited outside the door. He looked at their truck, then us. I could feel his gaze on me before he went back inside. A couple women were checking him out. That gave me an unsettled feeling in the pit of my stomach, too.

"Is Raize good looking?"

I hadn't meant to ask that out loud. Jake paused mid-bite. He started laughing, peeling the wrapper back. "That's funny, you asking me that."

I'd thought it once when I was drunk, but not after. And the women at the airport, now the women here... I just saw the deadness inside of him.

"Is he?" I didn't know why I was pushing this. I knew he was. But I wanted to hear what Jake would say. And I didn't know the reason for that either.

He paused, the hot dog in his mouth as he studied me a second. Then he swallowed and lowered his food to his lap. "You serious?"

I nodded.

He tilted his head, as if he could get a better look at me and maybe understand why I was asking. "Yes. I'm a straight male, but I can tell the ladies like him. A lot. Then again, most women are crazy in my opinion."

I nodded. That settled me.

The world felt right again.

Those women were just crazy.

9

CARRIE

We pulled up to a house two hours later. It was near some warehouses, but isolated from other houses. Really isolated. And it had a large chain fence set around it. The grass was brown—what grass there was. The house itself looked like it could fall apart any second, but Raize had parked and was unloading the bags.

When Jake got out, Raize said, "I want you to head out and grab what we'll need to live here for a while."

"Like what?"

"Food. Drinks. Whatever we need." Raize turned to me and added, "Clothes for her. She's got nothing."

Jake glanced my way before nodding. "Okay."

"Girl."

I thought I'd be Carrie, but no. Habits were hard to break apparently.

He didn't wait for my response. He indicated the back of the truck. "Help Cavers bring everything in."

I walked over and grabbed one of the large duffel bags Raize had put in the truck when he and Cavers went on their errands. It was hella heavy, and I recognized the sound of guns inside as I walked toward the house. Assault rifles. Jesus. I gave Raize a look, but he was busy with his phone. He had gotten enough guns that we could wage war, if we needed to. Then it hit me: that was why we were here.

Cavers came outside. His large shoulders almost didn't fit through the doorway. He gestured behind him. "Kitchen. You can start taking them out. Lay them on the table."

I dipped my head, moving past him. I stepped inside and took a sharp left turn to go into the kitchen, which was too small for a table except a tiny one only one or two people could sit at. I kept going into the dining room where there was a larger table. Putting the bag down, I glanced around. I needed to piss.

The whole house was small and made up of smaller rooms. The next doorway led into a living room with a couch against one wall and a loveseat against the other. A television sat up on top of a dresser, shoved back against another wall. There was barely enough room for two people to stand in the middle of the room. I kept moving. The other doorway from the living room led to a small hallway, and there was the bathroom. Going in, I shut the door and didn't move.

I didn't know why.

Maybe a sixth sense? A forewarning?

Instinct?

Whatever it was, I held firm.

I could hear Cavers' heavy footsteps going in and out of the house, then moving past the bathroom and into a back room. I heard the squeaks from a bed and a thud as something dropped to the floor.

Then I heard it—a lighter tread of footsteps coming in. I didn't know who that was. Jake was gone, and Raize didn't make any sound when he walked. He never did.

The footsteps went past the bathroom, moving slowly. The hairs on the back of my neck stood up. Whoever this person was, he wasn't one of us. When those footsteps stopped outside the bathroom, I silently moved up onto the toilet seat using the sink counter and the tub.

The person moved, and I held my breath.

I hadn't locked the door.

Closing my eyes, I cursed for a second. I needed to formulate a plan.

Then, the doorknob started to turn. Slowly, making no sound.

I was caught. I couldn't move from where I was. There was nowhere to go. A flimsy shower curtain was my only coverage, but pulling it back would make a sound. It'd be pointless, so I froze in place and prayed.

And boy, did I pray.

I prayed to baby Jesus. To Mother Gaia. To my sister. To any deities who'd hear. If mermaids were real, I was praying to them. Unicorns. I was willing to throw anything in. Yeti. If leprechauns existed? Why not.

My time would come, but I hoped it wouldn't be today.

The doorknob kept turning.

The latch unclicked, and the door swung open.

A stranger stared back at me—dark eyes, dark hair that was wavy and fell forward. A curl hung over his tan forehead. He was my height, and he looked a little chunky, but those eyes... They widened, and for a moment we stared at the other. He didn't seem to have expected to see anyone.

I swallowed.

The moment was over.

A hard look flashed in his eyes, and he stepped back, pushing the door out of the way.

I readied myself to launch at him. I had no other choice.

But as he moved back, bringing up a black-gloved hand with a gun in it, another hand came down on his shoulder. It startled him, and he jerked around.

Raize was there, a 9mm in hand, and before the guy could

think about his gun, Raize had thumbed a bullet into his forehead.

I flinched, but none of the blood got me.

The body fell back against the wall, and he slid down, in slow motion, to the floor as his legs crumbled beneath him. Raize lifted a foot, nudging him over.

Loud footsteps thundered in the hallway. "What the—"

Raize looked at me as he spoke to Cavers. "There's plastic in the truck. Grab it. Wrap his body."

Cavers came forward, and Raize moved aside so he could get by.

As he went out, I stepped off the toilet, but my knees were shaking. I took a breath, closing my eyes and envisioning it rolling through my whole body, steadying me. When I didn't think I'd fall over, I stepped out and around the body.

The guy's eyes were open, staring down into the floor. Blood pooled around him as it seeped out.

"I reached out for a meet," Raize murmured. "They rejected it."

I whipped my head up. "He's from the Estrada Cartel?"

He nodded, moving the guy's shirt aside to show me a star tattoo with eight points. "That's their sign."

Now I knew.

I swallowed over a lump. This was a bad sign, a very bad sign. "What now?"

Raize moved his gaze my way and spoke softly, surprising me. "Now we make them change their mind."

I swallowed again. That's what I was scared of. "It's going to get bloody."

"Yes. It will." Raize turned around. "Take everything back to the truck. We need a new spot."

Cavers came in with the plastic. He didn't look at me as he knelt and got to work, rolling the body into it. When he carried it outside, I started cleaning. So many dead bodies, so many shootings. I knew there was an effect on me. Damage. Trauma. But I swept all of it under a rug, and everything on top was numb. I went in search of something to clean the blood up as I let my feelings drain away—from my brain to my toes. I felt frozen on the inside, but that's how you got through this life. It was that or lose your soul. I was freezing my soul.

But back to work.

We didn't need to leave a record of what happened here, though I had a feeling a blacklight would make every inch of this house glow like a fireworks display.

After I was done, I helped carry all our things back outside. Raize was at the truck, putting everything in its place around the body. It took some packing skill.

When Jake returned, Raize told him to go inside and wipe anything down that we might've touched. After he started, I remembered I never actually went to the bathroom.

Damn.

10

CARRIE

Our next base of operations was the opposite of what we'd left.

Raize found a house on a real estate website. He made a call and arranged to tour the place with a local real estate agent. I can relay this with accuracy because I was the one touring the place with him. He said I wouldn't scare the lady away. Jake would've flirted, maybe, and Cavers definitely would've scared her. I think Raize had wanted to have Jake and me pose as a couple for the tour, but since he needed to be the one to sign any papers, it had to be him.

He was annoyed the whole time. And the real estate lady had tried flirting with him. That annoyed him even more. Not me. I found it just as entertaining as the divorced lady pack from the airport.

Then, while the real estate lady waited in another room, the sequence of calls went as follows:

Raize to a guy.

That guy must've called someone else.

That someone else called Raize.

Raize briefed him on what happened using coded words.

Apparently Raize had been getting set up in his hunting tree-stand when a pigeon wouldn't leave him alone. The pigeon kept finding him, and so he'd had to shoot the pigeon. Yes, the pigeon was dead.

Then whoever was on the phone with Raize hung up.

He waited, turning to stare at me.

Raize had been staring at me more and more, but I didn't find it creepy. That was also surprising, but I was going with it.

Anything that didn't make me numb was a good thing, or so I thought.

Then his phone rang again, and the mask slid over his face.

I hadn't been seeing the mask lately when it was just me and him, but he now moved toward the room where the real estate agent was waiting.

He placed the phone on the counter between us and hit the speaker button.

The real estate lady—Claudia—leaned forward, an eager smile on her face. "Hello! Who am I speaking to? This is Claudia Ronald."

"Hello, Ms. Ronald."

I tensed, recognizing Bronski's voice.

A hand clamped down on my hip, and Raize pulled me to his side. He was anchoring me, keeping me in place.

I wanted to run.

I couldn't run.

That voice slithered out of the phone again. "We need you to draw up papers on behalf of the house's owner. They'll be accepting a rental offer from my colleague who's standing in front of you."

Shit, shit, shit.

My skin crawled. Ice lined my throat.

Claudia had no idea what was happening here. Her head tilted to the side, and she leaned closer to the phone.. "I'm confused, sir," she drawled. "My clients aren't looking for renters.

They're selling their house, and I have to tell you that this house *will* sell. It's drawing a lot of attention from potential buyers."

"No, Ms. Ronald."

Sick. I was going to be sick.

"This is what's going to happen, because you're going to give my colleague your client's information. He's going to send some men to visit with your client, and we will all come to an agreement."

"What—"

Raize pulled out his gun, putting it on the counter.

Claudia's eyes went wide, and she froze.

I understood the feeling.

Blood drained from her face. "I..."

She couldn't talk. She couldn't—she was wavering on her feet.

I shot forward. "She's going down."

I caught her and eased her to the floor as Bronksi said, "Is that my Brooke?"

Raize picked up the phone. "We'll handle it from here."

Bronski made a hissing sound. "We'll send the transfer now."

Raize ended the call, studying me a moment before he knelt and dug out Claudia's phone. He swiped the screen, used her print to unlock it, and then worked his way through her information.

I shifted back, ignoring the storm in my body. "You'll need to wait for her to wake up."

He ignored me, still scrolling, and then he sent a text.

"What are you doing?" I rose to my feet.

Her phone buzzed back, and he read the screen before lifting his head to me. "I didn't know we'd have to go through Bronski today."

I didn't say anything. That was his apology.

A lump formed in my throat, but as with everything else, I ignored it and jerked my head in a nod.

He showed me the screen. "She keeps her clients under the

house numbers. The client is coming here now for a meet. Call the guys. Tell them to get ready."

I didn't want to do this. I'd never been active in this role, but I knew what would happen.

The client would come here. Raize would question him, get the information he needed. Jake and Cavers would be sent to find the client's loved ones and take pictures. The pictures would come back, and the client would be told to rent to us—at what would probably be a cheap price—and the client's loved ones wouldn't get killed. Say a word to literally anyone, and the loved ones would be killed.

I hated this life.

I hated it.

I hated myself so much right now.

And twenty minutes later, the client walked in, saw Claudia tied and gagged, and it began. This time, though, the client folded immediately. Raize still got the information he needed because we'd need collateral to hold over both Claudia and the client, but instead of Jake and Cavers having to go and be creepers, they helped us carry everything inside this giant house.

I chose the room in the far corner, the one that had a balcony, and I stayed in it the rest of the night.

THERE WAS A SLIGHT KNOCK, and my door eased open.

I knew who'd be standing there.

I was starting to sense his presence, or his lack of presence— the complete absence of anything human about him. Smells. Sounds. He was a ghost, just in a body.

"Why did you choose this life?" Raize asked.

I sat in the corner, since there was no furniture, and I could see out the window. But no one could see me since the room was dark. It looked so peaceful out there. We were in a normal neighborhood. Not normal. We were in an *affluent* neighborhood. This was a five-thousand-square-foot house, with a pool in the backyard. This should've been someone's dream home. It could've been mine, in another life.

Those neighbors out there were probably bankers. They might've golfed and wined—because wining could be an event. No. Champagne. Those people probably champagned for a hobby. And now we were right next to them.

Raize wanted to go somewhere the Estrada Cartel wouldn't find right away, and once they did, they might wait a bit before deciding to make another move. These neighbors were our camouflage.

He'd kept the light off, so he was just a shadow standing among other shadows.

"What do you mean?" I asked.

"I did my research. I knew who you were, what you could do, before I won you in that game. It's *why* I went to that game."

I'd never thought about it, but I realized he hadn't gone to another poker game since that night.

"Why?" None of that made sense. Why seek me out?

"A girl whose gut is always right? You're a weapon in living form in this life. You're more reliable than an actual psychic and less work than a lie detector. You save time from torture. But I researched where you came from, and I got nothing. The first mention of you was that Bronksi had bought a new blonde from Korkov. Korkov brings girls from Russia to use here. Or they trick junkies into working for them. You were neither Russian nor a junkie. Korkov isn't into randomly kidnapping American girls, so that made me think *you* made the decision. Why?"

I couldn't answer that. No one could ever know.

"You've got an attitude about what I did to get this house, but no one died in this business deal," he continued. "The real estate agent and the client are both alive. If they keep their mouths shut, they'll remain alive."

"And if they talk?" I shot out, my teeth grating against each other.

"They die. They know the score."

I shook my head. "No one should know the score."

He was quiet, and I felt him take a step back. "The cartels are here. They're operating in the Valley. Anyone who lives here, knows the score." He moved back again, his shadow separating from the others. "Jake picked up pizza. Your body needs to eat. If you're going to do whatever you're in this life to do, you need energy, no matter how much you hate living this life."

Then he was gone.

I felt his absence as much as I felt his presence. I didn't like that either.

My stomach growled, and I pushed up to my feet because he was right. I couldn't find my sister if I was dead, and that's what I'd be if I wasn't useful anymore. Like Jake had said, I'd hitched my wagon to Raize, and I had to see it through, no matter where our path was heading.

Fuck him, though, just because.

Fuck him.

11

CARRIE

A loud thud sounded, and I gasped, rolling over and jumping up at the same time.

It took a second to get my bearings. I was disoriented.

I'd fallen asleep on the floor—no blanket, nothing but me. I looked at the door. It was open. Cavers stood there, bending over to grab a bag from the floor. He looked over and grimaced. "Sorry." He lifted it, pausing to look at me again. "Since you're awake, the boss wants you downstairs."

Well.

I *"needed to be useful"*— Raize's exact words—so, ignoring the fact that my body so very much did not like sleeping on the floor, I moved into the bathroom. A quick piss, followed by a quick wash-up, and I felt a little... Nope. I didn't feel refreshed at all. I wasn't sure I would ever again, but still, I headed downstairs.

Jake was in the kitchen, making coffee with a coffee machine that he must've bought and brought along. He lifted his chin in greeting. "You want some?" He gestured to a pizza box on the counter. "There's a few slices left."

I ignored the offer of food and pointed to the coffee. "We have mugs for that?"

"Yep." He reached behind him. "I mean, we have Styrofoam cups. Best I could do." He glanced toward Raize. "Maybe we could stop and get actual mugs today?"

Raize stood at the table, studying a bunch of papers that were spread out. He looked up. "Get what you need." He started to go back to the papers, but his eyes narrowed on me. "You need coffee, and you need to eat."

I opened my mouth to protest.

He growled, "I don't give a fuck what you're about to say. Your body needs food. Eat."

And my mouth closed.

Jake smirked, dropping two slices onto a couple napkins for me. "You want these heated up?"

I glared, taking the pizza and the coffee he'd poured for me, and went over to sit at the table. Raize moved the papers over, giving me some space, and as I started eating, I looked over at what he was studying. It was a map of the Valley and the Mexican border. He had marked some points with scribbles going over the border.

My mouth dried because I knew I needed to ask, but I didn't want to know. Damn. "What is this?"

I could feel his gaze as a shiver went down my spine. I stuffed some pizza into my mouth and chewed, not tasting a damn thing.

"We're down here to make a connect. These are some options for us to do that."

Cavers came into the kitchen, dumping the bag he'd had upstairs onto the counter, along with three others. He started pulling out rope, zip ties, duct tape, and a bunch of other items. He left the guns inside, and I glimpsed a few thick bundles of cash.

"These look okay?"

Raize looked up. His eyes were cool, taking in everything Cavers showcased as he moved over to inspect the bags. He didn't answer, but his lips pressed tight and his jaw moved around, like he was chewing on something. Eventually he sighed and nodded. "Get it ready."

Cavers put everything back in, zipped up the bags, and hoisted all three of them on his back. He took them outside, and a second later, we heard the garage open.

Jake seemed stunned. "You're going to let him take off with that stuff alone?"

Raize lifted his eyebrows.

As if remembering his place, Jake flushed and lowered his arm. "I mean... Never mind. What do you want me to do today, boss?"

A different glint showed in Raize's eyes. It was one I'd never seen before.

"I need you to follow him," he said after a moment.

Jake looked up. "You serious?"

He nodded. "Don't let him see you. Take pics, and record what you think I'd need to know about."

Jake's face clouded over, but he grabbed his gun, his phone, and the other set of keys. He was out the door almost immediately.

I looked back, and was startled to find Raize had been watching me the whole time.

He showed no emotion, but he seemed to be inspecting me. "What are your thoughts about that?"

I frowned. "About Jake or Cavers?"

"All of it. Any of it."

I shifted back a step. A weird churning had started in my gut. "Why are you asking?"

"I'm curious."

"My gut doesn't work like that. You need to ask a yes or no question."

He moved closer. "I'm not asking for that. I had my setup all done and put together in Philly. It's different here. We're the ones creating a need, one the Estrada Cartel doesn't think they have. I have to create that need and reinforce it to them. I trust you the most in our group, and I am asking your opinion. What are your thoughts about what we're doing here?"

Jesus. I did not want to have this conversation. The churning in my stomach became twisting, but with knives. Twist, slice, twist, slice.

"I don't know what you're doing, so I can't have an opinion."

Raize moved another step closer, his voice growing softer. "Then ask what you need to know."

A lump formed in my throat.

It was that easy now? When it never had been? We were told to jump, so we jumped. We were never allowed to have a thought or an opinion. I answered Raize's questions on command. Now he wanted me to think for him? To be an active participant where people would die?

I knew what I needed to say. "Why are you changing the rules? You never asked before."

His eyes narrowed. "New situation. New rules. Now stop stalling and tell me."

I raised my chin and rolled my shoulders back. "I hate when you kill people."

His nostrils flared, but he didn't move back. His voice was still soft. "More."

Okay. More, then. "I don't understand why we have Cavers here. You don't want him, so why is he here?"

He stared at me, like he always did, but this time, his eyes were thoughtful. Considering.

I didn't know what he was considering...

"I worked for the Morales Cartel before I left them for the Estrada Cartel," he began.

I frowned. "I didn't know you could do that."

"You can't—not usually. I was a special case."

I remembered Jake telling me how Raize had his come-up. I was *so* not asking what had made him a special case.

"When Bronski made his move to get you back, Carloni saw his chance. He's been wanting to use my connection to the cartels for the last three years. I've been putting him off. You were there. You know a condition of me keeping you is him using me down here. He's got no in down here without me, and he knows it. The cartels also know it. They sent Macca for me as a nice *fuck off*."

I swallowed over that damn lump. "That guy in the bathroom was a nice fuck off?"

He grinned, taking out a knife. He ran his thumb over the edge. "I'm guessing Macca pissed someone off. They knew I'd kill him. Macca's stupid—always makes noise when he goes in for a mission. I'm surprised he's still alive all these years later."

Damn. He *knew* that guy.

"Did you like him?"

His grin widened. "I don't like anyone."

Right. Cold, dead—that was Raize. I forgot for a second who I was working for.

"You never said why Cavers is here."

He turned, heading back to the table. He laid the knife down and started to pile the papers together. "He's here to snitch on us to Bronski."

Hearing that name, I winced again. It was like an internal slap, followed by a roundhouse kick to the face.

"Why Bronski? Why not Carloni?"

Raize shot me a hard look, pausing before he put the papers in a bag and zipped it closed. "Because Carloni is pitting Bronski against me. Winner gets you."

Cold dread spilled over me. "How do you know this?"

"Because I bugged Cavers' room, his phone, and his vehicle. He's Carloni's man, but he's reporting to Bronski, which tells me Carloni doesn't want me here. I'm being used to make the relationship. Then he'll send Bronski down here to replace me, and I'm guessing you're the consolation prize. For Bronski."

"Why would Carloni do that?"

"Because even though I was sent to Carloni, he's not my boss. He must've found out somehow."

Did I want to ask? I closed my eyes for a moment. "Who is your boss?"

He shook his head. "That's not information you need."

I winced, feeling slapped by that refusal after he'd told me so much. But, okay then. Raize had a boss. That boss sent him to Carloni. Carloni is using his connections, and then he's planning to kill him and replace him with his own guy—who I refuse to think about—and Raize knew all of this.

Who was this boss? Maybe this might make more sense if I knew? Maybe? I didn't know. This was kind of the office politics of this world. You got used and then executed.

But I was here. Once I'd started on this path, there was never any going back. I had one choice now, keep going. "You can't kill Cavers then?"

"No, but I can send him on errands that will do nothing for us."

"Why send Jake to follow him?"

"Because if I didn't, Bronski and Cavers would both think I didn't give a shit what he's doing, and that would make them suspicious."

Right. Because all of that made sense. "You told Jake not to be seen when he followed Cavers."

Raize shook his head. "Jake sucks at tailing. There's no way Cavers won't see him, but Jake will at least try to stay hidden."

"And what are you and I doing?"

He picked up the bag and nodded to my pizza. "The real work. Finish eating and meet me outside in five minutes."

The real work. I wanted to make a joke about that, but I couldn't. Dread was my constant friend. It was in me, always. And hearing those words, *the real work*, my dread turned into an altogether different sensation.

Anticipation. I didn't like feeling that. I didn't like it at all, but the other surprise of the day? Raize was a lot smarter than I'd thought.

I'd underestimated him, and that alarmed me. Who else had I underestimated?

"Girl."

I had to go. I started for the door.

"Don't forget your food."

12

CARRIE

Raize had two items to handle. One, we paid cash for another truck. Second, we went shopping for me.

Jake had bought everything Raize asked him to—food and supplies like toothpaste and toothbrushes, hand soap, towels, sleeping bags, blankets, a fan, the basics for staying at an empty house for a while.

But as far as purchasing clothes for me, he hadn't done so great. He'd bought me a pair of socks.

So that's how I found myself at the local Target with Raize carrying one of those hand-held baskets. I was in the dressing room, eyeing what he'd handed off to me.

I took the jeans, size four. I eyed the sweatshirts and tops he'd also handed me. "Why am I trying these on?" I asked him through the door. "These are just basic clothes that I can eyeball whether they'll fit or not."

"Can you fit them?"

"Yeah." I tossed one of the pairs of jeans away, scooped up the rest, and went back out.

Raize stood as an older woman and a young girl came around the corner. "Oh!" The older woman looked like a young grandmother, her hair brushed back to reveal diamond earrings. The earrings got my attention first because they were classy. The granddaughter had the same blonde hair, same face and eyes. She wore a diamond necklace, and they both had their arms full of clothes. I was guessing the pink halter top wasn't for the grandma.

Interest filled their eyes as they stared at Raize.

There was that reaction to him again. I didn't understand it.

Raize's gaze cooled, and I was hoping he wouldn't call the grandma a skank cokewhore.

He stepped back, his hand went to the small of my back, and he murmured, "Excuse us."

"Oh *papacito!*" The older woman made a show of fanning herself. The younger one giggled and sent me a look of approval.

He was a killer. Didn't they see that? Didn't they instinctively fear him? They should.

They were stupid. Ignorant.

Raize was dripping in so much blood, he had no soul anymore. I railed at them silently, screaming inside my head. Why couldn't they feel that from him?

I stiffened, and Raize shot me a look, his hand pressing more firmly against my back. But neither of us said a word.

I walked briskly out of there, but not before pain sliced through me as a memory flashed before my eyes.

I was standing in a clothing store's dressing room.

I was bored. I wanted to leave, but I had a book in my hand. I gripped that book tighter and tighter.

"What do you think, Friend?" She winked at me. Friend. It was our 'code.'

The dressing room door swung open, and my sister came out, her hands on her hips, and struck a modeling pose—

No!

I would not let myself remember. If I did... I couldn't.

Acid filled my mouth, but I swallowed it, shoving it down,

down, so far down that I wondered how deep my tunnel went. Beyond my soul, beyond my body, all the way down into hell, that's how far it went.

I moved left, following the aisle, but Raize shifted and pulled me into the underwear and bra section. We were alone.

He stepped in, crowding me with a hand on my hip, holding me in place. "What's your problem?" His breath teased my neck and ear.

I couldn't suppress a shiver, but he didn't move back, and I didn't step away. "Nothing."

He pulled me against him, my side pressed to his chest. His fingers held my chin, and he angled his head to inspect my face. "What just happened in your head?"

"Nothing."

He knew I was lying. My mouth was so tight, my teeth were grinding so hard that my entire face hurt.

"Stop." He nodded to my mouth. "That'll give you a migraine."

"Like you care." I snorted before I could stop myself.

Raize released me, stepping away. "No, but *you* will when you're doubled over, puking in the bathroom. You'll be vulnerable when Cavers might be around."

God. I gritted my teeth again.

He drenched me in boiling water with that reminder. Never be vulnerable. I'd forgotten. At some point, with Jake asking me personal questions and Raize acting like he gave a damn—I'd started to soften. I could never do that either.

I was like that grandma and her granddaughter. I was being stupid, reckless, forgetting who Raize really was.

I pulled away, and knowing he'd steered me here because these were the last items we needed, I reached out and grabbed whatever was hanging in front of me. A pack of underwear, two sports bras. Some socks. We were good to go now. In the basket were two pairs of jeans, a few shirts, a sweatshirt, and now my underclothes.

Raize was still studying me, but when was he not?

He nodded and started for the front of the store.

I followed, not saying a word.

He took one detour, putting a pair of sneakers and sandals into the basket, and then we went to check out. Once everything was rung up, Raize pulled out cash to pay. He paused, reaching out to snag a pair of sunglasses. He added that to the pile.

Raize handed all of the bags to me, walking ahead of me once again.

I frowned, staring at the sunglasses. He'd added those for me, and I looked up as he pulled his own out and slipped them on his face.

"What do you think, sis?"

I rocked backward, the memory picking back up.

I couldn't shove it down, and I was helpless to stop as it played out in my mind.

I looked up, seeing my sister in jeans that were skintight and a top that wasn't a top. It was a bikini. She grinned at me, wiggling her hips as she did a slow circle. The tattoo was new on her side, so it was still bandaged.

I hated seeing that tattoo. It was his claim on her, like she was his property.

But before I could tell my sister she looked beautiful, because she always did—she was popular for a reason at school—he spoke up. "Those pants make you look fat. Pick something else."

My sister's smile fell flat and she swallowed. "Right." She hung her head and went back into the dressing room. The door shut quietly, a slow click, and I hated that almost as much as I hated him. My sister never shut a door slowly, carefully. She rushed through life with a zest that was annoying at times. She was a force.

The way that door shut? There was no force there.

He was taking that from her.

I didn't let myself look at him. If I did, I was going to smack him in the head with my book, and I wouldn't stop.

A tear slid down my face as the parking lot swam into focus.

I *should've* looked at my sister's boyfriend. I should've smacked him with the book, and I should've kept going until he was dead.

I hadn't wanted to go to jail.

What a silly notion now.

13

CARRIE

Raize parked, and when we got out, I was surprised to see him putting his gun in his seat's zipper pocket. He held his hand out. "Give me your gun."

"What?"

A few people walked past us on the sidewalk. They looked exhausted—maybe commuting for work. None of them were looking at us. In fact, I got the feeling this was a neighborhood where people minded their own business.

"I didn't bring it."

I ignored the flash in Raize's eyes and started for the end of the truck.

"Stop." He hooked his arm through my elbow, moving me closer as he reached inside and took his gun back out. He snagged the sweatshirt he'd just bought me and handed it over, unlinking our arms. "Put this on."

I frowned. "It's hot out."

"Put it on." He was back to being monotone.

I did, and then sucked in my breath when he reached for me, his hand snaking up through my shirt. "Hey!"

He ignored me, and I felt him putting his gun on the inside of my bra where there was some extra cushion in the sweatshirt. That's why he'd bought this particular sweatshirt.

I tried to stop myself from glaring at him, but it was hard.

Everything he did was for a reason, an angle. He hadn't bought me clothes to be kind. He'd bought them as an extra place to hide his weapons.

Raize stepped back, looking me over before giving a nod of approval. "They'll run their hands down your back, but the hoodie should bunch up. They won't do a thorough job with me there."

I eyed him as he looked toward a building. "Why won't they do a thorough job with you there?"

He lingered on the building for a moment. One story. Flat roof. The outside was of faded red brick. There were two narrow windows on both sides of the door. Both windows were blacked out. The door didn't look any better than the brick. It was painted in velvet red, but the paint job was old and chipped.

He looked back to me.

Heat flashed in his gaze, and I almost stepped back. Tingling shot through me—what the hell was that? He smirked. I'd never seen Raize smirk before, but there it was. *That's* how he looked hot to so many women. I saw it in that second, until I looked up and his eyes were still dead. That snuffed it out.

"They know me here. They'll be nervous about insulting me."

Well then. That explained nothing.

Everyone should be nervous about insulting Raize, as far as I was concerned.

He took off, and I stuffed my hands into the sweatshirt's pockets. Oh. He might not want that bulge to be outlined, so I took them out. I followed at a more sedate pace, which he noted with a slight frown. Once he was ten feet from the door, it opened and two giant guys stepped out.

They nodded to Raize, who jerked his chin up. "I'd like to see Oscar."

They both stared, not responding until one touched his ear. He had an earpiece there. He listened for a moment. "We gotta search you and your woman."

Raize's eyes were cool, but he didn't argue. He raised his arms and spread his legs. The earpiece guy went to him, and the other guy came to me.

Raize growled when he touched my arm. "Be careful with her. She's mine."

She's mine.

I gulped, a chill twining around that tingling sensation from before.

The guy gave Raize a dark look, but his hands barely skimmed me, and Raize was right. He didn't plaster the sweatshirt against me so he missed the part smack in the middle of my back.

They stepped back when they were done, and the door opened once more. A guy in a yellow suit flashed a grin at Raize. He was bald, ebony skin, and dark eyes. Those eyes were lit up in amusement, but there was something more there. Knowing? Something else? I couldn't tell.

A small grin tugged at his mouth before he ran a hand over his face, smoothing out the half-smile. "Well, well, well. I would never believe it if I wasn't seeing it with my own eyes. Can't believe you came back, *hombre*."

"Yeah. Well." Raize shrugged. "You know this business."

A more knowing look came over the guy, and his grin faded. "I do. You want to see him, huh?"

"I have to."

"Got it." The guy's gaze lingered on me before he jerked his head. "Follow me then. He's waiting."

I was noting that neither said each other's names. That was weird. Though, they weren't acting like it.

Then we were going inside, and I didn't know what I had thought it was earlier, but I wouldn't have guessed a strip club.

It was a strip club.

Everything was so dark. I knew we were walking past people, but I couldn't see them—could only hear them, sense them, almost feel the movement in the booths as we went past. The air in the room was heavy, with a lot of different smells. Cigar, sweat, booze, body lotion, self-tanner, perfume. I sneezed. I wasn't used to perfume anymore, though Broo—nope. I needed to shut down those memories.

Why were they coming to me? *Now?* After being in this world for over a year?

We were taken down a back hallway. It had little lights on the floor until we came to an office.

The guy knocked on the door as he opened it into another dark room, but not as dark. A few lamps in the corners gave the room a soft glow. Behind a large desk, a guy sat in a chair with a girl giving him a lap dance. Behind them was a large, glass room. It was like a wine cellar, but there wasn't any wine. Instead, a few heavily made-up girls lounged in bikinis behind another glass wall. Their hair was done in updos that must've needed an entire bottle of hairspray, and all of them were wearing high heels.

They looked miserable.

"Raize." The guy wheeled his chair back and smacked the girl's ass.

She got up, giving Raize a look before sauntering out of the room. None of the guys paid her any attention. All eyes were on Raize, with a few looks coming my way.

"Oscar."

Raize was guarded, but no surprise there. He was extra alert. I could feel it. I didn't know if this was a weird homecoming or we'd be involved in a shootout. Either way, Raize stood next to me, within reach of his gun in my bra, but he kept his hands free and loose at his sides.

Oscar looked tall and trim, his long legs kicked out and one ankle crossed over the other. He leaned back, his fingers drumming against each other. He wore what looked like an expensive suit with a few gold chains around his neck. His eyes were dark. His hair was dark as well. I couldn't place an age on him. But the more I looked at him, the more slimy I felt. This guy was dirty, and not just because of the strip club and all the girls. If I'd met him in Target, he still would've made my stomach roll.

Then his eyes slid my way, and the dirtiness turned into a rotten sort of feeling.

He tipped his chin up. "Who's this? I've never known you to take a traveling companion."

Raize barely flicked a gaze my way. "She's no one."

A quiet snort came from behind me, from the guy who'd met us at the door. It was so quiet, I was sure only I'd heard it.

"Right." Oscar's tone turned mocking, but it seemed we were back to business. He stood up, and his voice dropped, getting serious. "What the fuck are you doing here? Walking into my business? I know Estrada wants you dead."

I felt a bristling in the air at those words.

I tensed.

"I wasn't aware Estrada wanted me dead."

Oscar's eyes flashed, and his lip curved in a sneer. "Right. Where's Macca then?"

"They sent Macca for me as a nice fuck off."

"I don't know. I haven't seen Macca in years. How's he doing?"

"You're a killer, Raize. Not a liar." Oscar tilted his head to the side. "You a liar now?"

Raize's eyes narrowed, and his tone went cold. "We're starting with insults? It'll be a short meeting, if that's the case."

I heard the yellow suit draw in his breath, and found myself doing the same.

Oscar shook his head. "When you left Estrada, you left all of us. You're forgetting that."

"And you missed me so much?"

Oscar's face tightened. "Careful, Raize. I might kill your girl if you piss me off."

Frozen. Me. Right now.

If I thought the room was alarming before...

The hairs on the back of my neck stood on end, and I could feel Raize coiling up, rising. He was going to strike. I felt it in my gut, and I was now just waiting, looking around for where I should dive to avoid the bullets.

Then I felt a presence behind me, it was the door guy. He murmured softly, "It's a bluff, buddy."

Those words weren't for me, but Raize didn't seem to pay attention.

The room was stifling now.

"I came here as a courtesy," Raize said. "I'm in the area. I wanted you to know that."

Oscar had been reaching for something in a drawer, but he paused, studying Raize again before bringing out a bottle of tequila. "Why am I the one getting this courtesy? Word is that you reached out to Estrada. You're looking to work with him."

"You control the girls in this section. I'm down here on behalf of my employer, and I want you to know there's no interest in working girls. If you were worried I'd be competition, I'm not." He paused. "You didn't need to send Macca."

"Oh, damn," came from behind me.

Before I could sort out what had happened, Raize's hand shot out, shoving up under my shirt. He pushed me into a corner as he brought his gun up and around. He shot at Oscar at the same time he shoved the door guy away.

I heard a growl as my knees hit the ground.

People were shooting.

I kept my eyes on the floor.

Someone shoved me farther into a corner. I went, gladly, and hid behind a buffet counter.

Raize was in front of me, and I felt body after body hitting the ground.

One after another, and I could see them. Some had their heads turned our way, others had their heads the other way. One guy didn't have a head.

The room was thick with the smell of sulfur and blood.

When it stopped, I didn't realize it at first. My ears were ringing, and Raize touched my shoulder. I heard him shouting, "Come up!" But his voice sounded muffled.

There was someone else moving around the room. He and Raize were checking the bodies and yelling at each other. It was the yellow suit guy—both had guns drawn, but pointing at the floor.

"We have two seconds—" He was cut off by a thundering of footsteps down the hallway. He cursed, dropping a gun clip and jamming another in its place.

Raize was at the desk, going through the drawers. He stuffed something in his pocket. "I didn't ask for your help."

"You needed it."

A deep thump slammed into the door. Someone was trying to break it down.

Yellow Suit stepped back, pointing his gun at the door. "We gotta move, Raize. What's your plan?"

Move.

They were coming.

We needed to go to live.

I needed to live.

I pushed up. My legs were unsteady, but I looked around. The glass room where the girls were. They were gone. A door had been left open, but no one was coming through it. Not yet.

I pointed. "There."

Both guys looked, and Raize cursed. "Get over here. I need your pockets."

I shoved away from the buffet counter and went to the desk.

There were more thuds at the door, more shouting.

Raize's-I-Didn't-Who was cursing, but he backed up, going into the glass room. "The girls left their door open. We can get out that way. No one's remembered it yet. That's a back entrance. They have to go outside the building to circle around. We're not cut off yet. I bet we have thirty seconds." He shoved open the door connecting this office to the first glass room. "We gotta go now, Raize."

Raize kept looking through the door.

"*Now*, Raize! Right fucking *now!*"

Raize cursed, shoving things into my sweatshirt, but then he stopped and looked me in the eyes. "Are you okay?"

I lifted my chin up and down, not feeling connected to any other part of my body.

He cursed, but turned me and shoved me forward. "She's in shock," he told his friend.

The guy cursed again, but reached for me. Both guys had a hand on my arm, guiding me through the first door, into the glass room, then into the area where the girls had been and out another door. Raize's friend was right. It opened into what seemed like a different building. There was a thick wall immediately to our right, and we had to pass down a tight hallway with doors every few feet. Those were rooms, and I could hear moaning from inside.

They were still working after a shoot-out just happened feet, yards from their room?

I was going to be sick.

This was a sex building.

Those girls—that could've been my sister.

My sister could be in one of those rooms.

The thought raced through me.

I braked to a sudden stop.

I had to look. I had to make sure.

"Carrie!"

Now I was Carrie?

I ignored Raize. Running to the first room, I threw open the door.

A guy was on top of a girl. It wasn't my sister.

They didn't stop.

The girl saw me, but she didn't react.

I moved to the next room.

Different people, not my sister.

And the next.

"What are you doing?" Raize was in front of me.

I reached for the next door.

He blocked me. "We have to go."

"No!" I ripped away from him, lunging for the door.

I had to know.

I had to make sure.

Was she here?

"We have to go!" He was shouting in my face, grabbing my arms. He lifted me, carried me, but I was struggling.

I needed to look.

I had to.

I was blind to anything but that.

"Fucking hell!" He hoisted me up, ignoring my kicking legs and the way I scrambled, trying to reach for the doors.

Another door opened, and sunlight lit the hallway.

Raize carried me out.

"*No!*"

"What's wrong with her?"

I felt Raize's grunt through my body. "No idea."

Then we were running. I jostled up and down.

We rounded a corner.

Raize's arm left my legs. He was pointing a gun, but there were no guys outside the door.

We walked past, to our truck.

I was shoved in the middle of the front seat. Raize went behind the wheel, and his friend sat on my right side.

As Raize gunned the engine, shooting away from the curb, I turned back, as if I could still see her, if she was there.

No one was there.

It looked like nothing happened...

14

CARRIE

"Your girl is nuts in the head," Raize's guy noted. "You should put her down."

Raize yanked the wheel to the left, and we careened down another road. No one was chasing us, but he was driving like they were. "You shut the fuck up," he growled. "Let's talk about you. What were you thinking?"

The guy's laugh was a cackle. "Right. I ain't fucking stupid. You're Raize. Only reason you're walking into that place, asking for a meet with Oscar is if you're going to end him."

Raize cursed under his breath. "I didn't go in there planning on killing him."

"So what changed?"

Raize didn't answer. He kept driving, taking us to the outskirts of town, rather than back to the house.

I shot him a look, wondering what he was doing. He caught my eye and shook his head, just the slightest motion.

"I needed to know if he was the one who sent Macca or if it was Estrada," he explained.

This door guy/Raize's-Something?—I had no clue what to call him. Was he Ally Guy?

Whoever he was, he was quiet a moment, then started laughing. "Bullshit. He threatened whoever this chick is to you, and you went apeshit on him. I could feel you making your decision. You could've waited it out. You didn't need to throw it down, tell him you knew he was the one who sent Macca. But no, in a very un-Raize-like way, you killed first."

"I got his phone," Raize murmured.

"What?"

"I got his phone. He unlocked it, and I went for it."

The guy cursed, scooting low in his seat. He rested his arm on the window, his fingers catching the handle above. "That's why you killed him? For his goddamn phone?"

I kept quiet.

Raize went quiet, too.

The guy was still muttering to himself. "You killed Oscar, Raize. Oscar! You know who's going to come after you? After me? I knew if you started shooting, I'd have to choose. You or Oscar, and you damn sure know I ain't picking Oscar over you. We been through too much for this asshole to divide us. But man, Oscar? You started a war. I hope the fuck you know what you're doing."

Raize jerked the wheel once more, pulling off into a field, and he kept going until we reached an isolated spot. A group of trees blocked us from the road when he turned the engine off.

No one moved.

"What are we doing here?" the guy asked in a low voice. "You got shit to bury? Because you ain't putting a bullet in my head. No way, man. After what I just did for you—"

"Shut up, Basil."

Basil. I had a name.

Raize opened his door and got out, going to the back of the truck and putting down the tailgate. He dug through his pockets, laying out everything he'd grabbed. When I followed him, he started for my pockets. I stood there, feeling weird about him digging through my sweatshirt, but in an odd way, I found it pleasant.

That was super-duper odd.

Duper.

I'd never used that word before in my life.

What was going on with me?

"She's in shock."

That was it. I must still be in shock.

"What are we doing here?" Basil leaned a hand on the back of the truck, watching us. "Can we talk about this mute one here, while we're at it? If I'm joining your team, I need to know what I'm signing up for."

I frowned at him. "Your name is Basil?"

His eyebrows shot up. "That's what you're focused on? *Carrie?* Like that's your real name." He nodded toward Raize, who was studying everything on the truck bed. "What'd this one call you before Carrie?"

I put my hands in my now-empty sweatshirt pockets and rolled my shoulders back. That was an easy one. "Girl."

I caught the corner of Raize's mouth lifting up, just a bit before resuming its normal flat line.

Basil straightened from the truck and put his hand in his own pockets, his head tipping back. "Right. Girl. Carrie. I'm sure names are so important to us now, but you can call me Abram. Abram Basil. Raize and I used to work together, long time ago. How'd you and he meet up?"

Raize paused, his eyes sliding my way.

"He won me in a poker game."

Abram's eyebrows shot up. "What? Since when do you play poker?"

Raize turned to regard Abram. He looked at me over his shoulder. "Stop giving him information." He turned back to Abram. "Stop trying to needle her. She's not wired like that. You won't get a reaction."

"What *will* get a reaction from her?"

"Kill someone. She doesn't like that."

Abram pursed his lips together. "I'll take that into consideration. Nice officially meeting you, Raize's girl."

A low growl came from Raize.

Abram grinned. "There's the reaction I was looking for. Surprised it came from you, though. You going to tell me what the hell we're doing out here? You don't trust me to take me to your headquarters?"

Raize leaned back against the truck bed, his arms folded. "I need your phone."

Abram didn't move.

I didn't move. I knew he wasn't asking for mine.

When this clicked with Abram, he stepped back and his hands shot out of his pockets. "Say what?"

"Your phone." Raize wasn't fucking around. His eyes were steady on his friend.

Was he a friend? I was guessing since Raize hadn't shot him yet.

Raize leaned forward. "I've not worked with you for years. You put down with us in there, but that don't mean shit, and you know it. You could've been Estrada's man on Oscar, and now you see an opportunity to find what exactly I'm here to offer Estrada. I gotta know if I can bring you in or not."

"And if I refuse?"

"You walk from here, and I'll kill you the next time I see you."

See? Killing was not something Raize cared about.

Such an asshole.

I shifted back, ignoring the look Raize sent my way.

Abram smirked. "You're right. She hates the killing—don't even like you threatening it. Your girl is loony. I'm saying it again, you should put her down. She's a liability for you, *amigo.*"

Raize shifted, blocking me from his friend's view. "And I'll tell you again, shut the fuck up when it comes to her. She ain't your business."

I looked down as silence settled over us, except for Abram shuffling his feet in the dirt.

"I either give you my phone or I walk? Those are my two options?"

"It's not a bullet in your skull."

A shiver went down my spine. Raize was just... so... dead. He was back to being nothing.

"I can't give you my phone."

"Then start walking."

"Is this really how you're going to play me out? All these years? I throw down for you, and now I'm not okay with you going through my phone?"

"We have different employers."

"You don't know my employer!"

"Then tell me."

I closed my eyes, holding my breath for him.

I didn't want this guy to die, despite him saying the opposite about me, but I could feel Raize coming to a decision. If Abram said the wrong thing, he wasn't going to walk away, despite what he'd been told. And he knew it, too. I felt that in the air as well.

It was sweltering, pressing down on us.

I reached out, not knowing my hand was going to move before it happened, before my fingers touched Raize's back. I felt him shift, his body going hard as I trailed my fingers down, looping them into the back of his jeans and I hung there.

Two days ago, I'd never have thought to do this, but I was.

I had touched Raize of my own accord, and it settled me.

Was that why I did this?

No. I was trying to touch him, affect him. I was asking for his friend's life. He stepped forward, dislodging my hold.

"Who's on your phone, Abram? Who don't you want me to see?"

Suddenly, a growl erupted from Abram, and Raize shifted, his arm flashing up.

I jumped back, biting down on a scream, and braced, expecting to hear another gunshot.

"Look through it, you fucking asshole!" Abram yelled instead. "You piece of shit, making me choose!" He paced and flailed as he kept shouting. "*You* threatening to take *me* out? Who do you think you are? You're not above my paygrade. You goddamn—I helped you back there. I chose you over Oscar. You. I chose you and who are you choosing—"

"Shut up." Raize moved back to the truck.

I lifted my head to see Abram swinging his fists in the air. He paced back and forth, fists forming and unclenching. He shot daggers at Raize.

He growled, "You fucking asshole. Don't have any feelings in you."

Raize stopped thumbing through the phone. A sudden stillness came over him, and Abram felt it, too.

Both of us watched Raize again. A hot breeze blew over us, brushing the back of my neck, but I barely felt it. Different world, different life, I would've welcomed that breeze. Here, I worried what was trailing behind it.

Raize looked up at Abram. "You're working for Estrada himself."

Abram sighed, looking utterly defeated. "About keeled over when you threw that out, but yeah. Oscar reached out for a meet. I'm assuming he was going to tell us about you, about Macca. I knew nothing about any of that until Oscar dropped Macca's name. We never sent Macca. He hasn't been working for Estrada for two years. He's sloppy. You know that."

Raize glanced my way before returning to the phone.

The air lightened, or maybe that was just me. I could breathe easier.

Abram would keep breathing for another day.

He shook his head, rolling his eyes. "You're seeing everything, Raize. Everything. I need something back. I want to work with you, but if you don't reciprocate, then we got a problem."

"I'm working for the Russians in Philly now."

Abram was quiet. Then, "Marakov?"

Raize nodded, his thumb going back to the phone. He pressed a few buttons before he tossed it back to Abram. "I need to take Oscar out," he said. "All of his operations."

That perked my ears. Those girls—they could be set free.

Abram glowered, going through his phone. "You're such a dick. You sent this shit to your phone, didn't you? Normal guys would die for doing that."

Raize ignored him. "Tell me the rest of Oscar's operations. Set up a meet with my employer and Estrada."

"Right. Yeah." Abram's tone was mocking. "I'll just, you know, marry the Pope at the same time." His eyes went mean. "What are you smoking? You left Estrada. He will kill you if he knows about you. Those were the terms, Raize. You leave and never come back. You're violating those terms."

Oh.

OH!

Oh.

This was why Raize had to be forced to come back down, and it was because of me.

He watched me, waiting for my reaction, but I just blinked at him. What did that mean? For him to throw down like that for me?

A new intensity sparked between us. This was a whole new level. We weren't going to survive it, whatever this was.

I just wanted to find my sister. She'd been taken in by the Russians. We were going to get killed by the cartel in Texas, and I'd never get back to Philadelphia—if that's even where my sister was.

I grimaced, remembering the searing panic I'd felt when we

left those girls back there, how I thought my sister could be in one of those rooms.

I felt Raize's eyes on me, but he was replying to Abram. "Estrada still wants to know if Jorge killed his brother, right?"

"Yeah, but he'll never find out. He needs proof before he can make any move, and if he did, we're talking about the Estrada Cartel splintering in half. That ain't gonna happen."

"But he still wants to know?"

Abram waited a moment. "He still wants to know. He thinks it, but I don't think he knows it for sure."

"Set up the meet with Estrada. I have a bargaining chip for him."

Me. He was talking about me.

Shit. *Shit*!

They'd ask me a question about someone's life and... Okay... The pain wasn't there, not as much as usual. Thank God, my numbness was sliding back in place. I'd been feeling so much, too much.

Because of Raize.

He had to be the reason I was feeling things, remembering things, because he was making me feel like I was safe to feel, remember.

I wasn't.

I could not forget that.

"You sure about this?" Abram's voice quieted.

"I'm sure."

"You go in, you're going to need men at your back. Estrada knows you, knows what you can do. He'll have planned for that."

"I know. Make the call, Abram."

He walked away, putting his phone to his ear.

I could feel Raize's gaze back on me.

"He's going to come back, saying he needs to take a trip," he said softly. "His boss will want to see him up close and personal before deciding what to do, and then he'll make a decision.

Abram will text me a time and place, and we'll go. I don't want Cavers to know anything about this meeting, and that means Jake can't either. I'm going to make a call to my boss and ask for more men. But I have to know, before I walk in with you at my side, if you're going to go *fucking crazy again*?" He ground out the last three words.

I winced.

He wasn't asking *why* I went crazy. I didn't think he cared. He just wanted to know if I'd be a liability.

"I'll be fine," I said faintly.

"I mean it."

I lifted my head, my eyes finding his. He was angry, his guard not in place for the moment. I could see everything. He was seething. I felt his intensity seeping into me.

I didn't like this feeling of being tethered to him, but I also knew when that went away, that wouldn't be good either.

I swallowed over a knot. "I don't like the name Carrie."

"What?"

"Carrie. That's what you called me back there. I don't like that."

"What do you want to be called then? Girl?"

I kinda liked Girl, but it wouldn't work anymore. Raize and I were beyond that sort of cold, stranger work relationship. He needed me to live, and I needed him to live.

"There was a girl. Her name was Ashley, but I'd like to go by Ash."

He stared at me, then sighed. "Fine. Ash."

Good. Ash. I liked my new name.

15

ASH

When we returned to the house, bringing food with us, Raize's phone chimed just as we stepped through the front door.

"They're back!" Jake yelled from the kitchen.

"About fucking time."

Jake's smile stretched wide when he saw the large pizza box in my hands. "Nice. She *can* read minds."

Cavers grunted, coming forward and taking the box from me. He frowned as he looked over my shoulder.

I turned to find Raize had stopped back by the door, reading his phone.

Cavers' gaze moved back to me. "What were you guys doing today?"

"That's none of our business," Jake said before I could, glaring at Cavers, who ignored him as he put the box on the counter and opened it up.

Jake continued to glare as he turned to reach for paper plates and napkins on the counter behind him. He tossed them next to the pizza, but Cavers had already grabbed three slices.

We'd had pizza the night before, and this didn't seem too

appetizing now. I'd eaten two slices of pizza this morning. Raize had stopped to get soda, and water for me, and I regretted not grabbing food I liked from the store, too.

"Not hungry?" Cavers asked.

I lifted my head in surprise. Who knew Cavers cared?

Raize paused behind the counter. I met his eyes and shrugged. "You're going to yell at me if I don't eat that?"

"You didn't say anything earlier."

I lifted a shoulder. "I wasn't thinking about food then."

He frowned, just slightly. "What do you want? I'll make a run."

"Boss." Jake lifted his hand, half a slice in his mouth. He spoke around it, "Icanakearundoo."

Everyone frowned at him.

He shoved the rest of his slice in his mouth and held up both hands. "Wah?"

My stomach growled. "I don't even know what I'd want to eat," I told them. "I'll eat a slice. I'll be fine."

Raize slid the water we'd bought in front of me. "Grab a sleeping bag and a blanket from the pile. You slept on the floor last night. You'll need your rest."

"Why?" Cavers' voice sounded loud across the kitchen. His tone was gruff, and everyone looked his way. He didn't back down. "Why does she need her rest? What'd you guys do today? Why weren't Jake and I involved?"

Jake held up his hand again. "Don't look at me. I'm not questioning you. I want to make that very clear."

Cavers' eyes turned hard. "You sent me on some run-around errands today. If you're doing something, I want in." He frowned. "Can't prove my loyalty if I'm cut out."

Cavers works for Bronski.

Raize shook his head. "You're doing just fine. Those 'run-around errands' aren't useless. Want me to cut you in? Do what I say, stop bitching about it, and prove your loyalty that way." His words had a biting tone, and both Jake and I were quiet, waiting to see what Cavers would do.

He did nothing.

He went back to eating, but after Raize returned to his phone, Cavers sent him an angry look. He caught me watching him, and that anger transferred to me before he snuffed it out. "You still ain't eating, Girl."

"Her name is Carrie." Jake sent me a grin.

"She's asked to be called Ash," Raize murmured, distracted and not looking away from his phone.

Cavers gave me the weirdest look, like he'd just realized I was a person, and Jake gave me an approving thumbs-up.

"I like it," Jake said. "Mysterious. Somewhat linked to death. Very you. Carrie didn't fit you, unless you were going to turn all rageful."

I felt a laugh coming, and I tried to stop it. It came out as a snort-giggle, and I felt my face get hot. I just giggled.

I'd never been a giggler, ever in my life, yet I was giggling here, in this house, with a killer by me.

The earth was shifting under my feet. I was getting a new foundation—and I was thinking all these serious thoughts based on one embarrassing giggle?

I needed to get a life.

Wait. I couldn't.

Never mind then.

"Eat," Raize said. "Go rest after."

"I was hoping for a card game tonight," Jake said. "Anyone up to it? Raize, I heard you can play a mean game of poker." Jake smiled. He wiggled his eyebrows at Cavers. "What do you say? War?"

Cavers stared at him, long and hard. "I used to play gin rummy with my grandma before she died."

"Gin rummy it is! How about it, Ash? You spent all day with

the boss. I bet you need a card game to unwind. I know I would—
no offense, boss." He held a finger in the air toward Raize.

"What?"

I almost giggled again. Raize wasn't paying attention.

Jake looked relieved. "Ash?"

I considered it, but I didn't want to be around Cavers. I didn't
want to think about Bronski, but I couldn't avoid it, knowing we
had a snitch in the house. I shook my head. "I'm going to shower
and go to bed."

"Looks like it's you and me, Cave Man."

"It's Cavers."

"That's what I said."

I WAS DRESSED, leaving the bathroom after showering for bed,
when I stopped short. Raize stood at the end of the sleeping bag
I'd rolled out in the corner by the window, studying my setup
with a slight frown.

"What are you doing in here?"

The door was closed, but I could hear Jake and Cavers from
the kitchen. Correction, I could hear Jake laughing and Cavers
arguing.

"I wanted to check on you. Saw your face when we came in
and Cavers was there." He turned to face me, folding his arms
over his chest. "Can you handle being around him, knowing who
he's reporting to?"

I bristled. "I can be professional." I'd deal with it.

"You weren't earlier."

I flinched, but he was right. "Momentary lapse in judgment. It
won't happen again."

He stared at me, his head cocked to the side. He stepped
toward me, moving into the shadows. If he didn't move, didn't say
a word, I could've convinced myself that he'd left the room.

When he spoke again, his voice was soft, almost gentle. "I'm not pushing to know why you entered this life, but if it happens again, you will have to tell me. I won't give you another choice. Do you understand?"

My throat swelled up, but damn. "I understand."

"You'll be able to sleep with him in the house?"

"Yes, because if he does something, I'll kill him. I don't care who he's working for." I raised my chin, almost defiant.

He didn't respond.

He turned and went to the door. "I'm going to teach you to shoot tomorrow. You'll need to know from now on."

All the air left me.

He pulled the door shut on his way out, and I cursed. He was expecting me to fall asleep after that parting comment?

16

ASH

Raize woke me the next morning.

I rolled over and glared. I couldn't stop myself.

He chuckled—*chuckled*! I was so surprised I forgot I'd been glaring.

He stood up. "Get up. I want to do this before they wake up."

Right.

This.

He was going to teach me how to shoot.

I didn't want to learn how to shoot a gun. It was my line. Everyone had lines. But as I considered yesterday, I was going to cross that line. I'd need to learn or die.

I couldn't die yet.

I had my sister to find or avenge. At this point, it was an either/or sort of situation. That was the ultimate goal for me. Trudging to the bathroom, I made quick work of getting washed up and dressed. Today was my second pair of jeans, a new tank top, and the same sweatshirt from yesterday, mostly because it was my only sweatshirt.

I pulled my hair up, wrapping it up in a slightly loose/slightly messy bun. A few tendrils would fall through, framing my face. They always did.

I paused and looked at myself, really looked at myself.

I'd always been pale growing up. Brooke was the one in the sun, running around, mostly flirting with guys.

Me. I was the inside girl, the study girl. Brooke was lively and extroverted. I was just quiet, but we had the same face. Oval shape, flush cheeks, big lips. Dark eyes. Both Brooke and I had the same eye color. But I liked makeup.

I used to go a dark shade over my eyes. Frosted lips.

I did the slight pink hue on my cheeks.

Brooke didn't like makeup. She was almost a tomboy kinda girl, but she was the partier of us.

I didn't recognize that girl anymore. My skin was darkly tanned. No makeup. Lips were chapped.

My cheeks were gaunt, not flush or rounded.

With the weight loss, my chin stood out more. The oval face shape was almost a triangle one.

I had no clue if I looked better before or now, then I shook myself of that question. How could I look better? But I had dark hair before. Now it was blonde.

"You gotta change your hair color."

They decided to change my hair color, not me. They wanted me to have platinum blonde, but now with my roots, it was a beachy blonde look. I knew the back was super light, almost white on some strands. My eyes were the only thing I recognized anymore. They were the only thing I still had.

"...I can't use you until your hair is blonde."

That guy. A wave of nausea rolled through me and I grasped the bathroom counter, leaning forward.

I chose to go to him. *I* picked *him*. They asked my name and I told them Brooke.

That was the first name I used. She was the first one.

"You're gonna die with a needle in your arm..."

The lady who did my hair, because I argued, telling them they needed someone professional to turn hair from black to platinum said to me, "*Go to the bus station, buy a ticket, and disappear. They'll forget about you... Go far.*"

She tried to save me, but she hadn't known.

Hell. I hadn't known, and now here I was, seeing a stranger in the mirror who was wearing a brand new fucking sweatshirt. In Texas. Go figure.

No more memories. There was no point.

No going back. Only forward, and thinking about that, I might want to get a second sweatshirt, especially if we'd be using it to hide a gun because that meant I'd be wearing this thing everywhere and every day, and holy moly, it'd get stinky.

I was so tired.

I'd trudged to the bathroom, so keeping with the theme, I trudged down the stairs and through the kitch—I stopped as I passed the living room. Jake was sprawled out in the middle of the room, arms and legs akimbo. He was snoring. I felt it vibrating through the floorboards.

Movement caught my attention from the kitchen.

Raize was pouring coffee into a thermos... When did he get a thermos? He turned and grabbed a second thermos. My eyes went wide as he handed one to me, and I sniffed it, smelling the cream he'd added. He took his coffee black, so I knew he'd done it just for me.

"When did you get these?"

He gave me a look but didn't say a word as he stepped outside.

I couldn't discern whether that had been a good look or a bad look. It'd just been a look. It had me flabbergasted—and there I went again. *Flabbergasted*? I did not talk like that, or think like that.

So odd. What a morning *already*.

Raize got in the truck, and I slid in on the passenger side.

"Those two stayed up until a few hours ago," he informed me.

I glanced over, sipping my coffee. I would expect him to sound pissed. "You're not mad about that?"

He pulled out and turned onto the road. "I wouldn't have allowed it if it didn't work. Jake figured out that we're setting everything up, and his job is to either follow Cavers or distract Cavers. I'm guessing he got tired of following him yesterday."

Jake was a genius.

"Are you hungry?"

I shook my head. "I'm good. Maybe after shooting?"

Asking to wait to eat food until after an errand, that's what normal people did. I was hoping Raize would let me pretend we were normal this morning. Again.

He nodded. "That's fine."

He was going along with it. I was speechless.

He drove us to a legit shooting range.

Noticing my look, he shrugged. "I didn't have time to scout any land. Do you have your fake?"

I did.

We went inside, and an older guy with very keen eyes had Raize fill out some sort of form. Both of us showed ID, and then we were allowed through a door and into a shooting room. There were a few other guys there, one other woman. She glanced over, saw Raize, and her gaze lingered. She looked him up and down. The guys did the same, but likely for a different reason.

I needed to be honest with myself here, because it had become obvious that I was stupid in denying it.

Raize was hot. More than that, he was gorgeous, and the whole *dead-and-cold* vibe he gave off somehow accentuated his attractiveness. He was tall, six two and lean. But he was muscled. I'd seen his eight-pack, unfortunately. Now I couldn't stop thinking about it. But it seemed the men in this room saw what I saw, too—there was more to Raize. Not about the eight-pack. He had the quiet power of a killer, and these guys looked at him as if somewhat and reluctantly impressed.

The woman definitely wanted to fuck him. I was waiting for her to lick her lips.

"Stop looking at them." Raize was busy setting up our guns.

I snapped my eyes to the front, forgetting how Raize could see everything. He had eyes on the sides of his head and in the back.

"You should have a blind spot, like a freaking car," I hissed before I stopped myself.

He motioned for me to stand next to him. His next words were soft, and not what I'd been expecting. "You need a comfortable stance. There'll be kickback after you shoot."

"Huh?"

"Stance."

"Stance?"

He didn't shoot with a stance. He just shot. Sometimes running, sometimes not even looking.

"You need a stance." He patted the inside of my leg, and I jumped, feeling that touch shoot all the way to my chest. "You're new to this. Stop fucking around this morning."

I scowled. "I'm not fucking around."

It'd been a long time since I'd fucked around.

I'd had a boyfriend when I was a junior in high school, the year my sister was taken. He'd been my escape until I decided to *actually* escape and start down the path that had brought me here.

"I used to have sex regularly."

Raize went still. "What are you talking about?"

Oh boy. He didn't like hearing that from me. That was his *motherfucker* voice. I hadn't heard that tone since the motel room when he killed Bronski's man.

Bronski. I couldn't suppress my shudder.

I moved, putting my feet in some form of stance so I'd be comfortable for the kickback, but Raize was right. I *was* fucking around. "I have a list, you know," I heard myself say.

He'd been reaching for my gun, but stilled once more. "A

list?"

I took the gun from him and raised my arms.

"Wait."

"Huh?"

He slid the gun's magazine to me. "Load it. Press down, then slide it underneath."

I did as he said. He pulled out some noise-canceling equipment and eye protective gear and shot me a frown. "You have a sex list?"

"What?"

He handed me the gear. "You said you used to have sex regularly, and then you said you had a list."

"Oh!" Oh, gosh. That was kinda funny. I bit my lip, not understanding why I was in this mood this morning. "No. Sorry. I meant I have a *list*. Everyone who's hurt me or someone I cared about, or done someone wrong—their name goes on it."

Raize showed me the right way to hold the gun after I put the clip in it. He moved my finger to rest against the frame, moving my right thumb to lock over my left hand. "What's the point of the list?" he asked.

"They're people I'm going to destroy if I get the chance."

His body froze as his eyes shifted to mine. "Where do you have this list?"

"It's in my head."

He stepped back, putting my shoulders in the right position. Then he stood behind me, and I could feel his breath against my face. "Am I on the list?"

"No. If you were, I wouldn't be telling you about it."

"Who's on the list?"

My attention went back to the gun. "Am I good to shoot?"

"Keep your left hand on the gun. Don't break your hold. Keep your stance. Be ready for the kickback. Shoot when you're ready."

I shot.

I didn't need to go through the steps he'd just given me. I was always bracing for the worst in this life, and because of that, I didn't move. Not an inch. I felt the kickback. It reverberated up my arm, my shoulders, my chest. I felt the wave of pressure slam against my face, but I was ready for it. I'd been around enough guns being shot.

But I had *not* been ready for the emotions that surged through me.

I'd gone over my line. I'd just shot a gun. I was a step closer to making that list a reality. Maybe that's why I'd told Raize about it.

"Bronksi's on the list," I said softly.

His dark and penetrating eyes found mine. "We can make that happen."

Yes. Right. I told him I wanted to kill a man, and he said "we can make that happen." I was so far over the line now that I wondered why I'd ever drawn a line. It didn't make sense. I couldn't start on my list with that line being there.

"That last building, Oscar's, it's on the list, too," I confessed, my voice quiet. "I want to blow it up."

His eyes narrowed. I knew he was remembering my freak-out. "We can make that happen, too."

A wave of emotion swept through me, and I braced myself. I didn't know what I was feeling, but it was so much right now that I couldn't move a muscle. Not. One. Muscle.

Raize's hand went to my hip, and his fingers flexed there. "What's going on in your head?"

I went back to remembering that boyfriend. "I was thinking about the sex I used to have. That was a long time ago."

His fingers dug into my hip as he aligned behind me. I could feel him from my shoulder to my ass. He fit against me, almost perfectly.

He used to have sex regularly, too. I'd seen the women who left his room in the mornings. And his stint was a lot more recent than mine. Mine was years ago, probably three years ago. That would make me... "I should be in college."

Raize tensed behind me. I could feel his breath.

"If I hadn't decided, well, you know—another life, another world, and I'd be in college by now. Maybe a sophomore even." But I wasn't, and there was no point in dwelling on it. "You said you were going to destroy his operations. What are you going to do about the women?"

"That's important to you?" His forehead went to my shoulder, barely touching me. I don't think he realized.

My tongue felt heavy. I blinked a few times, and there was a wetness there I didn't want. "It is."

His voice got rough. "It have to do with why you started this life?"

Oh, damn. He went there.

This morning was just so weird.

"Yes," I whispered.

"We can take them to a shelter, wear ski masks so they can't identify us."

My knees almost gave away. I had to release the gun, grabbing for the table so I didn't fall.

Raize caught me, holding me in place with his front pressed against my back.

I could feel how long it'd been since he'd had sex. I don't know if he meant for me to feel it, but I was. I remembered how it felt when my boyfriend used to slide inside of me. So damned good, so distracting.

A slight growl left him as his fingers dug in one more time before he peeled himself away from me. "Shoot some more. I want you to feel comfortable."

Comfortable wasn't how I'd put it, but I raised the gun, turned my mind off, and kept going until I'd emptied the clip. Then he refilled it, and I did it all over again.

We went to eat lunch after both of us had shot all of our weird emotions away—or that's what I hoped I'd done.

17

ASH

There was a new awareness between Raize and me.

It was different. It was uncomfortable.

I almost wanted to spend time with Cavers to balance me out, bring me back to the way I'd been before. But when I really thought about that—nope. I shuddered.

Anyway, there was no coming back from where Raize and I had gone. I'd told him too much. I couldn't backtrack if I tried.

The new awareness was just there.

And actually, that new awareness had been developing for a while now.

Maybe I needed a new distraction? I was progressing, working toward my list, but without my line, maybe I'd lost the old failsafes to keep myself checked? Like they were anchors for me or something, a way to not lose my soul. Was I trying to find a new anchor?

Was that what I was doing?

Because that's what all of this was about. That was the real battle—keeping your soul. How far could you go, how much bad shit could you do, yet still keep your soul, no matter how much pain that entailed? Maybe I needed something else to counter all the pain I'd be feeling as I moved forward with my plans, because I *would* still have my soul.

Sex.

This was all about having sex. Me having sex with Raize, or me admitting I wouldn't mind having sex with Raize.

That was wrong. Right?

Right.

Indulging, having sex with anyone—much less Raize—was wrong. Well, different life and I could have sex with a boyfriend. It would be healthy and normal and respectful. I'd never looked at sex as a bad thing or something to be ashamed about, so when that was taken from me—violated and warped and twisted into something my sister was probably forced to do—I promised myself I would find her "boyfriend," I would find that guy's boss, and then *that* guy's boss, and I would murder all of them.

That had been the beginning of my list.

I watched Raize inside the gas station and wondered if his boss was on the list and neither of us knew it. Marakov. There was a family of Marakovs who ran the mafia we all worked underneath, but the way Abram had said that name, I wondered if Raize's boss was different, either more special or more in charge or... I didn't know.

I hoped Raize didn't care about the guy, because I wanted to kill him.

I *would* kill him. I needed to make that correction.

My phone buzzed, and I grabbed it—Jake calling. "What's up?"

He was quiet for a moment. "You sound weird. What's changed?"

"I learned how to shoot a gun."

"Ah. It's liberating, isn't it?"

That was one word for it. "I'm a bit more murderous now."

He chuckled. "That happens, too, but you're also spending a lot of time with the boss. He'd make me feel more murderous."

"True. It's a side effect."

Another chuckle from him.

I didn't know why he was laughing. This wasn't a funny conversation.

He sighed. "What are you guys doing?"

I pulled the phone away, looked at it as if it had grown an alien head, and put it back to my ear. "Why are you asking me this?"

"Because aren't you with the boss?"

"Yeah, but that's for him to answer."

"He's not answering my calls or texts. What's he doing?"

I looked up. He'd finished paying for our gas, and he was coming out, reading something on his phone.

"He's reading your text now."

Or he was reading someone's texts. Maybe Abram got back to him? That would be fast. Raize had said Estrada would want to see Abram in person, but Raize had made Abram, Basil, whatever, share all of Oscar's operations with him before he left. I hoped we'd start demolishing some of those buildings and networks today.

That'd require a bomb, and we hadn't made one yet.

"Cavers is with me. We're both waiting for his instructions."

"I'll pass the message."

He chuckled.

I didn't know why he chuckled. Again, this conversation wasn't funny.

I'd moved past the wanting to laugh or share weird facts I'd had going on this morning—or maybe that was just with Raize? This was a lot of thinking. A rule I needed to adopt: stop thinking so much. Except when I was trying to survive, then I'd need to think.

Raize opened the driver's side door. Thank God. I *really* needed to stop thinking.

I was getting a headache from so many conflicting thoughts and emotions all at once. I missed being numb.

Raize frowned, seeing something on my face. "What's wrong?"

I hung up on Jake, sliding the phone back into my pocket. "That was Jake. They're awake. You're not responding to his calls or texts, and he and Cavers need to know what to do today."

He continued to frown, still staring at me, but he hit a button and put the phone to his ear.

I tried to tune him out, but I couldn't.

"Send Cavers to get ingredients to make a cake," Raize told Jake. "You go with him, stay with him all day." A pause. "We'll need to make a few cakes."

Cakes. Now I was snickering.

Raize put the phone away and I said, "That's not very code-like of you."

Cake was code for bomb. *Everyone* knew that.

He started the engine. "Cavers is extra dumb."

True. "Jake's not," I told him.

He pulled out of the gas station and turned left. "I know."

Ugh. I was kinda hoping to go back to denying certain things to myself. That made being here a lot easier. Right now I felt all sorts of restlessness. I was on edge, and I needed a release of some form.

Gah. *No.* Not that kind of release...or maybe?

I hoped not. I wasn't ready for the kind of mental games I'd need to play with myself to be okay fucking Raize.

Why was I thinking like this again?

Maybe I should call Jake back. He seemed to distract me from these thoughts, from the other distraction I was obsessing about so I could be okay with what Raize was going to make me do this week—and I wasn't talking about sex.

I cursed, shifting in my seat. "I need something."

Raize glanced over. "What's going on with you?"

"Me shooting a gun wakened shit in me that I was keeping dead."

That made no sense, but Raize seemed to understand. "What do you need?"

I shook my head, frustrated. "I have no idea." Or I didn't want to admit what I needed.

I closed my eyes. *God.* I was going there. Raize was going there.

I'd have to brace myself for the self-hate I'd be piling on later.

"Drugs?"

"I hate drugs."

Realizing I'd said that to a former drug dealer, I froze a second, but there was only a ghost of a smile on Raize's face.

He nodded. "I don't want your mind altered anyway, so drinking is out, too."

Fuck.

I mean...well...that word. *Fuck.*

I closed my eyes, back to bracing because I didn't know what was going to happen next.

Raize kept driving, but then I felt him reach for me. He yanked me over to his side. "Unbutton your jeans."

Oh. Gawd.

I was flooded with need and was already wet, but this was embarrassing.

I didn't move.

"Ash."

Who...that was me. I'd given myself that name.

He was using it.

I didn't want to think about why that helped me do this, but it did. *He* did. I lifted my hips, unbuttoning my jeans and pushing them down.

I was not looking at him though.

"Move your jeans farther."

I did, hanging my head.

I could hear his voice growing rough, but he was still driving.

I felt his hand between my legs, and I hissed, jerking from the touch.

"Those gotta go down farther. I can't do what I need to do where they are."

Good.

Fuck.

Lord.

My whole face was heated by now, but I did as he said.

I peeked, I had to look, and relief flooded me when I saw he'd driven us out of the city again. He preferred the outskirts. After a few more moments he slowed the truck, turning onto an abandoned road and pulling to a stop behind some trees.

Then he was on me.

He pulled me down to lie under him. His eyes were on mine. "Do you want this?"

This. I knew what he was asking.

I had to admit this to myself. I couldn't talk around it anymore, so I nodded. "Yes." I made sure my voice was clear, articulate.

That's all he needed, and his lips found mine. I gasped as his mouth opened over mine. I hadn't expected this. I thought he'd finger me, bring me to a climax, and I'd be good for a while, but this was Raize. He was *so* thorough.

My mouth opened wider, and he groaned, pressing down over me, grinding up and into me.

I hissed, feeling him hit right where I needed him.

I was throbbing. Desire pulsated through me.

I was going to fuck my boss. That should be funny, right?

His mouth grew more demanding before he lifted his head to look at me. I was transfixed. I couldn't look away or do anything except compel him to keep going.

His eyes were nearly black, and he shifted, raising himself enough to pull my underwear and jeans all the way down. He splayed my legs out, and as his head went to my chest, tasting me there, his finger moved up and inside of me.

I gasped, not ready, but wanting more.

He gave me more.

Pulling out, pushing in. He kept going, going fast, almost too fast for me, but I grasped his shoulders. He was working me over, bringing me to a climax, and I could see him working on himself at the same time.

I bit my lip, watching him. That made me even hotter, even wetter.

I groaned, and he looked up. When he saw where I was watching, his finger slowed. A second slid in, and he went back to thrusting, but slower. He was dragging this out.

It was working—filling my brain with dopamine, the pleasure center, and it would help me settle myself for what else we'd be doing this week.

Fuck.

I'd probably need more of this.

I shifted my hips, urging him on, and I was writhing. I didn't want to think.

I was thinking.

That wasn't good.

There was an almost drunk need in me as I sat up, reaching for his cock. I replaced his hand with mine. When I felt my climax start, my lips parted and I let out a deep moan. My back arched because holy shit, that felt good.

So good.

I fell back, and he came on my hand, spilling over my legs. He reached up and caught my neck. He squeezed, turning my face to look at him. He didn't speak, and I just panted, breathless from that climax. The waves were still wracking my body. His gaze moved over my face, my body, and then stayed on my lips.

He moved back to stroking his dick, sliding up and down. He was getting hard again.

I knew what was next.

Was I ready? Was that what I wanted?

If I said no, Raize wouldn't do it. I knew him by now, knew he wasn't like that. But then I felt his lips on my throat, my chest, lower... He moved between my breasts, and my word, that felt good.

But this was wrong. This guy, he was all wrong.

I shouldn't be feeling any of this.

He epitomized the people who'd taken my sister. But even saying those words to myself, I couldn't bring up the resistance I should've been feeling.

It was now or never.

This wasn't about sex. This was about me moving forward toward being ready to kill. I couldn't find or avenge my sister if I wasn't ready to kill someone. I had to be honest with myself from now on.

I had to stop hiding.

Fucking Raize—I wanted to do that. I'd been wanting to for a while.

"Ash?" He had paused, his lips lingering over my clit. He was ready for me.

Desire lit me. I felt my whole body come alive, and I arched my back once more. "Yes" left me on a sigh, and he sat up and then slid inside.

I was gone. This was done.

The old me was dead.

This was the new me. This was the me from now on.

I could finally avenge my sister.

But first, I put my arms around Raize's shoulders and pulled him close. I wrapped my legs around his waist and met him thrust for thrust. I took what I needed from him, damn the consequences.

THERE WERE no pretty words or loving touches when we were done. Thank God for that.

Raize rested on top of me for a moment before he pulled out and grabbed some napkins from the gas station bag. He wiped himself off, then handed some to me.

He tucked himself back in, zipped his jeans while I put myself back together as well.

"There's sanitizer in there."

Okay. You had to do what you had to do in these moments. I washed between my thighs as much as I could handle.

Jesus.

Raize and I had fucked, and it was good. *He* was good. More than good.

I swallowed over a knot, because I knew I'd want to do that again. He'd just awakened a whole different appetite. I liked his cock. I liked how he used it.

He sighed, reading something on his phone before typing a response and putting it back in his pocket. He reached forward, starting the truck. He backed up and turned back down the road.

"We have three guys coming down," he informed me.

And we were back to work.

I pushed my back into the seat, lifting my hips and adjusting my jeans. "When?"

"Tonight. I want you to pick them up, take them to a motel, and set them up."

"You don't want Cavers to know about them?" That meant his boss wasn't sharing with Carloni, and he'd told Raize as much. That was interesting.

"You'll be driving this truck. Get 'em in their rooms and hand off the keys. I'll swing by and pick you up. They'll know what to get for what we'll be doing."

"You know these guys?"

"I've worked with them before, yes."

"And if Cavers or Jake asks me what I was doing?"

He glanced over. "They ask you that shit?"

My tongue felt heavy. "Sometimes. I tell them it's none of their business."

He scowled. "They shouldn't be asking you that shit. They know better."

"They're male."

His scowl morphed into a frown. "What does that mean?"

"That means they think they're above me, that they have the right to ask me when they wouldn't ask you. It's a guy thing. It's like man-splaining, but man-questioning."

He turned back to the road, shaking his head. "Don't say shit to them. Direct them to me if they want to know."

"They won't ask you."

"That's the point, Ash."

Ash. There was my fake name again.

Ash. I was Ash. I'd *asked* to be Ash.

I needed to adopt this name.

I refocused. "What are we doing until they get here?"

He gave me a slight grin. "We're going to scope out Oscar's buildings and figure out the best way to use those cakes."

Oh, goody. I'd cross something off my list soon.

A flare of want rushed through me, but I stuffed that right back down. It was wrong to get off on the thought of blowing up a building.

Wasn't it?

18

ASH

The guys Raize flew in were scary. Then again, Raize was scary. *Remember*? When had I stopped thinking he was scary?

I considered that. He was still scary. I just didn't think he'd be as quick to off me as I used to.

As the three guys walked out of the airport, I wondered how they were going to fit in the truck. When they saw the truck, they angled my way. They tossed their bags in the back, and two of the guys—with stony faces and black shades—climbed in behind them. The least scary one, the one that smiled, got into the cab with me.

They looked military, which made me wonder if Raize had been military at some point. He might've gone the mercenary route, and I was assuming that's what these guys were?

I had no idea. I didn't want to know.

"Hi." One in the cab gave me a nod. "Raize said you'd set us up?"

I nodded. "I got you guys two motel rooms."

"Cool." He settled back, leaning his head against the headrest, and his deep breathing a moment later told me he'd fallen asleep.

The two in the back watched the traffic as we drove.

In some places it was against the law to let humans ride in an open truck bed. But well, when would that stop us? I drove like I normally would, assuming they knew how to brace themselves if I had to brake suddenly.

We got to the motel with no problem, and they exited the truck without a word. They took the room keys from me, and I waited for them to get situated.

Raize's orders had been to let them do what they were doing, then they'd come out and we'd switch places. I'd go into the room and watch it while they took the truck to do whatever else they needed to do. I'd sit tight until Raize came to get me, or until I was told otherwise.

Twenty minutes later, the guys left, and I sat in one of the rooms. They had closed the connecting door and left all their bags in that room. They did not want me to see what they had in there, and that was fine with me.

My phone buzzed an hour into waiting.

Jake: I'm bored following Cavers around today. Tell me a joke.

A joke? I didn't have a sense of humor.

Me: No.

Jake: Why not?

I sat up in my chair. This was uncomfortable. Still, I texted back.

Me: Tell yourself a joke.

Jake: See? That was funny.

Me: I'm not funny.

Jake: You are sometimes. You don't mean to be.

I had no idea what that meant.

Me: You're making me uncomfortable.

Jake: I wouldn't want that. What'd you and Raize do earlier?

I frowned, typing back.

Me: I told you. He took me to shoot a gun.

Jake: That doesn't take all day.

Me: ~~If you want to know information, you need to ask Raize~~ —We went to shoot guns, then ate. That's all.

I waited.

It took a minute before I got his response.

Jake: You guys bond over shooting or something?

Me: No. Why?

Jake: You seem different around each other.

Me: Stop digging.

Jake: That's what I'm doing? I thought I was just having a conversation with you.

I didn't answer. I didn't know what to answer with.

Jake must not have either.

JAKE: Where are you?

Three hours later, I was wondering the same thing about the guys and Raize. I'd gone to the bathroom and done a few laps in the room, but I was going stir crazy. I wasn't used to sitting this long anymore, and I hadn't brought a book with me.

I sent Raize a text before replying to Jake.

Me: Jake is asking where I am.

He didn't reply, so I didn't say anything.

TWO HOURS LATER, my neck was cramping and my stomach growled.

Raize told me to stay and watch the rooms, so I had. But I wanted to leave. I was thirsty, and I wasn't sure if the water from the sink was drinkable.

I texted Raize.

Me: I need to go to the vending machine for water.
He didn't reply.

I never went to the vending machine.

WHEN I WOKE SOMETIME LATER, I had a dizzy head and stomach cramps.

Scooting off the bed, I made it to the bathroom. What time was it?

Checking my phone, it was after midnight. 12:48.

My head was still swimming, so I double-checked the doors. Both were locked, and then climbed back onto the bed. This time, I snagged one of the motel's blankets and pulled it over me.

I didn't know why I was cold, but I was shivering.

I went back to sleep.

A DOOR SLAMMED, and I jolted upright, gasping.

The room was completely dark.

I started to lie back, but there was a tingling at the back of my neck.

I wasn't alone in the room.

I screamed as a shadow darted forward. A hand slammed over my mouth. "It's me. Raize. Stop."

I ceased, gulping in relieved breaths. I didn't want to think about who might've come in.

A second later, when I relaxed, he pulled his hand away. "I have water and food for you," he whispered. "Can you sit up?"

I nodded. I'd gone days before without food and water. But I was still a little light-headed. He kept his hand on my elbow as he gave me the water bottle. A sandwich was next, but I wasn't sure I could swallow that. I pushed it away, pulling my elbow free, and drank the entire bottle before speaking.

"I'm fine. Just needed this."

I couldn't see him in the dark. There was no light from outside, nothing from the motel room—no alarm clock or light from the connected room, though I could hear the guys walking around in there.

I wanted to ask what they'd done, but I could smell sulfur and sweat on Raize. I didn't want to know who'd been on the other end.

A different thought came to me. "You didn't blow up that building, did you?"

He tensed before relaxing, a slight chuckle coming from him. This time it sounded nice to me, sliding down my back in a soothing way.

"No. It's on your list, not mine."

I grunted. "Good."

"You want to stay here?"

"You mean sleep on a bed?"

"Better than a sleeping bag."

"Won't Cavers get suspicious?"

"I can go back, tell him I have you on a stakeout."

"He'll still get suspicious. I wouldn't want to stay if you weren't here. Those guys are scary."

"They won't do anything. The door is locked."

"Right." I mocked him, not caring. "Because I'm sure that'll stop them."

He chuckled again. Why did that make my insides warm as well?

"They won't harm you. I know them."

"I don't, and that doesn't make me feel better." I nudged him back and stood. "Let's go back."

I moved around him, heading to the bathroom. When I came

out, he had the outside door propped open. Finally, light. A small ray from the streetlight was shining.

I walked past him, and he let the door go.

I started for the truck, but he made a sound, indicating the car Jake and I had driven a few days ago. I got in. That had only been three days ago? It seemed like a lifetime.

"How long do you think we'll be down here?" I asked.

"I don't know. Why?"

"If we do this, and get everything set up, you think your boss will install you down here permanently?"

Raize glanced over. "Why are you asking that?" His voice was rough, the edge was back.

"I'm wondering if it's worth it to ask for mattresses at the house."

I could literally see him relax, one muscle at a time. "It's not. We'll be transferring locations soon."

Oh.

Dammit.

That bed felt nice.

A little while later, he pulled into the driveway at the house. When I started to get out, he stopped me. "Wait."

I sat back.

He reached over into my pocket and pulled out my phone.

I gave him a glare. "You could've just asked."

"This was easier, less of a fight." He was already going through it, and when he paused, I knew he was reading the texts from Jake. His jaw clenched, and he hit a button before he handed the phone back to me. He'd deleted all the text messages, including the one to him. "I'm going to get you a new phone."

I started to protest, but then shrugged. "He'll need to have my number if we need to get ahold of each other for any reason."

"I'm aware, thank you." Still biting.

I ignored that.

"He's pushing you, and I don't like it. He shouldn't be pushing."

"He wants to get to know me."

"He shouldn't."

I could feel the glare coming from him, even though it was dark. A few shadows played over his face, and I could see his lips, his chin. He had a nice jawline. It was making me feel restless again.

What was wrong with me? Raize had killed a guy simply because he talked back when he shouldn't have. Actually, that wasn't altogether true. He'd asked me if the henchman would be a problem. The answer was yes. That's why he'd shot him.

How could I be this restless again? Twice in one day? I'd lost my mind. That was the only explanation.

As if reading my mind, Raize asked, "You okay now?"

"About Jake or...?"

"You need to get off again?"

I inhaled a sharp breath. It was like he was asking if I needed a hit of coke or something. So casual.

"I'm fine," I clipped out.

"Good. Stop being nice to Jake. I need to see if he'll stop pushing you."

I'd been about to ask what it would mean if Jake didn't stop pushing, but then I thought about it. I didn't want to know.

I went inside, not waiting for Raize, and I walked through the kitchen. The guys weren't here. I didn't know where they were sleeping, but I went to my room, flipped the light on, and locked the door.

It was then I realized I'd had it locked this morning, too.

That hadn't stopped Raize.

I didn't know how I felt about that, and then I was just so tired of everything.

19

ASH

I slept late the next morning, and when I got up, I found coffee, toast, and a note left for me in the kitchen.

Boss said to let you sleep. We're off doing recon. Call if you're bored –Jake

The toast was cold. The coffee was colder.

I had the house to myself.

I felt like I'd just scored a touchdown without ever carrying the football. *Score.*

I wasn't going to ask what recon they were doing. There were so many different agendas and lies going on—I was just following orders from now on. Doing what Raize said and living. My two main priorities as of now. The list would come. Raize would help, or he said he would.

So I ate my cold toast, drank my cold coffee, and grabbed a book. I went outside, found a tree in the backyard, and lay down on a blanket. All in all, this was the beginning to a great 'off' day, if those existed in this world.

I'D FALLEN asleep out there when I heard the voices and sat up.

There was movement inside the house.

The guys were back.

I stood and bent over to grab my book as a voice hit me—one I didn't recognize.

Lifting my head, everything went on alert inside of me.

I could see guys moving back and forth around the house, but I'd known. As soon as I couldn't place that first voice, I *had known*. Now that I saw, the alarm went flat inside of me. Dulled. Maybe that was my fight-flight mode? I didn't know anymore, but the guys I was seeing in the house weren't my guys.

They were strangers, and they were moving through the house on a mission. They went from room to room, shouting to each other. They rummaged through the kitchen.

Crap.

I edged back, my hand going to my pocket. Raize had taken my phone, but I had my fake ID in my pocket. That's all I cared about. Oh, damn. My gun. Where was my gun? Would the guys have left guns in there?

And why was I still standing here?

I scooted back, hiding behind the tree, and inched back until I could slide through an opening in the fence.

I heard more shouting, and when I looked back, a guy was in the backyard, staring right at me.

Fuck!

Run.

Run, run, run.

I shoved off, thanking God that I hadn't taken my sneakers off before I fell asleep. I pumped my arms and my book flew from my hand, but I kept going.

I couldn't stop.

I'd be captured—raped, tortured, drugged. I didn't know. I'd be interrogated for sure.

They'd be cruel, too. My heart pounded its way out of my chest.

The guy was in pursuit behind me. "She's here! Going west," I heard him yell.

Fuck.

Damn.

I changed course, spotting a path through a backyard, and I took it, going east now.

There was more shouting.

I had to keep going.

Damn, damn, damn. Why hadn't I kept myself hydrated? My body full of food? Those were energy reserves. I'd forgotten the reason I kept up on that shit.

I'd gotten lazy, soft.

I'd been lulled into a false sense of safety because of Raize.

I was always with him, thinking he'd always protect me. That was a joke.

I sprinted through the backyard, veering past a picnic table and around to the front of the house. I spied some gardening shears and grabbed them on the way.

An elderly guy came out the side screen door. It slammed shut behind him. "Hey!"

I whipped past him.

The other guy was right behind me.

"Oh hey! Stop!"

"HEY!"

"Why are you chasing that gi—" He stopped talking, and I heard the sounds of a tussle.

The house owner had waded in and gotten involved.

I couldn't think about that.

I had to keep going.

When I hit the street, I didn't see anyone following me—no vehicle—but I still kept going, finding another house that didn't have a fence. I went around the side to the backyard. A dog was chained up. I couldn't tell the breed, but he was big and dark, and he looked hungry.

A surge of anger burst through me.

I didn't have a dog, but we used to beg our parents for one.

The dog started barking at me, then he started barking at something behind me. The guy was coming for me, limping now, and holding his arm where he was bleeding. The house owner must've done something to slow him down.

I started around the dog. *Shit.* I eyed the house. Were these good pet owners?

I couldn't tell. My heartbeat was pounding so loud in my ears. I was sweating and panting, and I wasn't thinking straight.

I had to make a decision.

I ran over and reached for the dog's collar. He started to turn and bark at me, but I unclipped him from the chain.

He tore off, going right for the guy.

"*Hey!*" The guy stopped with a bloodcurdling scream.

"Oh my God! *Mom!*"

The screen door slammed again.

"Hey! That's our dog. Don't— Mom, he has a gun!"

I stopped.

Everything stopped.

That guy had a gun. Of course he had a gun. That would only make sense, and in that moment I knew he was going to shoot the dog.

The child. There was a child behind me.

I could hear growling and scuffling in the gravel behind me. They were rolling on the ground.

My heart beat firmly in my chest.

I knew.

I needed to make another decision, so I turned around.

The guy was trying to kick the dog off. A little boy stood frozen outside his house, his hand on the door, but no parent was coming after him. I saw no one.

No one was going to help.

This was my fault.

I let the dog go, knowing the guy was behind me, hoping he'd fight for me—and he had. But of course that guy would have a gun.

God.

I couldn't let... The homeowner had made his own decision. But this dog—I had a special place in my heart for dogs, especially a hungry-looking dog, one that was chained outside.

There was a child.

I knew what I needed to do.

A child. A dog.

No.

My mind shut off, and I threw myself at him. I was in the air, arms and legs poised for an attack. The guy didn't see me until the last second, and he never saw the shears coming.

He had the gun pointed, and the dog had backed up, maybe sensing he was about to be dust. I looked up for a split second and the kid was looking right at me. I tried to tell him to look away, but it happened so fast. Then out of nowhere, a woman swept him up, and just as she wheeled him around, my shears rammed into the guy's throat.

I landed in a crouch and knocked the gun—*my* gun, actually—out of his hand with my elbow as I reached for the shear's handle. Bracing myself, I pulled them clear through his throat. An unearthly sound roared through me from this motion, but then it was done and I couldn't move.

His blood was going everywhere.

But I couldn't move.

What had I done?

But then the dog was there, sinking his teeth into my arm. He was struggling, trying to do something.

I didn't feel his bite.

The lady was screaming from the house. I looked, and she had a phone to her ear.

Police.

It registered that she was calling the police.

I looked at the guy in front of me. He was dead, hunched over, and the dog was still trying to chew off my arm.

Move!

The command came hard and fast in my mind, and I jumped up.

Wait.

Fuck.

I used the edges of my shirt to wipe off the shears, as best I could. I wasn't going to run with those, but my gun.

Where was my gun?

There it was.

I jumped up to my feet, shoved the dog off, and ran, bending to scoop up my gun.

"Hey!" The lady was outside now, her phone by her side. She held the door open.

I stopped and pivoted back to her. "You tell them a different girl and I won't come back for you."

The blood drained from her face.

She was realizing I was at *her* house.

I knew where she lived. I knew she had a kid, too.

I didn't have time to wait for her decision.

Hearing a vehicle screech to a halt from the road, I started to run, but I yelled back, "Get inside! Lock the door. *Hide!*"

Then I turned and ran.

And I ran.

And I ran.

I ran until I didn't know where I was going, but I still kept going.

My arm was bleeding, and I stopped and ripped off my shirt. I wrapped it around my arm and looked behind me. I'd left a trail of blood. The droplets might be few and far between, but they were there. They could track me.

I hadn't been thinking.

My head was woozy.

I started to see stars.

I was spinning.

I was falling.

I was out.

I could still hear that dog barking, though.

20

ASH

I opened an eye, but only one because damn, the world already hurt so much for this early in the morning.

Wait.

No.

That didn't seem right.

I closed my eye again, and it registered that I was on a bed.

My arm hurt. I hurt all over.

What had happened?

"Boss."

I didn't know that voice.

"She's awake," he added.

I opened both eyes and wished I hadn't.

A light shone down on me, and I hissed, knowing it was supposed to be there and it was supposed to disorient me.

"Move that away."

"What? Oh. Sorry." The light moved away.

I could see a guy sitting next to me, inspecting my bandaged arm.

I lifted my head, looking over his shoulder to see who "boss" was, and a man stepped forward. He was dressed in an expensive business suit, and he had a handsome face. Classic features. High cheekbones. Full lips. He looked Latino—with dark hair, dark eyes. Tall. Almost skinny.

His lips curled up in a slight grin, as if I was amusing to him. He straightened to his fullest height. "You killed one of my men because he was going to shoot a dog. That's the most striking part for me. You didn't care about the old man he shot, but the dog." He shook his head, throwing a look at someone farther into the room, back where I couldn't see. "Abram tells me you're important to Raize."

Abram, as in Abram Basil, as in he needed to go talk to his boss, the head honcho for the Estrada Cartel before telling us about a meeting.

I was beyond screwed here.

"What's your name?" The guy had softened his tone, and he sat down, bending over to rest his elbows on his knees.

He was trying to make himself more appealing to me, coming down to my level. He was talking to me like I was someone who needed a soft voice.

Fuck him.

"Carrie." Abram spoke for me.

Estrada nodded to himself before narrowing his eyes. "Carrie what? What's your last name?"

I didn't answer.

Abram spoke. "I doubt anyone knows it."

Another nod from Estrada, and he motioned to me with an opened hand. "Do me a favor, Carrie. I doubt you'll give me a real last name, and I doubt Carrie is your real first name, so pick a name. Any name. I like to indulge myself and think I know someone when I talk to them."

He wanted a name? Fine. "Marakov."

The guy working on my bandage froze, and I waited.

There was a glimmer of a grin from Estrada before he sat up again. "Okay. We'll go with Carrie Marakov. Miss Marakov, if you were in my shoes, what would you do with me?"

The truth? "I'd let me go."

I would. That was the bleeding heart in me, the kind that would take shears to a guy about to shoot a dog. The dog that tried to tear my arm off seconds later.

He studied me and something must've clicked because he let out another sigh, glancing to the back of the room again. "Make the call. I have a feeling Raize will be motivated to get this one back."

"Boss. Marco."

Marco.

I tasted bile.

I didn't like that name.

Marco Estrada ignored whatever that was about, standing. "There's a reason Raize reached out for a meeting. I know him. He wouldn't have done it unless he had something he thinks I will want. Enough time has passed. I'm interested in seeing how he handles me having something he'll want. I have no heart to torture this girl. Not today."

He left and Abram appeared in his place, standing so I could see him. He had a phone in his hand, and he gave me a searing look. "You just got *incredibly* lucky. You know that, right?"

I did.

Man, did I know.

I grunted, wincing. "I liked the yellow suit." He was wearing a dark blue suit this time.

He snorted, but didn't answer.

I laid back down, needing to trust that Raize would come through somehow to get me back. I didn't know how he'd do it.

The guy finished my arm. "I treated you for any infection and gave you a shot, just in case of rabies. You should be good. You're stitched up, but keep them covered for another day or two. After that, let the air heal you. The stitches will dissolve themselves."

I raised my eyebrows. Dissolvable stitches. How fancy.

Then Abram spoke into the phone. "Raize, we have something of yours."

21

ASH

The meet was in the middle of a dirt road, somewhere far out of the city. They'd kept me blindfolded in the van, and only when we'd parked, did they open the door and yank me out. When I could see again, Estrada was standing in the front. Abram was with him. A guy I didn't recognize was holding me by the arm, and there were six others positioned around the van. Estrada had literally surrounded himself with men, and looking around, I could see why they picked this site.

It was flat desert around us. The hills were far away. Not many trees.

We could see Raize coming long before he pulled up. He brought two vehicles—his truck and the car. When he got out, Jake and Cavers came with him. Cavers had a large bag.

Raize stopped thirty yards away from Estrada, but Cavers came forward and dropped the bag at Estrada's feet. Then he bent over and unzipped it, spreading the sides so Estrada could see what was in there.

After he'd had a look, Cavers picked the bag up and returned to stand beside Raize.

Jake moved out until he had a clear line on me—or on the guy holding my arm.

"Raize." Estrada put his hands in his suit pockets, the epitome of calm and confident. "It's been a long time."

Raize's eyes went to mine, held, and then he blinked, the same cold, dead look on his face.

He focused on Estrada. "Give her to me."

"Who is she to you?"

"None of your business."

"That makes me want to know even more." He glanced around. "I'm surprised at you. You brought only two men? That doesn't seem like the Raize I knew." He gestured around. "I've learned from you. Picked this place on purpose—didn't want you to have a sniper anywhere within range." He sounded smug.

Raize smirked. "Right."

Abram jerked where he stood, and the guy holding my arm tightened his grip, just a reflex before loosening. These guys were on edge.

"I want my employee."

"For what? What's she worth to you?"

Raize's eyes narrowed. "My man showed you the bag of money. A trade."

"I don't need money. Give me something I need." Estrada's hand returned to his pocket. He turned, standing so he could see me as well as Raize. He looked between us. "I know you know I didn't send Macca. Oscar shouldn't have moved on my behalf, but then again, you made sure to create a job opening for yourself, didn't you? Oscar's family will be displeased with you, displeased with your boss."

Raize's tone was even, almost monotone. "I'll pass along that message."

"You wanted a meet. Let's have the meet now, and if I decide to take you up on your offer," Estrada looked my way, analyzing me, "you can have your woman back. She killed one of my men. Did you know that?"

Raize didn't react, but Cavers' head moved back a centimeter and Jake's hands flexed, forming fists.

"Interesting," Estrada remarked. "You've never given much away, but now you're worse."

"You still want me dead?"

"Of course." Estrada flashed a smile, and that seemed the most genuine thing he'd said. "But you know me. Business is business. You took out one of my men, and you knew Oscar ran his own women. That wasn't part of my business. I'm assuming you've been sent to offer your employer to take Oscar's place? He was my distributor into the US. That's the whole reason for your trip south. Am I correct?"

"You are. My boss would like to offer distribution starting here and extending toward the northeast in the US."

"But we already have distributors there. Why would we need more?"

Cavers frowned. Jake's eyes narrowed again.

"As of this morning, you don't," Raize said.

Estrada's face jerked back toward Raize, and his entire body stiffened. "What?"

"You employed the 63rds. You don't anymore."

Estrada's mouth thinned. "Do I want to ask what happened to them?"

"They're dead."

A dark cloud formed over Estrada. He lowered his head. "I don't do business like this. I won't be forced into an alliance. *You* know this, better than anyone."

Raize moved for the first time. He turned to Cavers and Jake. "Go back to the car. Drive away."

"Boss—" Jake started to protest.

Not Cavers. He dropped the bag and started for the car immediately.

"Go." Raize's tone was calm.

Jake swung his eyes my way, alarmed, but he did as he was told.

Estrada watched as both men got in the car and waited until the car had turned around. "Even more interesting. What are you setting up here, Raize?"

"I'm here on behalf of Roman Marakov."

I tensed, that name shredding my nerves.

The Marakov family ran the Russian mafia in Philadelphia, but over the last year they'd been expanding. I'd been a peon on the streets for them before I was sold to Bronski, and I knew the entire family worked together. Roman was the youngest of the brothers. There were three in total. Maxim was the oldest. Igor was the second. Roman was the only one my sister said she'd met, before she was taken.

"He's nice," she'd told me.

I'd snorted. *"He's mafia. This is dangerous. What are you doing?"*

"Leo trusts them. He works for them. He says he's going to go places."

"Leo works for Igor, doesn't he?"

"Yeah, but he wants to work for Roman. He says Roman is going to go places, and he's the one not to underestimate. And by the way, you're not supposed to know any of this. Don't say a word or they could kill us both."

A week later, she was gone.

Carloni worked for Igor.

Brooke's boyfriend worked for Igor.

I had no clue how she met Roman.

I knew Raize worked for one of the brothers. I'd assumed it was Igor since he was the one running Philadelphia, but hearing this now... What did it mean? *Did* it mean something?

"I'm assuming you still want me dead," Raize noted. "That's fine, but before you take your shot, Roman is aware that you've been trying to get into Russia with your product. He is offering *this* to you. Work with him here in Texas. He'll help distribute your product on the eastern side of the US, and you can expand into Russia."

"Russian mafia doesn't like the cartel."

"This Russian mafia does."

"Why, Raize? I'm aware of Roman Marakov's reputation, and he doesn't strike me as someone who needs me. What is he getting from this partnership?"

"He wants the 63rds out of business permanently. They're too reckless and dangerous for the United States. They kill too many innocents, and it's bad for business. They can't expand if the 63rds continue to work in the US."

"All of this was sent to get rid of the 63rds?"

"This was done so that further war wasn't waged when the 63rds were taken out, and so he's got a powerful partnership for expanding into Mexico. You work with the Colombians and you have a strong tie in Bolivia. That's an alliance that helps him."

"What's the drawback?"

"You work with him, and him alone. Not his brothers."

Roman Marakov was planning a takeover.

I got it then. All of it.

Well, almost all of it.

Wait. I had no idea, but that's the only thing that made sense.

And that filled me with so much excitement, I wanted to do a TikTok dance. I didn't know any. I didn't have TikTok, but I wanted to log onto a computer somewhere and learn one.

That meant Igor Marakov would die.

Igor was on my list. He was the boss over Carloni, who was over Bronski, and I hated them *all*.

"Raize."

"What?"

Estrada turned, holding out his hand to Abram.

Abram hesitated, giving Raize a look before he pulled a gun out and handed it to Estrada.

Raize watched the gun, his eyes darkening, but he didn't move.

"I allowed you to leave as a gift to *my* sister, but I said if I ever saw you again, I'd kill you. I'm seeing you again, Raize. You know what that means." He raised the gun, pointing it at him. "Have you considered that your boss knew I wanted you dead? He sent *you* to broker this relationship. Have you considered the thought that *you're* the gift from your boss to me?"

Raize drew in a breath, but had no other reaction.

No fear.

No anger.

Nothing.

He didn't pull a gun, and I looked around, wondering if his other guys were here somehow.

Then Raize spoke, "You think not having hills or trees around here would stop me?"

Estrada frowned. "What do you mean?"

"You're right, Marco. I didn't just bring those two men with me, and me sending them away wasn't for the reason you're thinking."

"What am I thinking?"

"That I sent them away to regroup and come up behind you."

Estrada went rigid, and I was pretty sure he *hadn't* been thinking that because his head and his men's heads whipped to look behind us.

That's when Raize moved.

He darted forward. Watching him now, I knew that I'd always be mystified by him. He moved quickly and soundlessly, and no one saw him except for me. All of Estrada's men had fallen for the trick.

When Estrada turned back, Raize was in front of him, his hand on Estrada's gun.

He took it, flipped it around, and had Estrada turned against his chest in an instant. Raize put Estrada's gun to his head and started barking orders.

"Release her now!"

The guy holding my arm let go, and I took off. Abram jerked forward to catch me, but I swung around him, anticipating his move. A gunshot hit the rock right next to Abram and he stepped back, letting me pass.

I ran past Raize and Estrada.

Raize had the gun back on Estrada...

Wait, no. Raize hadn't moved the gun. That meant he wasn't alone after all. The shot that moved Abram had come from out in the desert. And I wasn't the only one coming to that conclusion. Abram's eyes rounded, and so did Estrada's.

"Get in the truck," Raize told me.

I nodded, going right to the vehicle and climbing in. The windows were down so I could hear as he continued speaking.

"I'm not the idiot you think I am, Marco. I came with my own insurance and my own offer for you. Everything will be relayed to Roman, and we can go from there, but if you decide to work with him, that's between you and him. I have my own offering so you can lay down this death wish for me. I can't do my job to the best of my ability if the guy I'm supposed to be working with wants me dead."

"I'm listening," Estrada growled with his hands in the air.

"You want to know if Jorge killed your brother?"

"You know that?"

"I can't offer you proof, but I can offer you the knowledge if Jorge killed him or not. That's my bargaining chip."

Raize was banking a lot on this need Estrada wanted to know if someone killed this Jorge guy. *A lot.*

"And if I don't want it?"

"Then I walk and my boss sends someone else in my place to offer another deal—but with less benefits for you. You won't be getting into Russia anymore."

"You have that much faith in your boss?"

"I do."

Estrada was quiet, and for whatever reason, Raize let him go.

He jerked away, rounding and glaring at Raize, then at me.

"You care about that girl." He grinned, and the look was ugly. "*My* sister will be heartbroken."

"I don't know why she would be, but I left because you sent a death squad for my head. I'm back to set this up."

"What if I require that you're the go-between if this partnership is to start?"

Estrada was goading Raize. I just didn't know why.

Abram watched them like a hawk.

"You make that requirement and I retract the offer for you to find out whether Jorge killed your brother."

I couldn't see Estrada's reaction to that, but Raize was holding his own. He seemed unflappable, almost bored at times, though I didn't think anyone believed that. It was just his way of goading Estrada.

It was working.

There were lines of frustration around Estrada's mouth.

What was the history here? What had been between Raize and Estrada's sister?

"You've been given the offer, both offers. Take a day to decide."

Estrada clipped his head in a nod, and Raize turned his hand, emptying the gun into the dirt before tossing it back to Abram. Then he turned and walked back to the truck. As he did, three figures rose up from the desert, all wearing camouflage—Raize's second team. Each carried a long rifle, and I was sure they had other weapons on their bodies. They came over, climbed into the truck bed, and without saying a word, Raize started the engine and reversed.

We went one way.

Estrada went the other.

22

ASH

Raize didn't speak the entire drive back.

He looked me over before we left, but that was it. He drove to the motel. The guys got out and went inside, and we drove away.

"Are you hurt?" he asked once we were alone.

I shook my head, hugging myself.

"What do you want?"

My stomach growled. "Anything. How long was I with them?"

"Less than a day."

Oh. "I passed out. Came to when they were bandaging my arm. They had their own doctor."

"He's a good doc. I know him."

Right. Because you came from them.

"You killed a man?" Raize asked after a moment.

I nodded, a lump forming in my throat. I'd blocked that out.

"I don't want to talk about it."

Wait. I had to. "There was a woman and her son," I told him. "They saw me, saw what I did. There was a dog, too."

The air turned frosty, but I was too tired to hold my breath. Raize's reaction was going to be his reaction. I wasn't scared of him anymore, though I should've been. You should be scared of everyone in this world.

"A woman? A kid?" he said, sounding incredulous.

I nodded. "Yeah," I whispered.

"Give me the address."

My heart slammed against my ribcage. "Raize. No."

"Give me the address."

No.

No.

He could not—he'd kill them. I *would not* have a hand in that.

He lowered his voice, "If I don't take care of them, Estrada will —if he hasn't already."

I shrunk down in my seat, wrapped my arms as tight around myself as I could. "They're innocents."

"They saw your face." He sighed. "I need an address. If you don't give it to me, I'll have Jake look through police records. They would've called the police. I'll find them that way."

I shook my head. "Raize, I can't."

He fell silent and we drove for a bit, but then he spoke, "Estrada won't just execute them. He'll take the woman and sell her. He'll do the same with the kid. This happened today. That means if I don't get to them, they will. Tonight. They'll come in the middle of the night, and they will wipe out everyone in the house. Wife. Husband. Child. Teenagers. It doesn't matter. I need an address." He hit the steering wheel, barking out, "Now!"

I jumped.

Raize had never been violent toward me, but I heard his frustration, with rage simmering just underneath.

"Raize," I whispered, tears sliding down my face.

They were like my sister.

They were innocent.

That little boy...

"I can't."

He expelled a ragged breath. "At least let me find them and relocate them."

I looked over, not sure if I could trust the hope springing up in my chest. "What?"

"If I get to them first, we can control what happens. If I don't, they're gone no matter what. You have to see I'm the better option here."

Raize was a killer. He'd kill them.

But... Estrada.

He was right about Estrada.

"You don't think they've gotten to them yet?"

"No. Did she call the cops?"

I nodded. "I told her to give them a different description of me. She was already on the line."

"That means cops might already have them under surveillance, but Estrada has men on the force. I'm a ghost here. I can do this. Let me. It'll be more merciful. I promise."

God.

I couldn't.

He'd kill them.

But Estrada couldn't get them either. That was worse, so much worse.

I heard myself whispering the address, and a second later, Raize had the truck whipped around.

WE DROVE by the house first, and spotting a marked police car, Raize kept going. We went to get food for me, and I ordered extra, hoping I'd be able to give it to the woman and her son. I hoped against hope, because I didn't know what Raize would do.

But then we came back, parked around the block, and we waited.

When dusk settled in, Raize handed me my gun and gave me

instructions to shoot if anyone but him showed up. He left, pulling on a gray hoodie from the back of the truck. He put the hood up and ran down a back alley between houses. Then I saw him cut through someone's yard.

I rolled my window down, just a smidge.

I kept expecting to hear a dog barking or gunshots, but I heard nothing.

A minute passed. Nothing.

Five, still nothing.

My stomach twisted, and I knew something was wrong.

Fuck. Fuck! *Fuck!*

I hated this shit. I hated this life.

The image of my sister flashed in my head.

Could I give her up? Stop looking for her? Escape and return to my old life?

Who was I kidding?

What life?

I knew the answer before I started moving. In one motion I reached for the door handle and tucked my gun inside my shirt. I shut the door so it only clicked softly, because my life might depend on it.

With my head down, I moved through the houses, feeling my soul pull away from my body because I knew—I just knew that what I'd find in that house would change me. Again.

This was another line I was going to cross.

For them. The woman. Her son. For my sister.

And for Raize, too.

I crept forward until I got to the sidewalk.

My insides clenched, but I kept moving forward. It felt a little like I was watching myself from outside my body.

An eerie calm washed over me, even as I raged on the inside, *already* tasting blood.

When I got to the marked car, it was empty. Going along a

white fence between the house and the neighbors', I was listening. I heard nothing, from either house.

It was dark now. Dusk had come and gone.

Still. Nothing.

There was an opening in the fence. I slipped the lock, swinging the door open. One of the hinges creaked, and I caught it, holding my breath. After a moment I eased through and closed it, quietly this time. No creak.

As I moved closer the back door opened. A guy stepped out. He came out to the back step, looking around.

He was the guy who'd been holding my arm earlier.

Where was Raize?

Pop! It was somewhat muted. How could I hear that?

Then I saw—a window was open. The room had lit up on that *pop-pop.*

I knew what that sound had been, but as I jerked forward, a hand covered my mouth. An arm wrapped around me, picked me up, and eased us back to the side of the house, away from Estrada's man in the backyard.

I started kicking, making no sound, until a voice spoke in my ear. "*Stop.*"

Raize.

He moved us around the house, keeping as close to the fence as possible. Once we were on the sidewalk, he put me back on my feet.

I shoved away from him, whirling around.

His hand went back on my mouth, and he pressed me to the fence, moving me onto grass. "Stop." Still quiet, but firm.

I stopped, but I could feel my heart breaking.

More innocents, like my sister.

I hated this world. I *hated* this life.

He pressed in closer, his chest against mine, and dropped his mouth to my ear. "They were already inside. The kid wasn't here."

I stiffened.

He lifted his head, finding my eyes in the dark. "The mom was gone, too. I don't know what they shot, but no one was inside. I searched the place and got out just as they came in."

"There are no cops in the marked car."

Raize cursed, but shook his head. "They might be on Estrada's payroll."

"Who'd they shoot in there?"

"I don't—"

There was a sudden rustling sound and footsteps.

"Hurry!" came on a hushed whisper.

"Can't believe they kept a fucking snake in there. Insane. That thing was two seconds from grabbing you."

My chest spasmed. They'd killed a snake. I didn't know how to feel about that.

"Shut up. You gotta get out of here. We're going to roll up as if we're just discovering the house. You got three minutes."

"What about their dog?"

"Who cares about the dog?"

I grabbed for Raize, my hand curling around his sweatshirt.

He pressed against me, his head down, his mouth skimming my arm as he watched for them.

He moved us farther back, into the shadows.

The men rushed past us, not looking around.

"What about the dog?" I asked Raize when they'd gone.

He looked at me. "Are you kidding?"

I shook my head.

"He bit you."

"What about the dog?"

"That thing should be in an impound."

I pressed against his chest.

He sighed. "I drugged the dog."

Relief hit me hard. My vision blurred, and I rested my head back against the fence.

"I want the dog."

He stared at me.

Estrada's men were gone, but we could hear them at the car. We had minutes before this place would be flooded with blue and red.

I glared at Raize. "I want him."

He bit out a curse, and his teeth nipped my earlobe. "Fucking fine. Go to the truck. I'll grab the dog. *Jesus*."

We wasted no time after that. I went left for the truck. He went right, going back for the dog. I'd just gotten to the truck and opened the door by the time he was there. The dog hung limp in his arms as I jumped up into the seat. He deposited him in my lap and shut the door before sprinting around to his side.

We'd driven one block and were turning east as a cop car came careening around the corner. The sky turned red and blue after that.

"What will happen to that family?"

Raize shook his head. "They're gone. Police probably have them at a safe house. They might get witness protection, but who knows." He looked over, and I caught a flash of worry before the stone mask was back in place.

"What?"

"They saw you. They can identify you."

Dread lined my insides.

"But if they're being protected, I don't think it's because of you. You said you ran from there?"

I nodded.

"Estrada's guys tracked you down?"

Another nod. "I was bleeding from the dog bite. I didn't cover my arm in time. I was out of it."

"I'm thinking they saw Estrada's men—or they were able to identify the guy you killed as one of Estrada's."

"You think they'd take them and protect them because of that?"

"No." He shook his head. "I think the people got smart, called relatives, and took off. I think the marked car wasn't supposed to be there tonight. That's what I think."

"That's a lot of thinking."

He shrugged. "All I know is they saw you, and I don't like that."

What about the realtor? I wondered. *The other house's owner?*

They'd seen me, too, seen Raize. But I couldn't bring myself to ask.

All this happening, the personal shit because it was obvious there was personal shit going on, I heard myself asking, "How do you know Estrada? How do you know his sister?"

He went still, looking back on the road.

My chest was bursting, needing to know, but Raize didn't respond.

He just kept driving.

I didn't know if I liked that or not, if I should push or not?

Then I didn't. He went back to the house.

Raize took the dog, not a word spoken between us, and we went inside.

Jake took one look. "We got a dog?!"

23

ASH

I liked the new place. It was an older home, and it was set back on a big piece of land. I didn't want to think about how Raize had come to find this, but it had furniture. That was a bonus. I mean, the furniture was old. There were doilies on the wall as decoration pieces, and there were spiderwebs in almost every corner and under the beds. The place needed a full cleaning, which Cavers and I took care of the next day.

Now that things weren't so dusty, I *really* loved having a bed. My spot was situated in the back corner of the second floor. Raize waited until Jake and Cavers were off on an errand and then he'd showed me a hidden door that led to a secret room and to a back exit.

The new dog's name was Gus.

I'd wanted to name him Snake or Biter, but the guys outvoted me and Raize just left the room when asked for his vote.

So Gus it was.

After the attack, I got a better look at Gus and I still had no clue what breed he was. Cavers weighed him so we knew he was fifty seven pounds. He had short hair. Ears that stuck up. Smart eyes. His coat was a mix of all colors. He liked to smile and he'd nudged my arm more than once. I always took that as his apology for biting me.

I'd worried he'd miss that other family, but he hadn't. So far.

When he woke from being drugged, he'd been funny. Walking around with his back legs half dragging. His head down. Eyes barely open. He kept walking into things, as if he were blind. Once he really woke up, the tail started going and he hadn't done a search for his family. He was probably the most adjusted of all of us. That was saying something.

Raize had had one of his other men watch the house, to see if anyone came for the dog. After three days, no one showed, and Gus was officially ours. Jake confessed later that he'd always liked Gus the mouse from *Cinderella*, and that had sealed the deal for me. Consider me swayed.

It had been days since Raize had taken me on any errand, and I was getting restless. I didn't particularly want a redo of the sex, so one afternoon I asked him if he or Jake could take me out for some shooting practice.

He took me.

I practiced on the land, but we went far enough that we had to take the truck. As we returned, we saw Jake and Cavers coming back from an errand.

"I don't want either of them to know you can shoot a gun," Raize informed me.

"Jake knows you took me that one time."

"They don't need to know you've gone more then."

"Okay."

He nodded and pulled up behind the guys. Gus was in the back and jumped out, running over to greet the guys as they got out of their car.

"Hey, Gussy Gus Gus Boy." Jake knelt, giving Gus a rub behind his ears. He straightened when he saw Raize heading over, with me a bit behind. I tucked my gun into the back of my pants and pulled my shirt out and over it.

Since the whole Estrada kidnapping, Cavers had been less walled off toward me, even giving me a good morning and offering to cook a few of the meals. Jake, on the other hand, had been more cautious around me. I wasn't quite sure why.

"I'm going to walk Gus," Jake announced with a wave. "Be back."

Raize glanced back before stepping inside, but he didn't say anything. He headed for the back room he'd turned into his office.

It was nearing dinnertime, and Cavers was getting things set up in the kitchen.

The last couple days, I'd been helping him out, but today, as I lingered in the doorway, I decided to do something else.

I bypassed the kitchen, headed for Raize's back office, and opened the door to see him flicking on some machine, a set of wireless headphones in his ears.

He looked up and motioned for me to come in. "Lock the door."

He went to the window and peered out. I could see Jake going down the long driveway with Gus on his heels. Gus' nose was to the ground while Jake focused on his phone.

I waited, folding into one of the corner chairs.

A second later, Raize hit a button. Jake's voice came through a speaker. "...baby, yeah. How are you, beautiful?"

A moment later, a breathy female voice replied, "Hey there, sweetheart. I'm missing you so much."

"Yeah? How much?"

"I'm so wet for you."

My mouth dropped, and I could tell Raize was fighting a grin as he bent over some papers.

We were violating Jake's privacy. Then again, you didn't get privacy in this world. Ergo, I didn't get all uppity, though I was uncomfortable hearing Jake talk about how big his dick was. I could see him walking Gus down to the road as he explained how hard he was stroking it.

The call ended when Jake and Gus were halfway back down the drive.

"What was the purpose of—"

Raize stuck his finger in the air. "Wait for it."

I waited.

A moment later, we could hear buttons being punched and then the dial tone. Then a voice came over the line. "What do you have to report?"

I sat upright in my seat. That was Carloni.

Carloni, who was Raize's boss, and who I didn't think Jake was on a reporting basis with. But I sat back, stunned, and listened as he did just that.

"He made contact with Estrada," Jake said.

"Estrada is there?"

"He was. I don't know if he still is. This was the first time I could get away to call."

"Tell me about the meet."

"Estrada picked up the girl with us. Raize set up a meet to get her back. We were there with him, and then he called us off. He and Carrie returned an hour later. That's all I know."

"The girl? The Canary?"

"Canary?"

"That's what she's being called on the streets. She's a human lie detector." He paused, and I could hear his smirk as he added, "She sings, you know."

"Yeah." Jake's voice was a bit rough. He bit out, "Her."

"He has a weakness for her?"

Jake didn't respond right away.

I looked out and saw that he had paused along the driveway. His head was bent forward, and he was staring at the gravel driveway. "I don't think it's that."

"You're biased."

"I'm just saying it's personal with Raize and Estrada. It *seems* personal, but I don't know the history."

"He sent you away?"

"Yes."

"She was there the whole time?"

I stiffened, a shiver of wariness snaking down my spine.

"They were holding her, but he's with her most of the time," Jake replied, his voice a little muffled.

I glanced over and saw that Raize was also watching Jake. There was something different in his face I couldn't decipher.

"I want her phone," Carloni said.

I frowned.

"Get her phone, and we'll send you an app to download onto it. It'll give us full access."

"He has her phone."

"What the fuck?" Carloni snapped. "I sent you to watch him. You've reported literally nothing we can use. He's still icing you out?"

"I'm on Cavers-babysitting duty."

Carloni cursed again. "What's the point of me having you on him? I might as well let it go and pull you back to work up here for me."

Jake was silent for a beat again. "I'll work her."

"You told me that was impossible."

"I'll push harder. I'll do better. She's vulnerable. She said something about a sister. I'll work that angle, talk about my family. I got a grandmother. I'll talk about her, talk about my little sister. It'll work."

"You told me that wouldn't work, that she's locked down like you've never seen before."

"Raize got in with her. I can do it, too."

"You told me you didn't have a little sister."

"She don't need to know that."

There was silence on the line.

I held my breath, my stomach twisting.

"Fine," Carloni said after a moment. "Raize down there is my call, but he answers to my brother. I know this, and he knows this. So does my brother. I can't touch him. Her, on the other hand? She's disposable. I don't give a fuck if she's a human lie detector. Get something to use from her or die—you and her. Got it?"

"Got it, boss."

The line clicked silent. Carloni must have hung up because Jake stared at the phone for a full ten seconds before he ended his connection.

I could feel Raize's gaze.

"That's what they're calling me?" And by 'they,' I hadn't a clue who 'they' was.

He nodded. "Yeah."

My gut, I guess it made sense. My hair.

I didn't know what to say or feel or think about that.

But, Jake. I talked about something real with him.

Never show your cards. Never talk about anything real, anything personal.

I'd broken my own rules.

They didn't know my real name, though. No one did, and that was everything.

I wouldn't fuck up again.

I turned my eyes to Raize, finding him watching me. He was always watching me.

I showed my teeth. "Jake's on the list."

I GAVE Jake the cold shoulder for the next two days.

I know. Such a bad idea. So obvious. But I couldn't help myself. I'd talked about *her* to him, and this was how he repaid me? And if he didn't come up with something, both he and I would die? I wasn't worried about that.

I wasn't that girl anymore. I was me. I knew the stakes now. I knew what could happen.

I also knew who I was, and who I worked for, and I knew if it came to it, Raize would put a bullet in Jake's head. Whatever was happening here, Raize had it under control.

He told me later that he'd learned Jake used the sexy calls as a safeguard in case someone was listening. Anyone recording would stop listening when the phone sex started, so no one would record the real conversations.

Fucking. Genius. On both accounts—Jake and Raize.

Me? I just wanted to learn how to shoot better, so Raize took me out every time he sent the guys on an errand.

On day five since my kidnapping, we were still waiting for Estrada's decision.

Then it came.

I wished it hadn't.

24

ASH

"**M**om!" I came inside, the screen door slamming shut behind me. It was hot outside, and sunny.

"What are you doing?" My sister was in the kitchen.

My eyes needed to adjust to the inside. We didn't open the curtains. Mom never wanted them open. I was heading for the stairs, but Brooke was at the table. She was stirring something, and I wandered over.

"What's that?" Brooke was eyeing the order sheet.

"The neighbor is selling Girl Scout cookies. I wanted Mom to buy some." I frowned, glancing up. She'd been spending so much time up there lately.

"She's in bed."

"Yeah." And? When was she not in bed?

Brooke stopped stirring and glared at me. "So when she goes to bed, she doesn't want any of us to interrupt her. She's taking 'Mommy time.'"

Ask my opinion, 'Mommy time' was stupid. We didn't do anything to stress her out. Wasn't that why most the moms on our block said that? They needed a spa day or a pub day? Their kids were stressing them out? I swear that's what I always heard.

"What are you doing?" I leaned over, trying to see what she was making.

"Stop it!" She snatched her hand over, pulling the bowl away and to the side. Another glare from her. "I'm experimenting."

I half laughed at that. "Experimenting? That's what you said you'd be up for doing with Tommy Riskins last week, too."

"Shut up! You don't know anything about that."

I just rolled my eyes. I did. I knew a whole bunch about that, because Tommy turned around and asked me to experiment with him, too. Said maybe I was the sister who had some 'experience.' I told him to eat his own dick.

I asked, "Why are you experimenting?" She was trying to make something for us to eat. I could see that much.

Smelled horrible.

"Because someone has to, or we'll never eat real food again."

Oh.

We both got quiet, and as if on command, the floorboard squeaked above us.

Mom was up.

It wouldn't last.

ALARMS SPLIT THE AIR, and I jerked awake. I jumped out of bed.

Panting, with a pounding heart, it took a second to orient myself. Everything was going crazy. Red flashes were lighting up the house, and the alarms sounded like we had nuclear bombs incoming. Then my door burst open and a dark figure came in.

Before I could even scream, a hand came over my mouth.

It was Raize.

Only Raize.

Always Raize.

I tried to relax, but the alarms wouldn't stop. The red light flashed over his face as he moved his mouth to my ear.

"Estrada is coming. Go through to the secret room. Take your gun. Escape." I felt him push something into my hand. "It's your phone. Keep it on silent." He was gone in the next instant, and I felt almost bereft.

But then... *Estrada*!

My brain clicked on, and I whirled, going for the secret door when I remembered—I needed clothes, shoes, and my gun. Glancing at the phone, I saw it was four in the morning. That asshole. He'd come at this time on purpose, to catch us sleeping.

I heard stampeding footsteps down the hall below. Probably Jake and Cavers running. I heard shouting. I had to go!

Grabbing everything, I pushed through the secret door, shut it, and was in the secret room. I couldn't run in bare feet. Why hadn't I gone to sleep with my shoes on? I should've learned. I was getting so fucking soft.

Cursing, I pulled shoes on, and then I was running.

I went to the exit and paused.

Four trucks were speeding up the driveway. Men stood on the back of each one, assault rifles slung around their chests.

That was a terrifying sight, and I heard more shouting.

They started pointing. I saw Cavers running across the yard.

I'd already lost precious time. When would I learn?

I took off in the opposite direction. There were some trees I could use for cover, but no—even as I considered that, I knew that's where they'd go. So I veered a different way, not knowing where I was going, just knowing I needed to go.

I went three more feet before the shooting started.

Bang!

I started to scream, but clamped a hand over my mouth and turned, terrified at what I would see.

I cared. When had I started caring?

I didn't want them to kill Raize, Jake. Even Cavers. Despite Raize not trusting his boss, Cavers had never done anything except follow orders and cook for us. And Jake. I thought of how he cared for Gus—*Gus!*

I was hyperventilating now.

Where was Gus? Oh my God. Gus.

I couldn't—there was more shooting, more shouting.

I waited, but I couldn't hear any barking.

Where was Gus?

He'd gone to bed with me last night. He slept either at the foot of my bed, or right next to my bed on the floor. He hadn't been there when the alarms started, but God, where was he?

I turned around before I knew what I was doing.

I was going back for the dog.

So stupid.

Suddenly one of the trucks veered straight for me.

My heart hit my sternum, and I dropped to the ground. It was dark out, so I laid flat, and then I prayed.

The truck went right past me. Gunshots filled the air. A bullet hit the dirt ten feet from me. *Jesus.* My vision was blurring. I had to calm my thoughts. I had to slow my senses.

This wasn't the first situation like this that I'd been in. I should've been more prepared, more able to think clearly. I ran through the possible consequences.

I was having déjà vu from when I first ran from an armed man, but this situation was on steroids.

I could get shot.

I could get taken.

I could get sold.

I could be tortured.

I could die.

Okay. All those sucked.

God, I was so dumb. *So dumb.*

The trucks had moved to the other side of the house. I still couldn't hear Gus barking, but the shots continued like a steady rain.

I hurried to the back of the house and paused, listening.

They were fully engaged on the other side. I didn't know if anyone was in the house, but I crept up, letting myself *in* the secret doorway this time. There, a rubbery nose hit me and a tongue. Gus had followed my scent.

He'd found his way into the secret room. I had no clue how. The door was closed... Raize had done that! He'd put him in here for me, or for safe keeping.

I didn't know why Gus wasn't barking, but thank God. It might've saved his life.

"Okay, buddy—" The floor creaked, just on the other side of the wall.

Someone was in my bedroom.

Gus turned and started growling.

No!

I clamped my hand around his mouth, trying to stop him from making noise.

He shook me off, going to the door and scraping, still growling.

The floor creaked again as the person hurried forward.

They knew we were here, that there was another room.

The person ran. In the hallway, back to my bedroom.

They were looking, trying to find us.

I couldn't wait any longer.

Grabbing Gus, I pulled him after me, and he ran out when I opened the back exit. He started running, but he waited for me.

A blast of relief made my knees weak. Thank God for small miracles.

I jumped down next to him, and we took off, running in the direction I'd gone before.

More gunfire sounded behind me.

We kept going.

I glanced back a few times, but I couldn't see the trucks

anymore. They'd turned off their lights, and they weren't driving around. I didn't know if that was a good sign or not.

Gus sniffed the ground as we went, and I tried not to trip over the bushes and small trees scattered around the land. I tried to stay away from the denser pockets of trees. I assumed that's where they would look for me.

As we ran, the sounds faded. We went a little farther, and I heard a trickle of the creek. I hit the ground, my lungs burning. Tears had caked my face. Tears and sweat. I could taste the salt. I needed to keep going, but dammit. Dammit!

I didn't want to lose Raize. In all this madness, he'd become my anchor. I never knew. Without him, I'd have to... I couldn't think like that. I could try to get to San Antonio, but I had no idea where he'd stashed that bag for me.

I had no idea what to do, and I wasn't in the clear.

Estrada—if he won, if he was the surviving side back there— he would look for me. That's how cartels were. You got on their radar, and if you fucked with them, you were dead. No matter what.

Gus started licking my face. I realized I'd started crying all over again.

I looked at Gus, and he moved to clean out my eyes, then my forehead.

I let him.

I was so weak. So tired.

I knew I had fight in me, but for a moment, just a moment, I wanted to stay here.

I wanted to hide.

Gus nudged my shoulder, smelling my hands. He was looking for treats, and I was still clutching my clothes.

Right. My clothes.

I'd been running in my pajamas.

A slightly hysterical laugh came from me—softly, though.

Then, as I bent down—*bang*! A bullet hit the dirt just beyond me. If I hadn't bent down... Why the fuck was I thinking?!

I ran. But I only took two steps before a pair of arms caught me.

"*No!*" I screamed.

"We got her, boss. Tell the bastard to stop." That voice came from the darkness.

I saw two shadows. There were two men, not just the one holding me. Gus gave a primal growl and attacked. He lunged for the guy holding me, and I dropped to the ground immediately as the guy screamed. He hit the ground, and Gus went for his throat.

I heard a gun cock, and I whirled, shooting before I could think.

The other guy was going to kill Gus. I didn't know where I'd hit him, but I kept shooting until the gun fell from his hand and his body thudded to the ground.

I didn't look. I didn't want to see him, so I turned toward where the other guy was lying.

Gus stood over him and growled, right in his face.

The guy was bleeding from his arm and throat, but his eyes were trained on me. He tried lifting his free hand—in submission, I think—but Gus kept him from moving much at all.

This man had tracked me. He'd caught me. He wanted to turn me over to Estrada.

I shivered. I knew the ending of that story.

I would not go back—but dammit, I also knew I couldn't kill a man in cold blood. *That was a line I would never cross.* I couldn't say it enough. Never ever.

He seemed to understand my decision because he fell back in relief, giving up any more fight.

I went over and picked up his gun, and the other gun. I grabbed the radio they'd been using to communicate, and as I dressed in real clothes and not what I'd been sleeping in, I put it in my back pocket. The guy watched me, tracking my every movement. I didn't care what he'd see. I couldn't turn my back on him.

When I was finished, I stood. "What's going on back there?"

"Your boy is killing everyone."

"What?"

"Your boy. Raize. He's executing everyone. He's looking for you."

That didn't make sense. "You drove up with four trucks of men. There were four of us against all of you."

"That didn't last long. Three minutes in, we were getting picked off one by one. Sniper was set up somewhere. That's Raize's calling."

Raize was a sniper? "Estrada declined the offer?"

"Guessing. We were told to take out the men and grab the girl. I don't know why Estrada wanted you."

The head of a cartel wanted to kidnap me? I didn't like it.

I had to get going. I'd lost too much time talking to him. I wouldn't kill him, but because I wasn't seriously stupid, I took aim and shot him in the foot.

"*Ahhhh!* You bitch!"

The shooting lessons came in handy.

I sheathed the gun and started running. I had a plan in my head by now. I'd go along the road—not on the road, but beside it, and I'd wait for... No. Screw that.

I had my phone! And Raize was still alive.

I checked it, seeing he'd called me. Ten missed calls.

I hit one, calling him back.

He answered at the end of the first ring. "Where are you?"

"Came across the creek. The road isn't far."

"Estrada sent men after you."

"Two are down. Did he send more?"

A pause, then a curse. "He sent them all after you. Two are down?"

"Shot one dead, or I'm assuming. Shot the other one in the foot. Gus took him down."

"Gus is with you?"

I bit my lip. "Yes." I couldn't lie. He already knew.

"You went back for the dog?!"

"Lecture me later, how about?" I snapped.

"That fucking dog is your weakness."

As if understanding, Gus let out a small growl. I started to laugh, but then saw Gus staring behind us, stalking.

"Someone's coming."

"Estrada's men called in your location. I heard them on the radio. Get to the road. Cavers and Jake are driving, looking for you."

They'd gotten out. Another miracle.

My throat swelled, and I nodded, then remembered he couldn't see me. "Got it," I whispered.

Gus growled again, and he took off into the dark. A second later, more yells sounded.

I ran after him.

I had to save my dog.

25

ASH

When I got there, three men were trying to grab Gus. He circled between them. One was bleeding from the leg. A second from the arm. The last was trying to aim a gun at him.

I saw red.

Red!

Fuck these men.

Fuck Estrada.

Fuck everybody.

I was sick and tired of seeing guns pointed at *my dog*!

I emptied my clip toward the men.

I should've felt remorse. Sure, they were coming to get me, but they hadn't actually tried for me. Yet. They were just chasing me. But Gus didn't feel the same way, and damn if he wasn't one of the best things in my life right now, even if he had bitten me. I didn't hold that against him. He'd been scared.

He was more than making up for that now.

Once I started shooting, one of the guys turned his gun on me. Gus lunged, grabbed his arm, and he was down. His hand flexed, dropping the gun. He accidentally kicked it away.

Thank you, universe.

I hit one of the men, and he went to the ground, cradling his arm. The third ran off.

There was a crash through some bushes behind me.

I whirled, almost swaying on my feet, but dammit. No. I could still fight.

I would fight.

Raize appeared, and I almost fainted from the relief. A part of me had dissociated from what was happening here. That's all that made sense because I was appreciating the hotness of his whole soldier and ghost-look, appearing through the mist, sort of experience here. I mean, it was bushes and not mist, but he'd been off taking out Estrada's men, one after another and *whoosh*, he was here.

He drew up short. He was dressed in black, a gun hanging across his back.

He blinked once, taking it all in.

Then he scooped up the abandoned gun, flipped it around, and bent, bringing it down across the face of the guy fighting with Gus. As soon as the guy went unconscious, Gus stopped biting and stepped back. He looked up at Raize, waiting.

Raize repeated the action with the second man.

"A third guy took off that way." I pointed.

Raize nodded, bringing a radio to his mouth. "Estrada has a guy running your way. Scoop him up."

Crackle.

"Got it." That was Cavers, and then more crackling before nothing.

Raize put the radio back in his pocket and gestured to me. "Are you going to pass out?"

"Me?" I squeaked, feeling myself weaving. "Totally fine. Peachy even. I killed a man, and shot two others. I'm A-ok." I tried to give him a thumbs-up, but my thumb was two now. I raised my other thumb, and it was the same. I had four thumbs.

Thinking there was more than disassociating going on here, but who was I to say? I wasn't a professional, except in gut hunches. I was getting a reputation, with my own street name. How cool was that?

Yeah. Still dissociating. Or something was dissociating. Probably my sanity.

That felt more right.

Raize cursed, crossing and putting his arm around me. "You can't pass out. I can't carry you this time."

He'd carried me another time? When was that? Oh yeah. Oscar's. Well, I hadn't passed out that time. He'd taken me kicking and screaming.

I looked down and Gus smiled at me, his tail wagging.

There were three Guses. They were following each other in a circle.

I would've loved to have three Guses.

"Sit." Raize pressed me down to the ground, his hands on my shoulders. He wasn't rough, just assertive. He was good like that —always knowing the right touch, the right amount of pressure. And that had me remembering another time...

He knelt beside me and pushed my head between my legs. "Breathe. Don't move until the ground stops moving."

Yeah. Because that was happening. The ground was a constant ripple, like a gravel river. It was kinda pretty.

Raize was up and talking to someone. I ceased listening. Everything would be fine. Raize was here. He always kept me safe.

Gus licked my face. Man, I really loved my dog.

I threw an arm around him, cuddling his wiggly body up against me, and he started licking the other side of my face. He was having a grand time, cleaning all my liquids. There was probably blood there, mixed with the sweat and tears.

I lifted my head, but the trees started circling around me, so I went back to resting it against my knees.

Breathe in.

Breathe out.

Breathe in.

Breathe out.

I could do this.

I felt a little better, but this sucked—always almost dying and then being out of whack because of it. Or killing someone...

You'd think I might stop putting myself in those situations.

But my sister. Brooke.

I was doing this for her.

I didn't know how, but I'd figure it out. I just had to find her—or find out where she'd gone.

Raize could help me. Maybe I could even tell him about her.

Something bothered me about that... I didn't know what.

Maybe I wouldn't tell Raize about her, not yet.

Oh boy.

The ground had stopped its river impersonation, but now I could see stars blinking at me in the gravel.

I was about to pass out. Again.

"Bronski called you Brooke," Raize said, as if we were having a conversation.

Oh...

No.

Had I?

Dammit.

I looked up and he was staring at me, his phone in hand.

I gulped. "Is someone on that line?"

He looked, as if he'd forgotten he was using it, and shut the screen off. "Bronski called you Brooke before. That's the name you gave them?"

Shit.

So much shit.

"I was talking out loud?" I whispered.

He ignored that, coming closer. "What other names have you given?"

Brooke.

Miriam.

Suzie.

So many more.

All different names until Girl, then Carrie.

I didn't reply because he didn't understand. He couldn't.

He wouldn't understand.

But something transpired. He was doing his 'watching' thing, and he must've seen something because he knelt at my side.

He leaned in, but didn't touch me.

That was good.

For some reason, I didn't want him to touch me.

I felt raw. Exposed. I didn't know why.

Then I was crying again. Or had I stopped? Had I been continuously crying this whole time? Killing and crying? That was kinda badass... or wasn't it?

Everything was starting to swim around me again.

I didn't know what was going on.

Until Raize's voice was soft. "You asked how I knew Estrada?"

The ground was starting to settle, a little.

I heard more, "The sister he mentioned? I know her because she's mine, too."

My head snapped up. *What?!*

26

ASH

He stepped back, standing. "She's my half-sister—same mother. Her other half is Estrada's father. He took my mother as a mistress—didn't care what family she had to leave. My dad's from Connecticut, but was living down in Oaxaca." He paused. "He was there for the surfing, met my mom down there. Estrada's father knew my mom. He threatened to kill me when I was eight. He *did* kill my dad. I grew up in foster care, went into the army, and when I could, I went in search of my mom. Met my sister for the first time. My mom knew who I was the second I showed up. Morales. He runs the Morales cartel. Estrada was considered a bastard until he just took over another cartel. No one gave a fuck to question where he came from. Morales stepped back, let his son take power in the next region—because he considered Estrada his. But Estrada wasn't. They hate each other, but they also love each other. The two cartels are linked by blood, and no one knows except the leaders. When I showed up, I got a job for Morales. My sister grew fond of me, started joking that I was like a big brother to her. My mom freaked and sent me to Marco. I don't know when my sister found out who I was, but at some point, she went to him. She told him, asked that I be allowed into the family." He stepped closer, enough so I could see his eyes flash. Hard. "He sent a hit squad after me. I got out and went north to the States, as far north as I could. I needed protection, and at the right time, Roman Marakov found me. *He* found *me*. He recruited me." He took a break. I felt the conversation shift. He grew more, just more. I didn't know what he was before, intent? But it was more now. He knelt back down. "You gotta talk to me. I told you my shit. You tell me yours. You gave your sister's name because *why*? I gotta know what storm I'm walking into with you. I can't see the landmines if I don't know where to look for them."

I stared at him, overwhelmed by what he'd shared, but I couldn't respond.

A lump filled my throat, and I felt tears threatening.

His sister was alive. I didn't know if mine was.

"What's your real name?" he asked.

I could not go there. I would not. "Ash."

"Bullshit. What's your real name?"

"Miriam."

His eyes went flat. "What's your real name?"

I continued, "Sandra."

"You're lying."

I didn't wait to be asked again. "Melanie."

I stared at him. Hard. Fierce.

Again, "Suzie."

And then, "Brooke."

His eyes lit up, speculating. "Your sister."

"The first girl I found out he took."

I had a thing about names.

I saw the thoughts moving. He was connecting the dots.

He said, "Brooke. Suzie. Melanie. Miriam."

"You missed Sandra."

"Sandra."

I felt like fucking cement inside. "My sister fell in love—Leo this and Leo that. All she wanted to do was talk about him. She was obsessed. Then I met him, and I hated him. Didn't matter. Our mom died, and Brooke needed an escape. He was inside her already, got her taking drugs. Got her skipping school. She ran away. Cops never looked for her. They considered her another junkie runaway. Such a sad fucking cliche story, right?" I didn't tell him the other times the cops were at my house. I didn't tell him the looks I got, given the family history. Made so much sense to them, that's what one social worker said. I wanted to scratch her eyeballs out. "But I knew where she went. *You* know where she went. Her name was Brooke. Then I found out the other girls he took. Suzie. Melanie. Sandra. Miriam. You came along, and I was Girl. You never asked my name." I didn't wait. I whispered, "I have a thing about names."

He stared, long and hard. "Ash?"

"Ashley Cruz. I saw her missing poster once. It was old. She was taken as a kid, pretty blonde hair. Different life, but she looked like me. Doesn't matter if he's not the one who got her. Someone got her."

She was another missing girl.

So many.

Too many.

Too *fucking* many of them.

"He's on your list?"

"He's the first one."

Raize's jaw hardened, and he stood.

The conversation ended, just like that.

It left me aching. And Gus' licks weren't helping me.

Raize lifted the radio, pressing the button. "Where are you guys?"

"On the road, looking for that guy."

"Swing by, pick us up."

"Roger."

"We'll be on the driveway."

WHEN THE TRUCK APPEARED, Raize and I both hopped into the back.

As we drove up to the house, I saw the trucks had been abandoned. There were bodies splayed out over the grass. They'd been running for cover.

I watched Raize.

I couldn't not watch Raize.

He did all of that.

I stayed on the back of the truck, holding Gus, who was almost in my lap, and I did what Raize always did to me. I continued to watch him.

I watched as Cavers went to get a large roll of plastic. He kicked to spread it out, and one by one, they dragged the bodies over. They cut the plastic, rolled them up, and put them in the back of one of the trucks. When that was done, Jake drove the other trucks away, one by one. Cavers followed and brought him back each time. After three trips, there was one truck left—the one with the bodies.

Raize had walked through the entire house by now, going room by room. When he came out, he brought some of our personal items over to the truck where I was sitting—Jake's bag, Cavers' coat, Cavers' cooking knives, my book.

Cavers and Jake left again, this time taking the bodies with them.

Gus wouldn't stop licking my arm.

Looking down, wondering about a stinging I was feeling— there was blood trickling down my arm.

I'd been shot.

When had that happened?

No matter. I still didn't feel a thing.

By the time Cavers and Jake returned in our regular car, the smoke had started.

Raize walked out of the house. The smoke seemed to follow him. The flames were next, peeking out of the windows.

He'd set the house on fire.

That made sense. Destroy all the evidence? DNA? Something like that?

Seemed like Mafia 101: destroy any trail you might leave behind.

Cavers was the one who noticed my arm, and he shouted to Raize, who came over.

They gathered around, and Cavers prodded my injury, but I couldn't hear what he was saying. His voice was muffled, like I was underwater. I almost preferred it this way.

I no longer wanted to know anything.

I no longer wanted to hear anything.

I was so tired. I felt like I could sleep for months, but I knew I'd never be rested. Not now.

Not anymore.

Too much killing. Too much bloodshed. Too much violence.

There was a part of me that had always been like this, I think. Since I was a kid.

I was so tired of it *all*.

"Gus." Jake snapped his fingers, whistling.

I tightened *my* hold on *my* dog, but Raize came over and pried my fingers from Gus' collar.

Raize said something to me, frowning as Gus hopped off and trotted after Jake. They went into the car and Cavers followed. When I looked down, there was a whole bandage on my arm.

When had that happened?

I was on repeat, asking the same question to myself.

Then Raize slid his arms under me and picked me up. He carried me to the front of the truck and put me inside. He locked my door before rounding the hood to get in behind the wheel.

He seemed concerned about me, and I thought back to when I'd first started working for him.

"I had a rule with myself, not to look at you," I told him.

"Why?"

"Because I didn't want you to kill me for it." I started laughing, because that was funny.

Worrying someone would kill you for looking at them.

But it was true. That was the hilarity of it.

Right?

"I think I'm in shock again," I added.

He sighed. "Yeah."

I frowned, looking down at my lap. Movement caught my eye, and I realized we were driving. We had been driving. I was losing track of time.

"I'm really sick of this life."

Raize didn't answer.

But as I turned toward the window, I could've sworn I heard him say, "Yeah."

27

ASH

I was on the floor, sitting outside my bedroom door. It was closed. I didn't want to go in there, and it felt weird having these men being able to walk past, looking into where I slept. Not that they were all men. There were women, too. Police. Paramedics. Another lady was there, and she was dressed differently.

Jesus. I shouldn't be here.

I should go downstairs, to where Brooke was. To where my dad wasn't, but then again, that's why they were here. That's why that lady was here. We were underage. Both of us.

Our dad was gone, no one could get ahold of him.

I knew where he was, but it wouldn't matter. He'd been living there every day this last year anyway. At Marco's Bar. In the back corner, right up next to the jukebox. He liked being there. He made everyone who came over to pick out music, they had to talk to him. He was the song gate-keeper.

I'd heard him laugh about it enough when he came home, stumbling into the walls, sometimes falling and sleeping wherever he lay. He reminded me of the Shameless *dad, though that guy was funnier. Smarter, too.*

My dad was dumb.

So was Brooke.

So was I.

If we hadn't been, maybe we would've done something, but...

The stretcher came up. They rolled it past me, taking it into her room.

I saw the looks, knew what they were whispering about. They didn't need to whisper.

Yes. We'd all been so dumb.

We hadn't been watching enough.

Then again, no one had been.

I JERKED awake and had no idea where I was.

I freaked, to put it mildly.

I lashed out, kicking and screaming until a body covered me. Two hands caught my wrists, and a light flicked on.

For a moment, one heartbreaking moment, I thought I was somewhere else, a different age. I could hear her cooing to me.

"Calm the fuck down, woman."

Woman. Not Girl.

Not my name. Not a different name of a different girl.

It was Raize.

I sagged in relief. I'd registered it was Raize before he even spoke. I just couldn't get my brain to communicate with my body. I blinked up at him, then turned my head to see Cavers standing in the doorway, his hand still on the light switch. Jake was behind him. Both were staring at me.

Raize shot off of me, and I tried to ignore that he was only wearing sweatpants, and they dipped seriously low, deliciously low—and the guy was ripped. He had the whole penis-landing-strip muscles working there. Follow it down and...yeah.

"Where are we?" I asked as I checked my clothing. I was in a tank top and underwear. Note to self: keep the blankets over my legs. I looked around and realized we were in what seemed like a nice hotel room. There was a loveseat in the corner. A dresser. A desk. A nice television.

This was an *actual* hotel room.

I saw the blanket on the floor by the loveseat.

Raize raked a hand through his hair, his eyes tired, and went to the loveseat. He bent down, picked up the blanket, and stretched out. "Turn the lights off. Everyone go back to bed. I need at least one more hour of sleep before we hit the road."

Cavers gestured to my arm. "I'll check your bandage later today."

I looked down. *Right*. Because I'd been shot.

He'd bandaged me before.

How long had I been sleeping?

Cavers stepped back into their room, but Jake remained in the doorway.

"You okay?" he asked me.

Warmth flowed through me, but then I remembered his phone call to Carloni.

"I'll work her."

I shoved that warmth right out of my ass and said flatly, "I'm fine."

He frowned, but I rolled over, giving him my back as I pulled the blanket up.

The light turned off, and the door closed a beat later.

I thought I'd go back to sleep.

Yeah.

No.

Everything that had happened was rolling through my mind on replay. Gus' growls. Shooting the gun. I watched myself from above as I shot the gun and turned away, then steeled myself and kept shooting.

Kept shooting.

Kept shooting...

I had killed two men.

Two. Men.

I'd been so foolish thinking I wouldn't learn how to shoot, but I'd known that would happen once I did.

I had told Raize about my list. I'd even told him who was on the list. Not all, but enough.

God.

I'd messed up. Royally messed up.

"Do you need something?"

He sounded so tired, but my God—was he offering sex?

I growled, kicked off the blankets, and stalked to the bathroom. Or I assumed it was because there was nowhere else to go. I hit the counter, reached out to the right. Nothing. Was it a closet? A door? I turned on the sink by accident.

Raize never made a sound. He *never* made a goddamn sound, but I could feel him moving behind me.

He touched my hip, and a second later, the light turned on.

The shower and the toilet were in their own freaking room. With its own door.

I gritted my teeth as I moved past him. I started to shove the door closed but he caught it, his eyes stormy. "Do. You. Need. Something?" he asked again.

Did I need something?

My blood was starting to boil.

My heart rate had picked up.

I felt heat all over my body.

Did I need something?

I needed a life again.

I needed my sister back.

While I was at it, I'd like a mother back, too. A father would be nice.

A normal childhood, while we're asking for unrealistic favors here.

Please and thank you with a goddamn cherry on top.

Did I say any of that?

I opened my mouth. I was about to, but then his eyes flashed and he shoved me into the smaller part of the bathroom. He closed and locked the door and his mouth was on me as his hands lifted me up.

I'm thinking he understood me perfectly, right about now.

My legs wound around his waist, my arms around his back as we began a frenzy of losing our clothes.

Then we were in the shower. He pressed me against the wall.

I needed more. More of him. More of this feeling. More of everything, everywhere. Just, more.

I gasped, raking my nails down his back, and he turned me, pressing my chest to the wall. He kicked my legs apart, angled me back, and sheathed himself inside.

I groaned, my eyes closed, and savored the feel of him.

He pushed in, all the way in, and held.

I think he was savoring it, too, but then he began moving and my mind turned completely off.

I wanted him to fuck me hard.

I wanted it rough.

I wanted it long.

And when he was done, I wanted him to do it all over again. I wanted to escape, and judging by the way he gripped my hips, thrusting inside of me, I was pretty sure he needed this just as bad.

Good. Fucking good.

28

ASH

We never did blow up Oscar's building.

It was probably a silly notion to have, but I was pissed the next day as we piled into a rented minivan and headed out.

We were now entering Arkansas. We weren't flying because we were transporting guns. Guess that was a no-brainer. I did wonder if Raize had his other guys remain back in Texas or if they were ahead of us. I'd have to wait until we were alone, or... nope. Never mind. I didn't want to know.

I'd already shared too much with Raize. I felt in too deep, and it was uncomfortable—like there was something writhing around under my skin and I couldn't get it out. Part of me didn't want to get it out. With other bosses, I'd be thinking about the next guy I might be working for by now. But with Raize, I didn't want that. That was the "too deep" part of this situation.

It wasn't good either.

You can never rely on someone. I mean, big picture. If you're in a shoot-out, you're going to rely on the people shooting next to you, but that wasn't this particular situation.

I was thinking too much.

I needed to stop.

Other demons, other haunts tended to come out then.

Gus moved his head, laying it on my lap, and I petted him as I looked over into the car next to us on the highway. A bunch of girls were in it, all laughing, all drinking from travel mugs. One wore a University of Arkansas shirt.

Yeah...

Another life. Another world.

That wasn't mine anymore.

It never had been.

I needed to get over it.

29

ASH

Twenty-six hours later, we were in Philadelphia. We drove straight through, stopping for food and bathroom breaks and that was about it. Everyone took a turn driving, and everyone took a turn sleeping.

Except Gus. Gus slept the entire time.

Jake, Cavers, and I carried everything into Raize's house once we arrived. The boss took off. I was figuring he had calls to make, calls that I definitely wanted nothing to do with. We were just about done. I had the last bag and I was taking it inside.

Cavers was in the doorway. He was lingering there.

That's right, I remembered. *He doesn't stay here with us.*

Man. It felt like so long ago when we'd been here last, like a different life.

So much had changed.

Jake moved past Cavers up the stairs, Gus trailing behind him, his tail wagging.

Jake went to the second floor, giving me a lingering look. Gus sniffed my hands, but I didn't have any treats for him, so he went on up the stairs, too.

Raize hadn't come out of his office in the back. His bedroom was back there, too.

Jesus.

His bedroom. Where he used to party, with multiple women.

My mouth dried. Was he going to go back to those habits? Would I be mad if he did? Raize never went long without a sex party, so I needed to figure out my viewpoint on that issue real quick.

Fuck.

My mouth dried.

Yes. I'd be upset if he did.

My body was getting heated.

I'd be more than upset. I'd be pissed off.

So hell no, he wasn't going back to that.

Well, then. I had an opinion.

"I'm not standing here for any weird reason," Cavers announced, pulling me out of my thoughts.

I looked at him, surprised. Though supposedly working for Bronski, he hadn't done a whole lot to work against us that I could see. He followed orders and he cooked. If he was reporting to Bronski on the downlow, Raize never shared that with me, and I had a feeling Raize would know.

I frowned. "Why are you telling me that?"

He shrugged. He was such a big man, but he'd never looked big and uncomfortable until today.

"You waiting to talk to Raize?"

His gaze moved past me to the end of the hallway. "I don't know how long he'll be back there."

That was a fact. We'd just gotten back, and we hadn't accomplished what Raize had been sent to do. He could be in there all night, and all day tomorrow. Who knew?

I made a decision. "I'll tell him you want to talk to him."

His mouth quirked up before flattening.

"What?" I asked.

He shook his head, looking away. "Nothing."

"I saw that. You think I'm funny or something?"

"Just, you got a little spunk to you now. You didn't have that before."

Say what?

But I knew what he was talking about, and my stomach flipped over. It wasn't good to have anything in this life. Whatever you had, you could lose. Still, I kinda liked hearing that.

"I'll go tell him."

I was halfway down the hall when I heard him say quietly, "Thank you."

I glanced back and saw something shining in his eyes.

That moved me, but I didn't know what it was.

I knocked at Raize's office door and said, "It's Ash."

Ash. Not *me*. A different girl's name that I took.

Sometimes I hated names. Sometimes I loved them, but I always wondered, what was their point?

The door swung open. Raize's hair was messed up more than usual, his face stark and haggard, but also striking. He'd changed into a gray Henley over jeans. "What?"

I searched his face and jerked a thumb over my shoulder. His gaze followed. "He's waiting to talk to you."

Raize nodded to Cavers. "Come on back."

I stepped away as Cavers lumbered past me. He glanced at me. "Thank you."

Emotion filled my chest. I dipped my chin down, stiffly, and moved past him. This was all getting so odd.

I was on my way to my room when I heard a creak on the stairs.

Jake had come down, Gus in tow, his tail swishing. He came over to bump my hand and fit his head underneath it.

Jake's eyes moved to Raize's office. "You do that for him, but I feel like you want nothing to do with me."

Oh man.

I knelt, petting Gus down his back.

He wiggled, his tail thumping the floor in a steady staccato.

I didn't reply to Jake. Didn't know what to say.

"Did I change that or did he?" Jake asked.

He. Raize.

I didn't look up, focusing instead on how cute Gus' nose was twitching.

"Right." He sighed.

I'd answered by not answering.

Finally I looked up. "Don't dwell on anything. Okay?" And then I lied. "Nothing's changed."

He knew I was lying. I knew I was lying. I knew he knew I was lying.

But I lied anyway, and then we heard it.

Bang!

30

ASH

We took off running, Jake crashed through the office door. Raize and Cavers were both on their feet, looking stunned at a gun on the floor.

"What the hell?" Jake demanded.

They looked over.

Cavers was pale, and his hand came up in a helpless gesture. "I... Oh, shit." His eyes moved to Raize. "Boss, I'm so sorry. The gun fell and I—what a fucking rookie mistake." He slumped into the chair behind him. His hands caught his head, and he bent over. "Oh, fuck. Fuck. I'm going to die."

Raize's gaze was stormy, and he watched Cavers like a hawk. His hands were fists, pressing into the top of his desk. Then his eyes closed, and he breathed in, his shoulders rolling back as if he'd come to a decision. He looked over at Jake and me. "We're fine."

Cavers muttered to himself, shaking his head and rocking back and forth in the chair.

"He dropped his gun, and it went off," Raize said calmly.

I stiffened.

So did Jake, and then he launched himself at Cavers. He shoved him down to the floor. "What the fuck?! Are you insane?!"

Cavers didn't fight back. He just went to the ground and let Jake hit him.

"He's our fucking chance to live, you asshole! What are you doing, pulling that sort of shit?!"

He hit him a few more times.

I didn't know what I was the most shocked about—that Cavers looked genuinely remorseful, that Jake was going crazy like this, or that Raize hadn't killed him by now.

The hairs on the back of my neck stood up, and I looked over at Raize. He was watching me, again, and that storm was there in his eyes. He let it show, right out in front. He drew in a breath, his eyes closing, and when he opened them, there was a haunted look there. Agony flashed over his face before he moved.

One step, he grabbed Jake by the shoulders and launched him against the wall.

"What the hell?!" Jake's eyes bugged.

Fuck. I had a feeling where this was going, and I shut the door, just in case.

"He came clean with me. You? You've not done shit." Raize held Jake against the wall.

I noticed his shirt molded to his arms and back—his very defined arms and back. But Jake's feet were barely touching the floor. In that moment, everyone realized what Raize was capable of.

A shiver went through me. Alarm. But also awareness.

Desire.

I couldn't suppress a full-body shiver.

I felt Cavers looking my way, but ignored him.

"What are you talking about?" Jake asked, but his shoulders were already slumped. I was thinking he knew.

"You *know*."

Panic flashed in Jake's gaze before he looked at me.

"She knows, too," Raize growled.

Jake swallowed, his Adam's apple bobbing.

Raize was not letting him down, making it clear who he trusted and who he didn't.

I swung surprised eyes to Cavers. He slowly stood up and nodded, as if affirming my unspoken question. He shifted back, putting a few feet between Raize and himself.

Or no... Actually, he was giving Raize room to do what he needed to do.

"No." The word wrung from me.

I couldn't. Not Jake.

I couldn't see someone else I knew die.

Just, no.

Raize ignored me, putting Jake down and stepping back toward me, putting himself between Jake and me. His hands were loose, at his pockets. I could see a gun in the bulge of his shirt.

He could grab it so quickly, so easily.

I wanted to fold over. "No, no, no."

"I—" Jake looked around the room.

Looking for allies? Help?

Cavers had shut down now. I couldn't see Raize's face, but his body was primed. Ready. He'd kill Jake in a heartbeat, and he wouldn't feel a thing while he did.

Jake saw this, knew this, and his face clouded over. "Fuck."

His eyes found mine, and I knew we were both remembering that day the other henchman had been killed. Just one question. That's all it took. One question from Raize and one answer from me, and Jake had to dispose of two bodies that day.

"Carloni wants you dead," Jake confessed.

Raize didn't move.

Jake studied him a moment and let out a bitter laugh. "Right. You already know that. You already know that he put me in your employment to report to him." He continued to study Raize, and anger flashed in his eyes. His jaw went rigid. "You knew the whole time?" His eyes slid to me. "She knows, too? You told her, and that's why she wants nothing to do with me?"

Raize moved now.

It was mesmerizing.

His back straightened, and his head rose, but it wasn't just that. It was a whole transformation, as if he had shed his skin and a new Raize stood in front of us. A new predator. He had shed whatever was holding him back. We could feel his power rippling through the room.

"What'd you give Carloni?" he asked calmly.

"Nothing!" Jake's nostrils flared. He was enraged. He threw his arms wide, yelling, "I gave him nothing! That's the fucking joke here. I was loyal to you." His chin jerked at me. "To her." His eyes narrowed at Cavers. "Don't know about that fucker, but yeah, you and her. I chose you guys. I wanted to work for *you*, not Carloni, but it's the same shit. He owns me. He knows my woman, and he's keeping her." Some of the fight faded from him. His head hung down. "He's keeping her."

Raize shifted, turning to me.

No, no, no.

Oh no.

I shook my head. I didn't want him to do what I knew he was going to do.

Betrayal was betrayal to him. He didn't get involved. He did his job, and Cavers was one thing, but now Jake was muddying everything up. He wouldn't keep both alive. He'd have to eliminate one.

"Is he telling the truth?" Raize asked me.

Relief hit me hard, making my knees rattle.

This question I wanted to answer. I nodded. "Yes."

Raize took a step closer to me, lowering his voice. "Did he betray me?"

No! I shook my head. "You can't word it that way."

His eyes were hot, his jaw hard. "Answer me."

I wouldn't. "Ask it in another way." *Fuck him.* He wanted to kill Jake. I didn't.

Jake was like me—kind of. He was caught between one boss and another, but he didn't have an agenda. I did.

This wasn't right. It wasn't fair.

"Answer the question."

"No! I'm not answering." I gritted my teeth, showing him. "Say. It. Another. Way."

Jake's voice was soft. "I never gave Carloni anything on you."

Raize ignored him, now fixated on me. His eyes smoldered. "Answer the question, Ash."

Ash. That fake name again.

I shook my head. "I won't answer."

"Fuck's sake," Cavers bit out, moving.

I sprang, leaping at Raize.

He caught me, but he didn't stop me.

My arm was around him and I shoved away, his gun coming with me.

Everyone froze. The temperature in the room dropped.

Raize started for me, but I yelled, "No!" I hurried back, shuffling until I hit the wall. I gulped, shoving down a lump because I knew what I needed to do.

I wouldn't point it at him. I'd never do that. And I'd learned today that I wouldn't aim it at Jake or Cavers either, and I didn't want to ask myself why not. I really only had one move here.

I put the gun to my head and took the safety off. "I said no."

31

ASH

No one moved, or at least it seemed that way until Raize streaked over to me, ripping the gun away and holding me against the wall with his arm pressed against my chest. His eyes were wide, shocked. He dropped the magazine clip from the gun, letting it fall to the ground, then he tossed the weapon to a chair behind him.

All the while, his eyes didn't move from mine.

All the while, no one breathed in the room.

Then, a guttural sound ripped from him and he barked, "*Out! Now!*"

Cavers left first.

Jake moved at a slower pace and paused at the door. "Boss—"

Raize let me go, grabbing the door and slamming it shut. Jake had a choice to either get hit or move out of the way. He scrambled into the hallway and Raize locked the door.

I moved away from him.

"You'd kill yourself?" he demanded.

I opened my mouth, but no words came. I closed it again and hung my head.

"Are you suicidal?"

I closed my eyes, folding over to sit on Raize's loveseat. I rested my forehead to my knees and took a breath.

Just one goddamn breath. Tears blurred my vision.

What was I doing?

I didn't know anymore.

"You told me you had a list. You'd give that up?"

I said nothing.

"Answer me!"

I couldn't. I was choking on my tears.

A normal boyfriend, or even a normal friend, might move closer. They might've touched me, gently. They might've hugged me.

This was not that situation. This was *so* not that situation.

Raize hung back, staring at me until I lifted my face.

He winced and looked away for a moment, but then the wall slammed down over him. He was unsettled.

I almost started laughing. "You have no idea how to handle me."

He went still again, and when he finally looked my way, there was a glimmer in his eyes I'd never seen before.

He almost looked human, not such a robot. He could've been someone I'd known in my fantasy life. Maybe a hot college guy? A jock? No. A soldier—someone who'd come back from doing a tour, had some time off, and I met at a bar? That seemed more fitting.

"I'm not suicidal," I told him.

"You put the gun to your head."

"I..." I didn't even know. I couldn't explain what I didn't know. "Ask me about Jake in a different way."

"There is no other way."

"You know there is! Ask it in a different way." I shoved up to my feet. This was the fight here.

I was sick of the killing.

I could not handle one more body, especially not someone I knew.

My chest heaved. "Ask it in a different way."

I liked Jake. I was hurt by what he said, but he wasn't on my list anymore.

I frowned. "What happened with Cavers?"

"None of your business!" he erupted, his hands flying in the air, but he was moving farther away from me. His back hit the wall, and he let me see him, how haunted he was, how stricken. He let it all out for me to see and read, though I wasn't sure he knew it. "I don't run my decisions through some pussy I like plowing."

Okay, *now* I was mad.

"Take that back," I said quietly.

He swore, low and long. Then he moved, flipping a chair into the wall. It impaled there, and the wall held it. It looked like an abstract piece of art.

"Take it back!" I clipped out, folding my arms over my chest.

He looked away.

I didn't know what was going on here, but fuck him if he didn't take back calling me pussy he liked to plow.

I screamed, "*Take it back!*"

"*No!*" He was across the room and in my face in the next second.

I braced myself, but he didn't touch me.

He stopped just short of it, his breath in my cheek, his eyes taking me in, scanning my face.

He was panicking.

I saw it now, lurking there.

Good! That filled me with satisfaction.

My chest started pounding.

No, that was my heart.

It was thumping in my chest, getting stronger, faster—a

steady and powerful beat now. I could feel it all the way to my toes—in my fingers, my neck. His eyes lingered on my lips.

He couldn't look away.

Stark hunger flashed in his eyes, and he raised a hand, holding it in the air.

It curved gently, as if he wanted to touch my neck, or the side of my face.

But he didn't move. He just held it there, a few inches from my skin.

His eyes lifted to mine. "You bitch."

My heart still pounded, trying to reach him. "You're a murdering asshole," I whispered back, seething.

"What?" he sneered. "You want to fuck now? Forget you put a fucking gun to your head?"

"Don't kill Jake."

He pressed into me, his eyes wild, on the edge of control. "Why?" His breath was hot on me. He bent down, his eyes glittering now.

Then he found his control. He rested one hand against the wall, next to my head. The other found my hip and slid up, moving under my shirt, raising it.

God. I almost moaned.

Wetness flooded me, and I started to throb.

I wanted him.

So fucking bad.

He bent and his lips grazed over mine, my cheeks, my chin. Tingles raced through me.

Jesus.

I wanted him deep inside of me. I shifted, pressing against him, and both of us groaned from the contact.

I began moving, a slow grind, and he was quiet, grinding back.

This was different from the other times.

The terms had flipped. Roles were changing. Everything was being upended between us.

I moved again, my hand finding him, and I pulled down his zipper.

He let out on a hiss. "Fuck."

I palmed his dick, and it grew even harder. I began sliding my hand up and down, stroking him.

His eyes remained on me, but he rested his head against the wall next to mine. I turned, holding his gaze, and he moved with my hand.

"Don't kill Jake."

He panted, pushing up into my hand, "Fuck you."

I tightened my hold, and he groaned, his eyes fluttering, but he kept them open—to glare at me. I ran my thumb up the underside of his cock, and his eyes flashed, feral. Primal.

"Don't kill Jake."

His teeth bared, but he moved in, his lips finding my neck as he said, "Fuck. You."

Then he took over, tasting my neck, sucking there as he ripped down my jeans, hoisted me up, and thrust into me.

"I'll."

Thrust.

"Goddamn."

Thrust.

"Kill."

Thrust, thrust.

I groaned, my head falling back against the wall.

"Who I fucking want to."

The sex was hard, almost violent between us.

I pushed him back, but only to adjust my legs on his hips. He bounced me up and then turned to slam me down on the desk. He grabbed my hips, holding me still, and rammed into me.

I was writhing around, trying to move with him. I needed the friction, but he paused, so deep inside of me. His hand came to my neck, holding me still. "You're going to try to control me through your pussy?"

I groaned and grabbed hold of his shirt. I jerked him down, but he caught himself, moving to the side so he could still see me. I was fighting for something I didn't understand, but dammit, I needed it.

I kicked out, finding a chair, and I used the leverage to move us so he was inside of me, but we were bent at an awkward angle. He didn't want to pull out anymore than I wanted him to, but neither of us was giving in to the other.

He growled. "Stop moving."

I growled right back, pushing again. "Don't kill Jake!"

He stilled.

So did I.

I could feel our pulses, both racing.

A darkness flashed in his eyes, and he picked me up as he stood. He slipped out, but he turned me over, pressing me against the desk. He shoved my jeans down farther and ripped my underwear off. I felt his hand running over my bare ass.

"Jesus. You're so fucking hot."

My eyes closed, and I let my forehead rest against the desk. I just wanted him back inside of me. "Raize." I pressed against him.

He fit there, his hips reacting to my need, and he moved me back down on the desk, his body covering mine. I felt his hand over my ass, his finger finding that hole. He paused, his thumb rubbing around it before slipping inside.

I'd never had anyone touch me there, and I couldn't hold back the moan. *God.*

I should've been ashamed of being so transparent. He knew how much I wanted him, but I knew he hungered for me just the same.

"Raize!" I snapped, twisting my head around to glare at him.

His eyes were laughing, and he smirked, his thumb moving. "I can tell you like that." He pulled it out.

I opened my mouth, gaping, but damn. That felt so good. "Don't kill—"

"Stop saying another man's name when I'm inside of you, goddammit!" he snapped, his thumb shoving back in.

I moved with it, as if it were a button activating me.

Raize caught me and clamped down on my hip. He stepped in and brought my body back to his. I was spread out, aching for him.

"You're in my bed every night."

I held still. Was that...? Were we bargaining here?

"What?"

"I'll spare him, but you're in my bed. I want to fuck you whenever and wherever I want. Got it?"

Anger heated me. "I'm not going to be your sex slave."

"I'm not asking for that. I just want you."

"Me for his life?" Because that was seriously important here. I needed to know what this barter was for.

"No." He sighed. "I'm not going to kill him." He palmed one of my ass cheeks. "I just want you."

"Why, though?" I was pushing it. I felt like I needed to push it.

He held still. "Because I know that he hurt you. He said he was going to work you. Because you two were friends."

I froze. *Holy*... I got it then.

He wanted to hurt *Jake because of me, because of what he said he'd do to me...* I clamped down on my thoughts, not wanting to go any further.

Raize must've felt the same. His thumb moved, rotating and sweeping inside of me.

My thighs quivered. "Goddamn, just fuck me!"

He didn't respond, but he removed his thumb, and thrust his cock inside.

Halfway through, his thumb went back in and I climaxed, right then and there.

This guy.

He was going to be the death of me, one way or another.

I could feel him laughing against my neck as he turned me over and slid in from the front—missionary style now. I wound my arms and legs around him. We were almost having sex like a normal couple.

A LITTLE WHILE LATER, Raize carried me into his bedroom, shutting and locking the door.

I glanced at the clock next to his bed. Two in the morning. We'd been going at it for hours, and as he left the bed, my body shivered. This was ridiculous, because I wanted him back inside of me.

He went into his bathroom and turned on the water.

I closed my eyes, burrowing into the sheets. I hadn't moved when he padded back into the room.

He went to his closet. "I'm going to deal with Jake."

I sat up, watching him by the light from the bathroom.

He slid on some black sweatpants and bent over to tie his shoes. He straightened to pull a black Henley over his head and down his arms and chest. He smoothed it out, taking me in.

I was naked. His eyes flared, and he cursed under his breath. "This changes everything. You know that, right?"

I couldn't even begin to imagine how things would change. "Yes."

He shook his head, his eyes rolling to the ceiling as he reached for the nightstand and grabbed a gun. He checked the magazine before putting it in the back of his pants. Then his eyes flashed at me again. "You put a gun to your head." He looked at me for a moment. "Don't *ever* fucking do that again."

He stalked from the room, shutting the door behind him, and I collapsed back on the bed.

Had I just sold my soul to him? Because that's how I felt, but even now images of us flashed in my head—me against the wall, working his dick. Him bending me over the desk. Us sideways, and then all the other positions in his bed.

I was wet all over again.

Sick.

I was sick.

Was I sick?

But I got up, walked naked to his bathroom, and took a shower.

I didn't care.

32

ASH

I woke up when I felt the bed move.

Raize leaned over me, kneeling on the bed. "Want to start crossing names off your list?"

That got me awake, wide awake.

I sat up. "What?"

"You heard me."

"I don't know what that means."

He went to the closet, grabbed new clothes, and started changing. The clothes he pulled on were still black, but they were tighter, more form fitting. The hood of his long-sleeve shirt was a mask he could pull over his face.

My mouth went dry. I hugged my knees. "What's going on?"

He sat on the bed, pulling boots on.

"What do you think is happening?" He stood and began moving around the room, grabbing things, putting them in a bag. He tossed a second bag on the bed next to me. "You need to put all your personal items in there."

"We're running?" I'd not anticipated that.

"I got two guys out there who want to switch allegiance to me. What do you think that means in this world?"

"Someone's going to die."

"I gotta make a choice. No way am I going to trust them to go back and change their minds. They either get dead or their bosses get dead."

He went back to work, removing a section of the wall to show a safe. He opened it and my eyes almost bugged out. I got up and went over to have a look. Money. Weapons. He had passports, driver's licenses.

I felt like I'd just had sex with Jason Bourne.

He kept stuffing everything into the bag. When it got full, he grabbed another from the closet and tossed them by the door.

My head was spinning. Again. "You're going to kill Carloni and Bronski?"

"Yep."

He moved around me as I stood in just a T-shirt that fell to the tops of my thighs. I grabbed the end of my shirt, wringing it in a ball. "What's that mean?"

He had another bag ready to go and stopped behind me, tossing it to the door. "That means we're going to war."

I whirled, my heart in my throat. It was a common sensation by now. "What does that mean?"

He paused and let out a soft sigh. "Your list aligns with my boss' timeline," he said flatly.

"You didn't tell him—"

"No. I went to Roman. I reported in, and he decided it was time. I left that team behind for surveillance on Marco. They called in, said Carloni was down in Texas."

I stumbled back, but he caught my hand.

"Carloni made a move. He might've done it behind my back, I don't know. Maybe Carloni found out I'm really working for Roman, not the brother Carloni answers to. Again. I don't know, but Roman made his decision. I got the order to take Bronski and Carloni out." He was quiet. "You gotta pack everything you want because when we leave this house, it's going to get torched. Everything is going to change."

He tossed the mattress, flipping it over and shoving aside the frame. There was another safe in the floorboards, this one much longer. Raize began pulling out gun after gun.

We were going to war, and he had an entire arsenal for us.

33

ASH

I'd never been in a mafia war before. That's the stuff you see in movies, but being one of the foot soldiers, I didn't know what to expect. I thought we'd kill Bronski right away, but that didn't happen. We were five weeks in, and my experience was as follows: we'd set up somewhere, we'd wait, Raize would get a call, he'd go off—sometimes he took Cavers, sometimes Jake, and a few times me.

Then he'd come back, usually bloody, and we'd change locations.

Repeat.

Basically, Raize got his orders and then he gave us orders. We followed them.

What had changed was that our shit was out in the air—not that any of us talked about it. And the *it* was Cavers' first boss, Jake being under Carloni's control, and the relationship between Raize and me. But nevertheless, there seemed to be an easier camaraderie between all of us.

Raize no longer cared if I rode alone in a vehicle with Cavers.

Cavers said more than a few words here and there.

Jake went back to telling jokes every now and then.

And something inside of me was thawing.

The only one that hadn't changed was Gus. He got pets from everyone. He'd plop his head in anyone's lap, and that human was obligated to rub his ears.

34

RAIZE

I went to the coordinates I'd been sent, and an hour later, headlights came toward me.

This was how my meetings with Roman Marakov always began. Three cars drove up this time. Sometimes it was one, sometimes two, sometimes a truck and a guy gave me a phone. This time, all three cars circled around me, and when they came to a stop, Roman's head of security got out of the front seat in the third car. He walked around and opened the back door.

Roman Marakov emerged, taking a moment to regard me, smoothing down the front of his suit.

This, also, was habitual. The three-piece suit he wore was his uniform.

I waited until he approached.

He dipped his head in greeting, his security fanning around us. This, also, was routine, but it was an act.

"Clay," he said.

My first name.

"Roman."

He grinned. "I've been getting regular reports of your team hitting my family locations. You're doing good work."

I nodded. "I'm doing what you sent me to do."

"It was three years ago when I told you to start working for Igor. You've proven over and over that you are a worthy fighter for me. I am appreciative of your work."

Roman never complimented me. I waited because he was working up to something, and fuck, I was pretty sure I wouldn't like it.

He smoothed his suit again, standing as straight as he could. "Having said that, we're changing our scope. I'm going to step in as the new head of our family's operations. I'd like you at my side when I do that."

"What?" No. I did operations in the field.

When he'd sent me in to work for Igor on his behalf, it was a form of mafia undercover work. That's what I did. I was the guy sent out to kill, to take down. I didn't do management. I glanced over at Downer, his head of security. I didn't do that shit.

"Because of your attacks, Estrada's pulled back his support of Igor," Roman continued. "Carloni returned to Philadelphia. Your half-brother's decided a relationship with the Marakov family is not something he's open to anymore."

He wasn't my half-brother. "You sent me down to make a connection."

"Yes, that's what I told you, but I really sent you down to test whether Estrada would be a worthy ally. He's proven that he's not. Because of this, I've decided to stop waiting. I'll be coming to America permanently. When that happens, I'd like all obstacles for my family eliminated. You're aware of what I'm saying?"

"You're ordering the execution of your brothers and their heads of operations?"

That meant Carloni. That meant Bronski, finally. I'd been told yes, but not the 'when' it could happen.

That time seemed to be nearing.

"I am. You requested Bronski two months ago, but you never

said why. He's lower on the ladder for my brother. Why did you request him?"

All three Marakov brothers came from a long line of mafia background. They were each powerful, each ruthless, but Roman was the smartest. Him wanting me to "come in" and be at his side was alarming enough, but if I told him about Ash, that would be worse.

"I've heard you've taken a woman," he continued. "And that she used to work for Alex Bronski. You care for this woman?"

I looked around, counting the men, noting their locations. I took a tally of their weapons—the ones I could see, the bulges in their coats, and I could guess at the ones they had hidden. To kill them and attack Roman would change everything for me, for the group I now considered my unit. This was why I never took a woman. If she was threatened, there was no line I wouldn't cross and no person I wouldn't destroy.

But I didn't want to start here with this boss. I liked Roman as a person, and I was coming to respect him as a leader.

He respected me in return, or I'd thought he did.

"Stand down, Raize." Downer shifted, coming forward. He had military training, and he recognized what I was doing. "He's only asking questions."

"Uh, yes."

Roman looked between us, and it was obvious he didn't know what had triggered me. "We heard that Alex Bronski enjoyed raping the women in his employ," he continued. "I was alarmed when I heard your woman used to work for him. Is this the reason you requested permission to execute him?"

I hated saying anything, showing anything.

You either killed or you were killed. This, him asking about this, I did not like. I did not want to share anything.

"Clay," Roman murmured. "After Downer, you are my most prized man. What you can do in the field is unmatched by anyone."

Downer grunted. "Even me, man. I couldn't do the shit you do."

"I sent you to work for my brother. You rose up in the ranks until you got your own territory, and I know what Igor had you doing for him. You shed all of that, cut loose all your employees except for two men and a woman. We're aware both men had original alliances to Igor, but since they're both still alive and with you, we're assuming they've officially changed position. Am I correct?"

"Yes." I gritted my teeth, because fuck all of this. Now he knew about Cavers and Jake.

"You trust them?"

I didn't respond.

Downer laughed. "He's not going to open up, Roman. He survives out *there*, and not showing weakness is part of that shit. Just tell him what you want to say, but he ain't coming in. He don't want to come in."

I stared at Downer. I didn't know what to make of him.

He seemed to know this as he laughed again, shaking his head and moving back to the car.

Roman sighed. "Is he right? You don't want to come in?"

I eyed him. "No."

"You trust your men?"

I didn't respond, because I didn't. But I wanted to kill them less.

Roman seemed to move on, his eyes narrowing. "Bronski hurt your woman?"

He knew about her. He knew about Bronski. Why did I have to give the affirmation?

A sort of exhaustion seemed to settle over Roman, and he looked down. "I know your background. I sought you out because anyone who could evade one of Estrada's death squads, then get him to agree to a treaty is someone worth having on your team. Estrada is threatened by you, that's the sole reason he wants you dead. If he wasn't, he never would've let you leave working for him."

Why is he saying all this to me?

This wasn't what he paid me for. I wasn't the mastermind of anything, except maybe surviving.

"What Downer said was correct," he continued. "I'm aware of your qualifications, but I will need you at times to come in." His voice grew stronger. "I need a more open dialect between us."

"You want me to talk more?"

Downer snort-laughed from the car.

Roman shot him a glare before turning back. "Yes, Clay."

Okay... "I don't like being called Clay."

Roman's head moved back an inch. "You don't?"

"I go by Raize. Only Raize."

"Told you," Downer called.

Roman shot him another glare, more pointed. "Maybe you could take lessons from Raize and not be as forthcoming as you are."

Another snort. "Yeah. Right. You'd be so bored with me then."

A glimmer of a grin showed on Roman's face. Then he cleared it away, eyeing me. "You like the unit you have?"

Fuck. I had to talk again. "Yes."

He nodded again, one eyebrow rising. "Okay. You have your permission and your orders. Take care of them as you see fit, but I need it done within three days."

I—"All of them?"

That was a lot of hits to plan, coordinate, and execute in three days.

Roman seemed to read my mind because he inclined his head toward the car. "If you need a fifth member to your unit, temporarily, Downer has volunteered to work with you."

My eyes slid over to the head of security, a big man, and he was silently laughing to himself.

He was a dark-haired version of Cavers, but with attitude.

One Cavers was enough. My lips thinned. "Noted."

"You're okay with the change of plans?"

I nodded briskly. "You're the boss."

"Yes, but we won't be taking on Estrada. Are your sister and mother well? Do you know?"

"I made inquiries. They seem fine."

"That's something then. Good, but Raize, our fight with Estrada *will* happen. I promise you that. And if you ever do want to come in full-time, that offer is always open. I know you're loyal to those you respect. I have no intention of losing that respect from you."

I wished for a moment that Ash was with me, that I could ask her if I could trust him, but she wasn't because I *didn't* trust him. I didn't trust anyone, or I hadn't.

I trusted Ash.

And Gus, somewhat.

That was enough for me.

"Reach out if you need assistance."

"I will."

I usually waited for Roman to leave first. This time was different, felt different, and I left first.

He turned for his car, and I was gone.

35

RAIZE

I was almost forgetting which town I'd stashed my team in lately.

We'd had to move so many times, and we had to be low maintenance, small town, and hidden in the country. I knew everyone was used to nicer accommodations in the city, but for this shit, in this war, I wanted as low key as possible. And since Roman had made it clear I was different, since my unit ran our own rules and our own operations, I could do as I wanted.

Downer was right, I'd realized. I was used to being out in the field. It felt right to me.

It's what I knew, the way I survived.

Going in? What would that look like?

I'd slap on a suit? Follow Roman around with a shoulder holster for my guns? Were there politics involved? I had no clue. Would I glare at his adversaries? Do the kill when he ordered?

Fuck.

That's what I did.

I hadn't enjoyed being a drug dealer for Carloni, but I was there on orders. I'd fulfilled my mission, situated myself in place where I was able to bring Roman into a move before Carloni.

Estrada. Sucked that I'd been coerced to do it, but things were changing.

I needed to really think shit through.

There'd always been three Marakovs. Roman ran Russia. Maxim had been trying to move in on New York, but that wasn't working. Igor ran Philadelphia. Igor and Maxim, both shit stains on humanity, the worst possible fucking people I knew. But the problem was taking care of all of them.

If I hit one, the others would beef up on security.

If I hit another, the rest would go into hiding, or they'd start traveling in convoys.

Roman had said three days. I knew the reasoning. The faster, the better—less time to give anyone time to figure out who was coming, but hell. I'd been hitting the buildings, where they kept their girls, where they moved the drugs. Every target was done a different way. No pattern. No habit. They couldn't predict who was coming, why they were coming—but I hadn't gone after the heads yet.

Bronski was small.

Carloni was medium.

Igor, Maxim, they were huge.

Plus Maxim's men.

I'd do them all in one night. One day and a night?

I'd need help.

Once it was done, the landscape would change. I needed to be sure it worked in my favor, according to my wishes. And I needed to decide what those were.

When I'd worked for Marco, I'd been content with that. I could see my mom every now and then, and I was within the same circles for my sister. I never cared for more.

Didn't want more.

I was good at my job.

I was loyal.

Marco should've jumped at keeping me. Instead he'd tried to eliminate me.

When I left, I hadn't thought about future plans. Surviving and killing was what I knew.

Now, with Ash, it was time to think.

36

ASH

"I'm cooking tonight," Jake announced.

Cavers had just pulled into a fast food joint, but at Jake's proclamation, he pulled over, turned around, and glared. Jake was in the backseat. I was in front.

Along with our many location changes, we'd also changed vehicles too many times to count.

We were now in a Suburban, and I really thought it was Cavers' dream vehicle. He didn't let anyone drive unless Raize ordered him to.

"No," he growled.

Cooking was also something he'd claimed, though none of us had particularly fought him on that. Cavers was a decent cook, and he did it healthy, though he also enjoyed his fast food stops. Tonight was supposed to be a fast-food night. Every Wednesday was, and even more so because Raize had to leave for some meeting. He'd said he'd be back late, and he'd only have his second phone on. The first was for normal things. The second was for when we were under attack and had to go to ground—that sort of thing.

Yep. We were there now, having to plan in case that happened again.

Jake sighed, laying his head back. "It's my birthday, okay? I used to cook dinner for my grandma on my birthday." His shoulders rose and fell. "I kinda feel like we're more than what we were before. I just wanted to do something special, and the boss isn't around, so why not? We're not on the move or anything."

Once Jake said *birthday*, Cavers changed his tune. He nodded. "Hey. Yeah. Happy birthday, man."

"Yeah, man. Thanks." He saw me looking in the rearview mirror and tried to put a bit more oomph in his smile. "I kinda want to get shitfaced tonight, too."

"Let's run that by the boss first." Cavers hit the turn signal. "We need to go to the grocery store?"

"Considering we only have deli meat and buns at the house, I'm thinking yes."

Jake was sad, but his wit was still there.

I shot him a grin before turning forward.

Cavers pulled into the local grocery store, but as Jake and I started for the doors, Cavers indicated to the right. "I'm going to grab some other things."

There was a liquor store.

"Nice." Jake gave him an approving nod. "Appreciate it."

Cavers' mouth twitched in response.

I couldn't say which small town this was anymore. I lost count after the fifth spot, but I knew if someone came looking, they'd find us. We stuck out around here, which was evident as we walked into the grocery store. Women noticed Jake. A few men, and the bag boys, gave me looks. There was an old lady who harrumphed at me, literally sticking her nose in the air.

I didn't blame her. My soul was dripping in blood by now.

The gossipy ones alarmed me the most, like the woman who saw us and went right to her phone, typing away.

Jake saw her, too, as he grabbed a cart. "It's hard not to come into town every now and then."

I nodded. "We'll move on probably tomorrow."

"Yeah."

That was also the pattern.

Once we had to go into town, we moved. Because of that, we tried to do most of our shopping at gas stations, but there were exceptions. Like tonight. I kept hoping for one night where Raize would come back, tell us we were fine for the night, and we could let down our guards. Just for a night.

I wasn't holding my breath.

"So."

I looked over.

Jake's lips had pursed as he pushed the cart forward. He looked at me from the corner of his eye. "You and Raize, huh?"

Oh. Yeah. We'd never talked about that.

"Yeah."

"You didn't..." He paused, his head tilting to the side, but he wasn't looking at me. "You didn't do that to save my life..." He looked over. "Did you?"

Oh! Whoa.

I shook my head. "No! Oh my God. No. That, uh..."

He was following my statement, bobbing his head up and down. He finished for me, "That started earlier?"

I nodded.

"In Texas?"

We started forward again, and I gave another nod.

He sighed, his hand going to his chest. "Gotta say, I'm relieved to hear that. I mean, you seemed to be attracted to him, but I guess... You just never know in this life."

My stomach twisted. He'd thought I was faking it for his life? Damn.

"I *am* attracted to him," I assured him. "I'm not faking it."

"That's good. And, you know, congrats and all."

I frowned. "Yeah. I guess."

This was the weirdest conversation... I'm sure I'd had worse, but I wasn't going to go there. Hella awkward.

"What about you?" I asked.

Jake gave me a wry grin. "Me faking it with Raize for you?"

"No." I laughed. "You and that woman you talked about. You think Carloni is still keeping her?"

His smile faded and his shoulders slumped. "I don't know. I'm a romantic, wanted to hold on to something. I hadn't seen her in months, even before I started working for Raize. Also, I'm pretty sure she and Carloni were sleeping together. Just didn't want to accept it." He gave me a considering look. "You know what I mean?"

"What do you think, sis?"

I lost my smile. "Yeah. I do."

BURGERS.

Buns.

Coleslaw.

Chips.

Beans.

Cheese. Ketchup. A1 Sauce. Onions. Lettuce.

Watermelon.

Jake had wanted as close to a genuine barbeque as he could get, and Cavers showed up just as we finished loading the grocery bags into the Suburban. He had a pack of beer under one arm and a brown bag that clinked as he put it next to the food.

Jake shook his head. "Boss isn't going to let us get drunk."

Cavers stepped back, ignored him, and shut the back. "Maybe we can plan on the possibility he does?" He swiped the keys from Jake, going to the driver's side.

Jake and I shared a look.

They could hope, but it was a stupid hope. We all knew that.

37

RAIZE

A squad car was pulled over on the side of the road a half mile from the house, that pissed me off. Hitting my lights, I turned onto an abandoned road and crawled forward, getting out of sight. Considering we were out in the boondocks and the road was gravel, I doubted he saw me or anyone else going past.

This car was the first I'd spotted out here.

I was clearing the car when Jake picked up my call.

I heard the music first.

"What's up?"

Fucking hell. I was being too nice. *We were not friends.*

This was Ash's fault. I liked when people were scared of me.

Now this. Now all this friendly attitude.

"You got a cop staking the house," I snapped. "What the fuck are you guys doing?"

"What?" He pulled away from the phone and yelled, "Cave Man, hit the music. Any alarms going off?"

I could hear Ash asking, "Who is that?"

A thudding sound came over the phone, and his voice sounded even more distant. "It's the boss. He's saying there's a cop watching the house."

I could hear Ash's voice murmur, but couldn't make out the words.

"The perimeter alarms are flashing," Cavers said. "I got eyes on the cop."

I growled into the phone, "I need a name."

And I waited.

There was murmuring from their end, and whatever that *thud* was seemed to be blocking Jake from hearing me.

"Fucking hell, Jake!"

"What?" That came from a distance, then another *thud* and his voice came back, clearer. "What'd you say, boss?"

"Whatever the fuck you just did, don't ever do it again. I may not be able to kill you since Ash fucking cares about you, but I'll put a goddamn bullet in your ass. You getting me now?"

"Yeah—I mean, yes, sir. Boss. That won't ever happen again. What'd you say earlier?"

"I need the cop's name. After that, get your guns and your ass outside. I'm flushing him up to you."

"Cavers is looking him up. He says his name is Martinez."

That's all I needed. I hung up because my waning patience.

A cop on their front yard and they didn't know?

I wanted to do damage, but fuck. Needed to deal with this first.

There was good coverage around the house and driveway with thick forest, but I cut through an abandoned field, working my way around. Veering closer to the driveway, but still hidden by the trees, I flashed a light toward the cop.

Any good cop would pull forward to find out what was going on, and he did.

He inched forward, keeping his headlights off, which was smart.

When he was closer, I flashed the light again, farther up the driveway but still in the woods. He turned in, inching forward.

If someone came to the house, the protocol was that Ash

would get on the channel and listen. The guns would head out and surround. Jake and Cavers were waiting on the driveway—just standing there with guns in hands. They weren't raised or aiming, they were holding them.

As soon as the front of the squad car hit the driveway, he got a clear view of them.

If he was going to call for backup, he would be doing that now, but he wasn't.

Ash would've alerted us if he had been. Instead this guy paused, waiting, and I moved in behind him.

Then he shot forward in the driveway, turning his lights on. He let them shine on Jake and Cavers.

He was smart, which I knew from the file I had on him, but I wanted to know what had tagged us for him. He wouldn't have driven in if he was here for anyone off the books. He was in his squad car, wearing his uniform, and he'd opened his car door and stood just behind it. His gun was drawn, but he kept it angled down a bit. He waited, scoping out Jake and Cavers.

I rounded behind him, right at his trunk. I could've rested against it if I wanted, but I held off, waiting to see how he'd start this conversation.

I didn't wait long.

He raised his head. "I'm here for the girl."

Jake and Cavers both saw me, both saw I was waiting.

I wanted Jake to talk to him, get information out of him.

Jake frowned, but took a step forward. He kept his voice friendly. "It's my birthday tonight, and we were doing some cele-bratin', so you'll have to be more specific. What girl are you talking about?"

Barking erupted inside the house. Gus had gotten to the garage door and was clawing to get outside.

The cop straightened and almost took a step back, but instead he raised his gun. "I got a notice that a girl matching a missing person was seen in town. Got another tip that the same girl was shopping in the grocery store earlier this evening. And I'm standing here telling you I'm not leaving until I clear this girl."

Just then, the screen door opened.

Ash stepped out, her face like stone as she came forward. "That girl looks like me?"

The cop's shoulders sagged, and he nodded a couple times. "Yeah. She looks like you."

Jake and Cavers exchanged a frown, and Ash moved past Jake.

"Hey." He held a hand out, warning.

She only had eyes for the cop. "You got a poster or something?"

Jake and Cavers shared a look.

I knew who was on that poster. And I knew it would send Ash into a tailspin.

Determination flashed in her eyes and she rolled her shoulders back. Her voice got hard. "Show me."

I could see it on the passenger seat, and after scrutinizing her, the cop holstered his gun and reached for the paper. He offered it to her.

She stared at it, her head bent down.

She was so still.

Jake had locked on her. Cavers frowned in his direction, but to no avail.

Jake moved forward a step. "That someone you know?"

Ash didn't answer him.

She looked up, her eyes flicking past the cop to me before returning. "Can I keep this? Do you have copies?"

"Ma'am." The cop was being all gentle now. He nodded to the paper. "Is that you?"

She looked at it again, and I didn't like the look in her eyes, or the way her jaw seemed to be jerking around. She shook her head. "No."

"Beg your pardon, ma'am, but..." If he could've lowered a hat out of respect, folded it to his chest, he would've. His hand moved to the top of his car door, and his fingers curled around it. "You could be the girl's doppelganger. I'll need to ask for your identification."

Ash reached for her pocket and handed over a license. It would've been a fake. I watched as the cop added a sticker to the front before handing it back. His move was smooth and practiced. He'd been prepared—that sticker was on the inside of his wrist. Jake and Cavers wouldn't have noticed anything.

Ash looked at the sticker and without a beat said, "I'm sorry, sir, but we don't have any water here."

The cop's shoulders tensed. He grasped the car door tightly. His voice dropped low. "Are you sure, ma'am?"

She raised the poster again. "Can I keep this?"

He scratched the back of his head. "Don't know why you'd want it if it's not you."

She started to backtrack, but paused and looked at the paper again. Her words were muffled because she wouldn't look up, away from the poster. "She's my sister." Then she did look up, her eyes shining with unshed tears. Her voice was strong. "I didn't know these went out, but I know who took my sister. I'm trying to find him." Her eyes got hard. "There's nothing for you here, officer. I'd suggest you leave."

Jake's gaze moved to me, his eyes narrowed.

Cavers watched Ash go back to the house, open the screen door, and slip inside. A second later, Gus moved away from the garage door and a second door closed inside.

The cop reached for his radio. "Now, I don't know what's all going on here, but I think—"

Now it was my move, and I did it by cocking my gun.

The sound was clear, distinct.

The officer stopped talking, his hands in the air, and at that moment, I moved in, placing my gun at the back of his head.

"This is the time where you get into your car, Officer Martinez. You call in that you're off-shift and instead of stopping to see your partner for the usual dip you do with her, I suggest you head straight to your wife and your two sons. I suggest you appreciate what you have because tomorrow, your wife may not get to her shift at the local cafe and your sister may not get to your house where she watches your children." I let the silence settle a moment. "But if you do as I say, nothing will happen to anyone. In the morning, you can call in a house fire at Mrs. Rominsciez's home because it will be long burned to the ground by then."

I moved in closer and reached around him, taking hold of his gun. He tensed, but didn't stop me as I eased the gun from his grasp. "But I'd like a guarantee, and I think you'd hate to have your gun used in a murder, especially that of your own loved ones, so I'm going to keep this gun. When you return in the morning, it will be wrapped up." I tapped his left shoulder. "I need you to see where I'll put it."

He looked, and his hands flexed in the air where he'd been holding them.

"See the clump of white birch down there?"

He had to swallow before he grated out, "Yeah."

"It'll be behind the second tree, so no one else finds it before you get here."

He couldn't see me, but his eyes were down. He was trying to see my shoes. I'm sure he was trying to memorize every detail of me that he could get.

"You're cartel?" he asked.

"Something like that." I nodded to Jake and Cavers, signaling them to head back inside.

They did, but slowly, grudgingly.

"I know your job is about doing the right thing, and I get that. I do. But you came alone, and you didn't call for backup, and you knew you had to figure out what to do when you saw my men waiting for you with guns in their hands, because if you backed up, they might've started shooting. You knew that, too. So, I'm not saying any of this to stroke your ego, but I am saying you did the best you could in a situation without enough cops to police all the territory. You were smart about it."

I cleared my throat. "Here's my very real warning to you, though. In a week, maybe two, you're going to start rethinking who we are, and you're going to remember what that girl told you —that she's the sister of the missing girl. Because of that, I'm telling you *right now* that you won't remember her. Ever. Not any of us—not the dog, not the men, not me who you won't even get a glimpse of. Because if you do, I won't send men for you. I will come myself. If you disregard this warning, you and your entire family will go to bed one night and none of you will wake up. I'm that kind of killer."

I waited, letting him process that, and then I gave my last instructions. "You're going to get in your car, you're going to wait three seconds, and then you're going to reverse and go home to your family. No calls except to say you're ending your shift."

I started to pull the gun away, and he lowered his hands. "How'd you know I haven't called in yet?" he asked.

I eased back. "Because you never do until you go home to your wife."

Yes. I did my research, in *every* town we visit.

He noted that, an odd look flashing over his face, and then he got into his car.

As his taillights faded, I went into the house.

Jake and Cavers were already packing everything up.

Gus bounded up to me, jumping and wanting attention.

I ignored him. Well. Fuck. I gave him two pats and went to find Ash.

She was in the office, packing as well.

She looked up. "I'm fine. Take one of the guys to go get your truck."

"What was on the sticker?"

Her eyes flickered. "If I needed help, I was supposed to offer him water."

That was smart—really smart. I nodded to her.

Jake was waiting for me at the door, his keys in hand. Not one word was spoken as we retrieved the truck.

When we got back, the Suburban was packed. We left two hours later, after clearing everything out and making sure the fire would burn fast. We ditched my truck an hour into the drive, wiped clean.

It was an hour after that when Cavers broke the silence. "Gus needs food."

"I gotta piss," Jake added.

"I'm sorry about your birthday, Jake," Ash said.

Birthday? I hadn't known.

He shrugged before glancing my way. "Don't be sorry. I got a different show."

I'd had enough. "It's harder being the good guys. Think on that. Everyone else, shut up."

We rode in silence as Gus' tail beat against the vinyl.

38

ASH

Raize was on edge. I mean, more than usual. He was always on edge.

But he wouldn't talk to anyone, even me.

We drove to Baltimore and took up residence at a motel with two connecting rooms. We could park right outside the doors. No one watched anyone at a place like this. There were a few girls working the corner, so Raize sent Cavers to find out who their pimp was. After that, he laid a bunch of papers out on one bed in his room, his hands on his hips as he studied them.

He'd been studying them for an hour now. Maybe two.

Cavers came back and reported who the pimp was, but Raize only grunted when he told him. He never looked away from those papers.

I was standing and watching Raize, trying not to be obvious about it. He shut the door, then motioned for me to follow him. Jake came over. Gus as well.

"What's going on?" Jake asked in a whisper.

"No fucking clue," Cavers said. "He told me at a gas station to get a car for him tomorrow, make sure it was fully gassed, and put all the weapons in the trunk. He wanted a nondescript car. I don't know if I want to know what he's planning, because whatever it is, it ain't like anything we've done. Or I'm guessing anything he's done—"

"I have twelve targets."

Raize stood in the connecting room's now-opened door. His hands were balled into fists at his sides, his eyes shining with a fierceness I'd only seen in a few private moments.

"And I have two days to hit them. Two. Days. And none of them are in the same *fucking* city."

I started for him, but he jerked his hand up, his head twisting to the side. "No. Don't touch me, not now."

I ignored him, going right to him and plastering myself to his chest.

My hands tunneled up into the back of his shirt, letting him feel my skin against his.

He didn't hug me back. I didn't expect it.

But he did groan, and I felt that through his chest.

"I have to commit mass murder tomorrow night—enough to classify me as a serial killer," he said. "You do not need to comfort me."

I tipped my head back, finding his eyes. Some of that fierceness was gone.

Good.

Some of my Raize was back, and a rueful look flashed over his features as he put a hand on my back, pulling me close.

"Hey, man," Jake said, gesturing around the room. "We'll help. We're like the Criminal Squad. You know, we're elite and tight and..." Gus lifted his head from where he'd jumped up on one of the beds, his tail thumping on the blanket. "We have our own Rocket, except he's not hella smart and he can't assemble weapons, but he's the literal dog to beat in a fight. Which might not be a good thing, but you know, works for us." He clapped his hands together, smiling. "Am I right? I'm right. Everyone knows I'm right."

Gus woofed.

"Gus knows I'm right." Jake went over and sat on the edge of the bed.

Gus wiggled close, putting his head in Jake's lap. So much petting. Gus was in heaven.

"Who are the targets?" Cavers asked.

Raize went down the list, and yep, that was a lot, and none of them were small.

After a pause, he looked down at me. "Bronski is the last one."

Bronski.

Ice was starting to settle in my chest. "You got the all-clear for him?"

He nodded. "I did."

"I want to do it."

"Not a chance."

I zeroed in on Raize when he said that, but I could feel Jake and Cavers sharing a look.

They liked to do that now. It was their thing. They'd bonded.

I stepped farther back, folding my arms over my chest. "Excuse me?"

Raize sighed, and I didn't need to see him rolling his eyes to know he was rolling his eyes. He moved back into our room. I followed. He shut the door behind us, and I heard Gus whining.

I was focused right now. I'd let Gus in later.

Raize went back to studying the papers. "I can't entertain this conversation. It's not going to happen, and you don't want it to happen. You're just not admitting that to yourself."

My mouth dropped open. Rage shot up my spine. "Excuse me?!"

He groaned. "You're good—like, *good* good. You hate when I kill someone. You're traumatized from the two guys you did kill, and you don't like to talk about them. You killing Bronski—"

"My rapist."

He got quiet.

He couldn't say it, so I would. "I am not who I was when I started in this world. Things are different. I'm harder. Too many people have been killed in front of me, and it affects me. Every night."

"I know." His tone was soft. "I feel you jerk in bed, and shake, and I know you cry in the shower."

Right.

All that.

He *knew* all that?

I was blown away, but man, I shouldn't have been.

I closed my eyes, took one breath, and went back at it. "Have you ever been raped?"

"What?"

"I'm aware that men get raped, so I'm asking you if you ever have been?"

"No."

"Then you can't tell me who I do or don't want to kill. You cannot make that decision for me."

He leaned down, his eyes going tender, and I almost couldn't handle it.

It made my heart thump in a weird way.

"You killed in self-defense," he said softly.

"I didn't."

"You did. If you hadn't attacked that guy, he would've killed Gus, and you knew you couldn't just distract him because he would've killed you next. You made a decision, and you told yourself it was in defense of a dog. You hate when innocents get caught in the crossfire. No one enjoys that, but it's part of this job. Yet it torments you. I know you're worried I'll go back and kill that officer and his family, and that's the good in you. You. Are. Good." He tapped my chest. "I am not. I'm a killer, straight up. Nothing good about me. All bad. I get told to kill, and I do it. You're the closest thing I've got to a conscience, and even you know the bad guys gotta go."

He didn't get it.

He never would.

"If you don't plan for me to pull the trigger on Bronski, I'm going to slip away and do it myself. He's not the top of my list, but he's not far down."

Because I was a little petty, I went to take a shower and left the door open. He could hear me getting naked, and he knew he wasn't welcome in here. But once I stepped in the water, all that went down the drain, and it was just Bronski.

Me feeling him.

Me hearing him.

Him, him, him.

He was everywhere, and I couldn't fight against him.

He was... I gritted my teeth, raising my face and letting the water pound down on me.

Raize didn't get it.

39

RAIZE

She'd been in the shower for an hour, and I had no clue what to do.

The hours I had to get these targets done were ticking by, but I had a woman now, and I cared about her, and she'd been raped, and she wanted to kill her rapist, and she was in the shower, and I had. No. Fucking. Clue. What. To. Do.

The water turned off, but she still didn't come out.

I waited, trying to study what Downer had sent me about my targets, but the facts and locations and time schedules were all muddied in my head.

Fuck it.

I didn't know where Maxim's men would be tomorrow, but I knew where Carloni was tonight. I knew where Bronski was tonight. She wanted to kill Bronski.

Fine. We'd go kill Bronski.

ASH

I STEPPED out of the bathroom and stopped short.

Raize was dressed all in black, every weapon was packed up. His papers weren't spread out anymore.

And his eyes, a chill went down my back.

I didn't have a good feeling, so I tightened my hold on my shirt. "What's going on?"

He tossed my gun on the bed. "Suit up. We're getting this done tonight."

My mouth went dry.

Man.

My mind went blank.

40

RAIZE

We went over the plan. Everything was ready.

Cavers crawled into the cab of the truck he stole an hour earlier, pulling himself through the back window. Once he was in, he righted himself and glanced back. I was driving. Ash had refused to sit inside. She'd gotten in the back, scooted to the far corner of the bed, hugged her knees, and hadn't moved since. Jake was back there keeping an eye on her.

"Boss." Cavers looked back again, and I knew who he was checking on.

I had a feeling Jake told him to push this.

This wasn't Cavers. Even being a snitch, he sucked. He did nothing.

He did his job for me, and cooked.

Now he was coming in here? He was going to press me about Ash? Was that it?

Jake put him up to it, but I knew he did it because he cared.

Still. Bullet in the ass could be a thing.

"Maybe we should've left her with Gus."

Gus hated being left behind. Hated it. He'd been barking when we left, so we had to put him in the bathroom, which everyone hated. Even me. He was a good guard dog for Ash, but where we were going, he would've been a disaster. He was the opposite of stealth.

I shrugged. "She said she wants to kill Bronski."

"Yeah. I know, but..." His silence was long and suffering, so fucking suffering.

I growled, taking another turn. We were almost there. "Say your fucking piece, then get your ass back there, and don't fucking move again." I glared at him. "You're on her all night. You hear me?"

His mouth snapped shut and he straightened with a nod. "Got it."

"Now say your piece."

"Doesn't seem like I need to. You're going to let her go in anyway."

"Yeah."

He sighed. "Got it. Some shit never changes, huh?"

I swung the wheel over, hitting the brakes. Jake and Ash would be fine. They'd learned how to ride in the back of a truck. I slammed it into park and grasped Cavers' throat, pressing him against the side of his seat.

"You wanna say that shit again?" I squeezed. "We're doing it this way tonight, because things *have* changed." I tightened my grip. "When you going to fucking get that? Everything's changed."

Something cracked behind him, and I heard banging. Muted yells.

I could kill him. Right here. Right now. This way.

I could squeeze just a little harder, feel his throat pop and his neck snap.

The old me? He came to work for me to betray me. That enough would've put him in the ground.

This new fucking me? I didn't like this new fucking me.

My door wrenched open, and I tensed, expecting hands to yank me back.

Ash was on me, crawling over me, getting to my hands and digging her nails in, breaking my skin. "Get off of him! Let him go!"

He was close to death.

He knew it. He was looking right at me, and he saw it. He saw that I wanted to kill him, but fuck—I wanted to kill everyone. Panic flared, and he started fighting.

I liked having this power—a cold sweat broke over me. No, I *didn't* like this power.

I didn't like it at all.

But fuck him.

I squeezed one last time before letting go.

That's when my hearing cleared, and Ash was screaming at me. "Oh my God! You almost killed him!"

I withdrew my arm, now bloody, and Ash gave me a look of hate before she turned back toward Cavers.

He got out his side of the truck, coughing and doubled over. She scrambled with him, tending to him.

Jake came to my side, waiting for me.

He saw my arm and handed over a bottle of bourbon. "Thought you were going to kill him."

I grunted, upending the bourbon over my arm. I should've felt a burn, a good, solid one. I felt nothing. This was how it was when I killed. Everything in me shut down. I had to do what I had to do. And I would do it. Then I'd turn myself on again later, when it was safe to be on again.

"You sent him in there." I leveled him with a look. "I'm not the one to push tonight."

Jake swallowed, then nodded. "Figured I messed up enough, but I'm worried about her."

"That's why you're the one with her in there. Got me?"

He dipped his head quickly, briskly. "Got it."

"You and me, there's static because you're my number two. You can lead, if you need to. That's the reason for the static."

He dipped his head again. "I know."

Good talk. It was done.

I leaned back against the truck. I'd gone on countless missions, but not the blatant execution type—not like this, not with these stakes.

I should've warned them.

I looked over the back of the truck to find Cavers rubbing his neck and glaring at me. He was already starting to bruise.

"There's a diner just ahead," I told him. "You guys can stay there. Wait an hour and then call a car to take you back to the motel. I'll do this alone."

"Hey."

I looked up from the driver's seat.

"I know where you're going. I know what night it is. You're going to need at least one more with you." Jake shut my door for me, pounding down on the opened window. "I'm with you."

The truck shifted as someone got in next to me. Ash.

She had her gun out. "Let's go."

I stared at her a second, but she was shut down. After a second's hesitation, Jake climbed back in next to Cavers, then jerked his chin up. Cavers wouldn't look at me, but we were good to go.

"Ash—"

"Don't," she hissed. "I don't know what set you off, and I don't really care right now. You and me? I don't know what it is, and I don't know if I even want it, so you *do not* need to worry about me. My head is about my sister and killing Bronski. Do not put some weak-female shit on me, because I'm so far from that that I'm ready to wrap *my* legs around *your* neck and squeeze until *you're* dead. You got me?"

Shit. I started the truck and pulled ahead.

I got her.

41

ASH

We parked, and everyone suited up in the alley. It was dark, but I could make out Raize pulling out a box of some sort and hitting a button. A red light flashed twice, then went out. He gave hand signals to Cavers and Jake, and both nodded. Then he handed out silencers. Jake attached mine to my gun. He secured a second gun to my back.

Cavers distributed masks, and we pulled them down over our faces. Only our eyes were visible.

We also had earplugs, but Jake only attached mine to my ear, letting it hang down.

After that, Raize motioned for us to go.

He went first.

Cavers went next.

Jake indicated for me to go before him, and he brought up the rear.

We hit the building, and by the time I rounded the corner, the four security guards were down. Raize and Cavers were through the door and running up the first flight of stairs. The guards just inside the door were unconscious as well.

I started to go after them, but Jake touched my arm and motioned that I should proceed forward on the first floor.

I nodded.

He moved ahead of me, leading the way. We worked our way through the floor. Anyone Jake saw, he took down.

Body after body, and I had a moment, a short one when I faltered, but Jake kept moving forward. I needed to remind myself that these men were here for a reason. They weren't any better or worse than us, and God knew we deserved bullets as well. The killing we did, the evil we committed? That was the death I knew was coming.

I was okay with that.

So I shut myself down, summoned up the Ash I'd been in the truck with Raize not long ago, and moved forward.

I hadn't used my gun. Yet.

Above us, we heard slight thumps. I assumed Raize and Cavers were clearing their floor, same as us.

I didn't get why no one was calling ahead, sounding the alarm, but on our way up a second flight of stairs, I saw one of the men Raize or Cavers had already taken out. His hand was out, his phone in it, but the device was totally dead.

There was another phone by another body and the same thing.

I didn't pull my phone out to check, but I guessed Raize had hit a cell phone jammer.

The yelling didn't start until Jake and I were halfway through the second floor. The shouts were muffled, but clearly from the third floor. Jake took off sprinting. I was right behind him, and when we got there, the door to a large room was open.

Jake put his earplug in and motioned for me to do the same.

I heard *zaps* from inside the room.

People were running.

More *zaps*.

Gunshots were traded.

More *thuds*.

We stopped just outside the door, waiting until both our earplugs were in and then we entered.

I tried not to count how many men I had stepped over, until I realized what I was seeing.

It was a poker game, and some hadn't even left their seats before meeting their end. I saw Carloni and two of my previous bosses. There was another man in the corner, his security men surrounding him, but all were down. The guy's body had fallen back and slumped to the floor, a bullet hole in his forehead.

There was one man still alive, and he cowered under the table.

I swept over, seeing it was the dealer. He met my eyes and raised his hands.

I didn't shoot him, motioning for Jake to let him be.

Jake whirled to take down the few remaining men at the outskirts of the room with Cavers.

Raize was gone.

A door at the back of the room was open. Likely Raize had gone through it.

I scanned the bodies, the room. No Bronski.

Where's Bronski?

There was a last *zap*, and then Cavers was running, his footsteps like an entire herd of horses stampeding through the room. He disappeared through the door.

The shooting began again.

Jake had stopped to gather phones and wallets from the men. He produced a bag from somewhere—where he'd had that stashed, I didn't know—and I helped him. We did this to everyone in the room, the dealer as well once Jake knocked him unconscious. I didn't think that was necessary, but he didn't shoot him. That was something.

Then we backtracked, going through all the downed men in the hallways, and returning to the first floor.

When we got to an exit, Cavers came down the back stairwell, a bag in hand. He went through first, leaving the door open.

Jake followed. I was next.

Cavers took my bag and dropped it into his own, which was now opened, but he was zipping it closed.

Where's Raize?

Where's Bronski?

I didn't ask. We'd done all of this in complete silence. We ran, single file, back to the truck. Cavers got behind the wheel. Jake jumped in the back and gripped my elbow, helping me up as I threw myself in behind him.

Then we were off.

Cavers put the truck in reverse.

I gripped the side to brace myself. We hit the street, and he kept going, right into the next alley.

A door flew open, light hitting the alley's pavement, and Cavers hit the brakes, stopping right in front of it.

Raize appeared, his chest heaving and blood all over him. He had a body thrown over his shoulder, either dead or unconscious. Jake stood to help him, and when they put him in the back, I froze.

It was Bronski.

Raize met my eyes fleetingly before he gripped the side of the truck and launched himself up next to me.

Once he was settled, he hit the side of the truck and pushed me down to lie flat on the bed. Jake settled down as well, rearranging some of the bags they'd thrown into the back of the truck earlier. He used them to brace himself. I crawled forward and did the same as Raize flattened down behind us. He grabbed my leg and Jake's to hold himself still, before taking hold of one of Bronski's arms. Jake took the other. They anchored him as we drove out of the city.

Cavers took us from one road to another, slowing, then

speeding up. He was keeping to the darker side streets—fewer cameras, less lighting.

I couldn't say how long the drive was. It felt too fast, and it felt like it was days.

Once we hit gravel, exhaustion crept over me, and one last thought flashed in my mind:

I never used my gun.

"WHAT'S YOUR NAME, SWEETIE?"

I shook my head, shoving that memory away.

42

RAIZE

We stopped at a wooded lot, and right away, Cavers and Jake grabbed all the phones and wallets. They took the cash out, everything else went into a pile. A healthy dose of lighter fluid was added, and everything lit up.

Jake came back to the truck and grabbed one of the bags we'd pre-packed. He took the bag and dropped to the ground. Both he and Cavers stripped their clothes, reached in and put on the new ones.

Ash came over, still watching the guys. "Why are they doing that with the phones and wallets?"

"We took everything that could identify them to give us time."

She rocked back on her heels, her hands in her sweatshirt's front pocket. "Oh."

I looked over at Bronski, then her. I had to make a decision.

Jake paused, seeing where I was looking.

Catching the look, I nodded in Ash's direction. He moved his head from side to side in response, and there was that.

Going to the front of the truck, I grabbed duct tape and zip ties. Then I opened the tailgate, grabbed Bronski by the feet, and dragged him toward me. I looped the zip ties around his ankles, crisscrossing them and doing six more loops. He could cut it off, but it would take him a long time.

"What are you doing?" she asked.

I stopped, turning to her. "No bullshit?"

She raised an eyebrow, but nodded. "No bullshit."

"I grabbed him for you, but Jake told me you never once used your gun."

Her head reared back. "When'd you have this conversation?"

"Just now."

"Oh."

I did not want to do this. Not one bit. "Look," I began.

She focused back on me.

"I jammed the phones so they couldn't get any calls out. We have a few hours before their guys start wondering where their bosses are. The dealer will have a concussion, and he should be out for a while, too. I told Jake to make sure."

Her mouth flattened. "I know. I saw."

I could tell she hadn't liked that.

Tough shit.

"That was one side of our targets. I have five more men to take care of, and we need to do it fast. They can't know we're coming. You got me?"

A shared memory flashed between us, as I was using her own words.

A light flared in her eyes, but she stifled it right away. Her head moved down, just an inch. "I got it."

"I don't want to take you with me. I'm leaving you and Jake here, so what you do is up to you. You can let Jake kill him, you can kill him, or you can wait and I'll do it. Either way, he's gotta go. This is important, Ash."

Her head jerked back up, and her chin tightened. "I know. Just because I don't enjoy the killing doesn't mean I don't know it's sometimes necessary. I got it." She gritted her teeth as she spoke.

Fuck. I wanted to take her in my arms, take back all the bad shit I'd done, all the bad shit she'd been a part of, all the bad memories of everything in her life. That would mean a different life, a different Ash, but fuck. She didn't deserve this life.

She didn't deserve to taste death all around her.

But I couldn't do any of that, so I had to grit my teeth right along with her and push forward. We had another job to handle, and then I needed to start thinking about what would come after.

"You think he might know anything about my sister?" she asked.

I studied her a beat. Her words were soft, contemplative.

"He might, but he also might realize he could use that to bargain, stall for time. Don't give anything away about her. He's a conman."

"I know."

Jake and Cavers came back, fully reclothed, and cleaned up.

Jake handed the bag off to me. "Your turn, boss."

I nodded.

I motioned to Bronski, and both of them knew what I wanted done.

It felt nice, not having to speak when I gave orders now. This new unit had some benefits.

As they got to work, I carefully took Ash by the hand. I didn't know if she'd let me touch her, but her hand grasped mine, and she went with me.

I pulled her farther into the woods, away from their sight.

I waited to see what she'd do, but she only stood in front of me.

Not knowing what to do, but wanting to do something, I reached for her.

My movements were tender and slow as I gathered up her hair, moving it aside as I lifted her shirt up and off of her. She watched as I did it, not helping, but not stopping me.

Her bra came off next.

Then I reached for her pants, unbuckled them, and they dropped.

She stepped out of them.

I took her underwear off next and held my hand there, pressing lightly against her clit.

Her eyes closed, and she leaned into me, inhaling at my touch.

I wanted to make her feel better, but this wasn't the time or the place.

Still... I leaned down, my mouth finding hers, and she gasped as she surged up on her tiptoes, pressing into me. She opened her mouth, and I slid my tongue in, claiming her. While we kissed, I felt her reaching for my clothes. She undressed me, pants first, boxer briefs. Then she began raising my shirt, her hands skimming over my stomach and chest. I broke the kiss as she pulled the shirt the rest of the way off.

I waited to see if she wanted me to kiss her again.

When her eyes opened, I saw the hunger there.

I reached for her, unable to stop myself now.

My mouth sealed over hers, and she grabbed me, pulling me close, and I pressed her against a tree. Her legs came around me —*Jesus*.

This wasn't the time, but I groaned, pressing my mouth against her neck.

She grinded against me. "Please," she gasped.

I'd answered before I even knew I was answering. This was the power she had over me. It was heady, intoxicating—and alarming.

But I thrust inside of her, and *fuuuuuck*.

This needed to be fast.

Her legs tightened around my waist, and as I began pumping into her, I reached for her clit and rubbed there.

We were silent, but our movements were frenzied.

It was quick, though I held off, waiting until she climaxed. As soon as she did, I unloaded into her and stilled, holding her as our bodies quaked.

I bent down, my forehead resting on her shoulder.

She ran her hand up and down my back, gently, as tenderly as I had undressed her. She pressed a soft kiss to the side of my neck.

I looked up, my eyes meeting hers.

I didn't know what I was looking for. Was I making sure she was okay? Looking to see if she condemned me? Hated me? Still needed me? My head was a mess when it came to her, but I couldn't leave her. Though I should.

I *should* walk away from her.

I should send her off, make her live a new life, a normal life.

But I knew she wouldn't do that, and I knew I could never leave her.

I groaned, holding her close for one more moment, and then set her back down. Grabbing the bag, I found the wipes and cleaning products. We cleaned up.

Once we were dressed, we walked back to the truck, side by side.

I didn't hold her hand, and she never reached for mine.

43

ASH

"*T* *his is your new room, sweetheart.*"

She opened the door and inside were two beds. A little girl was sitting on one of them, a doll in her hand. She looked up...

I jerked upright, realizing I'd been leaning back against a tree.

A campfire was lit up in front of me. I was hoping it wasn't the one used to burn everything else.

Jake glanced over, "You okay?"

I nodded, a quick move up and down. "Yeah. Nightmare."

He frowned, his face lit by the small campfire he'd built. "I know you got Raize, but he ain't here. You want to talk about it?"

I almost laughed. He had no idea. "No. Just...different life. How long have I been out?"

He shrugged. "An hour, or so."

A snore came from the other side of the fire.

Bronski was still out, and the ground was hella uncomfortable.

Jake sighed. "I can do it. You want me to do it?"

Did I? "I don't know."

I also didn't know why I didn't just do it. Get it done.

It seemed so cold-blooded now, and maybe Raize was right. I

wasn't ready for this—to do it this way. Self-defense was a whole different ballgame, and maybe I was still sticking to some sort of line? I'd crossed over so many that sometimes I forgot I'd even had them.

"So, you have a sister, huh?"

I eyed him warily. Jake knew about my sister, but nothing else. We hadn't talked about the cop and missing poster incident from earlier either—not that he or Cavers would ask.

"Yeah," I offered.

When I didn't say anything more Jake asked, "What's going on with you and Raize?"

I frowned. "Thought the grocery store was our talk about him and me?"

He chuckled, reaching forward to poke the fire. "I'm bored. Give me something."

"What about you and that woman of yours?"

"She's free. Carloni's dead."

"Would you want to find her, if you could?"

He didn't answer right away, staring pointedly at the fire. "No. I'd steer clear of her, hoping she got free and stayed free." His gaze flicked back to me. "Can I ask you something?"

I eyed him. "About Raize?"

"No." He grinned, chuckling before he got serious again. "About your sister."

Oh. I steeled myself.

"Is she why you're doing all this?" He gestured around us. "It's kinda obvious you're not the normal girl that gets pulled into this life."

My heart felt heavy, because Brooke was one of those girls.

I just knew it. Felt it.

I hated it.

My voice came out raspy. "She got pulled in by a Romeo pimp."

He made an understanding sound, like a grunt tinged with sympathy. "I'm sorry."

I nodded, my eyes suddenly blurry. "Yeah."

"Leo Gettsicky."

Both of us jumped to our feet.

Bronski was awake and watching us, his eyes full of pain, his face one giant grimace. He shifted, trying to relieve the pressure on his arm, but he couldn't move. He closed his eyes, resting his forehead on the ground, and heaved out a deep breath.

"Don't suppose either of you is inclined to help me out here?"

Jake scowled, cocking his gun. "We're supposed to kill you."

"Of course you are. Let me guess—Maxim decided to make a move? He's taking out Igor and Roman? All their men?" He looked between us. "Which doesn't make sense. You're both with Raize, and he's with Roman. Isn't he? Was our intel bad about that?"

"Shut up while we decide what to do with you."

Bronski barely acknowledged Jake, his eyes only on me. Gritting his teeth, he was able to lift himself to a sitting position, though his hands were tied behind him, and he heaved another deep breath as his shoulders slumped forward. "That's better."

Jake snorted. "We're *so* glad."

I hadn't spoken to Bronski.

"I wasn't going to touch you again, when I sent a man to Raize for you," he informed me. "I'd heard what you could do."

My stomach rolled over, because I knew that wasn't true.

"I mean it."

"You're a rapist," Jake spat. "That kind of sick doesn't change. You're sick. You stay sick. Sick fucking monster."

Bronski shook his head. "Right. Because you're so much better? Raize doesn't rape, but he has just as much blood on him. The dude is a one-man army. Do you even know what he can do? Can *really* do? How many men he's *actually* killed?"

"We've both seen him in action. You can't say anything to shock us."

Bronski looked between us. "Is he fucking her?"

I shot Jake a look. I didn't want anything said about that.

Bronski smirked. "That's interesting. Are you two fucking?"

Jake heaved a sigh. "New topic, asswipe. That's old."

He fell silent. So did Jake.

I was grateful to feel the weight of my gun next to my leg. I'd pulled it out when Bronski first spoke, but I hadn't picked it up. It was ready to go, though. Just lift, aim, and pull. Then I'd be a different kind of killer.

I was still waiting, though I didn't know why.

"You told Korkov your name was Brooke, but no last name. Got me thinking. Once the rumors started going around about you—the canary in the streets—I remembered where Korkov told me he'd picked you up at. Massachusetts. I don't remember the town, but Maxim had a man working girls there. Picking them. Making them fall in love with him. A girl named Brooke came from that circuit, but she had dark hair, dark eyes. The face, though... I saw her last week and got to thinking. She still goes by Brooke. Same face."

My heart pounded. *My sister is alive?*

Bronski tried to raise his arms, but he couldn't bring them around. "She had a tattoo on the inside of her wrist. A four-leaf clover, or something like that."

It was a pot of gold.

God.

I wanted him to shut up.

I wanted him to keep going.

"Wait. No. It was... What was it? A pot of something. Not like *pot* pot—dope. Pot of... what? I got it wrong. Not a leprechaun—a pot of gold! Yeah. That's what it was."

He knew her.

He saw her.

She was alive.

There's no way he could make that up. No way he could guess that tattoo randomly.

Maxim?

Leo, my sister's boyfriend, had worked for Maxim?

I'd had it wrong? All this time?

I thought Igor, not Maxim.

How had I gotten that so wrong?

Bronski laughed to himself and ended up coughing. "Fuck, my ribs hurt. But yeah. I got her, right? That's your sister? I remember the story was that you approached Korkov. You wanted in the game, and he was all excited because he knew you were different. He told me you were a virgin—"

"Shut it, man!" Jake growled.

My body threatened to dry-heave, but not because of what Bronski had done to me. I had the power now. I wasn't scared. It wasn't that. It wasn't even my sister.

It was because I knew now what I was going to do.

"Leo worked for Maxim?" I asked.

Both heads swung my way. Bronski's eyes widened. He was surprised that I wasn't affected by him, not in the way he'd been hoping. I could read it from him. His lips thinned into a frown. "Yeah, but you came in under Korkov who works for Igor. You got that wrong, huh? There was a time period where Leo was hanging out with Korkov, until Maxim shut that down and moved him to a different location."

I nodded. "I got that wrong."

Jake stood and pulled out his phone. "I'm going to make a call." He pointed his gun at Bronski as he spoke to me. "None of the shit he spouts can be trusted."

I knew that, and I nodded, letting him know I'd be fine.

Bronski watched him walk away, his eyes darkening, and he licked his lips. "What's he doing? Who's he calling?"

"He's calling Raize."

Bronski shifted his attention back to me. I could see the calculation starting. "Why would he be calling your boss?"

"Because he's killing Maxim and his men right now." I stared at Bronski, feeling dead inside—what he was going to be soon. Very soon.

But not in a cold-blooded way.

I couldn't do that. I knew that now.

I knew my lines. I had always known my lines, but then I stepped over them. One after another.

This was another one, and this one I couldn't step over.

I knew that now.

I wished I'd known sooner.

It was all about the lines.

He licked his lips again. He'd be making his move soon. His head swung back, looking toward where Jake had gone. "You guys moved on Igor, then Maxim? I got it wrong? It's Roman making the move?"

I didn't respond. That's not the move either of us was waiting for now.

I just waited.

"Why'd you take me? Why not kill me there?" he asked.

"You know why."

He fell silent. "Guess I do."

Well. There it was. "You still rape girls?"

He looked at me. I saw no remorse, but he seemed to have lost his calculation. It was like he knew there were no more moves for him.

"Yeah."

"You must enjoy that?"

He shrugged. "Yeah."

"Right." I lifted my gun and shot him.

He was as surprised as I was, but by the time he saw the gun, it was too late.

I thumbed off the shot and got him in the chest.

He fell back, blood spilling from him. He began choking, more blood spewing up and out of his mouth. He rolled to his side, then the other side.

He was trying to crawl away.

I frowned. That wasn't how it was supposed to go.

Then again, I didn't know how any of this was supposed to happen.

I didn't follow him. I didn't have it in me to shoot him again. I already loathed myself. Raize was right. I was going to hold on to this for the rest of my life.

I twisted to the side and vomited into the ground.

Bang!

I froze before looking back.

Jake stood over Bronski, his gun smoking. The last shot was to his forehead.

Bronski was dead.

I threw up again.

I'd been wrong again. My last line.

ASH

I didn't want to be in my body anymore.
I decided this an hour later.
Not anymore. No, thank you.
So, I left.
I was gone, off, floating outside of my body.
It felt better this way.
Safer.
Not so scary.
I wanted to stay like this forever.

RAIZE

I'd had to send a text ahead of time to get the newest burner phone's number.

Downer picked up after the first ring.

"It's done," I told him.

I was about to hang up when he said, "That girl you have?"

"Yeah?"

"Roman asked me to ask around."

I didn't like that.

"There was a poster about a missing girl that got our attention. One of our guys said they looked similar. Don't know if you want to know this, but the missing-poster girl? I found the house she's working from. You probably did her pimp tonight."

"Maybe."

He gave me an address and a name.

Yeah. That guy had been done tonight.

"So you know, we're calling that house in—anonymous tip. Roman doesn't work girls. We'll be sending authorities to all those houses, so she'll be rounded up by the government. They'll be classified as sex trafficked."

He gave me the address where she was, and I hung up and made a second call.

Jake answered after the first ring. "Boss."

"What's happening there?"

"He's gone."

"Who?"

He paused. "Her, then me."

"Her?"

"Yeah."

Okay then.

"We're heading back."

"Okay."

46

ASH

The guys showed up and the body disappeared. I couldn't tell you a time. That had ceased for me. I was in zombie mode. Nothing mattered at the moment.

Then Gus was licking me, trying to squish me with his wiggly body.

There was a lot of Gus.

I showered.

Raize helped me change my clothes.

In the days that followed, I remembered being told to eat, so I ate. Being told to drink, so I drank. Being told to lie down, so I did. I couldn't fall asleep on command, but Raize had taken to holding me in his arms at night. That helped. It wasn't normally like that. We slept together, but usually there was space between us. He liked to be free in case he had to jump out of bed.

And Gus had taken to joining us on the bed some nights. Other nights, he went with Jake.

"Where are we?" I asked Raize one day.

He and I were sitting on the patio in the backyard of the house where we'd been staying. It was nice. There were mountains around us, a creek down the path.

Raize looked over to me, and I looked down. There was a blanket on my lap.

That felt nice, too.

"We're in West Virginia."

That made sense. By the mountains. We must've been in a valley. Did they have valleys? I didn't know much about West Virginia.

"Why?" I asked.

"We did a lot of bad shit. We need to lay low."

Oh yes. Right.

I blinked a few times. "How long have I been like this?"

"A week."

A *week*? Wow.

I remembered what Bronski had said...

"My sister..."

Raize's bench squeaked, and I was momentarily shocked by that because one, he'd moved and made a sound, and two, he'd sat in a chair that squeaked. The world was ending.

Also, I'd just made a joke. The world really was ending.

"We need to have a conversation about your sister."

Well, duh.

Right?

Wait...

"What about?"

"Your sister is alive."

"That's what Bronski said." Goddamn Leo Dipsicky. What a name. "I got the wrong boss."

He frowned. "What?"

"The wrong boss. I thought I did my research right. I didn't want to be too obvious and come in through Brooke's boyfriend's boss. But I got the wrong boss, under the wrong brother." A tear slid down my cheek. "I had it wrong the whole time."

"Listen."

Razie moved to sit next to me, and I didn't know how I felt about that. Raize wasn't a comforting guy.

He proved my point because his voice came out rough, like he was uncomfortable, too. "You're right that if you'd gone in under Leo's direct boss, you would've been flagged. You wouldn't have made it past the car doors. They would've killed you. Your face is too much like your sister's. Unless Leo worked you both, it wouldn't have been approved. They have certain protocols to cut down on getting caught. Certain types of girls they prey on."

Prey.

Protocols.

Fuck them. Just, fuck them.

"Tell me you killed them," I said softly. "You killed them all. Tell me you did that."

His tone was gentle. "I killed them. Leo. His boss. All of them. Your sister's newest pimp. I got them—anyone who knew enough to be a threat under Maxim and Igor. The operations had been weeded out before, and I worked it so Igor thought he was getting hit by Maxim, and Maxim thought it was retaliation for the 63rds."

"They never suspected Roman?"

"No. He's the youngest and kept his operations under wraps in Russia. They never knew how large he's gotten. Now he's moving everyone over here, almost everyone. The streets are going to be in chaos for a while. Cops, FBI, whoever, Roman kept everything off the grid. We had new burner phones every day. New ways to communicate. I was his lone wolf here, and now we're gone. We're supposed to stay low for a few more months."

My mind whirled. "Wait. You said Brooke's *new* pimp?" My mouth went dry. *How many had she gone through?*

Did I even want to know?

Yes. If she went through it, the least I could do was hear it.

"Roman sent in the authorities. Anonymous tip, though. They don't know it came from him. He doesn't run girls. It's a market he loathes, so all those girls got swept up by the cops. They should be classified as sex trafficking victims, but there's always a risk that the government will get them wrong. Call 'em regular working girls."

"What's the difference?"

"A lot, actually. One can get resources, help. The other gets charged, and if a new pimp moves in, they'll be back to work within the day."

"My sister?"

"She was charged with prostitution."

"Oh my God."

"But Roman sent in some information. They're watching to make sure her charges are changed." A pause. "There's a couple other matters."

"What?" My voice cracked.

My sister was alive. I had to run down my list again, but I was fairly certain Raize had single-handedly taken care of most of them. What else could there be?

"Your father."

It took a few seconds for his words to penetrate. "Huh?"

"You said your dad was a drunk."

"He was. Our mom died, and Brooke started going off the rails. My dad kinda went with her."

"He went to rehab."

"My dad went to rehab?"

Raize nodded. "He went three times."

My mouth dropped open. "Three?"

Whoa. Wow.

"What's the problem with that, though? That's good, right?"

His eyes were hooded, guarded. "It is, but people who come out of rehab after it finally stuck sometimes become problems. We need to know if he'll become a problem or not."

"Oh." I shook my head. "I don't know. We—we weren't close to him, ever. My mom's death wrecked him. He was gone by the time she died, but we all saw it coming. But then Brooke was gone, and I cared more about her than him. I chose to go after her."

Brooke.

I could taste the tears sliding down my face, but that was it. The salt.

Raize moved in, his hand cupping the back of my neck, and he lifted me onto his lap. This felt more like Raize, except the cradling was still new.

I relaxed, resting my head against his chest.

I grabbed ahold of his shirt. He was wearing a gray Henley. I always liked when he wore these.

"Do you want us to bring her here, too? She's not—"

"No." My answer was immediate and strong. I sat up. "Brooke and I were never close, but I loved her. We grew up together. I know the trauma she's endured, and she can't be here. She'll be a liability. Knowing she's not still there, still doing that work, that's good enough for me."

He cupped the back of my neck again, moving my face to meet his gaze. "Besides your dad, is there someone we can call for her?"

My throat swelled. "Maybe. Let me think about it."

"Okay. We'll wait."

My chest lightened. Relief swept through me.

"I never got to blow up Oscar's building."

Raize stiffened before a bark of laughter erupted from him. His arms tightened around me. He buried his face in my neck.

I liked that feeling. I liked that sound, too. I wanted to hear more of it. I reached for his hand, entwined our fingers, and settled into him. "Thank you."

"Yeah." He squeezed my hand. He ran a finger down the side of my face, tucking a strand of hair behind my ear. "You wanna stay Ash? Since we all know your real name now..."

I shook my head. I'd stopped being that girl a long time ago.

"I prefer Ash."

But not Ashley. I wasn't Ashley.

"Wait. You said a 'couple other matters.' What's the other one?"

He seemed to hesitate a moment. "You."

"Me?"

"Other reason we were sent to West Virginia is you. You were reported missing."

I couldn't—that didn't make sense.

Then he added, "A neighbor reported you. Not your dad."

...THE GIRL GOT off the bed and walked toward me.

She held her hand out. "My name is—"

47

ASH

I remembered what else Bronski said later and nudged Raize with my toe. "Hey."

We were in bed. I had no clue what time it was, but it was dark out.

"Hmm?" He opened his one eye and rolled his head my way. Gus was on the floor in the opened doorway. At our voices, his head popped up, and we could hear his tail starting to thump.

"Bronski said he'd heard rumors about the canary."

"Yeah. I heard 'em, too. It's why I came to get you at that game." He frowned at me. "We didn't talk about it before."

I shook my head and nudged him again. Something had been bugging me. I remembered tonight. "They used to use canaries in coal mines."

"You know those stories." He rolled to his side, propping his head up on his hand. I stared up at him as he fingered a lock of my hair, showing me the blonde.

I nodded. "They'd keep one down in the mines with them, and if it stopped chirping, it's because toxic gases killed it. That would alert the coal miners to get out. It's silence signified death was coming."

"Yeah."

"Canaries sing to save lives. I sing and someone dies."

A deep shudder went through me.

I pushed up, angling so I was resting on my elbow and staring Raize right in the face. "Don't use me that way again. I can't do it. Not anymore."

He studied me in the dark, seeing what he could see. I didn't know. I was able to make him out, but I felt like I was still in the shadows. He sighed, and it was soft and low. It seemed almost surrendering. He touched a strand of my hair. "When Marco learns you're the one who can tell him about his brother, he's going to come for you."

I sobered, feeling him tense next to me.

His hand slid around my neck, cupping the back of my head. He leaned forward, another soft sigh and his forehead touched mine. "I won't let that happen."

I slid my hand up his stomach, his chest, over his arm, his bicep, and then back down to his stomach. I tucked my hand under his boxer brief's waistband and opened my fingers, pressing against him. "I know."

He hadn't untensed, and his rough words drew my attention. "Roman is smart, but he's not as ruthless as Marco. I fear Marco. I don't fear Roman."

"But he's not sending sicarios after you?" I asked.

"He will." Raize's eyes flashed, and he flipped, sliding his hands up my arms and his feet down on the insides of my legs as he lowered himself over me. He pushed up against me, grinding a moment before he paused. "We're in a pocket of time right now— between one war and the next."

"Against Marco?"

He ducked his head, his lips nuzzling my neck. He slid a hand down my side, causing me to arch my back. I wound my arms around his neck.

"There are other players, and with Roman pushing to take

over for both his brothers, I don't know what the fallout will be, but yes—Marco won't stop." He skimmed his nose up my throat, his mouth settling over my jawline as he tasted me. "Shit will change when he finds out about you."

He switched to his side, wrapping his arms around me and taking me with him.

He held me there, tucked close, propping his chin on my shoulder.

"Do you miss Mexico?" I didn't know why I asked, but he lived there. He had a whole life down there.

"Yeah. I mean, I'm fine here, but Mexico is beautiful. It's not all about the cartels there."

"What do you miss about it?"

"The culture. The history. It's family-oriented. There's a warmth to the people down there, even to me. People smile a lot down there. Friendly. Helpful. It's... I had to get used to it at first, but then they'd learn who you are, who you're working for, and that'd go away. But there's wine country. We have the best tacos. And the beaches. The whales. It's a world away from a world, if that makes sense." He chuckled. "Gifts are opened on Christmas Eve and Santa's gifts come the next day. In the south, January 6th is when the three wise men bring the gifts."

"You celebrated Christmas?"

"Yeah. With Verónica a few times. Just a few times. And for Halloween, it's The Day of the Dead. We celebrate it in November, putting out altars with food, photos, and candles. It's an offering for the dead." He drew me close, dropping a kiss on my shoulder. "Yeah. I miss Mexico."

"What about the women?" I had to know.

He tensed, before lifting up to look at me better. "The women?"

"In Philly, you had so many women. They'd come to your room. I heard them, Raize. Do you miss that?"

He stared at me long and hard before his hand lifted, cupping the side of my face. "I was a different persona then. Had to be. Carloni must've learned at some point I worked for Roman, but for a while, he didn't know. I needed to be a different person."

He hadn't answered me. "The women? Do you miss them?"

His mouth curved up. "They were cleaning my room."

It was the mouth. Everything was straight face, monotone voice for that monotone answer and I hit him in the shoulder. "Are you kidding me?"

He laughed before lowering his head, pressing a kiss to the crook between my neck and shoulder. "I don't miss any woman except you, my sister, and my mom. I never will."

Well.

I might let it slide then.

Moving my leg between his, lifting it, twisting the curve of my foot to slide down the outside of his leg in a caress, I smiled at him.

He looked down, grinning at me.

"What do you think is going to happen with Marco?" I asked, knowing we needed to talk about it.

He held my gaze a bit and loosened his hold on me. "I don't think he'll make any move to progress into the US until he's taken over the Morales Cartel. That would require him killing his father, and I don't know what he'd do to my mother and sister. We share our sister, so he might leave my mother alive."

"But if he did that? Took over the Morales Cartel?"

A darkness flared in Raize's eyes, and he looked over my shoulder. "Then he'd come for me, and since I'm tied to Marakov, he would have to declare war against the Marakov family."

"Will there be fallout for Roman?"

His gaze came back to me, softened, and he shook his head. "No. It's him and his uncles now. They're in Russia. Marco is here. They'll follow the stronger Marakov, and that's Roman. He gets everything and everyone now. He's put himself and them in a position where they have to accept what he did."

"And if Marco comes for you?"

"Then I'll go to work."

He pulled me up and in one motion, stripped my underwear down my legs.

He said, "Enough war talk."

Rolling me to my back, he slid a finger into me. His mouth fell to my neck and he breathed there, his finger moving in and out of me. Pleasure and other emotions were rolling around inside of me, but for now; I let it go. I only felt him, what he could do to my body, how he could make me feel.

I was addicted to him.

My mouth found his, and I yearned for him to be inside of me.

This time felt different.

Every time with Raize was different, but right now there was an almost desperate, frenzied need to get our fill before that call would come, before the world changed again. Raize let me rest for a bit after the first time, but then he flipped me over to my knees, and he worked us both up all over again.

Carnal need pulsated between us, one that neither of us could totally satisfy.

Dawn came peeking through the windows as Raize brought us to another climax. Only then did we rest.

I shivered. *What would happen if we ever fully satisfied that need?*

I didn't want to find out.

"IT'S A CANARY."

"Yeah? So?"

"So," Brooke held it up and let it go. It flew away. "It'll come back if it's not safe out there."

It never came back.

The neighbor's cat killed it.
I should've told her.

48

RAIZE

We stayed in West Virginia for four more months.

I hated it. Mostly.

I wanted to be traveling, working. I'd gotten used to the constant go, but this staying, waiting, it had its benefits, too.

Ash laughed more.

She relaxed.

She ate more.

Cavers took Gus on daily walks. Sometimes Ash went with him. Sometimes she played with Gus in the backyard. She liked to spend time watching the creek. A lot of time.

I think she'd started meditating down there, but I never asked.

Jake was in charge of going into town, getting food for us.

He'd also started seeing a local woman, though he thought no one knew. We all knew. He giggled when he was getting laid. We learned that.

Every time Jake came back after seeing his woman, Ash and Cavers watched me. I knew Ash was concerned that I would kill the woman. She was a liability because eventually she'd get curious about Jake, want to see where he lived, what he did for a living. Cavers just watched me to see if he needed to help in any way.

But I'd followed Jake.

I'd bugged the woman's house, put a tracker on her vehicle, and was listening on her phone. So far she believed Jake was a traveling salesperson, and she hoped he'd marry her one day—or that's what she told her sister about him. So far, "Brian" was satisfying her in bed.

I'd have to have a conversation with Jake soon.

I was getting restless.

I wasn't the only one.

We were all on edge, feeling the end of our time was coming soon.

War was inevitable.

The killing would start again, but Ash, she was changing.

She *had* changed.

I just wasn't quite sure how she'd changed. Not yet.

I caught her twisting a lock between her fingers a lot.

She was missing her blonde hair. It had started to return to her dark coloring again.

Then one day my phone rang.

Downer was on the other end. "You need to come back."

49

ASH

Something was wrong.

The hairs on the back of my neck stood up, and when Raize stepped inside, I knew I was right. He was locked down. Completely. His face was blank, and that was *not* good.

Seeing him now, as he looked at me, we both knew.

It was done.

I gave him a small nod, because it was time. I had no clue what was going to happen, but we all knew our time here was a momentary break.

Jake was on the floor with Gus, who was tearing apart a couple of squeaky toys as if his life depended on it. Cavers was in the kitchen, cooking dinner, but it was like everyone felt Raize's chill. All heads lifted and all eyes went to him. He stood just inside the door, his phone in hand, and he looked right at Jake.

"You have two options."

A chill went down my spine. He was using his 'motherfucker' tone, and it was directed at Jake, and Jake knew what that meant. Raize was not messing around here.

Jake stood, slowly, and his eyes got guarded. "You want to watch how you talk to me?"

Raize wasn't deterred. He shot right back, "You want to watch how you've been lying to our group here?"

Jake straightened, his head shooting up and his shoulders falling back. "Excuse me?"

"You're not just fucking her."

Wait—what?

Cavers came into the room, a slow step until he was beside me.

A whole new level of tension filled the room, and Jake's head fell a little. So did his voice. "You want to say that again?"

"You're not just fucking the hair stylist in town. You're having a relationship with her."

Oh... No.

That was bad.

We'd kept to ourselves, or tried. I never left the property except for a walk with Cavers and even that, we kept to the woods. Ultimate privacy. Jake was sent to pick up food. He wasn't even supposed to go in and get it. He was supposed to order it since the local grocery store had that option, pull up and they'd bring it out to the car.

A relationship?

"You're doing that?"

Jake swung his head Cavers' way, a bit jerky. He glared at both of us, his jaw tightening, before he lifted up a shoulder. "Yeah, man. I did that."

"She talks to her sister about you."

Jake's head whipped back to Raize. "You got her phone tapped?"

I held my breath.

Raize's voice came out cold. "Of *course* I tapped her phone. She knows you. She knows how you feel, taste. She's got feelings involved and she's going to remember you."

"So—what? What do you want me to do about it? I ain't killing her."

"We're leaving."

That was the ball I was waiting to get dropped. I knew it now, knew why Raize was bringing up Jake's girl. If we left, she'd remember. She might start looking, talking more, and what then? Where would that lead to?

"Damn," a quiet word from Cavers.

Jake didn't say a word. His jaw clamped shut and a vein stuck out from the side.

Raize's eyes were back to being hooded. No. That wasn't right. He was back to looking dead.

A second shiver passed through me because I'd started to hate that look. It went away at times, mostly with me, mostly in bed, but it'd been less and less the last two weeks.

I detested that it was back.

He said, staring at Jake, "You leave her behind and what's she going to start saying to that sister of hers? Her sister is married to a probation officer."

Jake winced. He ran a hand over his face. "I didn't know that."

"Because you didn't vet who you wanted to stick your dick into."

I closed my eyes.

Cavers grunted at hearing Raize's words, but he didn't say anything.

"I thought, I don't know. She's pretty. She's nice. She's kinda funny."

"She's in love with you, hoping you're going to ask her to move in with you."

Cavers murmured, "She doesn't seem the smartest bulb."

I opened my eyes and Jake was shaking his head, his eyes downcast, and his shoulders slumped in a whole defeated way. "I can't kill her."

"Then what are you going to do? You can't bring her along."

I knew where Raize was going because Jake couldn't kill her and in Raize's mind, in this world, that meant he'd have to kill her. But damn. No. She was innocent. She didn't—I stepped forward. All eyes came to me, but I was looking at my man.

I raised my eyebrows. "Does she know his name?"

"No," Jake answered, and swiftly. "I'm not that stupid."

I kept on, staring *only* at Raize, "Relationships end for all different reasons. He can tell her his mom fell ill and he's gotta go see her. He can wait, break up with her in a week. Two weeks even."

"She's going to ask questions."

I shook my head, hard.

Jake and Cavers had fallen silent. This was between Raize and me, and I was bargaining for this woman's life.

"No," from me.

"He ends it now, she's going to start remembering all their past times and their past conversations. She's going to realize she knows nothing about him and she's going to start getting angry. She's going to feel duped by him and that's when she'll start searching for him. It'll be one internet search. She ain't going to find a 'Brian' and it's a matter of time before she's going to pull on the string she's got hanging in front of her." Raize glanced at Jake. "I can't use threats this time."

"You kill her and that'll set off the questions." My chest was tight and getting tighter.

Raize already had his mind made up, but no, no, no.

I was wrong again. I thought I didn't have any more lines left not to cross. This was it. Innocents. This was my stand.

I whispered, "She's an *innocent*, Raize. *No*."

He barely blinked. "She's a loose end. The sister knows a first name and that's it. The connection ends there."

"No." Jake stepped forward, his head swinging from left to right. "I go to the grocery store. The liquor store. Those have cameras. You kill her and the brother-in-law will make calls, get that footage pulled. They'll get a face. Ash is right. We go and I tell her my mom's got cancer. A week later, it's real bad. I can't get back. I'll string her along until I'm just gone. She'll hurt, but not in the way where she's going to get curious and start doing google searches for me. It'll be fine."

"I can destroy security footage. I can't stop a woman's curiosity."

He was right, but no.

Just, no.

"No, Raize."

His jaw clenched, and he stared right at me, his eyes dropping the dead affect. They were burning, and I almost winced because it was me. I was standing in his way, and in his mind, it was his way of making me safe.

"I just got a call. We need to go back. Roman's orders." His gaze swept the room. "Pack up and wipe the house. We leave in an hour." He turned to Jake. "You make that all about your grandmother, but do it from the road."

I almost sagged from the relief.

He was trying my way.

Jake clipped his head in a nod and he was off to start packing.

Cavers went to do the same.

Raize came over to me, standing so close, he was touching me. His eyes were on mine. And his finger reached out, stroking my stomach through my shirt. "Your way this time."

My throat got all full. I dropped my voice, barely a whisper, "Thank you."

His eyes were still burning, and I knew he didn't like it.

50

RAIZE

"I want to meet your whole team," Roman had said on the phone earlier.

We'd arrived in Boston, a city that I didn't understand why we were here, but it was where Downer told me to go. Now, an hour after that phone call, I was walking into a large mansion.

I hadn't cared for the whole estate or the gate that I'd needed to wait to be admitted through, but I was coming alone. I was taking this victory.

I had replied, "No."

Roman sucked in his breath and he got quiet. He got real quiet. "That's an order from me."

"Then you can give the order for my execution. I'm not bringing them in."

Another beat of silence. "You're not bringing them in, or you're not bringing *her* in?"

"She's on my team. I've become protective of my entire team."

Roman chuckled. "I am not going to lie that I don't know how to take this insubordination, and especially from you."

I was his best.

I knew Downer was good, but I was better and it was the

unspoken acknowledgement we all knew.

I wasn't the type of employee who started to think about what he was entitled to or had earned, but I didn't care. I was willing to risk that he wouldn't want to lose me when I drew my line. No Ash. That was how it was going to be for me.

"Fine." Roman sighed, then griped, "I'm allowing this one time, but I do not like having ghosts work for me. I will meet all of them at some point."

We'd see, but I said, "Where am I meeting you?"

He gave me the coordinates and here I was, my car getting valeted and I was walking into this mansion with thirty guns around me. It was making my back itch.

I preferred our other way of meeting, in the dark, with his men in their cars, where I could disappear.

Downer met me at the door, giving me a nod before indicating I should follow him.

In every room, there were men.

The kitchen. The dining room.

I was getting déjà vu from when we went to Carloni's home, sans the working girls.

Downer led me to a back office, also reminiscent of Carloni's home's layout and I stepped inside, seeing Roman standing in the corner with a phone to his ear. He turned, seeing me, and held up a finger. He went back to his conversation, and I glanced around the room.

Noting the exits.

A large window faced a pool and backyard that was tiled, with another poolhouse on the side, and a fence going all around the yard.

If I had to make a run, that was my exit. Over that fence, behind the poolhouse. I was guessing there would be the blind spot in their whole security system because the camera was facing the front of the poolhouse and there was another perched on top of the poolhouse, sweeping the backyard.

Yes. That was the blind spot.

"Raize! Welcome. Hope the trip wasn't too exhausting." He signed off from his call, slipping his phone into his pocket. Then he regarded me, his head cocking to the side. His eyes narrowed. "You look irritated."

Downer snorted.

I ignored both, asking, "Why did you call me here?"

The feeling in the room shifted, grew more tense, more alarmed.

Downer had been grinning, and he was still grinning, but it was fading. His eyes were alert, trained on me. He was studying me so intently that he didn't realize I was studying him back.

A feeling shifted in my gut.

Something had happened. Something concerning me.

Was this how Ash felt? When she just knew the answer?

I hoped not, because this feeling sucked. I didn't like it.

"There was a hit on Morales."

My mother? "On *only* Morales?"

The answer flashed in Roman's eyes first. "Your mother was killed, too. I'm sorry, Raize."

My mother.

I almost rocked back.

I should've been expecting it. A part of me had been. I knew it was a matter of time. She was Morales' girlfriend. Her time would come and I figured it would be a bloody end, but hearing it—that was another matter.

"My sister?"

"We don't know. Our reports say that she was with Estrada so she's probably alive. Or we can hope."

"But if he did that? Took over the Morales Cartel?"

"Then he'd come for me..."

"How?" That word gutted out of me.

"Sorry?"

He knew. He winced as I asked the question, and then he

pretended to misunderstand. He knew. He'd ask to know how his mother was killed if the roles were reversed.

I growled, my hands curling into fists. "Just tell me."

His gaze went to Downer before his chin lifted and his shoulders fell back, preparing. "Morales was decapitated. His body was found hanging from a bridge. Your mother..."

Jesus.

He had to pause before he told me. That said enough.

"...they were more merciful. An execution shot to the forehead. Her body was left intact."

Intact.

Jesus.

This world. This was my world, and I was bringing Ash *more* into it?

Intact.

That was a *merciful* killing.

I said, "It was Estrada."

"No." Roman started to shake his head, both his hands going into his pockets.

That was his tell, his only tell. When he got nervous or when a topic came up that he didn't want to happen, his hands went into his pockets. I picked it up long ago, but I'd never needed it against me.

I felt every inch of me cool. I was shutting down, or 'locking down' as Ash would call it.

I said, slowly and softly, "Yes. No one else would move against Morales."

"We don't know—"

"Do not bullshit me."

Roman froze.

I could feel Downer's alert go up a whole other notch. He was the best who could read me, and he knew I was close to violence. Because of this, I wasn't surprised when he said, as if soothing me, "Easy now, buddy."

I gave Roman a frank look. "You called me back because Marco made his move."

His eyes didn't shift. Nothing. There was no reaction. He was only listening to me, which told me he was aware of everything I was about to say. He had played it out in his head. He'd probably played out every response I would make and some of those weren't using words.

I asked, "You want me to execute him?"

I waited. I needed to hear what action he'd want me to take.

Roman lifted his head, inch by inch. "I'm not strong enough to take on Estrada, not yet. We have other adversaries here."

No, no, no.

That didn't make sense.

Marco made a move. He killed his father. My mother.

I didn't think he would've killed our sister. She was the only one he showed emotion toward. He was moving to take over the Morales Cartel, if it wasn't already done. No one would go against him. The Colombians would wait, see who came into power. The same with Bolivia. Belize. All of them would wait, but Marco wouldn't move their way. He would, if he wanted to take over their product, but knowing Marco, he would want to take over further distribution.

The US was the golden ticket. They paid the most for their product.

No.

I was right.

Marco was coming. He would come for me first.

He had decided to move against Roman, probably hearing how the family had been thinned. Or that was how he thought.

"Why are we in Boston?" I knew what I'd have to do, even if Roman didn't give me the order. I was going, but I needed to know where my boss' head was and Boston wasn't the 'where' we had eliminated his brothers for. This wasn't the targeted location.

"We're in Boston because it's open right now."

I frowned.

"The family that was controlling Boston moved to Chicago. They've had their own changes in the past years. That's why I reached out. There's been skirmishes, but no one has stepped up here. I want to take over. I already have Philly, DC, and the rest of the East Coast except for New York."

"You reached out?"

"I can't fight Estrada, but you're right. I think he did the hit, and I think he's planning on moving north. His first order of business will be to send sicarios after you."

"You're sending me after him."

It wasn't a request. Roman's nostrils flared and I knew he checked me.

His eyes went flat and his mouth thinned. "I send my best soldier after him, I could lose my best soldier. I need you alive."

No.

"You have to send me after him."

"No, Cla—Raize. No, Raize. There's another player here. I want to send you north, to Canada. Kai Bennett. He controls almost all of Canada. He's not big enough to take on Marco and neither am I, but together, *we* could."

It wouldn't work.

None of this was going to work.

They needed a lone wolf, or a lone group to go in and assassinate Marco. It was the only way to stop him.

"He has too many men."

Kai Bennett would not team up with Roman. Roman was too new. He'd just assassinated his two brothers. That was a bold move and it would be perceived as risky. Kai Bennett did not take risk, but Roman was set.

"The Bennetts are a family organization."

Roman's head reared back, a small inch, but he was listening.

"You just took out your two brothers. That goes against the grain of who Bennett is. Sending me to him to make a connect for you is a waste of time. It won't work and you'll lose that time for a surprise assault against Marco. Send me, just me, and I'll get it done. I know the area. I know Mexico. I can get in and get it done."

"I could lose you."

"It's worth the risk."

Roman's eyes flashed and he leaned forward, his palms going on the desk. He leaned over, his head toward me. "Not to me!"

Downer moved to stand between us, at the side of the desk. He had a hand on his gun, but his eyes were trained on me.

I was the wild card here.

I stepped back. I needed to use reason. That's what Roman would listen to, only reason. I needed more of it. My mind was trying to think.

"Send me to kidnap my sister."

The room's temperature dipped and I knew I had them. Both of them. They shared a look.

I explained, "She's the only person Marco cares about. I can go down, get her, and bring her back. He'll be tormented and he'll want her back. He'll lose time and energy trying to get her back. Sending me to Kai Bennett is not going to work, not yet. He doesn't work with others and if you want to recruit him, you need a solid and stellar reputation. Send me to take Marco's sister and that'll get back to Bennett. It's a move he might appreciate. It's not expected. It's a mental tactic."

Roman was regarding me again, his eyes narrowed.

He was thinking about it.

Downer noticed it, too, and he threw his hands up. "Are you kidding me?! You're actually considering this? This is insane."

Roman ignored him, asking me, "If you can get in and take your sister, why wouldn't you be able to kill Estrada then? You're taking the same risk."

I shook my head. "I'm not. I can get word to her. She'll tell me where to go and the best time to take her. My sister begged for my

life before. If she's still alive, she's not stupid. She'll know Marco
ordered the hit on our mother. I *guarantee* that my sister will want
me to come for her. She's his blind spot. We need to use that."

My pitch was done.

Now I had to wait.

Roman needed to think it over. He needed to come to his
decision, but I laid it out as best as I could.

"I've heard what your woman can do."

That surprised me. It wasn't what I expected from him.

I frowned, but didn't comment back.

Roman pushed up from the desk, going back to the window
and he reached for his phone. He turned his back to me. "Go. Get
your sister and get back here, *alive*."

I wasn't waiting for him to change his mind.

I started to leave.

He stopped me at the door, saying, "But Raize."

I turned back.

He was watching me, his phone in his hand. "Your woman. I
get that, but you're *my* man. Your woman is then therefore one of
mine. If there comes a time when I'll need to use what she can
do, I will. You will bring her to me to do that." His eyes were
harsh. His tone was unrelenting. "There is no room for negotia-
tions with this one, not if you continue to be in my employment.
Do you understand me?"

I had to give him the answer he wanted.

I said, "Yes," as I reached for the doorknob and I left.

I didn't wait to be excused, but I knew as I left, I was on a
leash and I would find how far that leash extended one day. As I
went back out, my car was brought up for me, and I drove away
because that day wasn't today.

Now, what we had to do was the reason Ash had come into
my life.

The irony wasn't lost on me.

We were about to kidnap *my* sister.

51

ASH

S omething was *really* wrong.

I sat up in bed, waiting for him until I saw a sweep of headlights pull into the driveway. I was in the middle of the bed, my arms hugging my legs, my knees pulled up against my chest. I was there, and it was a long time before he came in.

That said almost everything to me.

He didn't want to come in.

Why?

I didn't wait.

I moved across the bed, standing barefoot and I left.

I was in a tanktop and my underwear, but I hoped Cavers and Jake would be considerate, not come in if they were up? I didn't know. At this point, I didn't care.

I found him in the kitchen, a bottle of tequila next to him. The only light was a small nightlight that was left from the guest bathroom, and that'd been overlooked since we normally kept no lights on anywhere we stayed.

He didn't turn to me, and my gut clenched.

I went to him, crawling onto his lap, my legs straddling him, and I pressed my hands to his chest.

He didn't grab my legs. He always grabbed my legs.

"What happened?" I asked softly. I was treading with caution. I'd never felt this from Raize, whatever this was.

He didn't answer, staring off into the distance behind me.

"Hey." I slid my hand around his neck, turning his head to see me. I bent down, eye to eye. And I began rubbing my other hand up and down over his chest, slipping under his shirt. "Tell me."

Now he moved.

His eyes flashed, and his hands gripped my thighs, pulling me tight over him.

He swallowed, his Adam's apple moving up and down once before he rasped out, "There was a hit on Morales and his girlfriend."

I rocked back.

The only girlfriend that would affect Raize was his mother.

"Raize," I murmured.

He kept on, his eyes going back to staring at something behind me. "She was left intact. They executed her with a shot to the forehead."

I leaned back, trying to get him to look at me. He needed to see me, not whatever was in his head. "Raize."

"It was Marco."

"But if he did that? Took over the Morales Cartel?"

"Then he'd come for me..."

Our earlier conversation flared to memory. My question and his response about Marco Estrada, and a whole new slew of chills were slithering through my body.

I rocked forward against him, only half realizing what I was doing.

I said, "Roman is sending you after Marco?"

His hands gripped my thighs again before moving up to my ass. He cupped me there, and he helped move me with my already rocking motion. His hands were kneading my ass, slipping underneath my underwear. "No."

I frowned. "But—"

His eyes found mine, tipping up. "Roman's too new over here. He's not strong enough to take on Estrada, but we're going to buy time."

"How?"

His eyes skimmed the room behind us, the hallway. "He's sending us to go and take Estrada's half-sister. It's a stall tactic."

How he was talking...

He kept on, "He'll lose time and energy by looking for her. We'll let him know she's alive, but then she'll need to be hidden from him." He paused. "If that's what she wants."

I tipped my head back, touching his chin so he was looking into me and I asked through my eyes. He didn't want them to know?

His gaze flared, growing fierce, then burning, and then hardening. His hand kept rocking me against him so I was grinding on him.

I saw my answer. He didn't.

I gave him a small nod, knowing my own eyes softened, and he closed his, getting what he needed from me. His forehead went to my chest. I caught his head, my hand cradling his neck and I brought my other one around, sifting my fingers through his hair.

His mother was dead. We were going to get his sister.

Everything else could wait.

I moved my lips to his ear and said, so quietly, "I'm sorry about your mother."

His hand snapped up to the back of my neck, gripping me, but he only moved his head back, staring at me with such fierce yearning and a second later, his mouth was on mine. It was hot, demanding. His hands gripped my thighs, digging in, and I felt he needed more. Just more.

I closed my eyes, giving over, and Raize let out a growl, pushing me back.

He adjusted me, yanking my legs open, so I sank farther down on him. He tipped me back.

He was watching, his head back in the shadows, but I wasn't.

The moonlight was shining in. I was in its spotlight, and Raize wanted to see me.

He kept kneading my thigh, watching me, and I felt an inferno blazing inside of me.

I wanted him, just him, however he gave me right now.

He tipped me back even farther, I was almost half lying on his legs. Almost. He stopped me halfway there, ran his hand up over my stomach, spanning it, and moving up until he was between my breasts. He swiped them, slow, smooth, with his finger, running it over my nipple and I shuddered. Every touch, caress was a tease from him.

I wanted to grind on him, to make this go faster. I ached for him, but something in the air held me back.

He needed to control me.

His hand moved back, turned, grabbed my top and he ripped it apart.

I gasped, arching my back from surprise.

My shirt fell to the side, down and off my arms. He grabbed it from the back, crumpled it up in a ball and moved it back over my body, moving down.

I was fully displayed for him, until he ran that hand over my stomach, my shirt still in his hold, and I felt him grab the sides of my underwear. I heard a ripping sound, and I couldn't stop my body from responding.

I almost moaned, biting down on my lip.

Then he was touching me.

I felt the air against my clit, right before his tongue was there. He touched me with my shirt before another growl and the shirt was gone. His other hand came up and he shoved me down, all the way down. The back of my head was on his knees, but he cupped my back, yanking me up. I was arched for him, but he was tasting my clit, his tongue sweeping inside.

I couldn't hold much longer.

A dark pleasure was building. He was sending it through my whole body. I was for him, to do with what he pleased. My legs were trembling. My whole body was shaking. I kept biting down on my lip, trying not to make a sound, a cry, a scream. I needed the pain to keep me from coming.

Raize needed this dominance over me.

He thrust a finger inside abruptly as he shoved up from the chair.

I cried out from the shock, but my legs wrapped around his waist from reflex.

He was gripping my ass, keeping me in place, and he turned, putting me on the table. He wasn't gentle. This wasn't going to be that kind of night.

A second finger moved in, and he thrust deep, long, and he kept going.

He knew what he was doing. He was working me fast, he wanted me to come quick for him.

I opened my eyes, seeing his on mine, a stark hunger reflecting back at me.

He was in pain, it was buried deep down. His mother.

I reached out to touch him, cup the side of his face, but he caught my hand. Almost roughly, but he only caught it. His teeth bared a second, and he adjusted, a third finger shoving up and into me.

I opened my mouth, a guttural groan slipping out. But then Raize leaned over me, pressing my hand down to the table above my head, his hand still there, holding me captive.

He kept thrusting, working me, and I couldn't hold back.

I tried to squirm, lifting my leg higher around him, but he blocked my leg and kept thrusting. He was relentless, and then he leaned down. I felt his tongue at my clit and I couldn't hold back anymore. Ripping my hand free, I clasped onto his head with both of my hands, and he kept going.

A muffled scream burst out of me, and my feet found the table, pushing myself up.

I lifted myself even more into Raize's mouth and his fingers, but the release ripped through me. It was an almost out-of-body experience, and I could only gape, gasping for breath, as another scream tunneled down into my gut, leaving me in shambles from keeping quiet.

I got no time to adjust.

Raize reared back up, staring down at me.

His eyes were dark, hungry, angry. The lust was palpable, and this time we switched.

I was in the shadow. He was in the moonlight.

I saw everything, everything in him.

He rose up, tearing off his shirt, unbuckling his pants. He didn't push them down, just moved his boxers aside, took out his dick and stroked it. It was already rock hard, lying up against his stomach, but he ran his hand over it, watching me.

My body was still quaking from my release, but I was panting, my chest heaving up and down and I started to throb all over again.

Goddamn.

Every one of his muscles seemed to be straining as he was holding himself back.

I licked my lips.

I wanted that control, that restraint. I wanted anything dark and dangerous he had in him. I wanted him to unleash it on me.

Rising up, I was watching him back, daring him to take control again.

He didn't. He watched me come up to him. I was still on the table. He was standing between my legs, his hand moving up and down over himself but then it was my turn.

I replaced his hand, and bent down, my mouth going over his tip.

He sucked in his breath, and held still as I worked him.

Up and down. My hand moving around. Cupping the base. I was on his tip, sucking.

His hands grabbed the sides of my head, and his fingers sank in, tangling with my hair. He flexed, his hips moved closer to me and I sank in, taking him all the way in.

I made a choking sound, a deep grunt.

He started to pull out, I caught him, my hand going around, grabbing his ass. I kept him in place and then I pulled my mouth free.

I looked up, he was watching.

A deep and primal, possessive thrill seared me.

He was mine. *Mine.* No one else's.

I don't know what he saw in my eyes, but his flashed and my hand was knocked off his cock.

He bent, grabbed me, and I was up in the air.

He tipped me over his shoulder, one of his hands shoving up between my legs, his fingers back inside of me as he carried me from the kitchen to our room.

I was slammed against the door.

My legs were kicked apart.

He bent down, pulled me out, and then he slid inside.

I couldn't stop my groan this time, and he didn't quiet me.

His hand wrapped around my front, cupping my throat, and he held me in place as he fucked me.

I TOLD HIM LATER, when my body was so tired and my brain could barely function. "I love you."

It was important that he knew, especially tonight.

He froze, then rolled to me. He lifted his head, searched me, and then rolled on top of me.

———

"I LOVE YOU BACK." He said it back to me right before we passed out.

The sun had long ago rose. I ceased caring.

I just thought, *Good.*

I knew, deep down, but it was good to hear.

———

WAKING, I knew Raize wasn't with me. I rolled over, looking, but the room was empty. Glancing at the clock, I'd only been asleep a few hours and hearing noises from the kitchen, I knew the guys were up. Making quick work in the bathroom, washing, cleaning, and I pulled on clothes before heading out.

I wasn't sure what I'd find, but I wasn't quite prepared.

Blueprints were spread out on the table.

Cavers had something cooking on the stove.

I was assuming Jake had made coffee since I could smell a fresh pot being brewed.

Gus was chewing on a bone smack in the middle of the kitchen, his back legs spread out and his front two holding the bone up for him.

Jake and Cavers were dressed, ready to go.

Raize had his jeans on, and that was it.

His gun was on the table at his side, but he was shirtless and I could see evidence from our lovemaking last night. Yeah... I wasn't focusing on that, or the fact that Jake and Cavers both knew where those marks came from.

Moving on.

I also was so very not thinking about what they heard last night. Denial was my friend this morning.

"What's going on?"

All three heads lifted or turned my way.

Jake and Raize were going over the blueprints.

Gus' tail started thumping against the floor, but he didn't stop chewing on his bone.

"Morning. I made coffee." Jake gestured to the coffee pot.

We'd taken to bringing one with us, and kept stocking from almost every gas station we stopped at.

Cavers angled his head around the guys, holding a wooden spoon in hand. "I'm making omelets. You want anything special on yours?"

Omelets? The morning after Raize found out his mother was killed?

I just shook my head. "No, thank you." I moved to the coffee machine.

Raize didn't greet me, but I felt his gaze on me until I had my coffee in hand and I leaned against the counter, looking at his over my mug. He'd been waiting for that look, and his gaze swept over me before becoming hooded again. He turned back to the blueprints.

Jake flashed me a grin. "We got a new mission. Your boy share the details with you? We're going international, baby."

I slightly grinned back at Jake, but then Raize straightened. "Don't call her that."

Jake's eyes got wide, and he stepped back from the table. "I wasn't thinking." He held up his free hand. His other hand had a mug of coffee in it. "No disrespect intended."

Raize frowned at him, side-eyeing him. "Have you handled your shit with your woman yet?"

The grin was wiped clean from Jake. He lowered his hand, and his mouth went firm. He shook his head briefly. "I made that call about my mom, but I've not handled it yet. I will."

Raize gave him a brief nod before returning to the blueprints.

"What are you looking at?" I asked as I moved to stand on Raize's other side, sliding onto a chair with its back to the wall. I was facing where Raize was standing, but rested my coffee on the table by his gun. I moved that over, too, just an inch.

"This is Marco's main estate."

My eyebrows shot up. "You got blueprints for that?"

"I got 'em before I left there." His eyes were steadily on mine. "I knew what I was leaving behind."

Right.

I glanced at the guys and neither seemed to be paying attention. Cavers was still cooking. Jake was looking toward the living room, lost in his thoughts.

Gus, well, he was infatuated with his bone.

Cavers brought over a plate and handed it to Jake before asking, "When do we leave?"

Raize glanced my way, then to Cavers. "This has to be swift and fast. Eat, then pack, and clean. We go in an hour."

Jake paused before he took a bite of his omelet. "Do we not want to cross over at night?"

"Going down isn't an issue. We'll cross south of Phoenix."

Cavers nodded. Jake went back to eating.

I was the only one who kept watching Raize, and he went back to studying the blueprints.

I knew he'd have everything figured out if he didn't already, but we'd do what we did by now.

We'd go down. We'd get his sister. We'd come back up.

There might be some casualties. I was willing to bet it wouldn't be on our side, and then we'd handle it afterwards.

Raize said before that we were going to war, but that statement was about Roman going after his brothers. But this move, this was the first on a chess board and this was the first act of a whole different war.

And I was in love with Raize.

I'd follow him into any type of war.

As if sensing my thoughts, he didn't look at me, but he reached out and his hand intertwined with mine. Two of his fingers curled around mine.

We stayed like that until everyone was done with breakfast.

After that, it was time to start another war.

52

ASH

We didn't fly, but drove.

I was assuming the large arsenal of weapons in our two trucks were the main reason. Just a guess. Raize drove. I kept him company. Every six hours, we'd switch.

Jake liked gossiping. He mentioned once it was the romantic side in him. I wasn't sure if I agreed, but okay then. I got him to open up about his woman.

She was named Tracy.

She was a hairstylist.

She was funny.

A romantic.

She would snort when he'd tickle her.

She was also a reformed biker woman, but I didn't know what that meant.

I wasn't sure if Jake knew either.

She had big hair, and he missed her.

He didn't tell me that last part, but it was easy to figure out. Once he started talking about her, he wouldn't stop. When it got to Cavers, he was more quiet, but I found out that he was not into women.

"Really?" I sat almost facing him. "I had no idea."

He kept facing forward, only glancing at me with the faintest of grins. He tightened his hold on the steering wheel. "Why's that surprising?" He shrugged his big massive shoulder. "I'm strictly dickly." That got a full smile from him.

I smiled back. "Do the guys know?"

His head folded down on that, just a bit. "Raize does. He gives no fucks about who I fuck, which is cool because that's not always the case. Especially in this world."

He hadn't mentioned Jake.

I did then. "And Jake?"

He was quiet, still not commenting.

But, another shrug and his jaw tightened. "He made a 'gay' comment the other day, but I can't tell if he'll care. He might've just said it, not thinking. Some guys are like that, but... no. He doesn't know."

That sucked. A lot.

"Are you seeing anyone?"

He shook his head. "No. Not for a while. This life, it's too hard. I mean, it's not hard. There's apps, but I don't know. We've been locked down for so long and before that, I didn't know if I was going to live after I got sent to work for Raize. Bronski's a fucking dick. You worked for him?"

My gut tightened. So did my jaw. "For a few days."

"That's good." He glanced over, giving me a sad smile. "That it was only for a few days."

"I shot him."

He nodded, that smile turning grave. "I heard."

"Yeah."

We drove in silence after that. Somehow the need to fill the space wasn't there anymore and it was another two hours before I spoke up.

"Are you the boyfriend kind of guy or having fun type of guy?"

Cavers started laughing, the sound ripping through the cab.

The entire mood lifted and once his laughter faded, he said, "I'm both, and when I start seeing someone serious, you're the first one I want him to meet."

"Good." Then, "Raize knew?"

He nodded. "He saw a guy checking me out at a gas station. The only thing he said was that if I fuck someone, to keep my mouth shut about all of us and no relationships. Jake broke that rule."

Yeah. *Jake* was the one to break that rule.

"He really likes her, you know."

"Who?" The words were out before I caught myself. I knew who he was talking about the second I asked. I flushed. "I know."

"That's going to be a problem."

Another nod from me, and this one felt heavier than the last. "I know."

"Raize finds out, he'll go back and kill her."

I looked at him.

He was watching me, but turned back to the road ahead. "She ain't you. Don't know a lot of females who could get where you are. Jake either has to disappear or she will."

Yeah...

"Jake doesn't love her, but he likes her and that's the problem. His situation is an all or nothing sort of situation, but he ain't treating it like that. He's not thinking right. He doesn't believe Raize will go back and kill her. He thinks she's in the clear, but it takes one time, one moment when she gets curious."

Each word he said was making me shrink into my seat. Further and further until I felt so small.

"I know, Cave."

"He got mad at me for almost shooting Raize and I got it. I understood it. This world, Raize is keeping us alive. We go anywhere else and we're disposable. Just another guard with a gun. Raize treats us differently and Jake and I both know it's because of you. You changed the game. You and him. I don't want Jake fucking that up."

"We'll handle it. Somehow."

He glanced over, holding my gaze, and I knew he was thinking we wouldn't.

We rode in silence after that.

53

RAIZE

Only I went into Mexico.

I had the others stay behind. I couldn't risk Ash coming with me. She'd attract attention. Even though she hadn't changed her hair color back to blonde, there was an air to her that guys liked. She gave off class, elegance, but also a toughness and mystery. It was the mystery that drew guys to her. Jake and Cavers both gravitated toward her since the beginning, and it became even stronger after she stood against me to save Jake's life. They were loyal to me, but they were more loyal to her. And me traveling with the entire group would draw even more attention.

I kept with the lone wolf scenario, but as soon as I was past customs, I made a call.

A day later, a guy walked into a cantina and he swept the room.

Seeing me, he stepped back outside.

I followed him.

He was waiting, but we didn't talk.

I passed him, making my way to the motel and once inside, he stepped through the door.

The door was closed.

The light switched on and I held up my hand.

Abram shook his head, but smirked. His hand fit mine and we drew together, clasping each other on the back. Stepping back, he rolled his eyes, readjusting his baseball cap. *"Estas loco hombre."*

I nodded. I was. But we had business to handle.

"I didn't know if you'd pick up my call."

Abram gave me a long and hard look before sitting down at the table. He stretched his legs out, putting his gun on the table. He was still giving me that look.

I didn't move.

He shook his head again. "I considered not, because if I answer and don't report your call, you know it could go."

I still waited. I knew Abram. He had something to say, he'd say it. He'd just take forever saying it.

He glanced away, moving the curtain and glancing outside before letting it fall back in place. "Seriously, brother. Marco is out of control."

There it was. That's the real reason he took my call.

I got comfortable, leaning against the wall. "Where's my sister?"

"He's got her at his place in Guaymas."

"He's got one detail on her?"

A nod from him. "Four guys, plus the usual security team at his place, but that's his tourist place. He doesn't think anyone will touch it."

That was good, real good.

Abram added, "He's not expecting this."

"He's not expecting me?"

"He's expecting you, but not this way. You take Verónica and he's going to lose it. She's his *hermana*, but he's got a weird owner-ship over her."

I shrugged. It wasn't that unusual. "I'm sure he's hoping to marry her off to another cartel, make an alliance."

"He shot that chance taking out Morales. The other cartels are watching him to see what he'll do. He's already moved in on all the Morales ports. It came out that he was Morales' *hijo*."

"How was that received?"

A shrug from him. "There was less resistance to the transition. I think that's all that was achieved, also made sense to the other cartels about why Morales let Marco live so long and how he expanded so fast." He leaned forward. "But, *compadre*, I'm telling you, they are wary of him."

I eyed him, hearing what he wasn't saying to me. "You think a cartel war is going to happen?"

"Unless he leaves them alone and focuses only on moving north? Which, I don't think they think he'll do."

"But that's his plan."

Abram gave a wary nod. "I think so. He's pissed that his distributors up north were taken out. Blames you. *Does not* like your boss." He whistled, shaking his head. "I gotta say, I'd be shocked if he doesn't send sicarios after you and your boss at the same time."

I figured he'd go that route, but not after both of us. I'd need to warn Downer.

I asked, "You know who he'd send?"

He eyed me, then a stiff and slow nod. "I do."

I'd ask for those names after we handled this first order of business. "We have to move. Did you do what I asked?"

He paused, not answering, and then, "She knows you're coming and if we leave, we'll get there in the window she gave us for the approach."

That's what I assumed, coming in earlier so I could rest and scout the area. I needed to make sure Abram was coming in on his own. If I'd seen more police activity or any added Estrada men, I wasn't going to do the meet for Abram. He didn't know this, but I would've bugged him and tracked him, finding my sister on my own and making my own approach. Using him had been a risk, but I needed to see if he'd be an asset for me later.

"Raize."

I narrowed my eyes, hearing a sudden seriousness come from him. "Yeah?"

As if reading my mind, he said, "I know you want to use me against Marco, but I can't do that."

Alarm hitched inside of me. I straightened from the wall. "What do you mean?"

"You called and I knew I either had to turn you into Marco or go with you." He stood, picking up his gun. "Marco's going through his men like candy. He's either popping 'em or tossing them out. He's dangerous right now. I can't stay with him. He knows you and I were friends back in the day, that I did reach out for you in Texas. I'm shocked he hasn't ordered my execution by now."

Now it made sense. Some of the tension eased in me. "You're deflecting?"

"I gotta come with you. I've heard about your boss, heard he's ambitious. I figure if you're still working for him, that says something to you. You think he'd take me on?"

Now we were in a whole different game here.

Abram might've reported my call to Marco, and now Marco was being smart, trying to insert one of his men into Roman's employment. Or not and Abram was being genuine, needing protection when he deflected.

"You still in love with my sister?"

Abram's eyes got big, and a surprised bark left him. "How'd you know that?"

"You've been in love with her for years, the only reason I could think that you stayed with Marco when I left." It'd been a hunch, until now. "Marco doesn't know?"

"Hell no." A hollow laugh ripped from Abram. "He's—you're right. He's eyeing the Colombians to marry her off, and make an alliance with them. When she goes, there goes that connection and they're going to take it personal. When you whisk her off, he could be facing a war against them, too. You called and stated your case, I knew this was the right path. Not just for Verónica, but this is the move that'll cripple Marco enough where he might lose some of his power. You're going to be striking a blow, taking out one of his knees. He'll fall and we can then see who pounces on him, if they keep him down or not. Everyone's going to be watching and everyone's going to know who you are, and what you did. There's no going back after this, if we get her and get out safely."

"We will."

Another laugh from him, this one short and clipped. "Let's see, brother. But you gotta know that there's no turning back for you either. You'll either have to go all the way up the ladder or you become a ghost."

A vision of Ash flared in my mind.

I firmed my jaw. "Let's get Verónica first, and after that, if you're with us, then you're with us all the way. I got people in place. We just have to get across the border."

A short nod from him. "Sounds good." He checked his watch. "We have to go, or we'll have to wait another twenty-four hours to move in for her."

"Okay."

We had a four-hour ride ahead of us.

54

ASH

TWELVE HOURS LATER

W e were in Nogales, on the Arizona side when the call came in.

I answered, knowing it was one of Raize's burners. "Are you okay?"

Loud and harsh wind thundered over the phone first, then I heard him shouting. "You need to move. Now! Marco has men on the US side and they're looking for you."

I bolted upright from where I'd been sitting. The phone was clenched against my head, but I drew both Jake and Cavers' attention. I stood. "What's going on?" I didn't wait, already waving to both of them and pointing to our bags. I said to them, "We have to go now."

"Now?"

"Now!"

Jake clipped his head, but Cavers hadn't questioned me. He immediately grabbed a bag and threw open the door, running the bags out. I needed to free up a hand, so I plugged in a bluetooth earpiece that Jake had insisted we buy and stuffed my phone into my pocket.

"I'm here," I said to Raize as I ran to grab my things, and what items he left behind.

Gus started barking in the background.

I asked, "You got you—her?"

I winced, looking, but Cavers wasn't in the room and Jake didn't seem like he'd noticed I almost slipped. I didn't know when or how or where or even if Raize was going to fill them in, but that was not my decision.

"We got her, but as soon as we went through the border, an alert sounded. Abram's phone went crazy with texts. They know you're in Nogales and I'm sure they're thinking she's with you."

We had a cartel team heading our way. Lovely.

I was finishing grabbing the last of the weapons he'd left behind, my bag thrown over my back.

Cavers dashed in, grabbed what bags were left and Jake took Gus.

I stood in the opened doorway, and turned back. "We need to clean this room."

Cavers came back in, throwing bleach everywhere. He yelled over his shoulder, "Go! Get in the truck."

I did, hurrying in.

Jake was in the driver's seat. He saw my bluetooth. "Is he still there?"

I nodded.

Jake ripped the earpiece from me and put it in his. "Boss. What's going on?"

Since they were talking, I stashed my bags into the back area.

Gus was standing in the truck's bed, his head through the opened window. He started licking my face.

Then Cavers ran out, threw himself into the back with Gus, and pounded the side. "GO!"

Jake bit out a curse, but punched the acceleration and we were off.

He started yelling, driving at the same time. "Where?"

He swung through a parking lot, and soared over another one and then we were fishtailing and going in the opposite direction.

I cursed, seeing police. "Stop, Jake!" I pointed him out.

Jake cursed, too, but immediately hit another alley just as the cop was turning the corner. We were far enough up he might not have seen us, but just in case, Jake swung into another parking lot and turned onto the next street, going in the complete opposite direction. This time, he was moving at a more normal speed.

Cavers hit the window behind us.

I turned around to see him shooting Jake a glare. "What the fuck?" He had a tight hold on Gus, who was trying to break free.

"Cop," I told him.

He nodded, moving back and settling in once more.

Jake mouthed to me, "Sorry" but he was still listening to Raize. Ten minutes later, he said, "Okay. We're on the freeway." He motioned for me to take the piece. "Boss wants you now."

I fitted it back in my ear. "Where are you?"

"We're outside of the city. You guys are meeting us north of town, at the second rest stop. It's a drive so tell Cavers to settle in. No cops. Nothing. Got it?"

"Got it."

He hung up as I was turning around to relay to Cavers what Raize said.

A moment later, he was sliding down so no passing cars could see a guy holding a dog in the back of a car and call it in for state patrol.

I put the bluetooth piece away, glaring at Jake. "Dude."

He grimaced. "I know. I'm sorry. I heard Cartel and panicked." He tossed Cavers a quick look. "You think he wiped that room down adequately?"

I shrugged. "I don't know, but we didn't do anything. Let's hope it gets missed."

He frowned. "Are we talking cops or cartel?"

"I don't think cartels can wipe for any DNA traces."

"You'd be surprised what they can do."

True, but I didn't want to know.

I said, sliding down and trying to get comfortable, "We're in one piece. Raize said they're in one piece. Let's just get there and figure out what to do."

"He said, 'We got her.'"

"What?"

Jake was watching me, studying me before he turned back to the road. "He said 'we' when it should've been 'I got her.' Who's with him?"

I got quiet. But, dammit. "Why are you asking?"

He frowned again, then his eyebrows shot up. "You kidding me? We're back to this paranoia shit? I thought we were over that."

"If it's someone coming with Raize, then that's all you need to know. So I gotta ask again, why are you asking?"

"I'm asking to see if you know, and it's evident you do. You knew before he took off or are you just as surprised as me? Our boss isn't one to work with someone random."

I still didn't know why he was asking. "Interrogate Raize when we see him. I might know who it is, but I don't know any of the specifics and I don't feel comfortable about you asking me all of this. You either trust Raize or you don't."

I was studying him as I said that last part, and he got tight around the mouth.

That was it.

He didn't trust Raize.

Why didn't he trust Raize? When had this changed?

Then a different thought occurred to me. "Is this because of your woman?"

He jerked, his head whipping to mine. "What?"

It was about his woman.

This wasn't good, not at all.

"Are you not going to cut her loose?"

His jaw clenched, and his hand tightened over the steering wheel. He jerked up a shoulder, roughly. "I don't know. It's probably the wrong time to be having this conversation, considering we're running from a cartel. You know?"

"Just don't do anything stupid. Please talk to me or Cavers before you do?"

He sent me a restrained grin. "Gus count?"

I grinned. "Maybe."

He chuckled, but it was strained.

WE GOT to the rest stop, parking on one side of the building.

Jake started to reach for Gus' leash, but I got there first. "I'll walk him. You guys go ahead."

Cavers shot me a frown, but headed inside right away.

Jake was looking around. "Single woman looking like you out here isn't a good idea."

"Go. I'll be fine."

Jake had no clue what Gus was capable of. I did.

He nodded, his hand massaging the back of his neck as he went after Cavers.

I took Gus to a patch of grass, set up on a small hill so I could see who was coming in and out.

It wasn't long before I saw Raize was heading toward me from the opposite side of the hill. I hadn't noticed them parking.

Abram and a girl I was assuming was Raize's sister were walking for the rest stop. Abram had his arm around her, tucked into his side.

I watched them, seeing how her head rested against his chest a second and his hand dipped, rubbing a spot on her back.

That was... interesting.

"Guys inside?" Raize got to me, and bent down, brushing a

kiss over my lips before straightening, Gus' leash now in his hand.

I nodded and went back to watching Abram and Raize's sister.

She was tiny. Petite. Long black hair. She was in a dress and sandals.

I wouldn't expect those kinds of clothes if she'd been planning on running.

Raize looked where I was looking, and guessed accurately what I was thinking. "You got extra clothes she could borrow?"

I had to laugh at that, too. "Yeah."

"Why's that funny?"

"Because not long ago, I was the girl you had to take shopping when I had nothing."

"Oh. Yeah."

I gave him an appraisal. He sounded tired, and he looked tired, but there was more. "What is it?"

He focused on me again, blinking a few times. "What?"

"Something extra is going on with you. What is it?"

He didn't answer right away, his eyes trailing ahead even though Abram and his sister were inside by now. Cavers had come out, and he was heading our way.

"Just... we didn't have time to talk. We got her and took off right away. There was the car ride, but she was sobbing the whole time. And she wouldn't let me comfort her so Abram held her while I drove. I have no clue how to handle her."

Oh.

I reached for his hand, giving it a squeeze as Gus squatted to poop.

I ran my thumb over the back of his hand. "She's not thinking clear. That's all."

He tried to smile back, but it was taking effort from him. He ran his thumb over the back of my hand instead, and our hands fell apart as Cavers got to us.

"Boss. Nice to see you alive." He gestured to Gus. "Want me to take him?"

Raize handed over the leash. "We'll be a bit."

"Got it."

I didn't know if I should mention Jake, but then it didn't matter. Jake was coming out of the restrooms. Seeing us, he headed right for us. He skimmed over Raize, then looked for his truck.

"Boss," he greeted with a small upward chin lift.

Raize's eyes narrowed slightly. "Give us a second."

"Okay."

That was the exchange, but I looked back, noting Jake's tension. His shoulders were rigid. When I turned back, Raize had been watching me. "You want to fill me in?"

I opened my mouth, but then Abram was coming our way.

I shut it, just as he got to us, looking toward the women's restroom.

"Hey," he breezed, then did a slight twitch as he realized who I was. His eyebrows dipped in. "You look different."

"Different hair."

"Ah." His eyes lit up with comprehension. "No offense, but I liked the blonde."

I grinned. "Me, too. I'm going back."

Raize gave me a soft grin,before losing it. He asked Abram, "How is she?"

Abram gave him a wary and tired look, a very tired look. "It was bad for her at times."

"What do you mean?"

Abram was eyeing the women's door. "Let's talk later, yeah? Get to safety and then start debriefing all this shit because bruh, it's a lot of shit we gotta digest."

Raize grunted, then nodded to me. "Check on her, but don't approach."

"Got it."

He went his way and I went mine, and when I went in, I almost walked into the wall.

The girl standing at the mirror, staring at herself, was Raize's twin. Or the female version of him.

She was smaller, which I already knew. Her hair was dark and it hung limply down to the middle of her back, but her eyes were dead. Her cheekbones were gaunt. She had beautiful brown eyes, the same full lips as her brother, but her face was a little more rounded than Raize. His was hard with a firm and square jawline, but with the eyes, the mouth, the cheekbones, she was Raize's blood.

The guys would figure it out the second they saw her. All hell would break loose after.

I suppressed a shiver, not wanting to get ahead of myself with those fireworks.

I forced myself to keep going, into a stall and sat, but I didn't pee. I didn't know why I was waiting, but she hadn't moved when I went past her. She choked out a sob before the water turned on, but when she turned it off, she didn't let out another sound. She washed her hands, grabbed a towel, and slipped outside. All quiet-like, or as quiet as she could be.

I thought back.

I had stopped and stared at her. She hadn't noticed. Those eyes weren't even seeing herself, I didn't think.

Was the dead staring thing a family trait?

I was thinking it wasn't.

55

ASH

No fireworks happened after I came out of the restroom.

Cavers, Gus, and Jake were in our truck.

Abram and Raize's sister were in theirs.

Raize was waiting for me, studying both trucks. His attention moved to me as I came to his side and he touched under my chin. "You want to explain Jake's attitude toward me?"

I sucked in my breath. "I thought you'd wait."

His eyes barely flickered. "What's up?"

"I don't know. You said 'we' when you were referencing that you got your sister out and Jake asked me who was with you."

"Did you tell him?"

I shook my head. "He knows I know who was with you, but nothing else."

"You told him about Abram?"

"No, just that I thought I knew who the person was that was with you. That's it, literally. I didn't know, you know, but Abram made sense."

He started to step back, but I caught his shirt, holding him in place.

My chest tightened. I didn't like what I was about to do, but...
Raize had to know.

"He hasn't cut off his woman."

Raize tensed. "What?"

"He called her, told her the lie about his grandmother, but
he's been talking about her."

God.

What was I doing?

Had I just signed her death warrant? Because Raize would not
let it stand, especially now with his sister in the mix.

"And he's pissed, thinking I've been lying to him?"

"Well. Yeah."

Raize cursed under his breath, then sighed. "We'll deal with
this later. Go with them."

"Where are we going?"

"There's a safehouse I know in Colorado."

"Why Colorado? That's like, a twelve-hour drive."

He scanned over me, his mouth growing tight, but then he
sighed. "Because I want to be as far away from this border as I can
be, and somewhere that's nowhere close to the East Coast or
Texas."

"Well. Then. That makes sense."

He grinned, his eyes softening before he patted me on the ass.
"Get going. Sleep if you can, alright?"

I gave a small grin back. "You too."

He ran a hand over his jaw. "If my sister doesn't freak out that
her arm might touch mine, I'll try to get a nap in."

He leaned down, giving me another soft kiss, before we
parted.

SOME GUY

THAT GIRL...

A man stared at her. She was pretty. She looked like she knew the guy she was with, and he leaned down to give her a kiss. She smiled at him.

But then she turned and he saw her whole face.

He rocked back, stunned, but yeah.

He stared at the missing girl's poster pinned to the board in front of him. It *was* her.

Well, golly gee, his aunt's bee in a bonnet.

He pulled out his phone and dialed the number, hoping there was some sort of reward.

56

RAIZE

Verónica either slept or sobbed.

We stopped to fill up with gas, but she remained inside the car. Abram tried to get her out. She wouldn't go, kept saying in Spanish that she didn't need to go to the bathroom. We left her alone, and when she realized Abram was going to spot me, let me try to sleep, she scooted as close to him as possible. A bag was wedged between her and myself.

At that point, I started wondering why I got her out, and then Ash's face flashed in my mind right away. She did more than this for her sister, and she hadn't even seen her sister once Brooke was pulled out. Then again, there was no newsflash there. Ash was ten times the person I was.

Abram caught my look and said under his breath, "*Mantén el calmo mi compadre.*"

I grunted. "*Si, si. Solo estoy cansado.*"

Verónica settled after that, and I caught her sneaking a look at me a couple times.

I did what Abram told me to do. I calmed down, and what I said was true. I was tired enough where I was able to ignore my sister's constant tension and get some sleep. I needed it from the drive to Nogales, then to Guaymas, and we'd been on the run since.

When I woke, it was an hour later.

Verónica was passed out, her head resting against Abram's shoulder, and I took care when I stretched my legs. I studied her a bit, seeing traces of my sister in her face.

"I don't want to alarm you, but we're following a car."

"What?" I straightened.

There were two vehicles between us and Ash's truck. A small green compact and another truck, one that looked beat up. Two males were inside, both wearing cowboy hats.

Abram was speaking softly, and indicated ahead. "The green compact. It was behind us for a while, then when I fell behind, it went around. It's following your girl."

I took out my phone.

"I thought it was just local authorities looking for her."

He grunted. "Thinking it's not so local anymore. She's pretty. She still sticks out."

I knew what he meant, but I was dialing Ash's number.

"Did you get some sleep?"

"A bit, but listen. Put me on speaker."

I heard a button get pressed. Her voice sounded louder, "You're on."

"Who's driving?"

"Me." Cavers.

I frowned, looking at the back of their truck. "Where's Gus?"

Ash started laughing. "We brought him in. He's half on Jake's lap and mostly on mine."

"You're by the door?"

She was quiet.

Jake came on, more serious. "What's going on, boss?"

"You're being followed."

"I thought we were," Cavers added. "They came up on us thirty minutes ago, but haven't been moving anywhere. Just looks like a single guy. Can't tell if he's talking to someone else or not."

"What do you want us to do?"

Verónica was stirring, and I prepared myself for her horror at realizing I was beside her. She didn't do that this time, only blinking her eyes at me, bags under her eyes and her eyes took in the phone in my hand.

I asked Abram, "What are you thinking?"

"I can't see that being one of Marco's. It'd be a whole team or he'd go ahead, call it in and then a slew of vehicles would swarm in."

"They're behind our vehicle, not yours." That was from Jake.

Ash said, "I was on that hill."

That's what I was thinking, too. "Fall behind us. Let's see what that car does."

"And if he keeps going?" Jake.

"We take the next exit and haul ass. Stick to county roads."

"Got it."

"Leave the line open, just in case."

"Will do. I'm falling back now."

We hit the passing lane.

The green kept on them.

As we passed, the truck fell in behind us and then went ahead of us.

The green car, it stayed.

"They're sticking to us."

I said to Abram, "I want to drive."

"What? I got skills."

"Now."

He growled, but then nodded to Verónica. "Move over, V."

She didn't say anything, but then I opened the back window and crawled out.

Abram and I had done this before, a long time ago so he knew the procedure.

Opening his window, he moved over as much as possible, but still held the wheel.

I poised on the edge of the truck, grabbed under the door and then flipped around and back inside. My feet went first and went down immediately, touching the ground as I grabbed the wheel from Abram.

The truck had started to slow, so I hit the accelerator.

After that, I went back to the passing lane and hit the brakes.

I wanted to see who was in that green car.

"Raize!" Ash was yelling from the phone. "You're fucking insane!"

I smothered a chuckle. That'd really piss her off.

Abram chuckled. "Your blonde's still *loca*. I like that."

I flipped him my middle finger, and I was shocked to hear my sister let out a small giggle. Looking over, she had her head pressed into Abram's arm. She was holding the phone up as he had his gun pulled out, laying on his lap.

From the phone, I could hear Jake. "How'd he know your hair used to be blonde?"

"Shut up. One crisis at a time here. Did you not just see that Raize crawled out of their truck and crawled back in through the window?!" Ash's voice was rising.

"Yeah." Jake laughed. "That was awesome."

Cavers snorted, but must've taken the phone. His voice was more clear, closer. "What do you want us to do, boss?"

"I'm going to ram him, see what he'll do. If you see an exit, take it."

"You serious?"

I got behind the green car, hit the turn signal, and said, "Yes."

Then I hit the accelerator.

ASH

I DID NOT LIKE THIS. Not one bit.

Panic was rising up in me, clawing over my throat.

I'd just watched Raize go *out* of their truck and slide back *inside,* from the outside. Which meant he'd been on the *outside* of a moving vehicle. And we weren't taking a Sunday drive here. Speeds were interstate speeds. That meant *hella-freaking-fast!*

It was insane.

Crazy! Abram was right.

I wanted to murder Raize myself.

And then we proceeded to watch as he hit the back of the green car.

A bump, then he fell back and I knew he was waiting.

My heart was trying to pump out of me. "Oh my gawd, Raize. I'm going to kill you."

I couldn't handle this.

The green car swerved, ran onto the shoulder, then over-corrected and went into the passing lane. All the while, Raize's truck held back, waiting, being so controlled.

Once the green car was back on the highway, Raize was right behind it. Another bump, not as gentle as the first one. And again, he fell back to see the reaction.

He didn't wait long.

A gunshot sounded from the green car, and after that, it was over for him.

Raize rammed the car sideways, herding it off the highway and into the ditch. He kept pushing it. More gunshots came out and Raize's front window shattered.

Someone was screaming.

Probably me.

I could just make out the tops of Abram and Raize's sister's heads. They were crouched down, but Abram had a gun pointing over the dashboard, aimed out. I could see Raize directing him where to shoot, and I saw him say, "Now!"

A shot went out.

I couldn't watch this.

No way.

My hands were over my face, my fingers spread wide.

Oh my gawd.

Oh my God!

The green car jerked to the side, then Raize backed off and let it ram to a stop at the bottom of the ditch. There were giant rocks on the side. The car scraped against them. Once the car stopped, Raize braked abruptly behind it, the truck half blocking the car from any onlookers, and he was out and running to check on the driver.

His gun was drawn, pointing.

Abram ran out from the other side. As Raize approached from the far side, Abram moved in from the south.

Cavers was cursing, wheeling our own truck over and we all piled out.

"Clear!" Raize yelled at the same time as Abram and both went into the car.

The door was yanked open.

Raize was checking on the guy, but as I started to stop and see what I could do, Cavers grabbed my elbow. He pulled me with him.

Jake was ahead of us.

Gus—GUS! Where was Gus? But he was right beside me. Then he was darting forward, barking by Jake's heels.

That's when I got what Jake and Cavers were doing. They were grabbing anything that was in Raize's truck. His sister started screaming at the sight of both of them, but they ignored her, grabbing the bags and sprinting back to the truck.

Raize had pulled the guy out, laying him on the side of the road by now.

Abram was inside the car.

But then I was at the opened side door and Raize's sister was staring at me, tears streaked over her face. She was trembling.

Two hands reached inside my chest, took hold of my heart, and began squishing it together.

I was almost crying for her.

She was muttering something in Spanish. I couldn't make it out, but I edged closer and held up a hand. "I'm a friend of Raize's. Abram's, too."

At Abram's name, she quieted and looked at the car.

She blinked a few more times and straightened with each one. I knew what she was seeing. She was seeing her brother, but she was seeing Jake and Cavers running behind him and her brother not being alarmed by them. And he'd had us on speaker so she knew they were traveling with another vehicle.

I edged closer, my hand steady. "Come with me? *Por favor?*"

Jake darted in, grabbed a bag around me, and sprinted right back.

Cavers did the same from the other side of her, and by the time they were back for another trip, her hand was in mine and I had her out of the truck. We ran to the other one and climbed in.

After that, Cavers grabbed some gasoline. He went back and doused the other.

Raize and Abram were carrying the other guy with them, putting him into the back of ours and Cavers was dousing the car, too.

Blankets were pulled out, and spread out in the back. The guy was hoisted up.

Jake yelled at Raize, "Who do you want to drive?"

Raize was still bent over the guy, but looked up, checking out where we were.

He grimaced, then motioned for me. "You need to be on the outside. V on the inside." He hopped off the truck and grabbed the keys Jake was holding out for him.

I motioned for her to step out. She did, barely reacting. As soon as my feet touched gravel, she was going around me and into the middle. I hopped up, shutting the door.

He came in, starting the engine. "Lock your door, Ash."

I did.

V blinked again, looking between him and me.

I had no idea what was going on in her head.

Jake and Abram both hopped into the back, and Raize started edging forward.

Cavers had been waiting, but he lit a spark and tossed it into one car, then another.

Both were steadily smoking when he jumped in the back.

Raize hit the acceleration and we gunned forward.

We'd gone half a mile when the first car exploded.

A second one followed almost right after.

Then we were off, because who knew who that would attract.

ASH

We were off on the first exit, and driving as fast as we could down the back roads.

Once we hit the next big city, Raize pulled into a run-down motel. We got a room, and he pulled the truck to the back. No one said a word, Abram included. He was moving right along with everyone as bags were taken in. They brought the guy in, hands tied, duct-taped and a bag over his head, but he wasn't moving. He was breathing so that meant he was still unconscious.

Jake was sent out to buy another cheap vehicle with cash. The faster the better, and once inside the room, Raize hit the showers first. I went with him, but we were all business. A few slips might've happened. He might've needed me to get a couple extra spots, and vice versa.

Both of us were grinning when we stepped outside, but then we were changing into new clothes.

Abram jumped in after.

V waited, sitting in the corner on one of the beds.

Cavers was after Abram.

I didn't know the extent of how much English V might know. I was assuming she knew some since she understood me earlier, and also Raize, but still, I was going with what was the simplest action. I took out some extra clothes and handed them to her, giving her a nod and a small grin when she looked at them.

Raize rattled off something in Spanish.

She took the clothes from me, a returned smile back, then went to stand outside of the bathroom.

Cavers made quick work, and she slipped inside after.

Abram said something to Raize, and left the room.

"What was that?" I asked him.

He glanced at the closed bathroom door, but shook his head. "He's just making sure."

"What?" But I looked and ... that didn't make sense.

Make sure what?

Abram left...

A thought came to me and I almost gasped. "She'd leave?"

His words came out tight and clipped. "At this point, we don't know what she'll do."

I touched his arm and moved in close, lowering my voice. "She knows you saved her."

He paused, mid-packing his bag. "Did I, though?"

I squeezed his arm. "Yes." Feeling his bicep bulge under my touch, I slid my hand down, touching his and sliding my fingers through his. "Give her a beat. She'll come around."

He moved into me. His hand went to the back of my neck before sliding up into my hair. He murmured, his words husky as his forehead bent to mine, "Not everyone's you." Then his lips touched mine before he stepped back.

Cavers had stopped whatever he was doing, staring behind us.

I whirled.

Raize lifted his head.

His sister was in the opened bathroom door, my clothes on her, and a towel wrapped around her hair. She was staring right at us, her eyes back to not blinking, but then she did and she lowered her towel. *"Dónde está Abraham?"*

The hotel door opened and Raize nodded toward it. *"Aquí."*

Cavers took in the room and cleared his throat. "I'll—uh—I'll see if they have a vending machine."

He started for the door.

Raize said, "Wait." He bent, grabbed something from the bed, and tossed it to Cavers.

It was his wallet.

"There's fast food next door. Grab as much as you can carry."

He dipped his head. "Got it," and was gone.

Raize spoke, "You guys should both try to sleep. As soon as they're back, we'll be taking off again."

V congregated to the other bed, resuming her previous perch. She kept drying her hair, studying Raize, myself, and Abram, but she didn't respond.

Abram sighed. "When are you thinking we'll stop again?"

Raize didn't comment right away, but I felt how tense he was. After he finished repacking his bag, he zipped it up and tossed it to the floor by the door and then regarded Abram. "When I feel like I can breathe a little easier. That's when we'll stop."

Abram held his gaze for a long while.

I noticed that V had stopped drying her hair. She was now just holding the towel, but Raize was on the move again.

He went to the chair, tipped it back so he could see outside, and he tugged me with him. He pulled me on his lap, his gun on the table, and he moved the curtain to watch outside. He said without looking, his hand settling on my thigh, "You guys, sleep." He said this and urged my own head down and onto his shoulder, so I was figuring he meant me as well.

I wasn't going to argue.

I brought my legs up, curling into Raize's lap more comfortably. His arm moved up around me, anchoring me securely to him.

It wasn't long before I was sleeping.

———

THE SMELL of fast food woke me up, making my stomach growl.

I was being carried and then lifted into the back of another vehicle. Blinking, pushing past drowsiness, I saw that we were in a Suburban. With seats. And no one was on the outside.

Praise to the Gus.

And speaking of, his wet nose pushed into my face and I was given a Gus bath.

I took stock.

Cavers was driving.

Raize was next to him, and going through something in his seat.

I was in the next seat. Gus was with me, his tail thumping my seat and leg.

I looked back and Raize's sister and Abram were in the seat behind me. In the back was Jake, and with how he was sitting, I was betting the other guy was back there, too.

I went back to sleep.

———

WE DROVE through the rest of the day and night.

At one point, V, who I overheard was actually Verónica, but she told me to call her V, and I were stretched out in the second seat. Her head was at one side, her feet toward me, and I was the opposite. Our feet intertwined, but after a few hours, it didn't matter.

The 'guy' woke up a couple times, but he went unconscious right away.

When we stopped at a gas station, Raize brought me a coffee after I came back from using the bathroom.

I was sitting up, my coffee in hand, and I looked out.

Another car was just turning in, a few girls that looked like they were in college.

It took me back, to another time I saw another car with college girls inside, but I felt different this time. I *was* different. I was okay with where I was, who I was with.

If I'd lived that life, I wouldn't have met Raize.

In that moment, with that acceptance, I knew I'd never see my father and sister again. There might be a situation where I could go and view her from afar, but going up and talking with her— that was done. I was now fully accepting it. Raize had a guy keeping tabs on them for us, and I'd gotten a report that her charges were changed.

She was getting help now. Counseling.

But there was no going back for me.

Yes.

I lifted my coffee for a sip.

I was okay now.

Raize was getting in behind the wheel. It was his turn to drive and he turned back to me. He gave me a look, asking if I was all right.

I gave him a smile, settling in and taking another sip.

I felt him continue to study me, but it was fine. I was used to it. I *wanted* it.

Jake got in the front seat and he took in the exchange. He flicked his eyes upward, but he had a soft smile on his face as he did so.

Cavers grunted from behind me.

I knew Verónica and Abram were witnessing all of this, but it didn't matter.

I just kept sipping my coffee.

Gus jumped up and settled against me, stretching out and taking the rest of my seat.

No one argued with Gus.

58

RAIZE

"Where are you?"

We'd settled, finally, and I'd taken my phone outside with me as everyone was getting comfortable in a house that Jake rented for us.

I answered him now, "I was going to stop in Colorado, but we kept going. We're in Montana."

He was quiet for a beat. Then, a grating, "Where?! We're in Boston. Why the fuck are you in Montana?"

"Because Marco is going to send men after me. He already sent one and I want my sister to have disappeared before his next crew gets to me."

I was throwing a lot at him and I knew he was upset.

I got it. I did.

I was a soldier, but I was taking my own orders and I was explaining after the fact. Any other soldier, I'd be dead by morning.

I was banking on a whole lot that Roman wouldn't do that to me.

"He sent one after you already?"

I told him about the highway, what happened and added, "We

have the guy with us, but we've not questioned him. He has no ID, but his phone has an outgoing Mexican phone number. He had a police radio on him, too."

"You think he's a cop?"

"More like I think he was listening to the police scanner. We'll know more once we interrogate him."

"Right." He sighed. "Your sister. What's your plan there?"

"There's a network I know about. They hide people. I'd like to make contact, see if they'll hide Verónica."

"What network?"

I ignored that, saying, "That's the point. They typically hide people from people like us. I'm hoping they'll make an exception considering who my sister is hiding from."

"You're on a leash, Raize. Albeit, it's a long leash, but it's *still* a leash."

Meaning, he would tug on it eventually and if I didn't go back, he would send men after me as well. Probably Downer.

"I know."

"Use your woman to help interrogate him. She works for me as well now. I want to utilize her skill. When your sister is gone, report back here."

"Yes, sir."

"Immediately, Raize."

"Yes, sir."

"When you report to me in person, you're bringing your entire team. If you don't, you know what I'll do. You got me?"

"I got you."

The line disconnected after that, and I knew Jake was waiting inside the door.

He, Cavers, and Abram were all there, all waiting.

I gave them a nod.

At once, they walked outside, grabbed the guy and carried him to the garage.

I went inside and found Ash helping my sister make some food. "I'm going to need you."

Verónica froze, but Ash didn't.

She already knew and nodded. "Okay."

I said to Verónica, "You stay here."

Her eyes were big, taking in Ash and me.

I motioned to Gus, who came forward, his tail wagging. "You guard her."

He let his mouth open in a smile, that tail just got faster.

I left. Ash went with me.

Gus took position at the door.

Ash was quiet, following me to the garage and then inside, but I knew she was in turmoil. She wouldn't like seeing this anymore than I'd enjoy her seeing it. Still. This was the world we lived in.

The guys had him tied to a chair. He was awake, his mouth still duct-taped.

I gave the nod.

Abram ripped the tape off.

I started with my first question, "How'd you find us on the highway?"

He cursed in Spanish, spitting at me.

Okay, then.

Cavers had a bat in hand and I gave yet *another* nod.

The shit work was about to start.

59

ASH

The sounds of screaming, grunts, and sobbing filled the air.

The smell of blood, sweat, piss, and I didn't want to know what else filled the room.

And in me, I was nauseated but also annoyed.

Raize would ask a question. The guy wouldn't answer.

One of the guys would hurt him. Then the guy would answer.

I'd be asked if he was telling the truth, and after the tenth time of his lies being found out, the guy directed his threats and glares toward me.

Bad move.

That only pissed off Raize more. But also Jake and Cavers didn't take kindly to that so when the guy refused to answer, the guys got harsher in their punishment.

It was an hour into it, twenty minutes after I stopped watching what the guys did to him when he finally gave up. He confessed everything.

He'd been notified by someone in Marco's command to watch the highway on a small chance we got through. 'We' consisted of whoever had kidnapped Marco Estrada's sister. She was known as the Golden Goose to them, which Abram didn't like when the guy started to explain the reason she was called the Golden Goose. I didn't know what Abram did. This was at the time when I'd stopped watching, but I heard a tearing sound and then an animalistic scream ripped from the guy. It sounded especially worse than the other screams, which said a lot.

The guy went on to explain he hadn't known it was The Scooper who'd kidnapped her. He babbled on saying, "If I'd known, I never would've taken the job. No one wants to tangle with The Scoope—"

"Shut up," Raize growled.

A pause.

Then, from Jake, "How'd you know where to find us?"

He'd heard our location on the police scanner. "They were talking about a missing girl and they were on the lookout for your truck. I thought it was Estrada's *hermana*, but it wasn't. Wrong girl."

Jesus. Lucky break for him. Or not, considering his circumstances.

"What were your instructions if you found us?"

"I was supposed to call it in."

"Did you?"

He didn't answer, which was a wrong answer.

Thud!

I tensed. *Please stop lying.*

He started moaning, but choked out, "I did, but man, we're long gone. Estrada will never send men this far north."

There was silence after that. A long silence.

The guy asked, "What are you going to do with me?"

Raize came over and touched my arm. "You can go inside."

I nodded, suddenly exhausted. He brushed some of my hair back from my forehead and leaned in. I felt him give me a soft kiss to the forehead. "I'm sorry."

I didn't respond. I knew what he was apologizing for, and without responding, I left the garage.

It was dark when I stepped outside.

I realized I didn't know when we'd arrived here, what time it was now, or even what day it was anymore.

Then, I stopped wondering. It didn't matter in this life.

Going back into the house, the aroma of food was like culture shock after what I just left.

"I didn't know how long everyone would be out there."

More culture shock.

Raize's sister was standing in the kitchen, an apron tied around her waist, her hair pulled up into a bun, and she was looking normal. She was speaking normal, too. No sobs. No hysterics. No nothing. Her eyes were so big, so dark. They were Raize's eyes.

I blinked, jerking myself out of what dazed spell I was in and walked farther inside.

I stilled.

The table was set for six people.

Gus was laying on the floor, on his back, and his tail going back and forth. His tummy was exposed, his feet in the air.

I was guessing Verónica had just been rubbing his belly.

She smoothed a hand over her apron. "I—uh—I found some food in the cupboards. And that other man had brought some food from a gas station." She waved to the coffee machine. "And that, too. I noticed you all enjoy drinking your coffee, or most of you. The big guy doesn't as much. Clay doesn't either, not that much."

"Clay?"

She frowned at me. "Raize. You guys call him Raize."

In the span of an hour, I knew of two other names Raize went by. His first name and The Scooper.

I didn't know what to do with that information.

"Do you want to sit? I put it all together in a soup. There were crackers in the cupboard."

Soup?

I couldn't remember the last time I had soup, but I sat and she poured me a bowl, bringing it over to me. There were already crackers set out.

She poured herself a bowl, coming to sit across and down a few spaces from me. Her back wasn't totally toward the doorway this way and she kept looking over her shoulder.

"They'll be a while."

Man. I had soup and a guy was being tortured thirty yards from here.

I didn't know what to do with that information.

She moved to tuck some hair behind her ear, but it was all pulled up so her fingers finished the motion anyways before falling back to her bowl. She hunched over it, her head down.

"You're fluent?"

She looked up. "I went to boarding school. Private tutors, too. And then when Raize came, he and I practiced both languages. He knew Spanish, but it was choppy. He got a lot better fast. I like to think I helped him."

Right. The time he went down in search for his mother.

"I'm sorry about your mother."

She didn't look up, and she didn't respond. She stirred her soup.

I stirred mine, too.

Then, fuck it. My stomach growled and I decided then and there not to let what happened in the garage get in the way of me eating. I needed to eat. Raize would be pissed if I didn't so I forced that out of my mind, the smells, the sounds and I focused on where I was. Right here.

In this kitchen. Which was lovely smelling.

With Raize's sister. Who had cooked for everyone and was so shy, I was having a hard time knowing how to react around her.

I tasted the soup. It was made of beans and vegetables. I was guessing both came out of cans since there's no way there would've been fresh vegetables here or that the guys considered picking any up. It was delicious.

My stomach growled even louder.

Verónica heard and she looked up. "You guys eat a lot of fast food."

"This is a novelty. *Gracias*."

She gave me another shy smile. "*De nada*."

We both ate in silence for a bit longer.

"You and my brother are close." She lifted her head a bit higher, sitting up, and added, "I've never seen him like this."

"Like what?"

I was suddenly desperate for anything she had to say about how her brother was when she knew him. I knew he wasn't the same, but it was like a thirst was just teased and I realized I was dying for it now. My mouth was almost watering.

"He was," she looked down again, but kept speaking, "hard. He talked to me, but that was it. He stayed away from our mother. He was quiet. He did his job, but I could tell that the other men didn't want him there. They feared him. When Marco found out who Clay was, I'd never seen my brother like that. He killed everyone."

My mouth dried.

I didn't think she was talking about Marco.

"I missed him when he left, then I heard that he was alive. I was happy."

"When they brought you from Mexico, you acted like you hated your brother. What changed?"

Her eyes jerked to mine, and she stared at me. "I love Marco, but I've always been scared of him. He's never done anything to me except keep me away from everyone. Abraham was kind to me when he was around but then Marco started sending him away and for longer times. I'd lost hope until I heard the men talking about The Scooper and Abraham was sent off again. I knew something had changed. I didn't know what. No one would tell me and one of the maids came up to me with a phone yesterday. She gave it to me and it was Abraham. He told me what happened, with my father, my mother. I knew it was Marco who killed them, and then Abram told me that Clay was coming for me. It wasn't hate that I felt for Clay. It was guilt because I know that the maid who handed me that phone will die. Her entire family might die because she helped me." She lowered her face again, her voice coming out in a whisper. "I cannot even think of her name right now because it tears at me."

"I didn't know about the girl," a low, masculine voice from the doorway.

Raize stood there, a towel wrapped around one of his hands.

Verónica jumped up, scooting back her chair. She went to the kitchen. "Would you like a bowl of soup?"

His eyes went to me, but he shook his head to his sister. "I'm not hungry. Thank you, though."

She nodded, her head going back down. She stepped back from the counter, one of her hands covering the other, hanging low.

"Where are the others?"

He answered me, "They're coming in." He said to his sister, "They'll be starving, V. They'll appreciate the food."

Her eyes lifted and she gave him a small smile. It was a small beam, but it was something.

He went back to watching her in silence. And she was doing the same, but looking at the ground. She'd peek a look every now and then.

And yep, this was a family thing. I was seeing it now, but I also knew my man by now. I knew what he was covering under that towel, and I knew he needed me. So knowing all of that, I finished my soup, stood, gave it to Verónica with a thank you and a smile. She returned with another one of those beams I was quickly learning were hers.

I took Raize's other hand.

"Come on," I murmured, taking him upstairs and to the farthest bathroom.

Once inside, he saw that I had our bags brought up here. I say that like I had anything to do with it. I didn't. But I'd walked through the hallway earlier and saw someone had brought our bags to this room, so this was ours. We weren't on the main floor, but we had a patio and our own bathroom.

I wasn't complaining.

The patio would give Raize his needed exit, but judging by the slump of his shoulders, I was guessing he wasn't expecting anything to go down.

"The guy?"

He drew up short, giving me a look.

Right.

I wouldn't ask anymore about him, so I went into the bathroom and turned the shower on.

Coming back, letting it warm, I took the towel off of his hand and winced. "These are fresh?"

"He tried to make a run for it." Raize's head lowered to my shoulder, resting his forehead there. "He went for Abram's gun. I fought him."

I pressed a hand to his forehead, lifting his head up so I could gaze directly into his eyes. "I'm sorry."

He blinked. "For what?"

"For this being your family reunion."

He touched my hip, pulling me closer to him. He started to pull me down onto him, but I held back.

"I was thinking of taking a shower?"

"I'm too tired for a shower."

I stepped back, tugging at his hand. "Come on." I pulled him up and he followed me inside. The steam was filling the room and there was no fan. I shouldn't have, but I didn't care that night. I shut the door, locking it, and then Raize's lips were on mine.

Tired or not, we needed each other.

RAIZE

This woman.

I couldn't get enough of her.

I was pumping into her from behind, holding her up against the shower wall and she was like ecstasy to me. One taste and I was hooked. I needed more, just more.

Just. Fucking. More.

She gasped, her neck arching. She reached back for me, one hand grabbed onto my shoulder. Her other hand was against the wall.

I sank right back inside, knowing that was home to me.

So tight. So greedy.

Mine.

"Raize!"

Her hands clamped down harder, her fingers sinking in. I'd feel her nails scraping soon.

I didn't stop.

Jesus.

This feeling.

Being inside her.

It was the closest experience to heaven I'd ever get.

I moved my thumb down, rubbing her and needing her to come.

She always fought, wanting to come with me. No way.

Her first. Always.

But damn, I was close.

"Babe, you gotta come."

She started to lift herself up.

I clamped down on her hips, holding her and I just moved with her, thrusting even deeper.

A low guttural moan came from her, and she froze for a second. "Holy—Raize!"

I moved my thumb over her clit, pushing, rubbing, caressing.

"Now."

She was fighting it.

"*Now*."

She exploded in my arms, and I held her through the waves until she had stopped trembling. After that, it was all me. Taking her from the shower, I moved her to the bathroom counter. Her legs were positioned. "Arms up."

She snapped forward, pressing her palms against the mirror, and then I lined up.

I sank in, and bent over her, claiming her with every goddamn stroke inside of her.

I wanted her to feel me for the next month.

She started tensing again, and as I continued sliding in and out, she moaned again. "Raize." Her eyes were closed and she was panting.

I repositioned, pulling her up. I wrapped one hand around her chest, anchoring her to me, and continued moving up into her as I slid my hand down her front and back to her clit.

She fell back, her head and entire body resting against me as I worked her over once more, and as she climaxed, I was shooting myself into her.

We got her on birth control, during a stop and I was thankful.

Bare was the only way I wanted her from now on. We both collapsed and I waited until my legs could move again before carrying her into the bedroom and lowering her down onto the bed.

"You okay?"

She groaned, stretching out and smiled up at me.

The best satiated smile I'd seen on her face.

She whispered, "Yeah. I'm good."

I chuckled, but checked my phone.

The text stopped everything.

Unknown: We can meet now.

Unknown. Here. 2:30 am.

Unknown: image

"Raize?" Ash sat up, frowning. "What's wrong?"

I checked the time.

1:34 am.

They sent a map of where to meet. We had a fifty-minute drive ahead of us.

I said, "We have to go."

60

ASH

J ake and Cavers stayed back. I had no idea why, and so
did Gus.

When we arrived, I wasn't totally sure what we were
doing here. Abram had a grim set to his face so I was guessing he
knew and Verónica seemed as clueless as me. We were both
wired, because how could you not be?

It was the middle of the night.

We were meeting beneath the Canadian border, which was
on the other side of this gigantic lake. Or maybe the lake crossed
the border? I wasn't sure and driving up here, there'd been no
time to question Raize on what was going on. Or it didn't feel
right.

Raize talked the entire drive up, which was also different.
There was a sense of urgency to his voice, and he didn't talk to
Abram or myself. He talked only to his sister. He'd been a
different Raize. It was the brother version of him. He'd been
teasing her, getting her to smile, getting her to talk, getting her to
open up and relax. They talked, finally, as if they were long-lost
best friends and there was no tension or bad history or nothing
between them.

All that changed when we pulled into a back gravel road that wound through dense forest. The trees were almost intimidating, but then the road opened up to a beach. The sounds of lapping waves were almost refreshing, along with the smell. There was something about water. It was clearing, pure.

Raize parked, keeping his lights on.

We just saw water. There was no one else there.

That changed after we'd taken a few steps.

Two individuals came down from an embankment. They skimmed over the dirt, landing on the beach twenty feet from us and immediately Raize and Abram had their guns in the air.

The taller one, who was a guy, held his hands up. He came closer, dressed in dark clothing, a stocking cap that was pulled low over his head. Dreadlocks peeked out from underneath. He was wiry. The female with him was dressed the same, but shorter. A little more petite. She had orange hair and she held her hands up, too. She shared a look with her companion, then approached slowly.

"We're the ones you came to meet."

Raize didn't say anything.

Neither did anyone else.

The woman narrowed her eyes, but added, "I'm Carol." She motioned just behind her. "That's Blade. You reached out to us."

Raize studied both, giving the guy the longer stare before he glanced at me.

That was my signal.

I approached, bypassing Verónica and stepping between Raize and Abram.

"You can take them tonight?"

The woman started to respond, lowering her hands.

Abram cut her off, asking in a clipped tone, "What the fuck? Who are you talking about?"

"You and Verónica."

"What?" Verónica gasped, moving forward. Her eyes were wide as she was taking everything in. "What are you doing?"

Raize ignored both, asking the woman, "Can you or can't you? I need to know."

She lowered her hands all the way, but took a step back. Her gaze was flitting among all of us, but lingering on me before moving back to Raize. She raised her chin up. "We can take them."

The man moved to the side. He was almost completing a circle with him at the most northern point. "We know you, who you are. We just want you to know that."

I had no clue what was being said. They were being cryptic.

Raize's eyes cooled. "I reached out to see if you can hide both of them. That's all you need to know."

Guess I wasn't supposed to know.

"Clay!" Verónica snapped. "*What* are you doing?"

He turned to her. "Marco won't stop looking for you. These people are from a network that hides people. They're the best at their job, and as long as you're missing, Marco can't kill me."

Her eyes were getting bigger and bigger with each word he said.

And, wow. That made sense. A whole lot of sense.

Raize had been planning this the whole time? Was that why we came up here? These people were here?

"You know he's going to come for you anyway."

"Marco assumes you're still with me. He's not prepared for what I'll tell him. As long as I'm alive, I know where you are. He won't touch me. He won't dare because he does love you in his way."

Verónica stumbled back a step, her hands rising to knead at her temples. She bent over, muttering in Spanish under her breath.

"You *won't* know where they are." The woman stepped forward again. "We don't work that way. You know we don't."

"I know, but he won't," Raize said softly. "V."

She was shaking her head and turning to walk in a tight circle. Over and over again. Her hands went to her hips. "I cannot believe you did this. I left him for you. One bro—"

"It's for your safety. These people are the best. Marco won't know that I won't know. I can use that, string him along, and it'll work. He's irrational when it comes to his sister."

She stopped, her hands falling back down. A look of utter desolation settled over her shoulders. Her eyes brimming with tears. "I'll never see you again?"

"No." Raize continued, "It'll be a new life. You wanted a new life. You'll be normal. They'll help you with a home, a job. Papers. Whatever you need. It's a new life. Your mother would want that for you."

Verónica picked up on what he was saying, how he was phrasing it.

He didn't want these people to know of her relation to them.

"I can't," she whispered, the tears starting to fall.

"You have to. You leave, I can use that as leverage to stop Marco. You don't leave, he'll keep sending sicarios after me. He'll keep at it until he gets you back. You know this." He went to his sister, drawing her into his arms. "You and Abram. You go together. I've paid for both of you—"

"No."

Raize frowned at Abram. "What do you mean?"

He was shaking his head. "I'm not going with her."

Verónica started crying again. "I can't. I can't. I can't." She was in full meltdown mode.

The woman and man shared another look, both edging back a step.

Raize raised his voice. "I paid for you. You love her! You be with her."

"No, brother." Abram went the other way, gentling his tone. He tried to give Verónica a reassuring smile. It faltered and sadness emanated from him. "I'm sorry, Verónica. I am, but I've got too much blood on me. I'd never be able to live a normal life. But you can. You're a good person. In his way, Marco tried to keep that world away from you as much as he could. I'm going to stay. I'm going to protect my brother." He indicated Raize. "He's going to need me, and you know it."

"No," another cracked whisper from Verónica. "No, no, no."

Raize moved back, his gaze going to the couple. "I need your reassurance that she'll be safe. You're going to be hiding Marco Estrada's sister. You know who Marco Estrada is?"

They shared another look.

The woman nodded. "We do. We're aware of *all* the dynamics going on here."

Right. More crypticness. I was guessing they were indicating they knew who Raize worked for. That's the only thing that made sense.

Raize's eyes went flat. His lips thinned. "I need you to say that she'll be kept safe and alive."

She frowned. Her eyebrows dipped down, but she said it. "She'll be kept safe and alive. She'll be happy, too, eventually. We care about these people. It's our entire mission."

His mouth curved down, but he turned to me. "Is she lying?"

Relief flooded me. I was so grateful he worded it that way.

"She's telling the truth."

Raize's eyes went to the guy. "You now."

"Wha—"

Raize's gun was in the air. His words were rough. "I *need* you to say the same words."

"We don't do business like thi—" The woman started to step between them.

The guy interrupted her, his hand catching her shoulder and holding her in place. He raised his chin, too. "We will keep her safe and protected. She'll be happy. That is my promise to you."

I didn't know why or how, but this guy understood the need

inside of Raize. An understanding was there in his eyes, a dark knowing and it was enough.

I gave Raize a nod when he glanced my way. As soon as I did, he lowered the gun. The fight fled from him. His eyes closed for a beat.

Okay.

Now it was my turn.

I moved to Verónica, taking her into my arms. I hugged her and whispered, cupping the back of her head, "This is the ultimate gift your brother can give you. Both of your brothers. You need to accept it. Your mother would want this."

She was trembling in my arms, but her arms came up and wrapped tightly around me. She burrowed her head into my neck and shoulder. "I cannot. I *cannot*. Too much loss."

"You have to, but Verónica." I pulled back, framing her face with my hands and I rested my forehead on hers. "Do this for your brother. You have no idea how precious this gift is. Please take it."

"What do you think, sis?"

I was hugging Raize's sister, but it was someone else I was saying goodbye to.

Brooke.

Drawing in a breath, I stepped back.

Verónica was still crying, but she moved to Raize.

I turned away, wiping at my eye.

The hugs were hard to watch.

Verónica was sobbing and hugging Raize so tight. Then Abram.

She kept whispering his name, Abraham, over and over again.

In the end, the couple came forward and took her from Abram's arms.

"Cuida de él. Cuida su espalda. Guárdalo. ¡Prometeme! Prométemelo, mi amor. Yo te amaba Hago. Yo siempre."

Abram's dam broke. Tears fell from his eyelids and he choked out, "I will. I'll protect him." He had to take a breath. "I love you, too, *Verónica. Siempre te he amado.*"

Verónica broke again, falling to the ground.

I didn't know what he said, but it was beautiful whatever it was. It felt right not to know.

The man, Blade, bent down and picked her up. He carried her as if she were a child and walked back how they'd come. The woman, Carol, waited a bit before turning to us. She was blinking back her own tears, and her voice came out raspy. "When you reached out, we did our homework. We know you worked for two cartels and are now in the employment of Roman Marakov. We weren't sure about taking this booking, but decided to proceed anyways. This is the hardest part. It *will* get better. Estrada will never find her." She paused, glancing back before as if coming to a decision. Her shoulders set. "The *only* people who will know where she is, will be Blade and myself. No one else."

Raize dipped his head down. "Thank you."

Abram said, "*Gracias.*"

A sad smile came from her. "*De nada.*"

She looked my way, a question in her eyes, but she didn't say anything.

She turned and left.

I wiped away another tear.

61

ASH

"Heya, little baby doll."

My mom was at the door and I straightened back from my stuffies. She had that look, and when Mom had that look, it wasn't good.

I knew my stomach would start hurting soon, but I took a small breath. I held it. Dad told me this was the best way to calm 'it' when Mom was around. I never knew what 'it' was, but the breath holding and sitting real still always helped. Mom said what she wanted to say and left, and sometimes that look would go away. Other times...

I looked at my stuffies, deciding which ones I wanted with me if the 'other time' happened.

The stuffies helped, especially the wolf one. And the dragon one. Both were so soft and heavy.

I liked them a lot.

"Hey, baby." She came in, kneeling down beside me.

Her perfume was heavy today.

That wasn't a good sign.

She leaned in, smiling at me, and reached up. Her finger traced over my forehead, tracing a hair strand and tucking it behind my ear. She kept her hands on my forehead, a light and loving touch.

Sometimes Mom would lean in and kiss me, whisper her sweet things, and I liked that Mom.

I hadn't seen that one for a long time, though.

"Hi, Mom."

Oh man.

I expelled some air, sticking my tummy out. That came out all soft and whispery, like I was scared.

She didn't like when I sounded like that.

The look in her eye switched, and she pulled back a bit. Her hand pressed in to my forehead, but then she blinked a bunch and gave me another smile.

I relaxed a little then.

She was trying not to have 'that look.' I could always tell when she was trying.

Couldn't say anything about it, but I still knew.

I'd only need my stuffies to sleep tonight. That was good.

"I wanted to tell you that you have a friend coming over to play later. A neighbor girl. You guys are the same age, so I think you'll get along fabulously." She glanced at my stuffies and laughed softly. "You might have to share a stuffie or two. Is that okay?"

I smiled at her, trying to make her feel like I loved her with my eyes. She always liked that a lot, and I kept my smile stretched as far as I could get it to go. Sometimes it hurt, but that was fine. Always worth it. She liked it when I showed her my teeth, too.

She said that was cute.

"Of course, Mama. It's always nice to have a friend."

"Yes." She continued to watch me, then a softness came over her. She traced my hair again, a loving touch on my forehead before she blinked her eyes a whole bunch again. Leaning in, she rested her forehead to mine before moving and resting her cheek there. She tugged me into her arms. "I just love you so much. It's good if you had a friend. Right?"

She pulled back.

I nodded, that smile hurting my face. "Of course, Mama."

The doorbell rang.

REMEMBERING NOW, as we drove away, a tear slid down my face.

Over my cheek.

To the corner of my mouth.

It lingered, holding before it slid to my chin.

It held there.

I'm sure it fell, but I let it be.

Somehow it seemed appropriate.

I knew why this memory came today.

I knew why they were all coming back to me.

62

RAIZE

We were driving back when my phone lit up.

Recognizing Jake's number, I hit accept. "What's wrong?"

"We're in trouble."

Abram leaned forward. "Explain, man."

"We found a tracker on that guy. It was in his wallet."

"Get out of there. Now!" I hit the accelerator, already knowing we could be too late. We were thirty minutes out and I didn't know these roads.

Fuck. Fuck. Fuck!

"On it."

Dialtone.

No one said a word the last fifteen minutes. There was no reason.

Abram had his gun out and he was getting ready. He had two more guns on him. All were loaded.

He glanced my way, motioning with his head in Ash's direction.

I nodded.

Without a word spoken, he handed her one of the guns. She had her other gun out as well, and her hand reached up, wiping at her face.

I frowned, but seeing my look, she flashed me a tight smile.

She was nervous.

"Ash."

"What?"

Her tone was even. That was good. She wouldn't lose her shit. If anything, she'd kill everyone to save that dog of hers.

"You need to stick to me."

She slammed in the magazine for her gun and checked the safety. "I know." Then she rested that gun on her lap, and gazed out the window.

"Text Jake," I told Ash. "See if he responds."

"Should I call him?"

"No. If he forgot to put his phone on silent, I don't want to risk alerting anyone if they're hiding."

She thumbed off a text, and I went through what we might find driving back.

The worst-case scenario was that they had Jake and Cavers, alive.

This life, to me, that was always the worst case. That meant torture, prolonged death, dismemberment.

Me? Death was my first choice. But damn, that was before I had people who cared about me. Ash cared.

Ash was enough.

Maybe torture would be my choice, there was a chance of escape then. As long as you're breathing, there's a chance.

Fuck.

It was rising in me. I was locking down.

It was me or them.

It was my men or them.

I was getting ready to head to a gunfight.

It was Ash or them.

Them weren't them anymore.

The feelings went first.

They were people.

They were obstacles. They were weapons.

They were a threat against me or mine.

The emotions left me.

Any kindness. I no longer cared about the world, just *mine*. That was it.

I flipped a switch. All the color was gone. Everything was in different levels of gray. Black. White. Dark gray. Light gray. Someone would either live or die. I would either kill them or they'd kill me.

After that, the mind began to clear out the thoughts I didn't need.

My mission was to get in, assess Jake and Cavers, and proceed from there.

Kill, if people were between them and me.

Five minutes later, we arrived.

Jake never texted back.

ASH

I WAS A MIX OF EMOTIONS.

Fear. Anticipation. Readiness.

The same old, same old.

What number was this for me? Of fighting? With shooting?

I'd lost count by now.

And I knew Raize was turning his killer mode on. I could see it happen. He stripped himself of his humanity, keeping whatever was left that helped him become the murderer that he needed to be. Abram had been in that one fight with us, but I could tell he didn't know how to take my changes when I got my gun ready.

He had two.

I had two.

I didn't know how many Raize had or where his rifle was, but then it didn't matter.

We were going into this fight.

We were either going in to get Jake, Cavers, and Gus out or we were going in to avenge them.

It was actually simple, and I was past freaking out about it. Me and mine or them.

It was becoming like that to me.

Raize didn't turn into the driveway. He kept straight and took the first half road that led from the street. Once we parked, we moved fast.

Raize was out of the car and hurrying, getting his own guns ready. He had the rifle in the back of the Suburban, under a compartment, and he put it together, then slung it across his back. After that, he shut the door and we were off.

Raize first, leading the way.

I was second.

Abram brought up the rear.

The guys were going fast and quiet.

Me? I was fast, but not as quiet.

There was no way I could be like them. Raize changed paths, maybe because of my noise. We were hitting dense grass instead of leaves and sticks. Our feet were a constant and steady *thump thump thump.*

It was matching my heartbeat and I was trying to keep my breathing steady.

We drew up on a hill, overlooking the house and garage.

Nothing looked amiss.

Smoke traveled up from the chimney, but all of the hairs on the back of my neck were up. Straight up and I had chills running down my back.

Jake never responded. Jake would've responded.

They were inside, whoever *they* were.

Raize motioned for Abram with some hand motions. I wasn't fluent in hand language, but Abram was. He gave a nod and took off to the left.

Raize gazed at me.

I gripped my gun tighter and waited, knowing he wanted to tell me to stay.

His eyes narrowed.

So did mine.

Then he sighed and started down a path.

I followed right behind.

I won that fight.

The closer we got to the house, the more those chills were doubling, but nothing looked out of the ordinary.

We got to the treeline. Two steps forward and we'd be in the open.

Raize stopped and drew me close. His mouth went to my ear. "They've got three men inside. There's two in the garage."

I had no clue how he knew this.

"I need you to stay here. You see them, you shoot them, but only if they can't see you. Got me?"

I wondered how they were keeping Gus quiet.

Raize's hand tightened on my arm. "I need an answer."

If they hurt Gus...

"Ash."

Right. I jerked my head in a nod.

My lines were gone. There were no lines here.

Raize pressed one last kiss to my forehead, swift but strong. He pushed me down so I was hiding behind a fallen tree, and then he took off going south.

I waited, my heart still pounding.

My palms were sweating.

Nothing happened at first.

Different world and I'd be enjoying the weather, the scenery.

Montana was beautiful, but then a guy stepped out from the garage. He started going to the left, looking like he was going for a patrol.

Raize came around the corner behind him.

I watched, but no sound was made.

He stepped up, wrapped an arm around the guy's mouth. His other hand made quick work, slashing the front of his neck, and then he clamped down on the guy. He held him in some kind of hold, paralyzing him so he couldn't struggle. It didn't last long.

Blood gushed from his throat and Raize lowered the body, leaving him to bleed out. He stepped over him, checking inside the garage before moving. The door was opened; he slipped inside. I could hear thuds, but no shot.

Raize came back out a minute later, more blood on him.

I took all this in, but a part of me was thinking.

Raize was good at what he did. I knew this. There was a reason he was Roman's 'field' guy. But even if I hadn't known that, I would've known Raize was *extremely* good at what he did.

But. There was a big but coming.

I had no doubt Raize would do fine.

He'd go into that house and take out whoever was in there, *but* there'd be a day when it wouldn't work in his favor.

There'd be a day when he'd be on the other end of a knife or a gunshot.

Damn.

Just damn.

Blinding pain sliced through my chest and I blinked back sudden tears because *damn* again.

I was too far in, too far gone.

I was *in*.

I loved him.

I chose this world because subconsciously I chose him.

When I made this decision, I didn't know, but I made it. I was cementing it right now. I was choosing. Raize. It was Raize. It had always been Raize.

It was first about a girl given the name Brooke, then it became about Raize.

I took a breath because my chest was so tight right now.

I was so far in that I knew if I looked behind me, I couldn't see the starting line.

A shout sounded from inside the house, followed by a gunshot.

More gunshots.

Gunfire.

More shouting.

A guy broke out from the house, running to the garage.

He was directly in my line of fire, and this was the line.

I couldn't let him get free.

He was trying to get away. Maybe he didn't have a phone and he was going in search of one. Maybe he was going to the car. Whatever it was, he couldn't get away. I had to stop him.

I raised my gun.

I aimed.

I shot.

Yes. There were no more lines here. None whatsoever.

I missed the first shot, and he kept going. He didn't know that shot was for him. He didn't know he should duck or hide or shoot back.

I aimed. I shot again.

I got him, hitting him in the shoulder.

Abram crashed out the door, running after him.

The guy started to go down, but Abram had his gun up.

I turned, knowing I was also choosing not to see another man die in front of my eyes.

Was that a cowardly thing to do?

I knew he would go down and I knew Abram would make the

killing shot, and I still couldn't breathe any easier. I didn't know. I didn't care at this moment.

I looked back.

Abram was staring right at me, waiting. His hand holding his gun was still half-raised.

He started toward me, but then Raize yelled from the house and he turned, going back.

I stood there, not knowing what to do. But, I guess, there was nothing else to do. So I stayed and I waited, and I had my gun ready in case anyone else got free.

That was when my phone buzzed.

Raize: Come in.

I took off running, my chest still so tight until I heard Gus barking.

I hit the door and raced inside, and *then* I could breathe.

Cavers and Jake were both peeling tape from their mouths.

Raize came out from a back room, saw me, and let Gus dart around him. He came right for me, his collar and leash still attached. As soon as I had my wiggling pup in my arms, I burst into tears.

"Take him for a walk."

I nodded, my throat swelling up and I'd walk Gus for an entire day if that's how long they needed. I didn't see the men, but I knew they were in there and they were dead.

We went outside. I felt like my lungs could expand again, but everything was swirling inside of me. Emotions. Sensations. Thoughts. Memories. All of it was compounding me.

Because of that, I wasn't watching where I was going with Gus.

I wasn't thinking.

I was assuming we were safe.

I let Gus choose what direction we took.

So because of *all* of that, we were away from the house, down a walking path. I had no idea what direction we'd taken.

I had no idea how long we were gone.

All I knew is that we got to a clearing.

There was a car.

Gus burst forward, smelling something, and I heard the sound of a gun's safety being taken off.

"Nice to see you again, Miss Marakov."

———

"I WANTED you to have a friend, my sweet little girl."

63

NOT MISS MARAKOV

"Miss Marakov." Marco was leaning against the side of one of the SUVs, and he looked down, his shoulders shaking. A dry chuckle came from him. He had his hands folded over one another in front of him, the bottom hand holding a gun, but the safety was on. "I am assuming that your presence here," he motioned to Gus with his gun before his other hand folded over it, returning back in front of him, "is an indication that my men are dead inside."

His whole stance was casual. He wasn't alarmed. Scared. Nothing.

The corner of his mouth lifted up and he nodded to himself. "Right. Of course they're dead, because they're not my best men. My top man was Clay. My second was Abram, and I have myself to blame for neither of them being my men anymore." He pushed up, but he stood there. He made no move to advance toward me.

I was holding Gus back, whose tail was wagging at first. That was when he caught Marco's scent, or I was assuming for the reason he pulled me here. Now, seeing a man, Gus was growling and straining to get free.

I held on. I wasn't ready.

He had that gun.

I had a feeling he'd be a better shot than the other guy outside of Gus' original home.

"So, Miss Marakov." Another grin from him, like we both just shared an inside joke. "Let's talk, you and me. I figure I have precious time before there's more gunfire or a dog tries to attack me or, who knows what could happen. I won't get this chance again, not for a long time if ever."

With that said, he went to the second vehicle, a car, and he sat on the front. One leg could still touch the ground. The other was bent, his foot resting on the tire just underneath him. He leaned forward, an elbow resting on his knee. That gun was still in his grip, but it was being held casually.

I was dumbfounded. That was it.

Dumb. Founded.

"I did my research on you. I know your name, know your mother killed herself, your sister was reported missing. You were reported missing, and your father's done rehab. That's what my private investigator told me. Are we caught up?" His eyes sparked. He looked casual, but he wasn't. His gaze was sharp. "I also know what you can do. I'm assuming you're the 'gift' Raize was offering. You could tell me if a man named Jorge Miller killed my brother?"

My gut flared.

"I could tell you, yes."

His eyes narrowed. He raised his chin up, going to the side. "How does that work? If you're not 'psychic', how do you know?"

"...*your mother killed herself*..."

I was back there, sitting in the hallway, as they took her body from the room.

I pushed that aside.

"People get good at deciphering how a footstep sounds when a drunk father comes home, especially if he's angry. If a door shuts a certain way. How a bag is rustled. You know, you just know to hide or if you can keep breathing." I lifted up a shoulder, lying through my teeth but not at the same time. "It's kinda like that, I guess."

"You lived with an abuser, you mean?"

Goddamn.

"I've worked for six mafia bosses. My gut sharpened, real quick, after the first two."

It had nothing to do with them. Again. I was lying. He didn't get to know where I learned this skill, or where my gut did.

His eyes were steady on me, and he measured me. He raised his face. "Right. I guess that makes sense. Somewhat." He frowned to himself, looking around.

But he still wasn't worried.

Why wasn't he alarmed?

"So." He extended a hand toward me, waiting. "Did Jorge do it? Did he kill my brother?"

I knew the answer. "Go away and I'll tell you."

Surprise flashed over his face, and he let out a chuckle. "That's funny. I'm sure, I'll leave and you'll call me with the answer? Maybe you and I can start texting each other? How about we do that, too?" His grin faded and his mouth tightened. "Do not insult my intelligence." He looked over my shoulder before focusing on me again. "I'm not sure what Clay has shared with you, but I am not a stupid man. I might be selfish, ruthless, but when you think you've outsmarted me, that's when I've killed you."

My chest felt an invisible hand pressing down on it.

I stiffened.

"There's a reason I'm sitting here and why I haven't just shot you or your dog, and then driven away— because I could. Clay has let you out of his sight. He dropped his guard, and there's only one reason he would've done that, and that's the reason I'm staying. My guess is that Verónica is already gone. He's stashed her somewhere, and he's feeling that pain. It's the only time he ever messed up, when he was in agony over someone he loved. And don't take it personal. If he stashed you somewhere, he'd do the same thing then, too. I can tell that he cares for you, which is the second reason I'm sticking around."

Well, crap then.

"The other reasons are that I want you to come work for me." His eyes dropped to Gus, who was still growling. "If I hurt you or your dog, I have a feeling that wouldn't work out in my favor. And, yes, I'm intrigued if Jorge actually did kill my brother." A low chuckle slid out from him. "Though, that's a question I've had for years now and it's becoming a punchline in some joke. I'm the punchline, I'm sure."

I gritted my teeth. "I'm not going to work for you."

"Not yet, but you will." He stood from the car. "Maybe one day."

I jerked back and Gus tried to lunge free.

I held on to the leash.

Marco paused, watching both of our reactions before he put his gun away. "You can tell Clay I've changed my mind. I would like to accept his boss' offer on a working relationship. You can also tell Clay that I have a death order in place. When I'm killed, the first sicario to find my sister and kill her will earn my empire."

I was stricken.

That—no...

He laughed. "She's missing. I'll accept that, which I'm sure will shock Clay and his employer, but there is a part of me that loves her. Other than my empire, *mi familia* is the only thing that's important. The other part of me wants her dead when I'm dead, but we'll work with the good part today. Hmm?" He walked to the SUV's driver's side. "Tell Clay I'll be in touch, or tell Roman Marakov I'll be in touch when you see him yourself." Another smile, one that had me tasting bile. "Has Clay told you that his boss considers you his personal asset? If he hasn't, you can bring that up as well, too."

He left and I stood there, remembering...

"...*mi familia is the only thing that's important...*"

———

"Sisters, *sweetie. She's your friend that'll never leave. You'd like a new friend, wouldn't you? Family is the only thing that's important.*"

———

It was all coming back to me. All at once. All together.

The memories. They were haunting me, pressing to get out.

My brain was swelling.

They wanted out, out, out.

I couldn't—my head. It was like a chainsaw was being used on it.

My heart was thumping, so hard, so loud, so strong.

I couldn't do anything.

Then, arms picked me up and I heard Raize say, "What's wrong? What's wrong?"

———

"This is your new room, sweetheart."

She opened the door and inside were two beds. A little girl was sitting on one of them, a doll in her hand.

She looked up...

Thump.

...the girl got off the bed and walked toward me.

She held her hand out. "My name is—"

Thump.

"*—my name is Ashley. What's yours?*"

64

RAIZE

Ash was in Roman's basement, curled up in a corner of a couch, a blanket around her, and having that same pale color she'd been having since I found out Marco could've killed her. She was holding a mug of hot tea, her request, and she was staring at no one, talking to no one.

Gus was on her lap, curled in, his head on her stomach and looking up for pets.

Ash wasn't having it.

After that day, after hearing her screams, a sound that I will never get out of my head, Gus hadn't moved from her side. He would piss on the floor if she wouldn't go with him outside. It was that kind of relationship happening right now.

Roman came into the room, seeing Ash, me, and choosing to come to me first.

Good choice.

He stood at my side, looking around the rest of the room. He had his usual men positioned throughout his house, but he'd asked his usual personal blockade of guards to let him have the basement for this event.

He lingered on Gus, whose tail was thumping into Roman's

black leather couch, but moved and took in Jake, Cavers, and Abram, all who were lounging throughout the room.

"This is so *very* not smart."

I grunted. That was the most obvious statement of the century.

I gave him a look. "It's her stipulation. She's going to talk. This has nothing to do with you or me, but she's gotta tell someone. She's going insane."

"Plan a mafia coup, swoop in to surprise everyone, and what? Invite a detective to your house to let him see that you're here. This wasn't in my plan, Raize," he clipped out.

"You want her to work for you, this is her demand. Her and I have talked and I am not going to let you use her if she decides against it. This was her request. She's doing it here, where you are, and it's two fold. You know about it. You know what's being said. It won't look like we're snitching and again, you know what exactly it's all going to be about. You're my employer. If we went without you knowing, we both know how that would've looked. You control the environment. You control what detective it is. You're here and this works for you, too. You want to be somewhat legitimate, so you're going to deal with the authorities. This is a good start to that relationship."

He grunted, nodding to himself. "Right, because you haven't been a pain in my ass lately at all. I'm really controlling a whole lot."

Ash glanced our way, her eyes narrowing and no doubt, just seeing how we were standing. Both with our backs to the walls. Any firearms were supposed to be hidden, not that the Boston detective, whichever one walked through those doors, wouldn't know they were there. They would know, but after Ash told me enough that she needed to talk about, we both put together this plan.

Talking to the police at all was considered snitching. It didn't matter that it had nothing to do with anything illegal that we might've done in the last six months. But she was going to come forward, and I worked for the biggest Russian mafia boss on the East Coast. Everything was put in a way that Roman would look like the good guy. Statements were going to be kept to what Ash had to say, which had nothing to do with anything current. She was firm on that.

The police would know about her.

The police already did know about her. This way, they'd know where she was and that she no longer needed to be considered a missing person.

But the police would know about Roman, which was going to happen anyways. Roman wanted to set up legitimate businesses here. There's no hiding if that's the case. And myself, I guess they'd learn about who I was if they didn't already know because I wasn't leaving her side.

What Roman would be told after the meeting is that Marco decided to work with him after all.

I—I had my own plan to handle that, but we heard footsteps coming down the stairs.

One of Roman's guys came in. "They're here."

Roman nodded. "I want my men gone." He glanced around the room, and as it'd been talked about before, Abram, Jake, and Cavers all left the room, too. They were here, they had met their boss above their boss, but they didn't need the detective to see any more faces than what was needed.

We heard footsteps and a woman came in.

She was dressed in a suit. Slim. Sharp face. Sharp eyes, too. And a whole no-nonsense vibe to her.

She lingered on Roman, on me, but she went right to Ash.

"Hello." She sat on a chair not far from Ash and took out a recorder. "I'm Detective Maronzetti. And your name is Ash..." She paused and glanced at us.

Another detective had come into the room, quieter, but he was there. She looked right at him, letting us know he was there.

Not slim, a paunch on his stomach, and dressed in a suit. Balding head with the sides still trying to keep what hair was there. He also, which I found annoying, had smart eyes.

I didn't know who Roman had asked to come, but these detectives weren't the ones I'd hoped to get. In my life, you knew who would and who wouldn't. Neither of these two did.

"No."

Ash's voice drew everyone's attention back to her.

The feeling in the room changed, dipped, grew more somber.

I did not want to hear what she was going to say, but it was because once I heard, then I'd know what happened to her. I couldn't take it away. I couldn't kill anyone to make her feel better. The only recourse, literally the only recourse, was this.

"My name isn't Ash, actually."

"I don't want you by me, when I tell them."

"No."

"Raize." She sighed. She sounded so tired. "I have to do this on my own. I have to, for Brooke." She started crying, but she'd been crying on and off since we left Montana. "I can't explain it. I just can't have you by me."

"I'm in the same room. That's not negotiable."

"The police will know you—"

"It's you, Ash. You!"

That was the conversation we had two days ago. I hated it then. I hated it even more now. But, I was in the room.

I was in the room.

Then she began speaking.

65

ASH

I started at the beginning.

"She was sick, you have to know that first." My voice was shaky. Dammit. I couldn't be like that, not for this. I liked the female detective. She was strong. I could feel that, but she was going to be soft with me. I hated that, but I needed that and I swear, she knew that, too.

She told me her name, but I wouldn't remember it.

I wouldn't remember anything about anyone in this room after tonight.

I'd only remember what I was about to say, and how it would destroy anything I might've had.

"Who was sick, Ash?"

I had a feeling no one else would speak, just her and me. I'm sure it'd been talked about on both sides. That was the precedent here today.

I just had to do this. I had to get it done. Just, fucking say the words. Get it over and done with.

Mom, I'm sorry...

"My mom." My throat was clogged. "My mom was sick."

We didn't open the curtains. Mom never wanted them open.

"She—she took her life when we were in high school. Brooke and I. I—"

I couldn't.

How could you do this?

How could you do what you did?

"I wanted you to have a friend, my sweet little girl."

I couldn't. I just couldn't.

No words were coming to my throat. I couldn't speak.

"Ash." She started to scoot forward. She was going to touch my knee. And that touch would be kind, comforting. I could not have that.

"My name isn't Ash," I burst out. I was slowly leaving my body, but this—this had be to very clear. "I don't know what my real name is."

Now I had the room's attention, but it wasn't what they thought.

The detective frowned, and she started to look at her notes.

"I'm sure there's a name on my birth certificate, but I have no idea what it says. You don't understand. She—my mom... She was depressed. She was angry. She was irrational. She... she terrified me. She terrified everyone, but ..." She was my mom. How could I explain that? "She wanted me to have a sister and, then one day, I had a sister. I know she wasn't adopted, but my mom told me she was. She told Brooke she was. She wasn't. And I know this because I saw her missing poster sitting next to our fireplace. My mom was starting a fire. The doorbell rang. She went to answer it, and I walked through the room. I saw the paper. She was going to burn it. It was Brooke. My sister. My mom—Her real name was Ashley Cruz and my mom kidnapped her."

"This is your new room, sweetheart."

She held her hand out. "My name is—"

"What's your name, sweetie?"

"—my name is Ashley. What's yours?"

I couldn't look at Raize. I knew he would be tormented. I

knew he would want to come over and pick me up, take me away if I asked him to, and I wanted to ask him that. So, because of that, because he gave no fucks who would care, I couldn't look at him.

Though, God, I wanted to. I wanted so badly.

The detective hadn't said anything, so I kept going. Might as well get it all out.

"You can check your database, but she'll be in there." And now for the hard part. "Brooke—Ashley looked like me. That's why she was targeted. My mom did that. She targeted her, and she did it because she wanted me to have a sister. She used the word 'friend', but it was code for 'sister.'"

"Sisters. She's your friend that'll never leave. You'd like a new friend, wouldn't you?"

"She always said that loneliness could kill. She didn't want me to be lonely, and the thing is that I wasn't. I went to school. I had friends. I had Dad. I had..." My voice cracked. "I had her. But she was lonely, so she was convinced I was lonely. She didn't want me to be alone."

"Was your dad involved?"

I shook my head. "I don't know. He was on drugs most of my life, drinking if he wasn't high. I don't know."

"You said your—the girl kidnapped was Ashley Cruz?"

Ashley Cruz. I saw her missing poster once... Doesn't matter if he's not the one who got her. Someone got her.

I nodded. "My mom renamed her Brooke." A tear slipped down my face. This one I could feel. "My first name was Brooke. She took it and gave it to her."

"Why would she do that?"

I shook my head, my throat threatening to completely close up. "I have no idea."

And for the rest.

"My mom would lie, like, every day. Small lies. Big lies. Stupid lies. Things about big and major things, but also; she'd lie about what kind of toothpaste she used. Just, stupid things and I grew up in that. I got good, real good, at knowing what was a lie and what wasn't. But yeah, she lied. About everything."

What didn't she lie about?

What didn't you lie about, Mom?

"Do you have anything else to share with us?"

God.

My throat was so closed up.

"After Mom died, Brooke went off the rails. She was pulled in by a Romeo pimp and you guys have her in the database. She was picked up recently. I don't know if those charges changed, but you're going to pull her and you'll see for yourself. She was a victim of... " Jesus. I couldn't even say it all. "It's not her fault, what she did, what happened to her. None of it was her fault."

It wasn't mine.

I closed my eyes, trying to tell myself that.

It wasn't my fault.

It wasn't my fault.

I felt like it was my fault.

"Okay." The air was so thick, but the detective was trying to push forward. "Okay. So, we are going to need you to come down to the station. We'll need your DNA. We're going to pull everything. Your mom. Your dad. Ashley. Your file. Everything."

I wasn't looking, but her voice sounded far away for a second.

"My partner already sent in the search and you're correct. Ashley Cruz was reported missing in Colorado when she was six years old."

Six.

Colorado.

Oh my God.

A 'neighbor girl.' How long had my mom planned that?

"I have no doubt that her DNA will match Ashley's, and we can move forward from there." Her voice sounded different again.

She might've stood up. I still wasn't looking. "Do you, uh— I don't know how to proceed from here."

"Gail!"

I didn't recognize that voice. I was assuming it was her partner's.

She ignored him. "I'm not a counselor. My God, I'm not a counselor, but I know a little bit and you have—there's people you can talk to. Counselors. Allies. They don't need to report anything to the police."

"Gail," another groan.

"They are there for you. Only you."

I felt her hand again. It touched mine and squeezed, so gently.

She added, "I am so very sorry for what you have gone through, but what you did today was—it will help reset any wrong that was done. That's a good thing. I'll leave my card with your associates, and we'll be in touch for any more questions about *this* situation."

Another groan, "Detective Maronzetti, a word before you make any more promises."

"Yeah." She moved her head, as if sharing her thoughts away. She said under her breath, "I don't care. Right now, I don't care."

I didn't think those words were meant for me.

She started to pull her hand away, but I turned mine around and caught hers.

I squeezed it. Once. Just briefly.

As I looked up, her eyes were watering and she turned away. Her card was out, and she handed it to Raize. Not Roman. Raize. But she addressed Roman next with a small nod. "An eventful first meeting, Mr. Marakov."

He grinned. "Yes, it was."

They left.

Raize took one look at me.

He was across the room the next second.

I was lifted up in his arms, and I gave in.

I, simply, just gave in.

My legs wouldn't have been able to work anyways. I was done. Just.

I was done.

He carried me from the room.

"WE'RE GOING to be the best sisters ever."

Brooke was so happy.

"Yeah?" I was trying to smile, but this felt weird. I just didn't know why it felt weird.

"Yeah! You and me. Sisters forever. Right?" She had her hands in the air. She was that excited, but she paused and frowned. "Wait. What's your name again?"

66

JUST ME

They charged my father. Child endangerment, neglect of a child. It was why he never reported me missing, or Ashley. On the day they charged him, Raize took me to see her. She wasn't Brooke anymore.

We were told she was going by the name of Ashley again.

She was happy.

She had decent weight on her. She didn't look gaunt in the face, which she had been before she left and she was smiling now.

I'd also gotten pictures from the guy Raize had watching her.

One was her leaving a counseling office.

Another of her at the grocery store.

A third where she was having coffee with an older lady. And others. They looked like her. There was a family resemblance. A man. A woman. A brother. A sister. Could've been a couple aunts, too.

She seemed happy, but how could that be? After everything? But she was smiling. They were smiling.

None of that made sense to me, but they were.

We were currently watching Brooke cooking dinner with a woman. Both were in their kitchen.

Raize stepped up behind me. His chest grazed my back. "Do you want to talk to her?"

I shook my head, my stomach dropping, but my chest lightening at the same time. It was a bittersweet feeling. "No."

"She knows what you did. That you were the one who came forward. She knows that." His hand moved to my front, resting against my stomach.

A bittersweet feeling twisted inside of my gut. "Maybe one day, but not today."

A whole new wave of emotion surged up inside of me, this one making me bite my lip because I didn't want to cry.

But damn. I wanted to cry.

He moved to stand in front of me, and he touched under my chin, tilting my head up. A soft expression came over him, one that was loving and it took my breath away. I was blinking back tears for a whole different reason. Seeing them, he got even softer. He reached up, a finger tracing down a strand of my hair and sliding behind my ear and then moving to the back of my head. He took a breath and moved even closer, his body brushing mine. His forehead lowered, not completely touching mine, but he was that close.

I felt everything from him. His heartbeat. His heat. His breathing.

I felt a slight tremor course through his body, too.

"You need to know something. Your sister's case is getting a lot of attention, too much. Roman called today. He's ready to offer you a proposition. He said you can be free. You don't need to work for him. You can walk across the street and knock on that door. Ashley told the police that she'd like to see you, have a relationship with you. You could join that life. It's as simple as that."

I didn't react. I couldn't, and I think a part of me knew the other side. "What's the other offer?"

"You continue working for him, with me, and we disappear right now. But, you could be free. You joined this world to find your sister—"

I touched his chest, stopping him. "I joined this life because ~~Brooke~~ Ashley was taken again. The first time was my fault. The second time was my chance at redemption. Save her, and maybe I could save myself."

Oh man.

Oh boy.

I had no idea that's what was going to come out of me.

No. Clue!

But, whoa. Wow.

Redemption.

And all the 'lines.'

It made sense now.

But then I felt who was holding me.

I looked up.

Give up Raize for freedom. I knew that was the fine print for the first offer. It only made sense.

Roman wanted me to leave to help the spotlight fade away a bit, so it wouldn't get connected to him, but he wasn't going to give up Raize. There was no way.

That meant, freedom meant me giving up Raize.

I already knew my choice.

There was no decision to be made, at least in my mind.

67

UNKNOWN AT THE MOMENT

"R aize tells me that you've agreed to work with me."

With me. Not for me.

This guy was good.

When I first met Roman Marakov, I hadn't known what to expect, but going in and meeting this guy—he was in a whole other league. There'd been extraneous factors with the first meeting, so I was using this one as the official introduction. He wasn't like Raize.

No one was like Raize.

Roman Marakov was a thinker. That's what I meant.

He was the type of guy who not only played chess, won at chess, he was the guy who invented the board. That's who Raize's boss was and after the first three minutes, he started talking about Raize and I knew this guy also knew he was lucky to have who he had working for him. The admiration and respect wasn't to be faked.

That helped affirm my decision.

We were shaking hands and I released his, just going to lay out my cards. "I have a problem with killing. And ~~Brook~~—Ashley was trafficked. I have a problem with that, too."

His eyes flared and the corner of his mouth twitched. "So I'm told."

"Is that a problem?"

More deep amusement shone from him, but he kept a clear face. Nothing was twitching now. "It'll be good to have someone like you in the room. I didn't choose this life, but I'm going forth the best I can."

"I did."

His eyebrows lifted. "Hmm?"

"I chose this life." Twice now. "Just so you know."

There was a switch in his gaze, something deeper, darker shone there, but he only nodded. "I see."

Well, I didn't.

I had no clue why I wanted him to know that, but I did and he knew he did and now I felt an awkwardness between us, but it was also one that I wanted to be there. And again, I had no clue what was going on.

But he only grinned faintly before extending a hand toward the bar in his office. "I'm glad that everything is settling for Ashley, but I'm also glad that you've decided to stay on with us. Should we celebrate?"

I inclined my head, and as he made me a drink, he asked, "So, Ash. I have to ask, should I have killed Marco Estrada instead of deciding to enter into a business relationship with him? What's that magical gut of yours saying?"

"You want to do what?!"

As part of our agreement to 'join Roman' we needed to disappear. One might think we'd go to Hawaii or Turks and Caicos... Nope. We went back to West Virginia, and since it came out that Roman somehow had sunk claws into a certain brother-in-law that was also a local parole officer, Jake brought Tracey around to meet us all.

He was now exclaiming his disbelief not at me choosing to work for Roman Marakov, but that I was asking Tracey to color my hair blonde once again.

Tracey was lovely, by the way.

She had eighties' hair, with bangs that looked like they had an IV hooked up to an Aquanet bottle, and she was even wearing a tie-dyed shirt. The jeans skirt was modern, looking frayed and very trendy and showing a good amount of her ass, but judging by Tracey's makeup, I was thinking it was just how she liked it.

That, and her attitude.

She waltzed into our house as if it was hers and we needed to get out of the way for her to properly make it her own. She had a meatloaf in the oven within twenty minutes.

No joke. Twenty minutes.

Meatloaf.

I loved her immediately.

She told Cavers to 'take a load off' and myself to sit and eat. She felt I needed to pack on some pounds, or twenty. Her words. Abram was next and without batting an eye, not mentioning one bit how he was a solid two-fifty of straight muscle, she told him he could do a spa treatment on his pores. She also complimented his tremendously long and beautiful eyelashes, sighing with envy, and I had to admit that I understood. His lashes *were* something to die for. When she started for Raize, the words faltered in her throat and she just threw him a smile and mentioned, "Aren't you the hottie patottie one, huh?" And then she turned back to me. "Jake mentioned you were a blonde, and unless my eyesight is going a good forty years early, I'm guessing that was a color job?"

I laughed. "I was a blonde when I was little, but yes. It was a color job."

Her hands settled over my shoulder. "I'm a hairstylist, babe. I'm literally your godsend arriving to you. All that said, you want a new dye job or not? You got some frayed ends that need to be trimmed, too. What do you think?"

I put her right to bringing back my blonde, and once we were done, I gazed into the mirror and felt like I'd come home again.

It was an odd, but a settling feeling at the same time.

This.

This was me now.

The new me.

The 'canary' me.

Maybe I should take that name instead?

Feeling a warmth rush through me, I knew Raize was watching me.

I glanced over.

He was leaning against the kitchen wall, his arms crossed over his chest, and those eyes locked on me.

I liked Tracey a lot.

I also really liked that my blonde hair color was back.

———

I SANK DOWN OVER RAIZE, gasping as he was thrusting up into me at the same time.

Seriously.

This man.

His touch.

His body.

His cock.

I loved him. All of him.

I was gasping, feeling the sensations riding through me, threatening.

I didn't want to come, not yet.

I clamped down, my body slick as I tried to hold off.

He wrapped his arms tighter around me, his head moving and biting my neck. He growled, "Come!"

I shook my head, too weak to say anything.

I was almost blind from the pulsations inside of me.

Oh God.

I was so close.

But no, not yet.

Please not yet.

I tried to hold off, even though I felt the first roll starting.

When that first wave began, I knew what was after, and I growled, hoping desperately to hold off, but damn. Damn! I couldn't.

My climax ripped through me and I could only hold on. My arms and legs were wrapped around Raize, and he was holding me until my trembles had started to fade. After that, I was flipped over, he sank back in and went to town.

Gripping my ass tight, he pounded into me, his own growled climax coming not too far away, and damn again.

I seriously loved this man.

He collapsed on top of me, but I knew he wouldn't stay. He never did. I liked to feel his weight, but he always rolled to the side, and he'd pull me into his arms, cradling me as if I were something precious for him to hold. He'd pepper soft kisses over my neck, my shoulders, my face, and wherever else he could kiss.

I shivered, but the good kind, because damn for the fourteenth time, because I loved how he handled me.

I was 'precious cargo' in his terms.

Once he deposited us both back on the bed, I rolled to my back and looked over to him. He was starting to lie back down, his arm over me and his head finding my neck and shoulder. I held him off, murmuring, "I love you." I said it with a bit more oomph than normal.

He noted this, his head pausing and his eyebrows knitting a bit. He smoothed his hand over my stomach. "I love you, too."

More warmth rushed through me.

Usually that was enough and I could sink back into our happy oblivion, but this time, I held off. A nagging was there, whispering to me and I had to get it out of me. "Am I choosing wrong? Am I doing the wrong thing?"

He tensed, just slightly, and raised his head a bit higher. He sat up, resting on his arm, but he kept his other over my stomach. "Would you be happy out of this world?"

I knew the answer, so immediate that it gave me whiplash.

"No," I whispered.

I was torn because that isn't the answer I should've been giving.

I should've wanted to leave. It would've been considered a happily ever after to anyone else, but not me. That was the issue here.

Raize asked again, gently, "If you think about it, if you took Roman's offer and got out, what would life look like for you? Is that something you'd want now because if it is, we can figure it out. I promise you that. I love you. There's nothing I wouldn't do for you."

I believed him, and that cemented my gut, pushing my self-doubt out.

It helped.

A lot.

I spoke my truth, feeling like I could in his arms, "I would never be happy, living that life. This way, I'm in. I can do *some* good. I can't do anything to stop what my mom did, but maybe others. What Brooke's boyfriend did to her. Maybe."

Or was I just trying to sell myself on this decision? Was something still holding me back?

"You can try to do some good this way, but," his hand seemed to rest more heavy on my stomach, "you can't rely on that if that's your sole reason for choosing to work for Roman. If you want out, tell me. We will disappear within twelve hours. I've done the preparations. We can get to my sister and then we can all be gone, but, you have to make the decision. I will do what you want me to do."

There'd been wars started over territory, over vengeance, over women, but Raize—he was someone that Roman *would* start a war for. Raize was that good. I knew it. Raize knew it. Roman knew it. So did everyone else who came into Raize's life.

Could I pull him away? And for what?

To do what?

No.

The answer was solid. It settled in my gut.

I relaxed back in bed, Raize's hand returning to soothing over my stomach.

"I will only stay if I make a difference. If I can't, if there's absolutely no indication that Roman will listen to me, then I want out. I want out with you."

Raize's hand paused and he moved, rising above me again. His eyes found me, so dark, so somber, so serious. He said, quietly, before fitting his lips to mine, "Deal."

Deal.

Decision made.

I was okay with that decision.

My FIRST DAY I wore skintight jeans, boots, a black tank top, and a black leather jacket.

My hair was braided, and the color was on point.

I was known as 'the canary', but I decided I wanted to keep the name Ash.

It felt right. It felt like me.

It was also a nod toward Brooke/Ashley, but I wasn't Ashley. I was Ash. Only Ash.

I was ready to get to work.

EPILOGUE
RAIZE

I was waiting behind his bathroom door.

The lights were left off.

He didn't know that I remembered when I worked for him. He never had the house cleared before he retired to his bed. All his men on his property, around his home, in his home. He assumed.

He liked to walk through his room, then his bathroom, getting ready for bed. He always kept the lights off.

I never knew why. I never asked. Verónica thought it relaxed him, and if he put the lights on, he'd get wired again. He may not sleep as well.

I always thought it was laziness. He didn't need to be scared and turn the lights on. Tonight, he kept with the same routine except his walk was more shuffling. He had no girlfriend in bed waiting for him, and I knew he hadn't married.

He was in the bedroom.

He was taking his clothes off. He grabbed—something.

He was shuffling once again, coming into the bathroom.

This was when he'd sit on the toilet. The fan would go on. He'd enjoy his privacy.

He came in. A wine glass was in his hand. He was looking down, his other hand holding his phone. He never looked up. He would've seen me. I was behind the door. My shoulder was visible because I couldn't scoot anymore behind the door.

Clink.

He placed the wine glass down.

He was still focusing on his phone.

He hit the fan, turning it on. His heel lifted back, hitting the door, swinging it shut.

I was completely visible now, though I was dressed all in black. Camouflage over my face and neck, around my eyes. Ears.

He moved to the toilet.

He went one step and I was on him.

I shoved him against the bathroom counter, an arm around his neck. My gloved hand over his mouth, one that was thick enough he couldn't bite me. My leg twisted in between his from behind and I plucked his phone away, checking—he was on his social media. I tossed it to the side and then I jerked him.

He was struggling, but I had him in a hold he couldn't fight against.

He was trying to grab the gun tucked into his pajama pants.

I took it out, putting it on the counter behind us, and then I moved him so he could see me in the mirror.

He'd recognize me, and he did, his blood draining from his face.

That's when I smelled his fear.

Marco was my height, and he was strong. He worked out. He had bulked up in the last year, but it didn't matter. He couldn't fight me and he knew it.

When he stopped struggling, I reached behind and took out some rolled-up pictures. I put them on the counter, in the moonlight so he could see what I had. When he did, his entire body seized up, going rigid.

That was good. That told me he cared.

I moved my arm up, tightening my hold, and I angled it underneath his neck. I pulled on my grip, and he grunted, feeling the burn on his skin. If I kept applying pressure, I could snap his neck. I wanted him to know that, feel it coming.

"What do you want?"

He remembered he could talk. That was funny.

"You threatened mine. Now I can threaten yours."

The picture was of his most current woman and their child.

Marco didn't care about women, but he cared about his siblings, and I was guessing that would extend to any child of his.

I shook him. "Look at the picture."

He didn't, spatting out, "I know who it's of."

"You don't know where. Look."

His eyes flicked back up to mine, and he swallowed, but trying to inspect the first picture again. When he realized where it was taken, I felt him starting to tremble. Just the slightest. It was enough.

He was scared and he was at my mercy.

"This is how I felt that day when Ash walked our dog to you."

I would never forget that day.

I'd never get her screams out of my head, or the vision of her on the ground. She had curled up into a ball and let Gus go. He was bounding back to us, then to her, then to us, then to her until we got to her.

I lost five years of my life that day, in that small moment. Ash was mine. Mine to protect, and I had failed her that day. I would never fail her again.

I was reminding him of this today.

"You can't kill me. You do and sicarios will go after Verónica—"

"Bullshit."

I could do it, now. Tonight. I could end everything. I could end what future war I felt was coming.

"You will never let some sicario find our sister, kill her, and take over your empire. The day your son was born was the day you called that order off."

He slumped, resignation coming over him. I was right.

He asked, more wary, "What do you want, Raize?"

"I want you to know how it feels, knowing that I could've taken them when I took that picture. I was in the room with them, in their house. Just like tonight. No one knows I'm here. No one. Imagine how easy it is for me, especially when you are making *more* enemies. You're making powerful enemies. They enjoy having me as their ally."

"You're lying—"

"About what? There's nothing to lie about."

"What." He gritted his teeth, the white flashing in the moonlight. "—do you want?"

"Just this. I wanted you to know I can get to you, anywhere you go."

I couldn't kill him, though I wanted to. He was still needed. Roman needed him, but Marco was getting more powerful. He was allied with other cartels, whereas Roman was still by himself, but the day would come. It would.

I just had to wait.

When it would, when I was given the okay to take him out, I'd do it this way. I wanted him to die alone, within reach of help, but unable to call for it. It felt fitting.

And I'd given my message.

I tightened my hold, enough until he went unconscious, and then I eased his body down.

I grabbed his phone, synced it to the burner one I had with me, and took his gun.

Then I left, leaving through his blind spots that every estate had.

It wasn't easy for others, but it was for me. Ash had her skill. This was mine.

EPILOGUE AFTER THE EPILOGUE
THE CANARY

"I'm pregnant."

Good God, how did this happen?

Well, all the sex. That's how it happened, but I collapsed on our bed.

Raize was being sent out on a mission for Roman, but this happened often over the last couple years. I wasn't too worried. Roman never sent him on anything too harrying. He was always back within a day and over the last couple years, regarding our world, there wasn't much I could complain about.

Roman Marakov was true to his word.

He didn't traffic women.

And if there was killing, I wasn't in on those talks.

I'd been called in on mostly legit business meetings, but for Raize, we didn't talk about what Roman sent him off to do. I thought it was a good balance for us. I was still in the world. He was, too. We were together, but it wasn't how it was when we first got together.

In a way, life was almost normal...almost.

Except for my surprise, which showed up a few days ago, and after I lost it, called Tracey and lost it to her, and then she talked me into getting a doctor test done. I did that, and he called with the results and what was I doing?

"What?"

Raize had paused, packing his guns into his bag.

I said it again, whispering this time, "I'm pregnant."

I wanted to cry because who raised a child in this life?

Raize didn't have the same mentality.

He straightened abruptly and a wide smile came over his face. He took two steps, scooped me up from the bed, and then he sat back down with me on his lap. "You serious?" His hand came over my stomach, gently, so tenderly. He was looking down, a mystified and almost wondrous look coming over him. "There's a little me and you in there?"

My throat swelled up with so much emotion. I was fast blinking back all the tears.

My guy, I loved my guy so much.

I could only hold on tighter because my tears were starting to blind me.

I said, in a low voice, "You're not mad?"

His hand pressed tighter and his voice came out rough. "Fuck no." He couldn't keep talking. He choked off and he pressed his forehead into my neck and shoulder. We were both holding on to each other, emotion completely taking over both of us.

And damn, it was a lot.

I felt completely wiped out, from good and bad and nerves and happiness and everything in between. I was exhausted and wanting to run a marathon all at the same time. And terrified. I was definitely and completely trying to keep myself from doing a full body tremble in Raize's arms.

I just clasped on tighter, but then he was lifting his head and his eyes had their own sheen of unshed tears. "I never thought I'd have a woman I loved, a team behind you and me, a boss who's not that bad in terms of what a typical boss is like in our world, and now this? A kid? You kidding me?"

Oh man.

I couldn't hold back my tears.

They were slipping down my face, and some happiness was unfolding in my chest. It was like a flower that grew and rose up and was now ready to open. It needed sunlight and we'd been giving it so much sunlight.

"We're having a kid?"

The tears were just free falling by now. I could do nothing against his whispered wonder.

I nodded. "We're having a kid."

He touched his lips to mine, then murmured against them, "No matter what, you and the baby are safe. You got me?"

Not a normal endearment a significant other would want to hear on this announcement, but for us and this world, it just made me cry even harder. The good tears.

"I love you."

He rested his forehead to mine, his hand sweeping over my stomach. "I love you, too. Both of you." He moved down, pushing my shirt up, and I felt his lips touching my stomach.

I lay there, almost gasping in disbelief because I never would've suspected this would be our ending, but there it was.

This was our happily ever after.

Raize lifted his head, his eyes finding mine, and he paused, pushing some hair from my forehead. "You're happy?" He was asking about everything, and I nodded.

I said, "I am." And I would be because I knew Raize meant it when he said my safety and our baby's safety above anyone else.

Over the last few years, I enjoyed working for Roman Marakov.

I shouldn't, but I did.

He cared about his employees, and while he had to run a mafia, he seemed to give a fuck. I enjoyed being the one to tell him when someone was lying or cheating or wanted to hurt him. I enjoyed when he made it his mission to find out who his rivals were that were trafficking women and when he'd send Raize to go and 'deal with them.' Everyone knew what that was code for. I mean, we returned to Texas and I was able to blow Oscar's building up, finally and only after I was reassured it was empty, so yeah, I knew what the code meant.

Fighting that shit in my way, and now this? A kid? With Raize?

I was happy.

I was happier than I ever thought I could've been, so I'd take it.

This was my happily ever after.

Everything else? We'd deal because that's what you did when you found your place, right? You just handled it.

Jacob Cavers Raize was born almost nine months later.

A year later, we had Veronique Ashley Raize.

Ashley was there when both were born. So was her family.

Shit happened.

That was going to happen in this lifestyle, but like I knew, we handled it.

In the meantime, we were happy and we remained being happy.

And I officially became Ash Canary Raize a year after we had Veronique.

I kept my blonde hair.

If you enjoyed Canary, please consider leaving a review!!
They truly help so incredibly much.
Also, for more stories like Canary,

check out www.tijansbooks.com

Carter Reed Series
Cole
Bennett Mafia
Jonah Bennett
Frisco

Stay tuned because I have more mafia coming!

ACKNOWLEDGMENTS

A special thank you again to my editor, my beta readers, and the proofreaders. You guys either worked me into your schedule or read Canary so quickly for me. I truly appreciate it so much! Thank you to Heather and Crystal for helping with the audio of Canary! A special thank you to Gloria Gonzalez for helping me with some Mexico questions.
A very special thank you to the ladies in my reader group. You guys are so active in there and it truly helps me to keep writing.
I couldn't end this without a huge thank you to my cuddle partner, and the guy who is always checking on me, Bailey! My pup. Love you so much!

ALSO BY TIJAN

Mafia Standalones:

Cole

Bennett Mafia

Jonah Bennett

Frisco

Fallen Crest/Roussou Universe

Fallen Crest Series

Crew Series

The Boy I Grew Up With (standalone)

Rich Prick (standalone)

Nate

Other series:

Broken and Screwed Series (YA/NA)

Jaded Series (YA/NA suspense)

Davy Harwood Series (paranormal)

Carter Reed Series (mafia)

The Insiders (trilogy)

Sports Romance Standalones:

Enemies

Teardrop Shot

Hate To Love You

The Not-Outcast

Young Adult Standalones:

Ryan's Bed

A Whole New Crowd

Brady Remington Landed Me in Jail

College Standalones:

Antistepbrother

Kian

Contemporary Romances:

Bad Boy Brody

Home Tears

Fighter

Rockstar Romance Standalone:

Sustain

Paranormal Standalone:

Evil

Micaela's Big Bad

More books to come!

BENNETT MAFIA

CHAPTER ONE

"Die, you fly!"

I locked eyes with a black fly, or maybe our eyes weren't locked, but he was perched on the rock next to me. He was going down. He had been harassing me for the last hour. I was outside, trying to clean up the yard, but I was going nuts with this damn thing buzzing all around me.

He was teasing me, taunting me. He flew out of the way every time I swung at him. He was too fast, and as he paused on my shoulder, I swung at the same time the screen door opened. I heard its creak across the yard right before a numbing pain exploded in my shoulder.

"Ry—did you just clock yourself?"

Fuck. Fuck. Fuck.

I groaned, my knees buckling.

I had.

I'd swung with the rock in my hands, and now I felt blood trickling down my shoulder and arm. My shirtsleeve was rapidly turning red.

The fly fucker was trying to kill me, by outsmarting me.

"Shit."

The door slammed shut, and I heard Blade's feet scuffling down the stairs as he ran to me. The gravel crunched under his weight, and then he slid in behind me. His pants would be ripped up, but knowing Blade, he wouldn't care.

He rarely cared about clothes. We were just happy he wore them, most of the time.

"Fuck." He swore under his breath, his very tanned and slightly oily fingers gentle as he looked at my wound. His dark eyes seemed to penetrate my shoulder before he sat back on his heels, raking a hand through his dreadlocks. "What were you doing?"

I wasn't going to admit a fly had outwitted me.

When I was doing yard work, Blade made himself scarce. For the years he'd been living with us, he'd been content to clean the inside. He did most of the cooking, cleaning, and dishes, and it wasn't uncommon for us to come home from shopping and find him wearing a maid's apron and duster—and nothing else.

So for him to come looking for me outside like this wasn't normal.

"What is it?" I jerked my head toward the house, hearing the television blaring.

His concerned eyes lifted to mine, and a whole different look slid over him.

My alarm level went up three notches.

Of the three of us living in this little cabin outside of Calgary, or Cowtown as we called it sometimes, Blade wasn't the one who got concerned about things. He enjoyed indulging in marijuana, kept his hair in tight dreadlocks, and dressed like a child from the sixties in a brown vest, no shirt, and a tie-dyed bandana over his hair. Only instead of bell-bottoms, he wore tight, frayed jeans over regular runners. He handled all our computer stuff, and when we walked inside, I wasn't surprised to find he had switched over the news he'd caught on his computer to the main television screen.

I also wasn't surprised to be watching a report from New York City.

"—ennett mafia princess has been missing for forty-nine hours now."

Ice lined my insides.

A picture of my old boarding school roommate, Brooke Bennett, flashed on the screen, along with numbers to call if she was found.

Found...

As in, she was lost?

I felt punched in the chest.

Brooke was missing.

Dazed, I reached out for a chair to sit in. Blade moved to my side.

"That's your old roommate, right?" The chair protested. Blade's hand left my arm, and his voice came from my side. "The one you had at that rich school."

I almost snorted at his wording, but I was still in a daze. I nodded instead.

Brooke. *Man.*

The news was showing pictures from her social media accounts, and she was gorgeous. Fourteen years. I don't know why that number popped into my head, but it felt right. It'd been so long since I last saw her, or was it fourteen years since we first met? One of those.

"She was always so girly," I murmured, almost to myself. She'd been so full of life.

Not me. I'd been a numbed-down, post-traumatized zombie when I walked into that room.

"Oh my gosh! You must be my roommate!" She had launched herself at me from behind the moment I entered the room, wrapping her arms around me. Her face had pressed into my shoulder.

Janine had squawked. *"Oh my."*

I'd ignored my dad's secretary and had taken one second before the girl let me go and hurried around in front of me. Her hands went to my arms, just underneath my shoulders and she'd looked me up and down.

I did the same: black oval eyes, stunning jet-black hair, a pert nose, small mouth—but lips formed just like the ones that had been a stamp on my last Valentine's Day party invitation, full and plump.

I was slightly envious, or as envious as I could get since I wasn't usually the jealous type. She had a small chin to end her perfect heart-shaped face, and her eyes were glittering and alive.

That had been the one moment when I truly was jealous of her. Life. She had what I didn't. I wasn't jealous of her looks, though if I'd had a different upbringing maybe I might've been? In a way, that was something I was thankful for. Life meant more to me than looks or things. It meant yearning for safety, smiles, the feeling of being loved.

The other girls had been jealous of her money. For a "rich kids" school, everyone seemed to be pissed about how much money they had. They always wanted more, and they seemed to know who had the most. I was toward the lower end of the wealthy crowd, but Brooke—as it had been whispered around school—was at the top.

There'd been other whispers, other looks, but we were twelve in our first year there. I didn't understand what the word *mafia* actually meant. But it was used often as a taunt by our second semester at Hillcrest. The first semester there hadn't been that kind of bullying. Some girls liked us. Some girls didn't. A few hung out with us, and our room became known as the "hot guy" room. Not because we had guys there. Far from it. I would've died if a cute guy even looked my way. No, no. Our room had the name because of all the posters and photographs Brooke plastered all over our room. All gorgeous males.

It never made sense that some of her pictures didn't look

professionally taken, but the posters were real, and who wouldn't drool over a full-length shot of Aaron Jonahson, the best football player in the United States—or the celebrity actor from everyone's favorite television show, or the so-hot model that'd been a convict first. Brooke seemed to have all the guys covered, but some pictures seemed more like snapshots. Which was the truth.

I found out around the holidays: they were her family.

They weren't celebrities—not in the sense that I understood back then—they were her brothers, all four of them.

Cord was the oldest at eighteen.

Kai was fifteen.

Tanner was fourteen.

Brooke was twelve.

And Jonah brought up the rear at nine years old.

Brooke was quiet about her family, *really* quiet. But when I found out those boys were her brothers, and their names, I was fascinated. I couldn't lie about that. I just hadn't known who I was becoming obsessed about.

Cord kept his hair short, almost a crew cut above his more angular face. Brooke told me he was usually the reserved one, and artsy. She almost hissed when she used that word, as if it was a curse, but then she shrugged. "It's the truth. He wants to be a painter one day."

Next in line hadn't been Kai. She'd skipped over him and chewed on her lip, pausing before pointing to Tanner. As she did, her eyes lit up and a bright smile took over her face.

"Tanner has this shaggy hair that he bleaches blond, and sometimes it's dark when I see him. He's funny, Ry. He's *so* funny, but he also has an attitude. All the girls here would die over him, literally just die."

I still remembered all the emails she got from a tannerinyour-mama—almost her entire inbox was emails from him.

When she'd gotten to Jonah's picture, she'd quieted, but a

fondness had shone through her. She'd spoken almost as if he were in the room and words could break him.

"Jonah's the baby," she said gently. "He worships Kai..." She'd paused and scratched at her forehead before continuing. "But he doesn't look like the rest of us." That's all she'd said about him.

I'd inspected the picture of her and him together. She had pulled Jonah onto her lap, her arms around him, and his still-baby cheek pressed against hers as he smiled. His skin had a darker tone than the others, but they all had the most luscious facial features. All dark eyes.

Cord and Kai had black hair in their pictures. Tanner's was lighter, and Brooke's a lovely shade of dark copper. Jonah's hair matched hers, with a twinge of curl in it too. Tanner's was long and shaggy, sticking up all over. Kai's was short, where a hand could run through it easily and it'd fall back in place—just a touch longer than Cord's barely-there hair.

I returned my attention to the television now, coming back to the present.

In the photos on the screen, Brooke's hair was still the length it'd been in school. She'd kept it trimmed just above her waist and had been adamant that no one would cut it. She'd whispered one night about a fight with her dad, that her father went after her with a pair of scissors. But her hair was still long when she told me, so whatever the fight, he hadn't been successful. And like all the other times she talked about her family, she didn't go into detail. She always said just enough so I knew what she was talking about, and then she would close up. Her shoulders would shudder before a wall slammed down, and that night had been the same.

A soft sigh left me as I continued to watch the images on the news.

Brooke had her chin up, proud, as her braided hair curved around her neck. In another she struck a sultry pose in a bikini. She could've been a model, except maybe she didn't have the height—not like me. She'd been an inch shorter than me in school, though now I had shot up even taller to five ten.

They teased us about being sisters at school.

I had loved it, though I never said a word. I didn't know if Brooke enjoyed it. She never spoke for or against it, but I could see now why people thought that way. We both had dark black hair. Okay. Maybe I couldn't see why now. That was the end of our similarities. Brooke had a rounder face. I was fairer in skin. My eyes were more narrow. My face a little longer. And taller. I was always taller.

Brooke used to sigh that I could be a model, but she was wrong. She was the future model. I saw the proof now.

She looked like she'd gotten a tad bit taller too, maybe another inch, but that was it. It didn't matter. Brooke could've been a model just because she had turned into a celebrity—which was also why the story about her being missing had been picked up by a news channel from New York City, where I didn't think she lived.

"That's her, right?" Blade prompted again. He shoved back his chair to stand as I heard the sounds of an approaching car outside.

We lived near Cowtown, but we kept to the forest for a reason. The cabin we were renting belonged to a friend of a friend of a friend of another friend, and there were probably three other sets of friends before we actually got to the owner. There was a reason for that, just like there was a reason Blade hurried to his computer, turning off the news as he brought up the feed from the electronic sensors outside.

A second later, he relaxed and flipped the screen back.

All was clear. It was our third roommate, Carol. But I wasn't paying attention to her or to the sound I heard when the screen door opened and something dropped with a thud on the floor. Carol cursed.

My eyes returned to the screen, glued there because an image of Kai Bennett appeared now.

Just like the last time I saw my friend, the bile of loathing pooled in my mouth. Kai stared right at the camera, offering whoever had taken his picture the same look he'd given me before taking my roommate away so many years ago.

While I couldn't remember the last look on Brooke's face, I couldn't get *his* out of my mind.

Death.

His eyes were dead, just like they'd been back then.

A shiver went up my spine. I'd only seen Kai Bennett in person once, but it was enough.

I hated him.

Read more Bennett Mafia!